The Company of Comedians

First Published 2015.

Russell Press, Russell House, Bulwell Lane
Basford, Nottingham NG6 OBT.

www.russellpress.com - www.russellpressdigital.co.uk

Cover artwork by the author.

ISBN 9780993161223

The Company of Comedians

A Novel by Michael Payne

Leen Editions

For Kathy.

Part One.

One. *On Not Entirely Taking the Town.*

'Play actors,' declared the black cladded preacher, his voice and Bible raised high, 'are the most profligate wretches and the vilest vermin that hell ever vomited out. Play actors are the filth and garbage of the earth, the scum and stain of human nature. . .'

Ebullient buyers and sellers crowding into the market square were in no mood for such spoilers of good will. As of a voice in the wilderness, the pulpiteer was met with indifference by the festive crowd. Below him on the steps of the Malt Cross, several youths, drinking and lounging, listened instead to a fiddler whose cold fingers played a series of painful airs befitting the Christmas tide. Louder, more raucous calls prevailed.

Shouts of 'apples to roast,' 'hot spice cakes,' 'fine cooked sausages,' added to the clamour of trade before the coming winter holiday.

Bit by bit above the bustle two insistent sounds arose - the ringing of a hand bell accompanied by the beating of a base drum. This ungodly noise ricocheted down the pinched alleyways until it emerged echoing between the high houses of the Nottingham square.

A proclamation? A whipping, perhaps even a hanging? Surely not at Christmas. The answer when revealed caused wry amusement for the bell was being rung by a man outrageously clad in a suit of pink and white satin. Red stockings, bright silver buckled shoes completed his attire. For certain, this was a comedian. And a comedian gave promise of fun.

In front of the bell ringer a thin pale boy carried a drum which he applied with every aptitude of a carpet beater. The drum was so large and the boy so small that, being unable to see ahead, he crashed into a pottery stall toppling a column of dinner plates. The boy, receiving a cuff on the ear from the bellman and finding himself confronted by the angry proprietor, swiftly unharnessed himself from the instrument, which together with the drum sticks he dropped and fled the scene.

'You'll pay for this.' Pointing to the broken crockery the stall holder transferred his anger to the satin suited man.

'Restitution shall be made,' came the reply. 'You know sir, of course, who I am?' Turning to the small crowd that was beginning to circle he declared,

'I am James Augustus Whitley. Yes. He who will be appearing in one week's time at the fine new Theatre Royal in St Mary's Gate.'

Whitley was strongly built or stocky depending on the observer's judgement. Lately past fifty years of age, he was well preserved apart from being bald. This deficiency he covered with a powdered tie wig which almost added an inch to his height and gave him a dapper quality, useful in his profession. At five foot seven inches he wished with all his heart he had two or three inches more in altitude. High-heeled shoes helped, but still the disappointment in his stature remained. Conversely he wished he had several inches less around his waist, but a weakness for giblet pies and strong ales made this unlikely.

The tradesman continued to demand payment.

'Them's me best plates,' he insisted, ''that'll cost you a shillin.'

'My dear sir, you shall be well compensated.' Whitley gave a genial smile directed mostly at the spectators. 'But, I ask you. A lowly shilling - a mere twelve pence, a pittance when I speak of nothing less than a crown.'

Enjoying the interest he was engendering, Whitley's confidence grew. He knew that if he provided some waggery he may well hold his audience captive for a while.

He looked dramatically at his hearers 'How many of you have dreamt of a seat in Westminster Abbey at the crowning of our gracious King George III? For I offer each of you such a chance of a lifetime, the opportunity of witnessing the coronation of our beloved king!'

'Don't talk so daft,' said a man close by, 'that was way back.'

'No sir, I do not talk daft, for today week at the new theatre there will be re-enacted the Coronation of King George and Queen Charlotte. Complete in every detail and particular. All presented by myself and my illustrious company of comedians and each of you is invited to view the dazzling spectacle.'

'One shillin',' repeated the pot man showing increased anger.

Whitley put his hand into his pocket, removing a small disc.

'Sir I give you this token. Present it at my theatre and you will be given the best seat in the house, one that will transport you to. . . '

'You'll be transported if you don't pay up.'

This raised a laugh. Whitley sensing difficulties put the token aside, taking a coin from another pocket.

'Let me assure you sir that that I James Augustus Whitley do honour my debts.' The full shilling was paid and interest in the episode began to fade.

'But wait my friends,' cried Whitley as some began to leave. 'As I have offered a seat for the performance, it shall not be forsworn. If this gentleman refuses, then another shall benefit. The first to make his bid shall have this valuable token. Now, who shall it be?'

A dark eyed boy quickly raised his hand.

'Well chosen lad,' said Whitley throwing him the disc. The boy catching it smiled and carelessly tossed it up and down like a charm. At the same time he nodded at the discarded drum.

'What about that then?' he asked.

'Ah, yes, the drum,' said Whitley, 'it lies silent and unused.'

'Want me to play it?'

Whitley .was agreeably engaged by the impudence of the youth.

'Play a drum? Surely, a drum is but for beating.'

'Not so. Hark to this. . .'

The youth picked up the drum and put on the harness. Using only his bare hands, he beat out an impressive series of rhythms, far better than anything previously heard. So good it gained the approval of those who remained to listen. Retrieving the drum sticks the new drummer then proceeded to beat a commanding series of paces. Whitley was intrigued. For in spite of the youth's dexterity, he saw he was missing two fingers from his left hand.

'You are not a newcomer to the timpani?' he asked.

'Drummer boy, Colonel Hayter's Regiment of Foot.'

'Indeed?' Whitley saw a possibility 'Would you care to *sound the general* for me? To proclaim my presence to the public.'

'Worth a pot of ale?'

'By all means. Tell me, what name shall I call you by?'

'Thomas.'

'Come, Thomas, let us to the Malt Cross, You have your marching orders.'

Whitley resumed ringing his bell, newly accompanied by a superior tattoo on the drum which he was convinced would summon an audience.

By the time they reached the Malt Cross a small crowd was following. Of the black cladded preacher there was no sign. The same drinking youths remained and the old fiddler was yet scraping on his sad strings which were swamped by the approaching bell and drum. Mounting the steps, Whitley presented himself with the authority of a town crier.

'Hear ye, hear ye, my lords ladies and gentlemen. . .' he began. The fiddler protested at the competition but was ignored, Some bored soldiers joined the company to find what was afoot. It was a small gathering, leaving Whitley annoyed that he did not attract a larger number for on his appearances further north he had met with greater enthusiasm.

'Thank you Thomas,' he inclined his head and the youth ceased his drumming. 'My lords, ladies and gentlemen. . .' he declaimed,

'You've said that afore,' shouted one of the soldiers.

'And I shall say it again captain.' The man was a mere foot soldier but Whitley knew the power of flattery. 'For I have glad tidings to impart. What better way to welcome in the new year of our Lord seventeen hundred and sixty three than by visiting the new theatre in Mary Gate? For on this new year's eve we shall be presenting a dramatic musical offering.'

One of the onlookers looked towards the fiddler, 'Is 'e in it?'

'He is not,' said Whitley, 'for we employ only the finest players. But that is not all. There are many other delights. You will witness an exact representation of the Coronation of their majesties King George and Queen Charlotte with all the grand regalia and glorious robes directly new from Drury Lane.'

At this point Whitley's enthusiasm inspired Thomas to gave several resounding drum rolls. Whitley was pleased with this, feeling it indicated a flair for showmanship which might be encouraged.

'In addition,' he continued, 'there will be performed, without gain or reward, scenes from the celebrated tragedy of *Cato* by the greatly admired Mr Addison.'

Whitley looked sideways at Thomas who took this as a cue to beat out an impressive 'Pom, tiddeley-um-pom, pom pom.' Whitley smiled with pleasure. He was about to continue, when a deep female voice interrupted.

'Tickets, Mr Whitley. You have made no mention of tickets,'

'Ah, me dear wife,' Whitley bowed to a large gentlewoman taking her place beside him. 'Pray continue my love. . .'

'Tickets to be had of Mr Joe Parr,' she announced regally, 'at the White Bull near St Mary's Church and nowhere else. The performances to begin each night at exactly seven o'clock.'

Dressed in a similar material to the satin suit worn by her husband, Mrs Whitley's ornate gown was of a strong shade of vermillion which conflicted loudly with the pink of Mr Whitley. Her looks, if she had ever had them, were long gone. Being an actress it was allowed, even expected, that she should colour her face which she did with little skill. Her white painted countenance presented the appearance of a snowman in fear of an imminent thaw. She disported a impressive bust, not unlike two thirds of a pawn broker's sign. Upon her head she wore a high powdered wig from which sprouted several green ostrich feathers so that with the natural advantage of height she towered over her spouse like a tree over a shrub.

'My dear wife Cassandra, will be enchanting audiences with several songs during the evening, including that ever popular ballad *Cherry Ripe*.'

'What, in that dress?' came a shout. With this, people were about to go their way, when a familiar prohibiting voice was heard,

'Be gone, you sinners. We want none of your kind here with your filth.' It was the black cladded preacher, newly returned.

Several, sensing more free entertainment waited to see what reaction there might be. Whitley sought to find the owner of the voice.

'I beg your pardon sir?' He peered into the crowd.

'You heard, you sinful whore-monger. Here we are God fearing folk. We want no theatres in our town!'

'Sir. That is not the kind of welcome I expect from a fair place such as Nottingham,' protested Whitley, 'especially at this time of goodwill. . .'

'Get back to the hell hole you came from.'

'We came from Doncaster sir,' replied Whitley, 'Do you equate that delightful town with Sodom and Gomorrah?' It seemed as if Whitley might get the better of the moraliser for there was a laugh and some applause at this. But the preacher was not to be silenced,

'Players are the vilest debauchers of men's minds and morals. . .'

Here once more, young Thomas showed his sense of timing. Before either Mr or Mrs Whitley could maintain an argument with the troublemaker he beat his drum loudly enough to drown the preacher's onslaught.

Whitley and his wife, now looked upon with favour by those gathered around, graciously distributed playbills to their public, most of whom could not read but were nonetheless pleased to possess a copy.

The market was beginning to decline. As the throng diminished the Whitleys slowly walked from the square. Thomas followed nearby. After a few minutes he cleared his throat noisily.

'I am now ready sir, for my pot of ale,' he declared.

'When the drum is returned to the theatre,' replied Whitley.

'Sir, my thirst is very great. Without ale I fear I can go no further.'

'Not until the drum is returned to the theatre.'

'It's getting heavy,' said Thomas.

'You, a drummer boy complaining of the weight?'

'In the army I had a snare drum, light as a feather. Whereas this crate of old spilth grows so weighty I must soon put it down. Should I do so I fear it would roll away and doubtless come to harm.' He smiled roguishly.

'Don't you dare,' cried Whitley. But Mrs Whitley noticed a slightly lopsided grin from the young man seemingly aimed at her, which combined with his deep brown eyes, had a definite appeal.

'He's only funning,' she said to her husband.

'That's right, just a joke,' said Thomas, with a wink. 'I likes only proper ale,' he added, 'and if it's all the same to you I'd like it now.'

'You'll get what you deserve, no more no less,' muttered Whitley who also admitted to himself there was much he liked about the lad.

Not least was his stature, for Thomas had the additional height Whitley craved so much for himself. Wearing no wig, the youth stood above both Cassandra and himself. Strands of light brown hair fell across his forehead, the rest tied with a ribbon, lay in a queue down his back. Whilst not quite handsome, his appearance was pleasing, a quality given weight by the deft use of his eyes and engaging smile.

The trio's progress took them past the almost deserted Hen Cross. The last sellers were offering their remaining poultry and meat at much reduced prices. From the darkening sky a scattering of snowflakes began to fall. Thomas put the drum on his head.

'Don't do that,' shouted Whitley, 'it requires protection.'

'So do I. And me with no parasol ' said Thomas mischievously.

'We'd best take shelter.' Cassandra Whitley had removed her head dress, picking out the feathers and placing the whole into a wig bag. Whatever magic the couple had exhibited earlier was now gone. Thomas looked at Mrs Whitley, her grey hair cut short and uncombed, wondering almost if she was Whitley's mother and not his wife.

'This will never do,' she said crossly,'I'm not having this gown ruined.'

She looked at her husband who was peppered with snow flakes, 'And that suit of yours will be beggared if we stay outside.'

Saying no more, she walked indignantly into Bridlesmith Gate and entered the nearest tavern which happened to be the Old Rose.

The landlord Jud Drinkwater greeted them.

'My dear Mr and Mrs Whitley, what an honour! I was advised you have been pumping the square. Come, warm yourselves by the hearth.' He looked undecidedly at Thomas who stood awkwardly with the drum.

'Don't put that near the fire,' cried Mrs Whitley, 'It must dry out naturally,' Thomas laid the drum on the floor where it blocked the passage way.

'On its side,'said Whitley, 'did you learn nothing in the army?'

The tap room was dark but welcoming. Burning coals gave a flickering of light on the old wood panelling, black with years of tobacco smoke and soot. As the December day came to an early end, already candles were being lit.

'Warm gin with sugar?' asked Drinkwater.

'Very nicely,' said Mrs Whitley.

'I'll take a pot of your mulled Lisbon,' said Whitley. Eyes turned towards Thomas who stood at a respectful distance.

'Anything for . . .?' asked the landlord.

'A tankard of best ale,' Thomas proposed brightly.

'You cheeky young sod,' Whitley almost smiled.

'That was the treaty.'

'What's it to be?' The landlord looked at Whitley.

'A tankard of your best ale.'

Thomas grinned lopsidedly, the side being nearest to Mrs Whitley who again admitted to herself that he certainly had a way with him. She also noticed her husband had not seen this sly exchange and shuffled in her chair with secret pleasure. There was a moment's silence.

'Been a drummer boy have you?' asked Whitley.

'Yes.'

'You seem to have a faculty for it. Can you play anything else?'

'A bugle.'

'They go together I suppose,' said Mrs Whitley.

'Could be useful in the company,' Whitley whispered to his wife.

'We've already got a boy,'she said, 'What's become of him?'

'Absconded, cost me a shilling for breakages. I doubt we'll see him again.'

Here Thomas recognised his chance,'Then you'll be wanting someone else?'

'Not so fast,' warned Whitley. 'We know nothing about you. To begin with, how old are you?'

Thomas disliked this question, for he was unsure of his true age. 'When I was apprenticed my year of birth was said to be 1745.'

'Then you will be about seventeen,' said Mrs Whitley.

'That's right,' said Thomas, impressed by her arithmetic.

'Apprentice to what trade?' asked Whitley.

'Stockinger.'

'In that case you have not served out your seven years.'

'Nor shall I,' said Thomas. 'Two years of that slavery sufficed. Should you wonder why I absconded, you can see the stripes on my back and. . .' He showed where he missed fingers on his left hand to lay stress on his meaning. 'Only one good thing came out of being apprenticed.'

'What was that?'

'The master learned me to read and to write. In the hopes I might help keep his books, which he was not good at.'

The Whitleys looked at each other, for this was unusual in one of his kind. Cassandra leaned towards her husband saying quietly,

'If he can write sufficiently well he could copy out parts.'

'But you do that so beautifully my dear.'

'Indeed I do, but I would be glad to be relieved of the burden. It would free me to do so much else.'

'Quite so,' Whitley looked at Thomas seriously. He took a small volume from his pocket and passed it to him. ''Let me hear you read.'

Thomas examined the opening pages. He began, ' "*CATO a Tragedy, as is acted at the Theatre Royal in Drury Lane.*" '

'Go on. And it's not pronounced "Catt-o" it's "Kay-to." '

'*By Her Majesty's Servant Mr Addison.*' Thomas stumbled. *'Ecce, Specta. . . .'*

'Don't bother with the Latin. You say you can write?'

'Yes. Should there be writing materials to hand I can pen my full name, Thomas Hammond, that and more.'

'Penning a name proves nothing. Let me see you copy a speech.' Whitley lay open the play text and indicated a passage. He called to the landlord, 'Master Jud, a quill and paper if you please.'

With the arrival of writing materials, Thomas looked scornfully at the dog-eared quill.

'Might as well scrawl with me big toe as write with this,'

'Particular isn't he? said the landlord. Thomas moved to a table lit by one candle, trimmed the quill with his own penknife and began his copying.

Drinkwater sat down with the Whitleys. 'Well my friends,' he said, 'I bid you welcome to Nottingham. But you're either brave or barmy bringing a play to this town. Here such things are prohibited.

You'll be arrested as sure as rooks is jackdaws. I'll wager that was one of Fairlight's men harangued you in the square.'

'Fairlight, who might that be?'

Drinkwater laughed, 'Alderman Fairlight is our leading puritan and a mighty hater of play acting. As sure as fourpence is a groat he'll be after you.'

'Whitley smiled. 'Recall, landlord, we have been invited to perform here by Mr Marmaduke Pennell, the mayor no less. What's more he has built a theatre for us. That must surely guarantee our immunity from prosecution.'

'Far from it,' said Drinkwater. 'Mr Pennell has now ended his term as mayor. He may have built you a theatre, but in so doing he's made many enemies. None moreso than Alderman Fairlight with his whigs and chapel folk. They consider a theatre worse than a brothel, for it promotes idleness and corruption.'

'I shall not be thwarted by some local Tartar.'

'Then moderate your billing. Lay stress upon the musical part of your evening and not the play. That way you might avoid prosecution.'

He pointed to the playbills, 'It's this, "*The celebrated moral tragedy of CATO*". That means spoken words, which you know full well is unlawful.'

'But we present only scenes "without gain or reward,"' said Cassandra, 'that surely is sufficient to exempt us from prosecution.'

'Won't do. The harm's been done. It don't say that on your bill.'

'You talk as if it were the old days,' said Whitley, 'when we were branded rogues and vagabonds.'

'And still you are by Alderman Fairlight.'

'Fiddlesticks,' Whitley stood to add stress to his words, but realising his voice lacked conviction changed the subject. 'Well dear boy,' he moved towards Thomas, 'how much have you copied? Let me see what you've done.'

Waving the paper to dry the ink, Thomas handed over his work.

'Mmm. A tolerable hand. What d'you think my dear?'

Mrs Whitley taking a spying-glass from her bag took in the page.

'Could you read that on stage?' asked her husband.

'Possibly. But I would prefer it larger.'

'A penny a length would you say?' Whitley turned. 'D'you know what a "length" is my boy?'

'Can't say I do.'

'A length is fifty two lines of text. You will be paid by the number of lengths. You don't copy the whole play, only each actor's lines together with his cues. That will require ten parts. At the rate of a penny a length I could pay you something like. . .' he paused, 'what d'you think my love, shall we say a guinea?'

'Fair to the point of generous,' agreed Cassandra.

'A guinea?' Thomas was interested. Having exhausted his meagre army gratuity he was almost without funds.

'The landlord laughed. 'You robber! In a good company he could earn fourpence a length. You watch him my lad.'

Whitley struck as imposing a stance as he could. 'I am not a wealthy man. I am not a Garrick. I am not a Tate Wilkinson. . . .'

'No and yours isn't a company of that standing,' said Drinkwater.

'Ignore this publican, this vendor of pussy piss masquerading as beer. My boy, I am offering you a foothold on the ladder of success.'

'It's a fine offer,' added Cassandra, 'no matter what this villain says.' (And, she thought to herself, it will save me hours of the most tedious drudgery.)

Thomas thought. In spite of the landlord's words, after weeks of wandering the streets this was a wage. And also work in a theatre, which he had long desired. 'All right. Depending you add two pots a day of best ale.'

'Agreed,' Whitley and Thomas shook hands. ' You have undertaken a noble task. I don't hold with contracts. My word is my bond.'

Cassandra smiled at the two of them. 'A wise move,' she said, 'We start rehearsing directly after Christmas by which time we shall require the completed work. So the sooner you get your head down the better.'

'Quite right,' said Whitley draining his drink.

'Well now my love,' he said to his wife, 'I see the snow has abated, for sure a good omen. Brighter skies await. Let us wend our way, like the torch bearers we are, to the playhouse; that home of dreaming hopes and hopeful dreams, that world within. . .'

'Don't fuss! Lord, how he does go on,' Mrs Whitley sighed, at the same time half smiling at Thomas. She and her husband picked up their accessories and went out into the cold and dark of the winter street, Whitley shivering in his thin satin suit. Thomas struggled into the harness of the drum which was really the only comfortable way of carrying it. As he followed the couple who now appeared to have become his master and mistress he began to sound a drum roll.

'There's no need for that,' Whitley said, 'we're off duty and you'll get no extra beer for it.'

'Never mind. Helps keep the flies off,' answered Thomas.

*

Two *Gilded Scenes and Shining Prospects.*

The Theatre Royal, St Mary's Gate was not deserving of the splendour of its name. The new building might be correct in calling itself a theatre but it had no right to consider itself regal. Nonetheless, without a majestic name a theatre was not held worthy of public regard; in truth the title gave status without any legitimacy, like the royal bastard that it was.

The stage door was down a narrow passageway of no more than a yard in width. Thomas, accompanying the Whitleys, came to a green wooden door which opened onto a paved court, traversed overhead with washing lines from which hung fabrics and costumes, supported by a forest of prop sticks.

Regarding them from one corner, chewing hay from a manger, was a doleful looking horse its bridle attached to a lamp bracket. This was 'Gunpowder,' Mr Whitley's own steed. The name, perhaps befitting during the horse's younger days, was now reduced to 'Gunpy,' which, as the animal was well past the age of retirement, seemed appropriate.

'Bracer,' shouted Whitley as they threaded their way through the thicket of prop sticks and washing to enter the theatre.

'In 'ere,' replied Bracer from inside. Thomas had never been backstage before and the chaotic atmosphere was, for all he knew, a normal state of affairs. Even though it was a new building the amount of clutter looked old. As he later learned it was what Whitley had managed to salvage from his previous theatre in Manchester. Mildewed props and battered scenery vied for space with paint pots, basins of glue, sacks of artificial snow, ladders and sawdust everywhere.

'Bracer,' Whitley repeated, 'I gave you instructions for Gunpy to be stabled.'

'I know you did,' replied Bracer a small red-faced man curiously clad in a bearskin cap and a blacksmith's apron.

'Then why is he secured here in the yard?'

'You've not paid the stablers that's why. You owe four weeks from the last time you was 'ere.'

Sighing loudly Whitley proclaimed, 'Oh, the avarice of the age. Where is the generosity of spirit? The largesse of yesterday. . .?'

'And where are the robes and regalia?' asked his wife waving a freshly read letter.

Knowing that her husband ignored all correspondence, she had made it her business to open several documents awaiting attention. She wished she had not.

'There has been no delivery of the costumes for the coronation,' she revealed. 'Not so much as a garment nor garter is come.'

'No, nor will there,' said Bracer with an air of 'I told you so.' 'The whole lot's been took by the Fishers of Norwich.'

'Impossible. I've paid the deposit. I have a receipt - somewhere.'

'Ah, but the Fishers settled full in advance. Cash down for the lot.'

Whitley clasped a hand to his forehead, 'How all things do conspire against me,' he moaned.

'Did I not warn about it?' asked his wife. 'But you would have it blazed abroad, " *a dazzling spectacle. . . . as seen at Drury Lane. . . .*" Husband, I believe we are faced with ruin.'

With a sigh of weariness Whitley sat on the execution block last seen in *Jane Shore*. The optimism demanded of him was, for the moment, quenched. It seemed as if all the years on the road, the endless struggle to survive had at present defeated him. He felt for a snuff box and tapped it sharply, sniffing powder into each nostril. A volcanic sneeze was followed by the blowing of his nose into a lace handkerchief, which he then used to wipe off the mixture of snuff and snot from his frontage. He rallied.

'The Coronation will have to be. . . postponed.'

'Explain that to the public ,' said his wife with sourness of aspect.

'Due to unforeseen circumstances.' Whitley replaced the snuff box in his waistcoat pocket. 'We will have to present *Cato* in full, to replace the coronation. A risk, I know, but there is no alternative.'

'And what of *Cato?*' asked his wife. 'If we offer the entire play it must be in costume.'

Whitley thought for a moment. 'Where's Mrs Kenna?'

'I'm 'ere as always.' An ancient sewing lady pushed her way through a rack of dresses. Her mouthful of pins did not prevent her sipping gin from a bottle in her free hand.

'Ah, Mrs Kenna. We are in need of miracles in the wardrobe.'

'I'll say,'retorted Mrs Kenna, 'like the miracle of me getting paid.'

'Come now, Mrs Kenna, let not cupidity dull your needle. Tell me, what dresses have we for *Cato ?* Those still remaining from *Julius Caesar* I trust.?'

'*Julius Caesar?* Huh! So long as 'e's on 'is ownsome.'

'What do you mean, "on 'is ownsome,"?'

'I mean I've but one *equipage* remaining. You sold the rest to pay for *The Wrangling Lovers* in Retford you might recall.'

'We didn't sell everything did we?'

'Two breastplates, that's all what's left.'

'Well. . . we must improvise. Togas . . . sheets . . . towels. The men can wear sheets as togas.'

'They won't like it. Oh dear me no.''

'Purple edging will enrich anything, even a dust sheet when it's been laundered. The line of beauty, Mrs Kenna, the line of beauty.'

He turned to his wife, 'We shall manage, my love'

'Manage? There's more. Listen to this,' Mrs Whitley read from yet another official looking letter. '*You are hereby informed under the Licensing Act of 1737 that no person can be authorised to act for hire, gain or reward. . .'*

'But we are not acting for hire gain or reward,' broke in Whitley. '*Cato* will be played for gratis. Have we not performed in other towns with impunity?'

'But not in Nottingham. As Drinkwater said, here there is much opposition.'

'And much support. Remember, we come at the invitation of Marmaduke Pennell, the mayor himself.'

'The *former* mayor. This is signed by Alderman Fairlight, chairman of the town council. Mrs Whitley continued, '*persons acting within a public place shall be deemed rogues and vagabonds and as such be liable to six months' hard labour . . .'*

'It's all very well,' said Whitley, his bravado badly dented, 'but we have to play *Cato,* otherwise the evening is too short. We'd be finished by nine o'clock, just when the carriage trade arrives.'

'I can always sing my selection from *The Maid of the Mill,'* said Mrs Whitley.

An acid look from her husband said much. 'I believe we must risk a hazard and trust to luck,' he said, 'unless. . .' An idea came to him. 'I wonder if we could get Saunders to do his act? Always pleases the public does Saunders.'

He turned to Thomas who had been totally overlooked in the midst of the developing drama. 'You've seen Saunders, of course?'

'Can't say I have,' said Thomas.

'Popular with all classes,' said Whitley. 'Balances an egg on two straws, whilst playing the Dead March from *Saul* on a penny whistle. Blindfolded all the while. Greatly admired. Yes, we'd do well to get Saunders. . . '

Whitley began to leave, maybe to find the admired Mr. Saunders but Thomas intervened. For Thomas had plans of his own. Now, he thought, was conceivably the moment for his ambition to be revealed. Copying parts was all very fine, but it was only a shoe horn to a life upon the stage. He wanted more - Thomas wanted to be a comedian.

The desire was a new one. Caught with the rage of a fever only a while before in London, when he had been rousing with a band of drunken soldiers. After the newly declared peace with France and her allies, many like Thomas were no longer required by the army. Paid off, then befuddled with alcohol he had found himself in the gallery of a theatre where his new purpose was discovered. For in that squeezed noisy space he had witnessed a beatific vision - something that was called a Harlequinade. A bespangled comedian in multicoloured patches had danced and tumbled, somehow changing himself into a lion, a bird, even a lover. Thomas was one of the delighted spectators madly applauding and shouting for more of his drollery.

Immediately his mind had cleared with a certainty that this was to be his destiny. He had to be that man. He had to become a comedian and play Harlequin. Somehow he must find a way. But how? Where to start? Wherever he asked for guidance he was met with ridicule.

London was filled with the likes of him. Layabout lads hoping for a life on the stage. Such dreams were folly. 'Go thee to the provinces,' he was told with scorn. 'You might find something there. Here you're only a smatterer. London is for professionals.'

So he had been wandering north, where it was said dozens of new theatres were opening daily. There he was certain to find work. But it was not the way. Nobody wanted him. That is not until this day, when Whitley had given him the drum to beat and brought him into his theatre. This must be the moment to act, or at least begin to act. . .

'Sir, I am thought to be good at tumbling. Would that serve to entertain?'

'No, lad, no. You will be at your copying.'

'But I wish to act. Can I serve an apprenticeship in the theatre?'

This caused amusement among the onlookers. Whitley almost regaining his old complexion.

'In time I might allow you to dress the stage,' he said.

Thomas thought,' You mean put up scenery?' More amusement.

'It means to stand in silent character on stage, be it as a citizen of Harfleur, a nobleman of Corinth, or a Roman soldier. . .'

'I could do the last,' said Thomas.

'At present, you 'd pass only for a country yokel.'

Bracer interrupted. 'I'd 'ave a better use for 'im. Since our other lad's gone, I require more 'elp back stage.'

'Possibly, but the replicating must be done first,' said Whitley. 'After that I dare say we'll have one or two jobs for him. Howsoever,' he sighed, 'I think that concludes the business of the day. Christmas tomorrow I'm told. No doubt we all have plans for the season.'

'I have no plans,' said Thomas.

'Pardon me, but you have. You have a task with your pen. You can work and bunk here if you wish. Does that suit you Bracer?'

Bracer, like Thomas, had no family and it seemed few friends.
He used the theatre as his home which suited Whitley who was glad to have an unpaid watchman on the premises. It was clear that Thomas and Bracer were to be left alone in the theatre.

'Sir,' said Thomas, 'you have not yet shown me how you want the copying done'.

'Neither have I.' In less than five minutes, Whitley hurriedly explained what he required. Thomas, far from fully understanding, said yes he followed, in the hope that all would work out for the best.

'Husband,' said Cassandra, anxious to begin her Christmas preparations, 'we must be away.'

'Indeed we must, replied Whitley as he and his wife made to leave, at the same time Mrs Kenna gathered her pieces together.

'Remember Bracer, rehearsal, day after St. Stephen's day , ten o'clock. Full cast mind you. A fine if any are late,' he hesitated, 'and a merry Christmas to you both.'

Thomas pointedly looked at his pocket.

'Sir, it being Yuletide I have with me but tuppence. A sum hardly sufficient for me to eat drink and be merry. A shilling would keep good company with the two coins that I have.'

'Bracer, can you be of assistance?' asked Whitley.

'What, a penny father like me?'

'Recalling the token you gave me to see the Coronation,' said Thomas. 'Could I redeem it for the price of a place?'

'Indeed not,' replied Whitley, 'tokens are not returnable.' Then, perhaps realising that he and his wife would soon be enjoying an ample meal at their lodgings; a capon with trimmings, no doubt a fig pudding attended by a bottle or two of wine, a small stir of generosity touched Mr Whitley.

'Here's a sixpence. As an advance,' he said, 'it will be subtracted from your final payment. That should suffice for a plenteous celebration.'

He handed the small coin to Thomas with the same magnanimity as if it was a nail removed from his thumb.

*

'But where are all the actors?' asked Thomas.

'Hon root' replied Bracer.

'What's that mean?'

'On the road. Walking down from Doncaster. Should be 'ere soon. They'd better be, they've got the scenery.'

'Why isn't Whitley with them?'

'You won't catch Whitley walking, nor 'is missus neither.'

. 'Do they have a carriage?'

'A carriage?' Bracer laughed. 'Poor old Gunpowder couldn't pull a cork never mind a carriage. No, Jemmy rides Gunpy and Cassy 'ires a norse. Whitley makes out 'e's got to be first in a new town so 'e can pump around like you saw today. Then Cassy 'as to get the bills printed, 'cos if you don't tell the public what's 'appening you get no custom. But 'e 'asn't took the town yet.'

'What d'you mean "took the town?" ' asked Thomas.

'Got the right to perform. Trouble with Jemmy, 'e's been welcomed in too many places. Most magistrates likes seeing a play and gives permission straight off. But not 'ere in Nottingham. If 'e don't get no licence 'e's in trouble. What's more 'e'll 'ave a job to get one with Alderman Fairlight breathing fire and brimstone.'

Thomas looked around wondering where he might do his copying. He was astonished at the collection of what seemed to be little more than clutter.

'Don't touch nothing,' said Bracer, 'I knows where it all is,' he presented a small brown volume. 'This'll be what you're wanting.'

Thomas opened the book. 'This isn't *Cato.'* he said, 'This is a play called *O-roo-no-ko.'*

Bracer examined the volume carefully as if unsure if it was a play or prayer book. Eventually he said quietly, 'I 'aven't got the reading.'

'Where's he put *Cato* then?' Thomas was tempted to ask, 'Do you really know where everything is?'

Bracer walked to a pile of small books. ' 'e calls this the library. You'll maybe find it 'ere.' Thomas looked through the jumbled collection of plays, not recognising any until, with relief, he found the missing volume of *Cato*.

'Where does he keep paper and ink?' he asked. Bracer rooted into a bag and uncovered a bundle of paper together with a stone bottle of ink and a bundle of quills.

'Before you start,' said Bracer, 'you'd like a bit to eat? You're welcome to share a sausage if that's your liking.'

From what appeared to be a coal box he produced a frying pan with a string of uncooked sausages. 'These be all right?'

Thomas looked round, 'Is there a fire some place to cook them?'

'There is that,' said Bracer, 'Downstairs.'

Thomas asked, 'What about ale? I could pay for a jug.'

'I've got that an' all,' Bracer pointed to a pitcher in the midst of the paint and glue pots. 'Well 'idden eh? Come along, It's time you 'ad a look around the 'appy 'ouse'old.'

He lit two candles. 'I don't use candlesticks. I always carry a candle like the miners do 'twixt me fingers in me palm, much safer.' Bracer then noticed the youth's damaged hand and hesitated, but Thomas smiled, took the lighted candle and followed Bracer into the depths of the theatre.

Much of it had been built on old foundations. The lower walls were a mixture of bare sandstone and aged brick, cold and damp to the touch. They descended a flight of worn steps which must have been part of an earlier building, long forgotten. Bracer led the way in the darkness, their shadows flickering, changing shape from grotesque dwarfs to mighty giants.

'We're under the stage,' he said, opening a hidden door and beckoned him through it. The acoustics changed immediately, for they had moved into the auditorium where their voices were no longer muffled but beginning to echo.

Bracer lifted his light, 'There now. . .'

They were standing in the pit, an area filled with a muddle of benches around a brazier in which glowed a low fire. Candles provided little light until their eyes grew used to the darkness making it possible to see the distant form of the boxes and gallery. Bracer drew up one of the benches scraping it noisily over the stone floor. Patting a place at his side he bid Thomas to sit next to him. From a coal box he put fresh lumps on the fire and with a poker began riddling the ash to create a draught. He lay the frying pan on top with the sausages within.

'Proper 'ome from 'ome you might say.' Thomas did not reply, for he was still staring at the surroundings in the mutating light. He turned his back on the galleries to face the stage rising above him. The black void was bordered by a white proscenium arch. On each side were elegant columns framing a panelled door opening onto the stage. Even in the dim light it was impressive.

'Is it marble?' asked Thomas innocently.

Bracer laughed, 'Marble, no, it's painted wood, but it's well done you'll agree. Wait 'till you see it all proper lit.'

He pointed above his head, 'With all them candles afire, very grand I can tell you. If you gets took on, that'll be one of your jobs. Fitting all the candles in the chandeliers. To be done quick, but you'll learn soon enough. So, let's be 'aving a bit more light.'

He moved to the wall where a rope was wound to a clamp Untwisting it, he lowered from the ceiling what looked like a large wooden wheel lying flat. Around its circumference were holders for twelve or so candles. Bracer lit several and the increase in light showed more detail, until as he raised it high, the swinging of the glowing wheel cast crazy shadows making everything pitch and toss like a ship at sea.

Thomas looked with excitement at what the the swaying lights revealed, as Bracer next applied himself to the frying pan from which came a comforting sizzling of frying sausages.

'Let's be having that jug.' He took a deep draught from it.
'Yes,' he said wiping his mouth, 'queer place this, very old.'

'I thought it was only built last year,' said Thomas.

'Up top yes, but down 'ere no . . . Are you bothered by ghosts?'

'What manner of ghosts?'

'Old Saxons maybe. It's said there was once a great Saxon 'all 'ere 'till the Normans came and cleared them out. There's probably been many a killing on this very spot.'

'You don't know that.'

'You're right, I don't. But when you're down 'ere on your own in t'middle of a windy night like this, there's noises that gets you wond'rin'. Us theatre folk is as superstitious as sailors, so take no nonsense from such as me.'

He took another drink from the jug and passed it to Thomas,

'Any road, Merry Christmas.'

Thomas took the jug, 'Merry Christmas,' he replied and took a drink from the jug whose contents he found were almost gone.'

'Sausages are ready,' said Bracer, 'Got a knife?'

Thomas took the pen knife from his belt and they speared links from the pan which they ate, blowing on the hot food.

'Not much I know, said Bracer. 'Still as the saying goes "Hunger finds no fault with the cookery." '

Thomas looked at the brazier. 'Is this always kept alight? he asked.

'Lord luv yer, no. There's a performance comin' up that's why it's 'ere. Day before a show there'll be more like these. *Good fires 'ave been kept* it'll say in the papers. The customers likes it warm.'

When the food was finished and the jug finally emptied, mostly by Bracer, he said, 'Been a lobster 'ave you?

'A red coat? Yes. I was drummer. With a fine uniform of my own. Colonel Hayter's regiment.'

'Don't know 'im.'

'Up in Yorkshire.'

' 'ow come you're in t'midlands then?'

'We were on the march down south,' said Thomas, 'when news came of peace with the Frenchies, So we were sundered and paid off. Near London it was. I had a look round there, then started up north again. I was headed for York. They say it's the best playhouse there outside London.'

'Why be in Nottingham then?'

'It's on the way. And I'd heard tell a new theatre was opening.'

'And so there is,' said Bracer. The small amount of food finished he stood up. 'And you'll be wanting to start your copying. You'll be warm 'ere by the fire.'

'I need a surface, a flat top.'

'Oh my word! You'll be wantin' a writing desk .'

'No, just somewhere I can write with an inkwell.'

'We'll 'ave a look back in the green room. He stood, extinguished the candles, then hoisted the wheel to its place below the ceiling.

'Why is it called the green room?' asked Thomas.

'Some says it's 'cos when actors is waitin' there to go on onstage, many of 'em looks fair green wi' fear. Who knows?'

Once back in the oddly named room, Bracer lit two more candles and looked round. He pointed to a table and stool. ''ow will this do Master Scribe? You can have two candles if you're good, and don't tell the mester.'

Thomas gathered together the sheaf of paper and sharpened a quill. Finding a cloth he wiped clean the surface, putting his quill and ink in place, then drawing up the stool he opened the edition of *Cato*.

'That's got you settled then,' said Bracer with satisfaction.

In the distance they heard a watchman calling the hour - *eight o'clock of a fine night.*

'That gives you four hours at best don't it? So, seein' as 'ow you're goin' to be occupied for a while, you'll not mind keepin' an eye on the premises if I slips out for ten minutes.'

'To the nearest tavern?

'It might be. But after all it's Christmas ain't it?'

'Yes, it is Christmas,' Thomas said as Bracer left.

Examining the text, he dipped the quill in the ink, trying to follow Whitley's instructions. 'Leave out the prologue. Fair copies only for the five main characters. The others can share. And don't bother with the epilogue.'

Thomas considered the day just ending. Here he was. Working in a theatre! Far from he wanted. but it was a start - a start with prospects.

He put the pen to the page,

'*CATO, Act One, Scene One. Portius and Marcus* (they can share.)

Portius: The dawn is overcast, the morning lowers. . .

He heard the watchman call midnight. He was cold and he was tired. His hand was cramped with the writing and he could not be sure that he was copying the text in the way that was required. Many of the words puzzled him and he had to copy them with care, letter by letter, names like. S-Y-P-H-A-X and J-O-B-A. They made no sense.

'Ten minutes,' Bracer had said, but he had not come back. Rarely had he felt so alone. Was it a fool's errand to be copying these words? He had earned but sixpence so far and promise of a guinea however much that might be. Should anyone return, would they roar with laughter at his gullibility?

It was the cold. Cold that penetrated like a blade of ice. He left the stool and looked for something to wrap around himself. He found a doublet, discarded from a long mislaid play, red velvet, dark with grime. It was too small but he draped it over his own thin jacket. Drawing it about him, he felt little benefit; it was damp and mustied which decided him to return to the theatre pit, to seek warmth and comfort from the coals in the brazier.

He lifted the candlestick from the desk and began to search for the way back into the auditorium. Before, he and Bracer had walked down a flight of stairs to get to the pit. Somehow he had missed the stairway and taken another direction, which was wrong. He was in a different unknown place.

He shuddered. Somewhere far away he heard a creaking followed by an unrecognised sound which made him think of the Saxons of times past. He wondered, was he being watched? He stood still and listened. He could hear a movement but it was hard to tell from what quarter it was coming. Outside there was a high wind blowing. Yes, it had to be that. He hated owning to the truth, but he felt anxious.

Perhaps he was not alone after all?

No it was nonsense. Probably rats, the place must be full of them. But which way to go? A step forward and he tripped over a ridge in the floor. Losing his balance, the candle fell from the stick. Now he was in complete darkness, quite lost until he saw that the candle, still alight, had rolled onto a pile of discarded paper which was rapidly catching fire. Near to panic he began stamping on the flames attempting to extinguish them before they took hold. As he did so he understood where he was.

He was standing on the stage.

Briefly, the flames had illuminated the surroundings enough for him to see that there were flats on either side and before him was the empty auditorium. He continued to stamp his feet until he was certain the fire was gone. The exertion warmed him slightly and he retrieved the still burning candle.

Consider! Here he was, on the stage. Looking downwards he could see the faint glow of the brazier in the pit, his original destination which was now of minor consequence.

It mattered only that for the first time ever he was standing on a stage. It was like being inside a great mouth. The stage was the tongue.

The galleries before him like surrounding rows of teeth. He longed for more light to see better until moving one foot slightly he found more sheets of old newspaper. For the moment he felt slightly mad as he knew exactly what he was going to do. He placed the candlestick on the stage floor and taking a page of old newsprint rolled it into a torch.

It was a moment in his life that needed marking and nothing would prevent it. Perhaps it was a surfeit of the poetic lines he had been copying. Or was ot light headiness caused by an almost empty stomach? Whatever it was at that very instant a force took hold of him. Once rolled, he lit the end of the paper and stood centre stage looking out directly at the auditorium. At his feet he saw the empty footlights. He held the burning paper high as a beacon and proclaimed, his voice resounding,

'Look at me! Listen to me! I will be worth your while!
Give me time. For I will deliver such scenes, such songs,
That you will marvel. You who are not yet here.
You will know me and demand all I have, and I will give it.
This I declare for I am here. And I am Thomas Hammond!'

Thomas believed he was alone. It was not so. Deep in the dark of the theatre, there was a listener; one who noted and made remembrance of his vow from the stage, but for the time being held it secret.

*

Three. *Each Actor on his Ass.*

The production of *Cato, a tragedy* was still in its infancy, the actors having been handed their parts only that morning. The cast list when displayed for examination was met with glum resignation .

MEN

Cato . . . . Mr Wheeler
Lucius, *a senator*. . . . . Mr Sweeny
Sempronius, *a senator* . . . . Mr Naylor.
Jura, *Prince of Numidia* . . . . Mr Willis.
Syphax, General *of the Numidians*. . . . . .Mr Mitteer
Portius]. . . . . Mr Mitteer.
] *Sons of Cato*
Marcus]. . . . . Mrs Mitteer
Decius, *ambassador from Caesar* . . . . Mr Willis.

WOMEN

Marcia, *daughter to Cato* . . . . Miss Proctor.
Lucia, *daughter to Lucius* . . . . Mrs Willis.

'Play as cast' was engraved upon the hearts of the players who accepted their roles as they might a prison sentence. Two of the cast, Mr Mitteer and Mr Willis, saw that they were to double for which there was no extra payment and they would be subjected to the additional perils of frantic costume changes in the confined backstage conditions.

The day began with the serious matter of the initial play reading with everyone gathered in the pit around the same brazier shared earlier by Thomas and Mr Bracer. At a first rehearsal Whitley marked the occasion with a short address. This never varied, always ending with the same joke, 'Well cast, shall we cast off?' Today he followed this by asking, 'Mister Sweeny, we await your Lucius with pleasure.'

Mr Sweeny, well-built with a good voice was an actor able to tackle any role be it young or old, tragic or comic, poetic or vulgar.

It came as a surprise when, after regarding Thomas's newly hand-written text, instead of his opening speech he said petulantly,

'I cannot read this. This is not in the usual hand. It is indecipherable.'

Whitley sighed, 'No, sir, it is not in the usual hand, but it is quite clear nevertheless.'

'I beg to differ. I repeat it is indecipherable.'

No-one else was brave enough to agree openly with Mr Sweeny, yet several pages rustled in sympathy.

'Mr Sweeny, if you please,' insisted Whitley.

'Under protest,' replied Sweeny. He stared disdainfully at the page in his hand, until with his strong voice he began,

'The down is overcoat, the moaning lawyers,

Act heavily in clubs flings on the dew. . . . It makes no sense.''

'No Mr Sweeny. Your reading does not.' Whitley breathed deeply to keep his temper, 'the lines are,

The dawn is overcast, the morning lowers,

And heavily in clouds brings on the day. . . .'

'I need the book,' said Sweeny. This was unheard of. Only Whitley possessed the text and would no more part with it than with his purse.

'No Mr Sweeny, you do not need the book. I suggest we skip your speech so you can examine it, with a magnifying glass if need be. Miss Proctor will you read in the next speech?'

Dora Proctor was the youngest in the company. Though aged about twenty, when needed she had the great asset of seeming on stage to be no more than twelve years old and could pass as either sex if carefully costumed. She could bring the house down as a dandiprat, turning cart wheels and playing a medley of tunes on the musical glasses. Often, she was absent from stage work, due to an arcane activity which seemed more lucrative than her earnings as an actress. Indeed Dora was never short of a shilling and being a generous girl was always willing to give whatever she could. Not for nothing was she known as 'everybody's sweetheart.'

Perhaps because her eyes were clearer or because she had been studying her lines in advance, Dora spoke with eagerness.

'Thy steady temper, Portius, can look on guilt, rebellion,

Fraud and Caesar in the calm lights of mild philosophy. . .'

Excellent,' smiled Whitley at the end of her speech, 'Quite in order.' Dora smiled with satisfaction and the others regarded her with annoyance.

The rehearsal was underway. . .

Whitley did not reveal who was responsible for the newly hand-written scripts. He had made no mention of Thomas, believing he should be kept at his writing desk until the task was complete. As the reading continued, numerous deviations from the original were suspected and mostly passed over. It was not until Cato himself proclaimed,

'Bathers let us meet in Cornwall,' that a major error was identified. A hurried consultation of the original showed the line to be,

'Fathers let us meet in Council.' Corrections were made. Other inaccuracies were dismissed in the belief that, 'We may see it but the clods in the gallery won't,' which was probably true.

In the late afternoon, Thomas having finished his pages, took it upon himself to approach the company with his completed work. Whitley was not pleased and grasped the scripts from him, curtly handing them to the cast whilst ignoring his presence.

'Who is this?' asked Miss Proctor, 'Do we have a new *confrere* in our midst?' She laughed cheerily. She was always glad to see a fresh face and this one she thought was a rather pretty fellow. Thomas blushed as all eyes examined him.

'Name of Thomas,' said Whitley. 'He may be with us a while.'

'Indeed I do hope so,' said Dora. Knowing glances were exchanged. Several members of the cast greeted Thomas in a friendly way, some did not. Mr Sweeny spoke his mind.

'Are you are responsible for this travesty of a script?' he asked. 'I shall be fortunate if I am not blind by the end of the day.'

'If you are,' Mr Naylor replied, 'We'll all know what you've been up to.'

Whitley raised his voice over the laughter, 'Come along now, time is passing and I want to be cast off before the evening tide.' Nobody laughed at the joke. They had heard it too often. ~

What finally emerged as Mr Addison's *Cato* was only an approximation. Mistakes in the copying together with ad-libbing by the actors left, what the scholarly would call a *palimpsest*; i.e. the faint reappearance of a once rubbed out text. Understanding of it might have been helped if the play had been staged with authentic settings and costume. Such lavishness was not one of Whitley's attributes. Scenery to him was a nuisance, to be provided as cheaply as possible. The original play was divided into seven scenes, with only one being stipulated, namely *The Senate (sitting).* For this Whitley used an ancient back cloth from *Julius Caesar* thus revealing that the Roman senate sat in the street outside the *Colosseum (restored).*

The whereabouts of the other six scenes was not specified. Dialogue at times suggested domestic settings, perhaps even Cato's own house. For this was used the kitchen-parlour set from the *The Distressed Mother* which had recently served as Gertrude's Bedroom *(Hamlet),* a council chamber in Pomfret Castle *(Richard II),* and many other interiors. But as Whitley said, it depicted the inside of a home thus fulfilling the main purpose of any scene which was - location.

As feared, the costumes caused the most upset. The edict that togas were to be made from towels and bed linen was not well received. Only Mr Sweeny, always proud of his physique, was happy with the notion. His offer of appearing bare chested in the interests of economy was not thought helpful. The point being made that he was playing a Roman senator, and not a Roman gladiator. This ruling was a relief to the other men in the cast who found themselves clad in miscellaneous nether garments surmounted by purple edged material which approximated as togas. These were constantly slipping off shoulders, the hitching back of which was a continual irritant to both actor and observer.

Miss Proctor also cast as a Roman, one of Cato's daughters, followed Mr Sweeny's example insisting that an off-shoulder toga would be sufficient for her. When this fell frequently, revealing her admittedly delightful breasts, she was persuaded to wear a bodice (low cut) to conform with the other Roman apparel.

Mr Huntley Wheeler, a senior member of the cast, was given the lead role, only when Whitley decided not to play it himself. The part of

Cato being lengthy and unspectacular was not to Whitley's taste, so it had been designated to Mr Wheeler.

An imperious man in his middle thirties, Wheeler stood more than a head above the others and was certainly better suited to act the noble Roman than the slightly rotund Whitley. As the eponymous Cato he was privileged to be awarded the only full Roman costume. Even so, he did not feel this gave him the authority his tragic role demanded. After some rummaging in property baskets, he had found a full bottomed Restoration wig which he felt gave him the required gravitas. After angry exchanges with Mr Whitley, which included threats to leave the production altogether, he was allowed to wear the wig.

This led to jealousies. A similar wig was also found by Mr Sweeny who, playing a leading senator, felt he too should have a head-dress. After more ill temper, the realisation that Mr Wheeler's wig was taller than Mr Sweeny's, allowed the difference to be resolved, if not hierarchically at least amicably.

By this time the other men in the cast also insisted on some form of head gear. There being no more Restoration wigs to be found, the lesser members were satisfied with brightly coloured turbans and in one case a Cromwellian helmet which gave a perplexing insight into the attire of ancient Rome.

Properties too caused divisions. Long swords Whitley would not permit. Not because they were wrong with togas, but because there were not sufficient As a reparation the remaining men decided amongst themselves to appear cross gartered. By now Whitley hardly cared what they wore. If they came on as Peruvian warriors he would not have minded as long as they knew their lines.

In this area the elderly Mr Mitteer was having his usual problems, for sadly a bad memory combined with poor hearing made his acting prone to difficulties

But he believed he had hit on a brilliant solution. From studying pictures of Romans he saw that most such senators carried scrolls. With Whitley's reluctant approval he copied out his lines onto a paper roll and the difficulty was solved to some extent. Unhappily his eye-sight not being what it was, he was almost reduced to kneeling down by the footlights in order to read the text or find his cue. ~

Later that night, Jemmy Whitley, sitting up in bed beside his wife continued to complain. 'Never before have I had such a troupe of misfits and incompetents,' he chuntered,. It is without doubt the worst company I've ever known.'

'You always say that at the start of rehearsals,' said his wife.

'They can't speak, they can't move, they can't act.'

'You engaged them.'

'I had no choice. The craft of acting has gone. The lack of talent will be the death of the theatre, of that you can be certain.'

'Don't fuss. Remember husband - Rome wasn't burned in a day.'

With that, Cassy blew out the candle.

Once Thomas had completed his copying of the parts, he was given further tasks, answering the needs of the actors and backstage staff. Trips to the pie shop and the tavern for beer dominated his day. In no time he discovered not to undertake such errands unless he received money in advance. The disposal of bodily wastes was an undertaking also regarded as his responsibility. The needs of both sexes necessitated two containers in the dressing rooms which Thomas was expected to empty and maintain as often as was thought needful. Understandably it was a duty he avoided until ordered to 'empty the bloody shit box,' which he did by disposing of its contents in the street as far away from the place of origin as possible. As the other property holders carried out the same practice the whole roadway was no place for a sensitive pedestrian.

He became a messenger for many including Dora Proctor for whom he ran routine errands. These were mostly concerning young gentlemen in offices and clubs who were anxious to learn when and where they might call on the lady should she have half an hour to spare. Miss Proctor took an instant liking to Thomas, commissioning him from her small and pretty lodgings. Here Thomas repeatedly found her in state of *dishabille* which troubled him at first but soon bothered him not one bit.

Mrs Mitteer he found to be equally amiable but in a maternal way. She was prone to patting him on the cheek and calling him 'my lovely lad,' as time and again she asked him to lift or move heavy loads or shift furniture, as her husband was no longer able to carry out such tasks. 'Mitteer used to be as strong as an ox,' she said, 'but now. . , ' her voice trailed away in sad reminiscence. Thomas carried water for her, fetched coals, threaded needles, uncorked bottles and searched for missing shoes and keys which both she and Mr Mitteer mislaid hourly.

The men in the company paid little heed to Thomas. Mr Wheeler with his haughty manner had few friends. He never indulged in gossip or pranks and when not required on stage kept himself apart studying his lines.

Mr Sweeny was more approachable, yet aspects of his behaviour were troubling. Quick to take offence, he never looked anyone in the eye when conversing, but at other times he could be found studying people when he thought they were unaware of his scrutiny.

Thomas spent most of his time with Mr Bracer. He was after all the backstage manager and supervisor of lighting in the auditorium. Candles used in the *chandeliers* were made of tallow derived from animal fat which emitted smoke of an offensive odour. When Thomas commented upon this Bracer replied,

'You think that's bad, but wait till you smell a full 'ouse full of sweaty bodies, food, drink and piss pots runnin' all over the floor.'

Bracer liked Thomas's youthful eagerness to please. He had never known a lad so keen to learn. It was a pleasure to have him readily accepting tasks and he believed that soon the youth would be an asset to the entire establishment. For Thomas, the older man was an encyclopaedia of theatrical knowledge and the close companionship that quickly developed between them enabled him to learn much .

As the day of the opening drew near, there was less laughter and more outbursts of bad temper. Worrying reports from Mr Joe Parr, in charge of advance booking, revealed that many on hearing that the *Coronation of George III* was withdrawn, had asked for their money back . Booking in general could have been better.

A tryout of the musical items was arranged before the full dress rehearsal of *Cato*. Characteristically Whitley would not buy or rent a keyboard instrument so three amateur musicians on violin, cello and and flute provided a standard of playing acceptable for the majority. Serious music lovers stayed away. As for those in the gallery, it was rightly assumed they were no more able to appreciate good music than read Mycenaean Greek.

PROGRAMME.

SONGS

For 'tis rare to find a True Love. . . . . **Mrs Willis.**

(With this sentiment few disagreed.)

While Happy in my Native Land . . . . **Mr Mitteer.**

Bucks Have at Ye All. . . . . **Mr Naylor.**

Duets.

Sweet is the Breath of Man, (words by Milton no less.)

Said a Smile to a Tear. . . . . **Mrs Willis and Mrs Mitteer.**

Musical Interlude.

Selection from *The Maid of the Mill. . . . .***Mrs Whitley.** (Again!)

Musical Novelty.

Miss Proctor and her Musical Wine Glasses.

Songs.

Four and Twenty Fiddlers . . . . **Mrs Mitteer.**

No Flower that Blows is Like a Rose. . . . . . . **Mrs Willis.**

Scottish Ballads

Tak Ye Ould Cloak About Ye! with the rousing song of Bruce's address to his army, *Scots Whae Hae wi' Wallace Bled. . .* **Mr Naylor.**

(As both songs proved unintelligible to the English it was thought Mr Naylor's Gaelic tongue must be truly authentic.)

By Popular Demand **Mr Whitley** will sing his celebrated song in the role of a French Valet. *Fol De Rol Tit, La La.* And a new song written especially for this evening in celebration of *Nottingham Ale.*

Grand Finale.

Hearts of Oak, Rule Britannia . . . . The **Full Company.**

God Save the King.

(It was thought that with this part of the evening at least, the patrons would be given good value for money.)

.

The final run through of *Cato* evoked the spurious tradition that the worse the dress rehearsal the better the performance, although nobody believed it for a minute.

Whitley's temper with his cast grew worse and Mrs Whitley as prompt almost read out the entire play herself, the 'drys' were so frequent.

'Why can't any of you act?' he asked furiously, 'You mumble, all of you. I ask for fluency - you give me flatulence. I ask for drama not dregs. I want to be moved. I want performances! I want attack!.'

Pointing to Mr Mitteer he called, 'You there, who are you?'

'What?' poor Mr Mitteer asked in a state of alarm.

'He wants to know who you are,' his wife tried to help.

'I'm Mitteer. . . ' he stuttered.

'In the play you fool! What's your name in the play? You're Lucius aren't you?' shouted Whitley.

'No I'm Syphax at the start and Portius later on.'

Mr Sweeny stepped in. 'I believe I'm Lucius,' he said ,

'I don't mean you, I mean the other Lucius,'

'But I'm not Lucius, I'm Syphax or Portius,'protested Mr Mitteer.

'I know that,' Whitley snapped, 'and Portius should come in by the left door.' Whitley had a constant difficulty in recalling his stage left from his stage right, particularly now that he was standing in the auditorium.

'But I did come in by the left door,' Mr Mitteer was bewildered.

'I don't mean that left door I mean the other left door,' Whitley shouted. 'Don't let him come in by the left door. Bolt it somebody.'

'My next entrance is by the left door,' Mr Willis pointed out.

'Then you'll have to unbolt it before you enter,' Whitley insisted. 'I don't think it has a bolt,' said Mr Willis.

'Then it should have a bolt. Bracer! Where's Bracer? See there's a bolt on the left door.'

The rehearsal continued. . .

Later in the day Mr Wheeler shocked everyone when he said, 'I would like to make a suggestion.' Such a challenge to Whitley's authority was rare. There was a silence.

'Yes, Mr Wheeler?' asked Whitley coldly.

'I think the production would benefit if there were some music.'

'What sort of music, Mr Wheeler?'

'I'm not an authority on ancient Rome,' continued Mr Wheeler, 'but I think some trumpet calls would help. Especially when Cato enters.'

Whitley had to admit that this was not a bad idea, but there was a deficiency. 'Mr Wheeler we only have a flute. I don't think trumpet calls can be achieved on a flute.'

'We have got a trumpet. I came across one the other day in one of the property baskets. I think Mr Saunders may have left it.'

'Mr Wheeler, the man who plays the flute can't play a trumpet.'

It seemed the whole idea of trumpet calls was about to be forgotten when Thomas spoke up from the wings.

'I can play a bugle,' he announced. His audacity created as much excitement as did Mr Wheeler's interruption.

'He can you know,' Mrs Whitley said from the prompt corner.

The tension was now palpable. Whitley realised the idea had merit. He considered for a minute then asked for the trumpet.

There were a few moments of relief with the rehearsal coming to an unexpected break as the search for the trumpet took place. Mr Wheeler came on stage wielding the instrument.

Whitley looked at Thomas, 'Can you play it or not ?'

'I'll have a go.'

Thomas was wise enough not to come down stage, but at a modest distance he cleared his throat after which a series of blasts filled the theatre with sound. Not that it was a very good sound and to tell the truth it was inclined to be flat, but it was a recognisable trumpet call. When he finished there was tentative clapping from some in the cast.

Mr Whitley nodded his head in approval. To his admittedly tin ear it sounded more or less authentic.

'That sounds tolerable,' he declared, and some in the cast agreed. 'Very well,' he said, 'we'll use it. Mr Wheeler, if you can say where trumpet calls might be inserted please let me know after the rehearsal. Thomas you'd best come as well to decide on cues.'

Fortune smiled on Thomas. It had been an achievement. And it meant that even though he would be heard and not seen, Thomas was now an acting member of the company.

*

Four. *Latecomers will be Welcome.*

New Year's Eve and opening night. Costumes and properties were checked and checked again. Actors in various parts of the house muttered to themselves as they went over their lines. Mr Mitteer, still trying to learn his, was followed everywhere by his wife giving him the cues to which he responded,

'Don't tell me, don't tell me, I knew it full well this morning,' which he did not.

Scene changes were in the hands of Mr Bracer with Thomas his main helper. Flats were to be slid into position, back cloths lowered and raised in full view of the audience. Also their responsibility were the lighting wheels above the stage as well as the footlights. The candles being of the cheapest make, burned for less than an hour which meant their renewal several times during the evening.

Candle stubs could burn and the hot fat scald. At speed, a dozen candles had to be removed from each wheel and dropped into buckets of water, with new ones in place and lit before being hoisted again. The same applied to the lighting in the auditorium which also became Thomas's concern. Timing was complex, for he was expected to perform these duties as well as provide the trumpet calls recently assigned to him.

Until then he had only played the bugle and he found the valves on the trumpet an annoyance. In the end he did not touch those seductive taps and used his lips and breath as he knew best. Whitley prudently had told him to practice outside in the yard, where strange blasts had caused babies in the neighbourhood to wake screaming and several cats to disappear, never to be seen again.

From four o'clock in the afternoon rumbustious members of the public waited for the main doors to open with strident laughter, singing and pushing for a position. Added to this, street musicians, one with a dancing bear arrived in the hope of entertaining the crowd. Although the performance was not until seven o'clock, the pit and gallery doors were opened at six.

The gallery filled first, being the cheapest part of the house. Its seating was a series of deep steps down which many young blades leapt to get the advantage of the front row. Babes in arms were not admitted but such was the crush that several infants slipped past unnoticed. Later their screaming disturbed the few quieter moments of the evening, until their mothers thoughtfully put them to the breast.

The pit did not fill so rapidly due to the higher price. Benches, carefully laid out in orderly rows were soon knocked over and many a shin was bruised in the pursuit of a place. Fruit (mostly oranges), pies and nuts were on sale in all parts at inflated prices and were consumed by customers as if they had not eaten for a month. Waiting for the entertainment to begin led to boredom which in turn led to horseplay.

Orange peel and nut shells rained down from the gallery onto the pit causing great merriment. Insults too were traded between the two parts of the house. A young man in the front of the gallery found the audience enjoyed his animal impersonations, so that his rendering of a cockerel crowing and the mooing of a cow helped pass the time agreeably.

When eventually the three musicians took their places, excitement reached new levels with deafening cheers, clapping and yells. At seven o'clock Mr Whitley came on stage to welcome the audience with a poem he had written especially for the evening. Truth was it had been written months before and could be adopted for whatever town he was appearing in. Hence the opening line,

Dear town of ---------- (insert locality) *which is the muses seat,*
Where players in performing find their happiness complete.
Where drama, music, art so strongly do survive
As culture in this town by all is always kept alive . . . . .

Each couplet when complimentary to the locality was received with loud applause.

The concert, making up the first half of the evening went well. Ballads by Mrs Mitteer and Mrs Willis were much liked, as were the duets by Mr Mitteer and Mr Naylor. Mr Whitley's song in the guise of a French valet was encored. In addition to playing her musical glasses

Miss Proctor was prevailed upon to appear in her celebrated role as a pretty little girl of twelve. She sang a seemingly innocent song with so many nods and winks to the gallery that she took a whole series of reprises to the aggravation of Mr Whitley. Eventually she had to ask the audience to excuse her for not giving more, but she had a part to play later in the evening and she feared for her voice.

Nobody had seemed to miss the Coronation, so Whitley's policy of saying nothing appeared to have been warranted. All the *artistes* added additional songs and monologues from their repertoire so the gap was happily filled.

At nine o'clock Thomas and Mr Bracer again renewed the many candles and there was an expectant pause before the performance of *Cato* . Thomas was concerned to see that the boxes were almost empty until Bracer reminded him that the carriage trade never arrived before that hour.

It had been decided that a fanfare would be ideal to indicate the start of the play. Thomas, suddenly anxious about his ability, suffered his first attack of stage fright, but after an extra mug of ale played more than tolerably well, his trumpet calls commanding attention throughout the house which was moderately full for the second half.

Cato did not receive the success the concert had enjoyed. Those in the gallery grew restless, unable to follow the political vicissitudes of ancient Rome. More orange peel and nuts were thrown onto the stage, even a bottle was hurled, narrowly missing Mr Wheeler at the height of one of his noteworthy speeches. With disdain he kicked it into the footlights.

About nine thirty, towards the end of Act One, further disturbances began, this time caused by new arrivals in the private boxes. With the lighting in the auditorium as bright as on the stage, leading gentry and local personalities were recognised by the audience, taking attention away from the play.

Society ladies timed their entrances carefully, showing off their finery in what amounted to a parade of fashion. New gowns were met with loud buzzes either of appreciation or disapproval, with *Cato* by now almost a distraction. When the former mayor Mr Pennell entered, there was loud applause which he acknowledged modestly from his box, bringing the play to a complete halt. The hold up was disastrous for Mr Mitteer, who was in the middle of one of his most difficult speeches. The poor man lost his place, completely forgetting his line, 'My voice is still for war.'

His prompt was given first by Mrs Whitley but he seemed not to hear, then by both Mrs Whitley and Mrs Mitteer, which was heard by the entire house. Still he hesitated until the audience shouted in unison,

'My voice is still for war,' and he was able finally to recover his place.

But the grip of *Cato* had been lost. Those in the private boxes talked loudly amongst themselves as well as opening bottles of sparkling wine and hampers of food. Some even called across to friends on the other side of the auditorium saying how pleased they were to see them,

'What a fine gown it is, I demand the dressmaker's name.'

Even social engagements were discussed,

'Are you going to be at the Hartlocks this coming Friday?'

Yet finally, in a way, the success of the evening belonged to Thomas. For his fanfares were so ear splitting that the entire audience was silenced by them, something that was never achieved by the acting of the players.

*Cato e*nded at half past eleven and was received with modest enthusiasm. Those in the private boxes were content to stay for a while and chat as the lower orders vacated their seats. Eventually, assisted by their servants, they made their way to their conveyances waiting outside. Many of the coaches and carriages in the narrow street were facing in opposite directions resulting in a monumental tangle. Angry drivers shouted at each other as wheels were locked, shafts wedged and bridles jammed in a gigantic snarl. Eventually some carriages at the rear were turned round and the street finally made clear, but many ladies and gentlemen were obliged to walk to their means of transport in the far from clean road way.

Backstage, the actors were so relieved the evening was over that past differences were forgotten and thanks given that things had gone as well as they had. Even Mr Mitteer was told his performance was 'remarkable,' and 'no, of course nobody had noticed the drys.'

When asked what he thought of the evening. Mr Whitley, never one to lavish praise, had said, 'I've seen worse.' He was quietly pleased for it had been an almost full house which promised a good return at the box office. He told his company that he was confident another performance on New Year's Day would be forthcoming.

Miss Proctor had a most profitable evening. Several fresh admirers sought out her acquaintance backstage and did not mind one bit that she was only able to greet them in a state of near undress. Compliments were showered upon her like rice at a wedding, to which she replied with affecting modesty,

'Sirs, have done with your flattery, such sauce, will be my undoing!' Yes, I should be most happy to take supper with you, though I must warn I *never* touch the strong waters!'

All this suggested that her daytime engagement book was filled for weeks ahead which meant that the number of errands Thomas had been asked to run was noticeably reduced.

Thomas found the first night joviality exciting. Nobody had mentioned his bugle calls but he felt he had in his way contributed to the evening's success. He hovered around the many exchanges of compliments in the hope that one might be inclined to him. Nothing was said. At last he asked Mr Bracer cautiously,

'Was I all right? The trumpet calls I mean?'

'Yes, yes,' replied Bracer, his mind clearly elsewhere.

'Nobody's told me,' added Thomas.

'Nor will they if it went well. But if it doesn't you'll 'ear enough. That's the 'umour of it.'

As is the custom after the exhilaration of the first night, the second performance of a play is invariably flat. Next evening, in a quiet business like manner preparations both backstage and front of house were put in place. The cast assembled, make-up was applied and costumes donned.

All seemed to be ready, until something was noticed.

Where was Mr Wheeler?

Several felt a little ashamed that they had not noticed his absence. Whitley was the most concerned.

Has anyone seen Mr Wheeler? Where can he be? Heads were shaken, shoulders shrugged, nobody knew.

Mr Wheeler being such a private man it was not known for certain where he lodged, so word could not be sent to him there. It was too late anyway. The mystery was complete. Even worse, the house was already beginning to fill. Nothing like the numbers of yesterday but there was an audience and if disappointed, audiences could turn nasty.

Someone said, 'As he's not in the first half, perhaps he's coming later.'

'He knows my rules,' snapped Whitley. 'Roll call here before curtain up.'

'If he's not come by the concert interval, you'll have to take his place,' said Mrs Whitley, coming straight to the point. Her husband replied,

'But I don't know the part. . .'

'Then you'll have to read it,'

'That means using the book. You won't have it to prompt from.'

'You'll have to prompt as well as read from the book.'

To herself, Mrs Whitley rather liked the prospect of an evening without being on the book. She might perhaps go home and examine the latest London news sheet and at the same time enjoy a glass of port.

Her husband's anxiety continued, 'The costume - it won't fit me. Wheeler's so much taller.' he complained.

'Don't fuss. You'll have to be pinned up. Let's see to it.' Whitley showed signs of near panic as his wife took over. Soon, Mrs Whitley's hope of an evening at home faded as she realised she would have to adapt Mr Wheeler's costume to her husband's stature.

'The skirt will have to be let out, if there's enough material. I expect the breastplate will cover a great deal.'

'I shan't wear the wig,' Whitley pronounced.

'No, you'd be lost in it . . .'

As emergency plans were rapidly put into place, Bracer broke into the conversation.

'Someone to see "Sir". '

'I'm far too busy, get rid of them whoever it is.'

'It's a constable. 'e's got a warrant.'

Mr Whitley blanched. 'Say I'm on stage, say anything. Send him away.'

''e says 'e's not leaving 'till 'e's served it.'

'I don't deserve this. This is too much. Where is the bastard?'

Tired and jaded the Whitleys went slowly to the green room. Here waited an unpleasant looking man with a weasel-like face.

'James Haugustus Whitley?' he asked in a superior tone.

'Yes,'

A sealed document was produced by the weasel.

'High am 'ereby ordered to 'and you this hinjunction, with a warning that forbids you to perform hany dramatic presentation that hincludes spoken words. Hiff you should break this horder, you and your company will be harrested and charged under the vagrancy hact.'

The official document was handed to Whitley. 'From whence does this come?' he asked with dignity.

'By horder of Halderman Fairlight, chairman of the town council.'

Mr Whitley shook his head. 'High 'ave,' he cleared his throat, 'I have a hall full of people who are waiting to hear a concert of serious music.'

' Singin' hand dancin' his not ag'in the law. Talkin' is.'

'Am I not even allowed to announce the titles of the songs?' Whitley asked, using his most commanding of tones. The weasel hesitated.

'High shall 'ave to look hinto that.'

'Please do. Meanwhile my public awaits, I cannot disappoint.'

'Ah! Hexactly what the prisoner said.'

'What prisoner?'

'Name of Wheeler. 'e now lies hunder arrest at the Guild 'all. Refused bail, due to appear before the magistrates tomorrow morning at heleven. Charged with hacting the role of. . .' he examined a paper, '*Katt-oh.'*

'Are you in earnest. "Acting the role of *Cato?*" '

'That is correct. Court at the Guildhall, heleven o' clock sharp.'

'Eleven o' clock?'

High 'ope high made myself clear. God save the King, Harmen.'

All was well ready for the second performance. The audience, though smaller in number, showed the same enthusiasm for the pleasures that lay ahead. But unlike the previous evening Mr Whitley did not begin the entertainment with his poem. Instead he addressed the house in solemn tones.

'My friends. Last night I was able to thank you for the warm and generous welcome given to me and my humble band of players. Tonight I have to tell you that the town council has rejected this kind welcome.' *(Murmurs.)*

'Not only have we been forbidden to perform, but our very own Mr Wheeler, who last night dazzled with his brilliant performance in the arduous role of *Cato*, has been arrested and imprisoned for doing so. *(Louder murmurs.)* I ask you. Is this hospitality? *(Cries of No.)* Tonight we are forbidden to act before you. *(Cries of Shame, Miserable buggers and worse.}* But, my friends, you can have your say. *(Let's have it! What's to do? etc.)*

Tomorrow morning at eleven o'clock, the stalwart martyr to our cause, Mr Wheeler, is to be put on trial. He faces imprisonment, perhaps worse. *(Anger increases.)* If you believe in the freedom of speech *(We do!)* If you believe in fair play, and I don't only refer to our presentation, *(Sympathetic laughter,)* then I implore you to be at the Guildhall tomorrow morning at eleven o'clock and make your feelings known. *(Loud cheers.)* Show these kill joys that we are Englishmen and that our blood is fired! ' *(Loud and prolonged cheering.)*

Whitley asked for calm. 'And now for your delight, here is my dear wife who will sing a new song, appropriate to our mood this evening "*The Deuce Take Him.*"

Never before or ever again was Mrs Whitley to receive such overwhelming applause as she began to sing.

*

Five. *When the Battle's Lost and Won.*

The magistrates court assembled promptly at eleven o'clock. It was a chamber that had changed little over the decades. The last major innovation had been fifty years earlier when the royal coat of arms had been taken down upon the death of Queen Anne. With the accession of George I, the altering of the initials AR to GR, had been accomplished. Georges II and III were greeted with relief that the tiresome operation did not have to be repeated. Had it been known that George III was to reign for nearly sixty years, his name would have been blessed by generations of carpenters and porters.

For those who toiled within the court, its otherwise unvarying state was both a comfort and a support. Here, criminals met their just deserts with cold indifference and were sentenced with little leniency. Most were assumed to be guilty unless proved otherwise, whereas those found innocent were silently reprimanded for wasting the court's time.

On the bench that day was Alderman Fairlight himself, a JP known for his rigourous and obdurate policies. He took his place with the eagerness of a small boy having a plum pudding set before him, for Alderman Fairlight was looking forward to his confrontation with the comedian, Mr Wheeler. He had decided that an example was to be made of the miscreant and this morning he hoped to show that plays and players were the enemies of order, peace and moral purity, thus consequently of Christianity itself.

The court was full, with only standing room available as Mr and Mrs Whitley and their followers crowded together in the public gallery. Today they were in the unusual role of spectators, with a drama in prospect more gripping than any fictional piece.

Mr Wheeler was called and once in the dock after being sworn, the charge was read. Alderman Fairlight began his examination

'Your name is Huntley Wheeler?'

'It is, sir.' Mr Wheeler paused, 'Well. . . not quite exactly.'

'What's that? Explain yourself. Tell the court. Are you or are you not Huntley Wheeler?'

'I am and I am not. For it is not the name I was baptised with.'

'But you answered under oath to the name of Huntley Wheeler.'

'Yes. That is my stage name you see.'

'No I don't see. What exactly do you mean by "stage name"?'

'It is the name under which I act when I appear on stage.'

'Indeed. Then you might equally say that your name is "Hamlet, Prince of Sweden"?' This gave rise to great laughter in court which his worship received with an indulgent smile. He paused to allow the assembly to recover from its mirth.

'Take care sir. I am firmly of the opinion that you are a fraud,' he continued, allowing his austere gaze at the prisoner to be seen by all assembled. 'You appreciate gentlemen what we are up against. The man is a trickster. Deceit it must be said is his trade.' He frowned at Mr Wheeler. 'Pray tell the court sir, what is your real name?'

'Cuthbert Dilkes.'

'Cuthbert Dilkes? I have to say that sounds an honest enough name. Why have you chosen to change it?'

'We in the theatre sometimes like to have a more. . .' Wheeler tried to find the right term, '. . . a more resounding appellation.'

'In other words you confess to being a charlatan. Take care sir. I warn you there are severe penalties for masquerading under false names. That is the way counterfeiters and fraudsters delude honest folk. What is the charge again?'

The clerk to the court repeated. 'That on the night of December thirty first without licence or permission he did act upon a stage the role of *"Cato."* '

'Enlighten the court, Master Dilkes, what is this, this . . . *"Cato"*?'

'It is a play written by the highly regarded Mr Addison your worship, about the famous Roman senator. It has been much praised in many places.'

'Not in this court it hasn't. Why any right minded man would want to appear in public pretending to be a Roman, whether it be a Roman road or Roman catholic is beyond my understanding. It reveals the depths to which play actors can sink in their depravity which it is the duty of this court to expunge. Cuthbert Dilkes, how do you plead?'

'Guilty,'

'Ah, guilty.' Alderman Fairlight was greatly disappointed. This plea robbed him of further cross questioning, when he had hoped to air in detail his hatred of playhouses. If he could keep the prisoner in the box a little longer he might play him like a trout and possibly still be able to propound his views.

'Mr Dilkes,' he asked, 'would you tell me what is meant by the word "guilty"?'

Mr Wheeler being much annoyed with the magistrate replied,

'If you have to ask me what the word means, you have no right to be sitting in judgement on me.'

This spurt of anger although highly satisfying for the moment was a serious error. Even worse, it got a louder laugh than did Mr Fairlight's earlier jocundity. Mr Wheeler was to regret his unfortunate remark.

'Silence in court!' A furious Alderman Fairlight banged his gavel.

'I will not tolerate levity in my court. Cuthbert Dilkes, you have pleaded guilty to acting the role of *"Cato"* as charged. This court condemns such immorality to be a symptom of the wickedness that I and my fellow citizens will not tolerate. You are hereby sentenced to six months imprisonment with hard labour. You will be taken from here directly to the House of Correction where your term will be served. Send him down!'

Mr Wheeler smiled sadly as he was led away.

From the public gallery Mr Whitley and his companions shouted, angrily 'Shame!' 'Call this justice?' 'Is there to be no defence?' Not waiting for answers, the enraged friends moved swiftly from the gallery to an expectant group who were waiting in the street to hear the verdict.

'Six months hard labour!' Once heard, the four words inflamed the passions of the angry mob outside the Guildhall. That is if some twenty or so disparate persons can be termed an angry mob. Whitley looked at them, unable to decide what next to do. He felt he should lead the crowd in some sort of demonstration. But how? Although a veteran director of scenes of mob violence on stage, (his *Coriolanus* lingered in the minds of all who saw it), the role of rabble-rouser was not in reality his *métier*.

It was Bracer who knew how the crowd should be managed and possibly a rescue achieved. Bracer had always kept his early life a secret for having served in the army for a year in the American colonies he had been involved in the repression of the aboriginals of that land. Now a strong republican, he deeply regretted his past actions which were the main reason for his secrecy. Nonetheless, he had been twice ambushed by the native Americans whose tactics of attack he understood and which he was now about to employ to bring about the rescue. With his voice in conspiratorial vein, he said,

'Listen lads. It's no good staying here. That's what they expect. We'll do better to take them by surprise somewhere else. They'll take Wheeler from 'ere to the jail by going up Stoney Street, that's the usual drill. We'll wait in one of the side streets. Thomas, you're quick on your feet, you keep watch. As soon as you see 'em leave 'ere, you run to us and give the signal. We'll be waiting for 'em.'

There were undertones of agreement. 'We must seem to disperse, so all of you go different ways and meet together in Woolpack Lane.'

Bracer raised his voice, shouting for the benefit of any within the Guildhall who might have been eavesdropping. 'Well lads it's all done and dealt with. It's a shame, but that's the law. We best get off 'ome.'

With a melodramatic stance the group pretended to saunter away, some kicking pebbles along the street, others whistling to convey their nonchalance. As soon as they were out of sight of the Guildhall they scuttled along alleys and secret ways to take up their position on Woolpack Lane.

Thomas, as instructed, kept watch in the shades of a nearby doorway. This was more exciting than the first night. It seemed he was to be in a battle, something he had never experienced even as a drummer boy.

The officials at the Guildhall were in no hurry to take Mr Wheeler to the House of Correction. Sensing mischief, they delayed the walk in the hope that any would-be troublemakers would disperse.

*

It was nearly four o'clock in the afternoon when the prisoner left under escort. In the growing dark Mr Wheeler, his hands restrained behind his back, was accompanied by four constables and their assistant watchmen. Once spotted, Thomas ran to the waiting liberators with the news. Bracer had already given instructions that the attack was to be made when the troop had passed by and they would take it by surprise from the rear. There were about ten in their party and they lined themselves in a single row along the lee of the street, hidden in the shadows. Armed with cudgels, clubs and even one shillelagh, they waited as silently as any Cherokee or Mohican.

'Go for their legs,' Bracer ordered, 'Attack their rear. Make as little noise as you can. We don't want them to know what's 'it 'em.'

There was no sound apart from the tread of feet on the cobbles as Mr Wheeler and his captors approached and walked past the end of Woolpack Lane, unaware of the imminent attack. After a signal from Bracer his pack rushed upon them from behind wielding their weapons.

In a few seconds several of the enemy had been floored, blows to the legs laying them out on the roadway. Stepping over the fallen, the rescuers set about those still standing. The first advantage of surprise was gone and battle was returned by the lawmen. Clubs and staffs met quarter staffs and blackjacks. The skirmish was strangely silent, broken by gasps and muffled cries as ribs were cracked and heads buffeted.

In the midst stood Mr Wheeler amazed at what was happening. Jemmy Whitley, unused to such scenes of actual conflict, waved a wooden sword with as little effect as a fly swat. However, he called to his former colleague, 'Wheeler, Wheeler, this way.' Managing to reach him, taking his arm he attempted to pull him away from the fracas. Mr Wheeler in an effort to follow, tripped and fell over a figure lying in the road. Whitley threw away the wooden sword and putting his arms under Wheeler's shoulders tried to lift him. The actor was able to get up without aid when a constable saw Mr Whitley effecting a release of his prisoner. With an angry cry of, ' Oh no you don't,' he felled Mr Whitley with one blow to his head.

Jemmy Whitley slumped to the ground where he lay, blood spilling from a wound above his ear. Thomas had seen the incident and was torn between helping one of the two men. Quickly deciding it would be best to take Wheeler, who was still on his feet, he took the actor's shoulder guiding him into the safety of Woolpack Lane. Returning to try and help Mr Whitley he saw he was by then being carried away by two of the constables.

The clash which had lasted little more than three minutes was over. The road was littered with discarded hats, weapons and men trying to get off their knees and examine what damage had been done to their personages. Some dark patches on the cobbles denoted that blood had been spilt. One of the constables had been injured, but the remaining three took command of the situation, which included the arrest of the now unconscious Whitley.

Mr Bracer as leader ordered a retreat to plan their next move. It was quickly decided to take the freed Mr Wheeler to the safety of the theatre. As so often happens in a conflict, the encounter ended in confusion with the rescue of Mr Wheeler achieved but the capture of Mr Whitley the unforeseen outcome.

*

'He'll be transported, I know,' wailed Mrs Whitley. 'It's for seven years at least, is it not? It might be for life. And what if he's killed somebody? Then it's the string. I knew he should not have gone but he's always been so wild, so impetuous. . . . .' She wept into a large handkerchief as she was assured that there had been no murder and the worst charge that could befall her husband was that of common assault.

'But that's punishable by a whipping,' she was not to be consoled. 'To think of him in a cell, it is beyond bearing. And all to rescue that wretched Mr Wheeler.'

Mr Wheeler (or was it now Mr Dilkes?) tried not be upset by this unkind remark. He was, as he insisted, hugely grateful for what everyone had done to engineer his freedom. At that moment he was preoccupied with Mr Bracer's attempts to cut through the chain binding his wrists with a hacksaw. He winced at the closeness of the blade, consoled by the fact that should any cuts be inflicted, help was near at hand.

This would come from Miss Proctor, who had always believed herself to be a nurse by nature and was applying her home-made medicament to the many cuts and bruises. Made up of a beaten raw egg in a mixture of turpentine, camphor and spirits of wine. It had been her mother's remedy and although she could not recall the proportions accurately, she was certain the mixture would work. She was also adamant that cuts and bruises whether deep or superficial should never be washed but the edges brought together and bound with a bandage. Onto this her balm was applied and if it burned that was a sure sign that it must be working. Fortunately, amidst the wounded under her care there seemed to be no broken bones, only damaged pride.

Yet the main misgiving was the future of all the players. If Mr Wheeler could be arrested for the acting of Cato then they were all at risk. Was it safe for them to stay in the town? If not where should they go? Mr Wheeler was under a double threat. The original sentence of six months still stood, but there was now a further offence of being involved in an affray if not a riot. He was become a fugitive from justice. He was a man on the run. It was obvious he must leave Nottingham.

'I best not go to my lodgings,' said Mr Wheeler, 'for it was there I was arrested.' Out of curiosity some asked where this was.

'With Mrs Stirrup, the dressmaker on Castle Gate,' he told them.

Mr Wheeler now had both his hands free. He thanked Bracer again for his rescue, warning him that he too might be wanted by the authorities for leading the skirmish and should consider removing to another town.

'As for me I shall remain here,' Mrs Whitley declared, a little more recovered, 'so long as my Jemmy lies in the condemned hold.' It was pointed out that dark though his future seemed, it had not yet reached that extreme.

'Perhaps we should repair to our lodgings,' suggested Mr Sweeny, 'if they are after us, this is the first place they'll come to. Get your belongings together and we'll meet at the Blackamoor's Head tonight. We'll decide then what next we do for ourselves and Mr Whitley.'

Everyone prepared to leave, gathering their few belongings together when a loud authoritative knock was heard on the stage door. The ladies gasped, the men froze. All looked at each other, apart from

Mr Mitteer who had not heard the knock and wondered why everyone was suddenly standing still.

'Is it locked?' asked Mr Sweeny. 'Yes it is,' said Bracer. The knocking came again, even more demanding of attention.

'Shall I go?' asked Thomas. It was agreed. The summons must be met. Thomas unlocked the door to find facing him a gentleman in a fine grey frock coat with a dark red collar. A double row of bright silver buttons ran down the front of the garment, below which could be seen white velvet breeches and grey stockings. In his hand was a silver capped stick with which he had been knocking on the door.

'Good evening,' said the gentleman,' I am Marmaduke Pennell. I hear there's trouble at the Theatre I built.'

*

When he regained his senses Jemmy Whitley found himself in a bloody, if not to say dangerous condition. For him, there was no Dora Proctor to comfort with her soothing balms, only a rough warder who gave him a basin of cold water and a cloth with which to tend his wounds. He had a swelling on the side of his head the size of a quail's egg and a headache so severe he could hardly tell where he was. This was perhaps as well, for he lay in a cell below the House of Correction that was damp, dark and dirty.

It contained only a trundle bed and a bucket. He had never imagined such privation. Daylight had come and gone, so he believed he had lain there for at least twenty four hours . A bowl of what he supposed to be gruel and a jug of water was brought for him. He was aware that from time to time someone looked at him through a grill within the cell door.

On what he took to be the second day of his incarceration the warder visited him. 'Now sir,' he said, 'we must tidy you a bit for your public showing.'

'A showing?' asked Whitley, wondering if it was the stocks.

'You're to be up before the magistrate. So we must get you looking well favoured. We can't have people think we do not care for our guests.'

'What am I to be charged with?' asked Whitley.

The warder laughed, 'As if you didn't know. "Disorderly conduct and incitement to causing riot," you naughty man.' He told Mr Whitley to stand and taking a cloth, poured water on it and gave it to Whitley to wipe his face. A rough brush of the hand was used to remove dirt from his clothing; his wig was handed back to him.

'There, a fine sight for the ladies eh? Now what sort of jewellery will you be you wantin'?'

'What do you mean?' Whitley asked, feeling himself still in a nightmare.

'Allow me,' the warder opened a large metal box. He brought out some cruel and heavy looking manacles. 'These were very fashionable last season. Worn by some of the best gentlemen what stayed 'ere.'

'Am I to be put in these?' asked Whitley with horror.

'That all depends on the "garnish." '

' "Garnish?" '

The warder rattled some cruel looking leg-irons.

'These 'ere ornaments comes at a charge of one guinea. But there is little pleasure to be 'ad in such unseemly garters. Whereupon these comely bracelets . . .' he brought forth a pair of handlocks from the box, '. . . are of a more delicate capacity being at a cost of just three guineas. Nevertheless, I would venture for your best cheer this pattern being from our top array which is a gift at a mere five guineas.' He revealed a lighter looking pair of handcuffs. 'So soft and delicate you'd never know you was wearin' 'em sir.'

'And for this you require - "garnish"? '

'Entirely at your discretion sir, but without such niceties I fear 'tis our leg-irons and a ball, which I would not recommend one bit.'

'It is a wicked system.'

'It is a charity sir, and charity does not come cheap.'

'I would much prefer the handcuffs, yet I cannot pay you here and now.'

'Oh that is no obstacle. We 'ave the address of your wife and if your wish is for the cuffs, once she 'as paid, we'll be 'appy to oblige. I'll send word this day, so we can make ready for your appearance tomorrow.'

Mrs Whitley must have agreed to the demand, for next morning, Mr Whitley, lightly handcuffed, was taken back to the Guildhall.

It happened that on the previous night, the Chamber of Manufacturers had held their annual dinner. Amongst the guests were most of the town's JPs, including Alderman Fairlight. The lavish manner with which the party had been entertained had regretfully led to Alderman Fairlight's indisposition that following morning. On waking, so poorly did Mr Fairlight feel, that he wondered if a man could die in his sleep and not know about it until the next day.

As a result, Mr Justice Swift, a younger and less experienced JP was commissioned to deputise for the alderman on the bench.

Jemmy Whitley subsequently arrived in court, was sworn and the charge of disturbing the king's peace read out. When asked how he pleaded he replied with clarity, 'Not Guilty.'

At this moment he saw Marmaduke Pennell sitting close by. This gentleman, having been instrumental in the building of the theatre, had subsequently felt a moral responsibility for the problems that were afflicting the actor manager whom he looked upon as both a friend and a colleague. When Mr Justice Swift was about to question Mr Whitley, Mr Pennell interrupted the proceedings by rising to his feet,

'May it please your worship. . .'

Mr Justice Swift was annoyed. 'What's that?'

'With your worship's consent I am here to assist in Mr Whitley's defence.'

'In what capacity?'

'That of a friend, your worship.'

Mr Justice Swift knew that plaintiffs were sometimes supported by lawyers, but he was not sure if such help was to be given to a defendant. He was dimly aware of such newfangled practices in higher courts such as the Old Bailey, but he was unsure if this procedure had reached the provincial benches. Not wishing to enter any tangle of new legal pursuits he preferred instead to examine Mr Whitley about the violent events in Stoney Street.

Answering his questions, Mr Whitley described how he had tried to come to the aid of Mr Wheeler after he had fallen in the affray.

'Doubtless to help bring about his escape?' implied Mr Swift.

'No sir, only to enable him to stand up. He had tripped and fallen.'

'So you say. Tell the bench, what happened after that.'

'I was attacked.' Whitley pointed to the constable waiting to give evidence against him. 'When I went to help Mr Wheeler, that man knocked me down I heard him say, "Oh no you don't." '

Mr Pennell rose. 'Your worship will, I'm certain, be well aware that Mr Whitley has grounds to bring about a counter charge of assault and a claim for damages.'

'Has he?' Mr Swift was surprised and unhappy, for this was moving into territory of which he was uncertain.

'But was not Mr Whitley disturbing the peace?' he asked.

'On the contrary, he was trying to restore order, by offering help.'

'I can't allow that, he was involved in an affray.'

Mr Pennell looked sternly at the magistrate. 'May I ask, Is your worship seeking a mere summary conviction?'

'Yes, yes, I suppose I am.'

'Then your worship is aware that this could lead to a judicial review with a referral to the Quarter Sessions and all that that entails?'

His worship was by no means aware of this. In truth his worship, the youngest son of a local landowner, had little knowledge of the law and was rather at a loss. He had no wish to prolong the case having a long standing arrangement to travel that very day up to Scotland for the deer hunting.

'Quite, quite,'he looked knowledgeable. 'That is to be avoided.'

'Then can it be taken that your worship means the charges by both parties are to be withdrawn and settlement made out of court?.'

'Indeed. . . yes. . . . that is precisely what I had in mind.'

Whereupon Mr Justice Swift, after seeking Mr Pennell's further advice on judgemental proceedings, to the deep disgust of the clerk to the court, saw that the charge against Mr Whitley was dropped. Some fifteen minutes later, the handcuffs were removed and Jemmy found himself summarily dismissed and free to leave but without receiving costs which troubled him not one bit.

Not long afterwards, celebratory drinks were taken at the Blackamoor's Head. The happiness soon dissolving when it was realised that although Jemmy Whitley was free, others of the company were still in danger. Thomas, Mr Wheeler, and Mr Sweeny had been actively involved in the disturbance. It was thought advisable that to avoid arrest, the three should quit the vicinity of Nottingham, for at least the time being.

Whereas Mr Bracer had stated his obstinate intention to remain,

*

Six. *Breaking Up.*

A hand-written bill was nailed to the door of the theatre informing the public that it was closed until further notice; the players and staff gathered together to be paid their dues by Cassandra Whitley. This sharing out of takings was an occasion that filled Jemmy with unease, which was why he left the ritual for his wife to deal with. Mrs Whitley held command of a large metal box referred to as the treasury. For this, she alone kept the keys and it was not until everyone was assembled that the coffers were opened and the financial situation disclosed.

'The first night was tolerable,' she announced, 'it wanted nearly seventy pounds on the door.'

'How near did it want?' asked Mr Sweeny.

'Sixty nine pounds, sixteen shillings and three pence ha'penny,' replied the lady reading from a small cash book. Another compartment of the treasury was a removable metal tray, divided into sections in which lay a mixture of guineas, shillings, and coppers as low as farthings.

'The takings for the second night was much less.' continued Mrs Whitley, 'below nineteen pounds, for as you are aware numerous customers asked for their money to be returned, and the box people never took their places. So the the sharings were lower than hoped.'

'Like skinning a maggot,' commented Mr Wheeler.

'Now, now Mr Wheeler, civility please,' said Mr Whitley.

'I'm told that nowadays, in the better companies, actors are paid by salary' said Mr Sweeny

'When you are sufficiently talented to join a better company, Mr Sweeny, then perhaps you may be salaried. For the time being you are fortunate to be sharing with us,' said Mrs Whitley tartly.

Mr Whitley felt he must stress the problems besetting his company for any rebellious undermining of authority had to be prevented.

'This has been an especially difficult time, he said, 'there is great expense at the opening of a new theatre. New scenery, new costumes.'

The communal laugh that followed sounded like a shout of scorn.

'In the division of our takings have we ever shown signs of unfairness?' asked Mrs Whitley indignantly.

'Aye,' shouted everyone. Cassandra Whitley slammed down the lid of the treasury box. 'Mr Whitley and I have been through sufficient anguish these few days past without having this insolence. You should be grateful we are not one of those beggarly managements who disappear with the takings and leave their company destitute.'

'Oh we are,' assured Miss Proctor who, as the saying goes, knew which side her bread was buttered.

'So I should think,' said Mrs Whitley. 'As to expenses, we have fairly deducted our share for management and administration. There are ground rents to be paid, printing costs, purchase of oil and candles, coal for heating, an insurance for wear and tear on scenery and dresses. So here is the share to divide within yourselves. Be fair to each other and thank God for it.'

She glared defiantly as she emptied the cash from the metal tray onto the table. It fell with the rasp of shingle on the sea shore, leaving the company like scavengers with the takings before them.

'Shall I do it?' asked Mr Wheeler. The others agreed.

Like players round a gambling table everyone sat as Mr Wheeler sorted out the few coins that there were, for the money was in low denominations, crowns, florins and less. He was watched in silence as he divided each sum into piles.

'Nine of us to share the fortune?'

'Ten, including Thomas,' said Mr Bracer.

'He should not be included. He's been with us less than a month.'

'I was promised a guinea for the copying,' said Thomas.

'That is so,' Mrs Whitley said from a distance, 'less sixpence.'

Without a word, Mr Wheeler counted a guinea less sixpence and passed it to Thomas. 'You, being in the part of an apprentice, take no more.' The hush that followed denoted that this was the decision of the company which Thomas had to accept as the way of things. Slowly, nine piles of coins were awarded. The money did not divide exactly, there being a quantity of farthings that amounted to an odd number. This was put into a separate bank and still the formality continued in silence.

Here, for it was obviously a tradition, Mr Sweeny reached into his pocket and produced two dies. In turn, everyone threw the pieces. Each time a double appeared a farthing was taken from the pile by the lucky thrower. Within a few minutes the outcome was settled and Mr Mitteer found himself richer by three farthings.

'Now that's done, for those of you who wish there is a boon,' said Mrs Whitley, 'a box of candle ends which is yours for the sharing.'

The mood that followed was bleak. Nobody was happy with the situation and everyone knew that it would be some time before they worked again. Mrs Whitley was unmoved and merely sniffed. Mr Whitley addressed the gathering.

'My friends I am sad that things have ended thus. For you must know that our future is unsure. We may continue to offer entertainment for the town, but only if we sing or mime. This means , Mr Wheeler and Mr Sweeny, I can offer you no province, for as you know your talents do not lie in this field. Mr and Mrs Mitteer, Mr and Mrs Willis and you Mr Naylor if you choose to stay, it may be that I can give employment, but you must decide what's best for yourselves. If you find occupation elsewhere, you must take it. Miss Proctor I would ask you to remain, for although I cannot promise you a major singing role I feel sure you will have a place in any future vocal presentations.'

Mrs Whitley intervened, 'The situation is, if we are to perform it will have to be in musical pieces which will mean employing trained musicians. There is a great demand for ballad operas containing English airs which are vocally highly demanding.

'Such as *The Maid of the Mill,* eh?' asked Mr Sweeny, 'You can sing the whole bloody thing on your own. That'll be a cheap evening.'

'Please, please,' said Mr Whitley, 'Let us see that this parting is well made for, *If we do meet again, why we shall smile!* '

He signalled to Mr Wheeler, 'a word in your ear.'

Whitley drew Wheeler aside and spoke confidentially.

'I advise you strongly to leave Nottingham,' he said, 'we have a good friend in Mr Pennell who has told me you might well be arrested again if you remain. Do you have anywhere you can go?'

Mr Wheeler replied that he had no friends nearby. He came from Gloucester and had no means other than walking back there, which was something he did not wish to attempt alone and in January.

Mr Whitley agreed, then continued,

'My wife and I have a daughter in Stamford in charge of the theatre there. She may be able to offer you work. Stamford is a good location for anyone in your situation for it borders on four counties.'

'That too is a long way to walk alone,' said Wheeler.

'Young Thomas and Mr Sweeny are also facing likely prosecution for your rescue and should leave Nottingham as well. You could form a threesome.'

'Yes. they would make good companions.'

'Then the three of you should set forth without delay.'

Mr Wheeler still hesitated. 'It is midwinter ,' he said, 'At any moment the weather could worsen.'

'You can journey to Stamford by way of Melton Mowbray and Oakham, they are each within a good day's walking. Should the weather worsen you can find safe haven at one of them. Go talk to them and decide.'

Whitley patted him warmly on the shoulder. Wheeler was affected by his concern. Of course it cost nothing to give advice and if he had offered some additional funds for the journey, he would have valued Whitley's counsel more. He found the others gathering their possessions together, after collecting their shares. Only Mr Bracer elected to stay. He was prepared to face his fate and was not keen to go to Stamford, believing there would be no work for him there. Wheeler, Sweeny and Thomas were agreed that their departure was unavoidable and plans were made to begin their journey early the next day.

It was fortunate that it would be the Sabbath when it was unlikely that any arrests be effected. From the almanac it was discovered that the moon was entering its full phase, which meant that walking could be done by night if the weather be clear. Thomas, Wheeler and Sweeny bade farewell to their colleagues. As they disbanded, past animosities were put aside with tears and fond tidings.

In the realm of experience, Thomas had encountered so many

hindrances to happiness, that he never thought such a state could be his. Yet within this short while he had been so at ease, with such a sense of belonging, that he cursed himself for being vulnerable to fresh disappointment. Once again he must move on; was it his fate in life never to settle?

Miss Proctor too was deeply upset,

'We shall never meet again,' she wept, 'I know it for sure, I feel it in my bones.' She flung her arms around one and all, finally embracing Thomas,

'Oh Tummy,' as she called him, 'what shall I do without you?'

'Same as what you've been doing all long,' said Thomas. Such honesty caused Miss Proctor genuinely to blush.

Hugs and kisses were exchanged, even Mrs Kenna remembered to take the pins out of her mouth before bestowing her lips to any who wished to partake of them. Only Cassandra Whitley stayed apart, pretending to read the London news sheet full of the latest fashion and gossip. She knew she was not liked and although this pained her she was unable to understand why this should be so. At last, when she felt the emotional exhibition had lasted sufficiently she clapped her hands,

'Come along all of you. This won't be doing. These men must be setting forth. See to it Jemmy.'

Mr Whitley cleared his throat and in a voice far from steady said, 'We wish you all and everyone God speed until next we meet. For those of you remaining here, please keep close in touch and we will inform you as soon as we know of our future strategies. How true, *parting is such sweet sorrow.'*

With this, the company of comedians separated and went their several ways into an uncharted future.

That night at their lodgings the Whitleys had the pleasure of entertaining Mr Marmaduke Pennell. However disappointing the box-office takings had been, the Whitleys had retained money enough to put before their guest a saddle of mutton and a brace of snipes, accompanied by three excellent bottles of Chablis. By their normal standards this was lavish but the Whitleys wanted to show their gratitude to a true friend.

In turn, Mr Pennell was anxious to meet with the Whitleys, being also troubled by recent events. When he built the theatre he understood full well that many in Nottingham regarded it unlawful as well as being an edifice of sin. Knowing this, he had been cunning enough to call his new building a *Musick Hall,* opening with a grand concert funded by private subscription. This first performance was of Mr Handel's new oratorio, *The Messiah*, with which no-one could take exception.

By way of celebration, Mr Pennell next arranged for a Grand Ball to follow in the resplendent new Assembly Rooms he had also built recently. This great social event took the town by storm, being long remembered as a glittering occasion with over fifty couples dancing cotillions and quadrilles until dawn.

Having once provided this memorable event Marmaduke Pennell was besought by many to give more of the same and being a generous man he was glad to comply. He ventured to present a further concert, again for the benefit of charity, to wit the wives, widows and children of soldiers *'who had so gloriously served their King and Country throughout the long and bloody war.'*

Surreptitiously the artful Pennell, in between the many musical pieces, slipped in a play; the tragedy of *The Orphan* or *The Unhappy Marriage* which being a spoken drama unlawfully turned the musick hall into a theatre. This sleight of hand was so adroit that the suspicious Alderman Fairlight and his associates came to know of the episode only after it had happened. Their fury ensured that on the following Sunday, chapels throughout the town shuddered with sermons denouncing this vanity of vanities in their very midst.

However, Mr Pennell's one theatrical success had given him a false conviction that there was in Nottingham a public hungry for the drama, whereby he set upon engaging a permanent company of comedians to play in his new theatre. He invited James Augustus Whitley who was seeking a new base for his activities to join him in the venture, both men blissfully unaware that they were to fall victim to that entrenched hater of all things theatrical - Alderman Fairlight, who with his supporters brought down the force of the law on them.

'What a state of affairs it is,' sighed Mr Pennell, 'when fire-eaters and dancing dogs are permitted to appear in public, yet to speak the words of the poet Addison is considered a crime. My friends, we must regard this closure as a set back, not a defeat. I believe there are many in our populace who are not killjoys. They must be cultivated until they can insist on regular dramatic presentations. Meantime, we must do our best with musical diversions.'

'Could Mr and Mrs Lascelles' girls give a dancing display?' suggested Cassandra, 'I'm sure the young ladies would delight in showing their skills in gavottes and chaconnes.'

'A kind thought,' said Pennell, 'but audiences would be merely watching their own daughters which they can do any time. Almost as bad as staying at home to play whist with the family. No, within the law we must find other fare.'

Mr Whitley said, 'I have heard good reports of a satirical fellow named Foote who gives what he calls "lectures on heads". He has a series of busts which he uses to great comic purpose. This is permitted because it takes the form of a lecture to the audience, and so contains no dialogue. Those who have seen him say he is excellent.'

'A good start. He must be sought out and engaged,' said Pennell with enthusiasm.

'Where do you suggest we find the supporters you ask us to cultivate?' asked Cassandra.

'To begin there is Lady Grandby and her cronies. They usually plan a concert or something similar for the Assizes. My wife tells me they are wild for a ballad opera which could be presented at the theatre with impunity.'

'A ballad opera?' Mrs Whitley lowered her eyes modestly as she remarked that *The Maid of the Mill* was a piece she had often sung and would be happy to encore. This was noted as a possibility then gently put to aside by the two gentlemen.

'There's Theobald Plumptre,' suggested Mr Pennell. 'Mad as a march hare, but crazy for the theatre. He gave a lot to my building fund.' He looked at Whitley. 'You might consult him for ideas, for he might well further support our enterprise. Meanwhile. I will cogitate on who else could help us.'

Plans were soon being made for a possible new season of music and mime that would not be liable to prosecution. Yet as the third bottle of Chablis was emptied the muse inspired Jemmy Whitley to extemporise with a toast,

Though now we only dance and sing,
In days to come - the play's the thing!

*

Part Two.

Seven. *Winter and Rough Weather.*

'Let us hope the weather holds,' said Wheeler. He, Sweeny and Thomas set out at first light for Melton Mowbray. There had been a week of clear skies and winter sun giving cold and frosty days ideal for walking; the air sharp and fresh, the ground hard and firm.

The three left Nottingham by the flood road to the south and in a short time the town with its buildings were left behind. They walked the causeway, across the Meadows, a low lying area of marsh which, when spring came in a few months, would be covered in sweeps of blue and yellow crocuses. From the old bridge across the Trent they noticed the flow of the river was sluggish with ice forming on both banks and a collection of water birds floating midstream.

'Seagulls,' said Mr Wheeler. The word was sufficient to imply that the birds had come inland from the coast, predicting bad weather ahead. But still the morning was clear and cold. Conversation was minimal, each man involved with his own thoughts.

Thomas, still of an age when silence was uncomfortable, tried to chat as they walked. 'Did you know Mr Whitley had a daughter?' he asked.

'Not his,' said Sweeny. 'It's hers, from an Irishman, name of Parker. Jemmy took her on as his own.'

'When was that?'

'Years ago, in Dublin.'

'Gossip,' said Wheeler.

'She may have more, who knows?' said Sweeny.

'Gossip,' repeated Wheeler.

'That's right, gossip. Keeps our trade alive. Who ever heard of an honest actor?'

'Is not Mr Garrick an honest actor?' asked Thomas. 'You've acted with him have you not Mr Wheeler?'

'Who says so?' asked Wheeler.

'I've heard it said.' replied Thomas.

'If you've heard it said, then it must be so.'

After this exchange there was no more talk. They progressed towards the vale of Belvoir, a rich pastoral area with few villages. The roads were no more than tracks, frozen hard. Deep furrows where carts had sunk in the autumn mud, together with hollows trodden by many hooves were now petrified ruts and pot holes glazed with ice. To stumble in these could mean a twisted ankle or worse a broken limb, so they trod at the sides where the grass was greyed by the hoar frost. Each man took a staff to be sure of his footing, their progress slow as they walked in single file. By mid morning it became apparent that the sky was changing, first with high cloud catching the pale sun, followed at a lower level by a bank of dark coal sacks as they were called.

A wind began to rise.

Climbing upon a gate, Wheeler pointed to the distance.

'The Fosse,' he said, 'we'll have to cross it.'

'I've walked the great north road more than once,' said Thomas.

'All of it?' asked Sweeny sarcastically.

'I walked from Stamford to York when I was fourteen.'

'You'd walk that and more if you're ever an actor,' said Wheeler.

The track they were using steadily widened into a fan of churned up land as it joined with the Fosse. They picked their way carefully.

It was now that the first flurries of snow appeared. Blown hard by the wind, it began with grits of frozen rain scattering across the marbled land. In little more than five minutes a blizzard was upon them, a white confusion shuttering their sight. By the time they had left the track and climbed to the edge of the Fosse carriageway the sky had darkened and curtains of snow swept over the empty landscape.

'We must watch out for rattlers,' said Wheeler. They hesitated at the roadside trying to see across the ancient highway for signs of any traffic. It appeared to be deserted but the snow was now so heavy it reduced visibility to that of a thick fog.

Sweeny shouted above the wind, 'Can't hear anything.'

Wheeler stood still, looking and listening like an animal, using every sense he possessed to detect danger. The others waited for his guidance. But winnowing shreds of cloud obscured the view.

'All right, let's go,' said Wheeler rashly 'but make haste.'

In the half light they ran across the broad expanse of the Fosse like hunted creatures leaving the safety of cover.

'Look out!' shouted Wheeler.

From nowhere it was upon them, the wind muffling the sound as the stage coach bore down. Galloping horses sided by lamps with the great burdenous bulk behind. The three dived out of the way as the vehicle appeared. Next came the noise. The thundering of hooves, the rattling of harness, the grinding of loaded wheels over hard ground as the machine flew past in its frenzy.

Then it was gone. The snow already settling into the new made tracks.

'Fucking bandits!' shouted Mr Sweeny. 'No warning! No post horn!'

'It's our doing,' said Wheeler. 'Only fools like us go abroad on days like this. Come, we best pick up our trail .'

The three said nothing for some time; the shock of the near fatality had chastened them. Once more it was Thomas who spoke,

'None of the roads are signed,' he said.

'Course not. Those that live here know the ways,' said Wheeler. 'Strangers get no telling.'

Goose feathers of snow stuck to faces and eyelids, whitening their clothes into shrouds. Twice Thomas found himself separated from the others until their shouting told him where they were. As the wind eddied and veered the snow played crazy patterns with their vision, at times flying upwards making them feel as if they were falling.

'Keep together,' shouted Wheeler.

The darkness increased as the blizzard took command. It became impossible to see where tracks were leading, humps and hollows were hidden under folds of sculptured drifts. They relied on Wheeler to lead them as he headed forward, his staff prodding the blankness ahead.

'We've got to climb the Belvoir ridge,' he shouted, 'once we're up there it's straight on for Melton.'

'Can we do it before dark?' asked Sweeny.

'Got to,' said Wheeler, 'at the top we might find somewhere to shelter. There's nothing down here, it's all pasture.'

'Can you see the ridge?' called Thomas.

'Aye, it's there. That black line ahead.'

Both Sweeny and Thomas doubted that it was the Belvoir ridge. More likely it was a strand of cloud luring them like some winter will o' the wisp.

Yet neither of them had any idea of the direction to follow, so it was best to make after Wheeler. For a time there appeared an area of clear sky which could have been the setting sun, but it fast disappeared. In this white wilderness there was an imminent chance they could be benighted.

'We must keep on,' said Sweeny, 'the worst thing is to stop moving, that's how you freeze to death.'

'You're right,' said Wheeler, 'so let's get the ridge climbed.'

Still the snow came. Their feet and hands were numb, their walking no more than a series of staggers as drifts increased in depth.

Eventually Thomas had to state what he thought.

'I don't think we're on a track,' he said.

'Shut up,' barked Sweeny, 'think you know best do you?' Thomas felt for a moment that it wasn't his place to criticise, but he became sure of his convictions. 'There's no hedges, no fences,' he said.

Wheeler stopped and listened. He turned and the others saw how exhausted he looked. His chest heaved as he laboured to breathe before managing to speak. 'What's that you say?' he asked wearily.

Thomas replied, 'Up 'till we now we had hedges and fences on either side. Now it's only banks. I think we're in the open, in fields.'

Wheeler stood still. Shivering with cold the three of them considered their plight. At last the snow had stopped, with a tail end of cloud clearing the sky. Their minds too had a new clarity. A realisation took hold which none dared to admit. They each knew they were lost.

Because he was the oldest, Wheeler felt he must make a decision. 'Sweeny's right,' he said. 'We've got to keep moving. The snow's stopped. Over there it looks to be level.' Tapping through the snow with his staff he confirmed, 'Yes, this seems right. This is a track.'

He continued forward, Sweeny and Thomas close behind. It was almost too dark to be certain, but Thomas looked warily at the snow around his feet. For a moment he thought he was wrong, but then he understood what he was seeing. The snow was turning black - black and wet. It was water rising upward. It was not a road at all.

'It's ice!' he shouted, 'we're standing on ice.'

They stopped. Wheeler stamped his foot to test the ground and there was a deadly crack beneath him.

'Get off, get off!' he shouted.

'Where?' called Sweeny.

There was a villainous creaking and Wheeler with a look of astonishment fell sideways disappearing as the ice under him gave way.

'Lie flat,' shouted Sweeny, and Thomas fell onto a mound of snow. Neither of them knew what to do. A few seconds later they saw that where Wheeler had fallen was a spread of ink black water. On the surface were several sheets of ice which tipped and rocked, the water lapping over them.

'Wheeler, Wheeler!' shouted Thomas. He crawled through the snow to the edge of the dark patch. He grasped at pieces of ice, the cold so bad his hands felt scalded. Calling his name repeatedly Thomas reached into the water trying to find the lost man.

'Don't go nearer,' called Sweeny, 'you'll have us in.'

'I can't see him,' shouted Thomas, 'he's gone.'

Sweeny said nothing, for he had already started crawling back in retreat. Thomas, his arms and hands deadened with cold lay still, staring into the water. The plates of ice in the hole closed together and for one dreadful moment Thomas saw what he knew was Wheeler's upturned face and a hand stretching from the water. With a scream he tried to grasp him, but Wheeler was gone, sunk below the surface. There was another keen crack of ice and the entire table creaked and groaned beneath them.

'Come back, for God's sake,' cried Sweeny who had managed to reach a place of safety. Thomas, now beyond the bounds of reason, allowed self-preservation to control him. Painfully he crawled back to where Sweeny waited. When he finally reached him, Sweeny tapped the ground at his side. It had the sure dull sound of solid earth.

'You were right.' said Sweeny. 'We were miles off the track.'

'Damn you, damn your bloody eyes,' cried Thomas, 'you did nothing.'

In a passion of despair he beat at the air trying to strike Sweeny until he fell sobbing into the snow. It was impossible to tell if the shivering of his body was caused by the intense cold or by the horror of what he had just seen.

All sense of time was gone. A lambent moon shone like a white sun. The ghostly landscape reflected the light with the compliance of a dead world. The wind long stilled gave way to the grip of frost. Nothing on earth stirred.

Thomas lay unconscious in the snow. Sweeny could think of no way to revive him. All he could do was to hug the boy and hope that what little warmth was still in his own body might reach him. He shouted for help.

He tried calling out three times in succession, thinking that if there was anyone within distance that way he might be heard. He was aware of the moon rising higher and growing smaller and brighter in the winter sky which now trembled with cold silver stars

Both he and Wheeler had said they must keep moving and he knew if he didn't that would be the end. But he couldn't shift without Thomas. He was a big lad, too heavy to carry and the idea of dragging him was ridiculous. Yet he could not leave him. Already he was troubled in mind that he'd done nothing to save Wheeler. To have Thomas on his conscience as well was too much, even if it required his staying with him.

His head could not deal with the problem. Sleep was fast taking possession. He was exhausted, so exhausted he could scarcely shout. As he sat with Thomas in his arms he tried calling again. His cries were growing weaker. His imagination had started bluffing him.

He could hear voices from the past . . . His long dead father from far away. . . strange voices with no meaning from far away. . . snatches of tunes from far away. . . the jingle of harness from far away. . . .

'Stand up. Get up, you've got to help me . . .'

The man's voice sounded distant, as if at the end of a long cavern.

'Come on, I can't do this alone.'

Sweeny looked up, he thought he could see a figure looming above him. He shut his eyes, all he wanted was to sleep.

A man slapped the side of his face. 'D'you hear me? If you don't stir yourself you won't live. Now get up.'

Sweeny looked again and saw not only a man but a horse alongside. It was the movement of the horse's head that had jingled the harness. He lifted his hand which the man took, pulling him to his feet.

'Move about, beat your arms, it's your only chance.'
The man drubbed his own arms as if to show how it was done. Sweeny followed his style gradually waking himself, but as he did the pain of cold cleaved every part of him. His teeth chattered and speech was impossible.

'Come on man, stamp your feet, keep going.' Sweeny tried to do as he was bid. 'We mun get the lad onto the horse.' He looked at Thomas lying corpse-like in the snow. 'There's life in him, but not for much longer. Help me move him.'

Unable to speak, Sweeny's senses returned to him slow footed. The whole situation was dreamlike as he moved himself behind Thomas attempting to lift him by his arms.

'That's no good,' said the man, 'get him upright and over my shoulder.' He knelt down in front of Thomas, 'now, sit him up.'

Somehow, Sweeny managed to do this and the man, who was obviously used to lifting loads, shifted Thomas onto his shoulder. With a great heave he stood and threw the unknowing youth over the saddle of the horse. The animal stepped backwards in protest as it took the sudden load.

'Whoa, angel, whoa, ' the man said, holding the reins in his hand. He turned to Sweeny. 'Now you've got to walk, understand?'

The man led the way, pulling the harness. Sweeny walked alongside steadying himself against the horse. The animal gave off a steamy warmth and Sweeny was glad to lay his hand on its shanks. There was little sound apart from the crunch of snow as feet and hooves trod their way on the frozen track. Several times Thomas had to be hitched further onto the saddle to prevent him falling. When this was done he groaned, the only evidence of life.

Sweeny could not see far ahead as he followed the man until they approached a long structure, which looked more of a barn than a dwelling. Without warning the man gave a loud whistle as they came to a doorway. It was opened by a woman, who stood her outline black against a faint glow of light.

'There' two on 'em,' said the man. 'One's far gone. You're to help me down with him.' Without speaking the woman took the horse's reins to lead the animal towards the building. The man turned to Sweeny, 'Get inside,' he ordered.

Sweeny stumbled into the building. A mixture of warmth with an overwhelming stench greeted him. It was, as he had thought, more of a barn than a house where these people obviously lived. In addition to the smell was the noise. Cattle, sheep, pigs and horses, few of which could be seen, neighing, bleating and mooing. The animals probably brought in to provide winter warmth. He felt he was inside Noah's ark.

Two other things were apparent. First, the great timber roof as lofty as a church and a free standing brick chimney rising from over a fireplace, which was almost a room in itself. A massive beam spanned the opening revealing a hearth of old flag stones blackened with smoke. A fire smouldered beneath an iron stew pot hung from chains and hooks hidden somewhere in the flue.

Opposite, at a high level, was a wooden floor or shelf, with a ladder to give access. Sweeny guessed that this was a sleeping area away from the animals. Outside he heard the man giving sharp instructions to the woman. Soon the two of them came inside carrying the inert Thomas, whom they laid on the floor, shooing away several chickens whilst a cow looked on curiously.

No words were spoken as straightway the woman went up the ladder to the shelf coming down a few minutes later with an assortment of cloths and blankets. As if it was a regular routine, she removed Thomas's wet clothing, busily dried him and wrapped him in woollen blankets, the young man barely conscious of what was happening.

When she gave him some drink he coughed noisily, beginning at last to take notice of his surroundings. Finally she lay Thomas on a bench and smeared his body with handfuls of grease from a jar the man held, whilst he watched her circumspectly. Once this was done

Thomas was again wrapped in blankets until the man putting him over his shoulder as he would a sack of grain carried him up the ladder to the shelf above.

Up to then no exchanges had been made with the couple. When the man returned, Sweeny finally spoke, 'My name is Sweeny,' he said, 'there were three of us. One's dead.'

The man looked at the woman. He turned to Sweeny,

'Croft by name. This be my wife Rachel.' She barely smiled at him.

'The boy is Tom, Tom Hammond,' said Sweeny. 'The dead one was name of Wheeler. He fell through the ice. We thought we were walking on a road.'

Croft grunted grimly, 'Pastor's Dyke,' he said looking at his wife.

Still in his wet clothes, a fierce shiver convulsed Sweeny, 'I would welcome a brandy if you have it,' he said.

'You'll not find no such drink in this place.' Looking at Rachel he charged, 'give him some of the broth from the stew.'

Rachel went to the fire. With a mug she scooped liquid from the top of the cooking pot and handed it to Sweeny.

Croft said sternly, 'That's all you're getting. Nothing more. Frost has to leave the body unhurried.'

When he had finished the broth Sweeny was told to take off his wet clothes. Under the careful scrutiny of Croft, Rachel covered him with the same ointment that had been applied to Thomas.

'What is it you're using?' Sweeny asked. Before she could answer, Croft said, 'It's her own remedy to counter the cold.'

She wrapped him in a blanket.

'Can you get up the ladder?' asked Croft. Sweeny nodded and managed to climb slowly. Croft indicated a mattress with a bolster of straw and a blanket next to where Thomas lay.

'Sleep, that what's needed. Let nature and distemper fight it out,' he said and left the two of them lying alongside each other in the dark.

Back by the fire Croft looked at his wife. 'See what's befallen them. Unpossessed of foresight. No provision for hazards. Town folk.' He spat with scorn into the fire. Rachel said nothing.

*

Eight. *Meanwhile, back in Arcady*

'To eat a kipper correctly,' said Mr Theobald Plumptre, 'requires the skill and sensibility of a surgeon.' Although it was past midday he was breaking his fast in bed with Jemmy Whitley nearby in attendance. On Marmaduke Pennell's advice Mr Whitley had sought a meeting with Mr Plumptre to see what financial support might be gained from him. Mr Plumptre was propped up with pillows and bolsters, his embroidered night-cap still in place and a patchwork quilt over his shoulders. A large clean napkin was tucked into the front of his night-gown. On his lap was an unusual tray containing numerous sockets in which were placed silver bowls, tureens and cups.

Mr Plumptre, still only in his early thirties, had decided some time ago that his health was not sturdy and mindful of this he was of sufficient fortune to see that he was well cared for.

Pointing to the kipper with a knife he said, 'You see the brown flesh here. . . there is a line down which the blade must run. . .so. . . and then it lifts from the skin in one piece like this. There's the craft, what?'

From his bedside chair Jemmy Whitley noted this with faint interest. Although their acquaintance was of less than fifteen minutes' duration, he had already decided that Theobald Plumptre had more money than sense.

Mr Plumptre prattled on, 'One can't tolerate people who hack at a fish. A fish is a beautifully constructed thing and should be dissected with feeling.'

'What about the bones?' asked Jemmy.

'Oh the bones. I have them removed before it's cooked. Nowhere to put the bones up here, what?'

By 'up here' was meant his bed chamber on the first floor of Plumptre House, a fine mansion on Stoney Street, not far from the theatre.

Some years before, Mr Plumptre's father, who prided himself on his modernity, had had the old family house 'improved' by a London architect. As current fashion deemed it vulgar to have roofs exposed, the elder Mr Plumptre required that a Palladian facade be applied; the type that he had seen whilst making the Grand Tour. Such foreign proclivity with its Italianate showiness had caused distrust in Nottingham and the Plumptre family were viewed with suspicion by those of a more bucolic turn. Despite these eccentricities their wealth could not be dismissed so that when Mr Plumptre invited Jemmy to share breakfast with him, the summons was accepted with curiosity.

'Is the chocolate to your liking?' asked Mr Plumptre. Although the drink was almost cold, Jemmy assured him it was delicious.

He was roasted on one side by a fire in the bedroom, even though it was a fine bright morning with sun from the window adding to the heat of an already warm room.

'You've been before the bench I'm told,' said Mr Plumptre.

Jemmy replied that this was so.

'Well, that's no disgrace. My nephew, Hollis, appears in court monthly. Like the curse of Eve his mother says. Usually on charges of drunkenness. What were you up for?'

'Disturbing His Majesty's peace,' replied Jemmy.

'Just like Hollis. Yes, I remember now. Some business over the actor man wasn't it?' At this point, Mr Plumptre's breakfast tray almost slid off the eiderdown, he caught it with his one free hand.

'Did you see that?' he asked indicating the objects in the tray. 'All still in place. Everything in its own niche you see, even the slop basin. Entirely my own invention. Ingenious, what?

Jemmy agreed that it was.

'Thinking of having it patented and manufactured. Sort of thing people would pay good money to buy, what?'

Jemmy agreed that it was.

'Yes, it's the Fairlight man isn't it?' said Mr Plumptre returning to the court case, 'damn nuisance that clown, poking his nose into things. Time he was taught a lesson. It was him wasn't it?'

Jemmy agreed that it was.

'It's the theatre I want to discuss with you . Your place isn't it?

Jemmy agreed that it was.

'I write plays you know,' Mr Plumptre was by now onto toast and quince jelly, 'and I want to have a play of mine given at your theatre.'

Jemmy suggested that this was difficult at present, due to the closure on Alderman Fairlight's orders.

'Yes, I know. But once that's settled, then you can play it.'

With the meeting not going as Jemmy had wanted, he was about to excuse himself when Mr Plumptre's next remark took his attention.

'Now I realise the drama has to be paid for, so I'd be willing to cover any expense. What would it cost?

Jemmy decided to be outrageous and make an impossible demand.

'At least a hundred pounds,' he suggested.

'As much as that, what? Didn't realise it was so costly. But never mind, I'm not one to spoil the ship for a ha'peth of tar, what?'

Here, Jemmy decided to enquire about the subject of Mr Plumptre's dramatic work. He was told, 'Very fine piece. . . . Historical. . . . Ancient Rome. . . . Julius Caesar, what?. . . . His life and murder. . . . Damn good part. I'm not an actor, otherwise I wouldn't mind having a stab at it.'

'Like Brutus?' Jemmy resisted asking as Mr Plumptre continued, 'D'you know what gave me the idea?'

Jemmy admitted that he didn't.

'That play of yours. *Cato* wasn't it? Thought to meself there's a good subject to be had also in that fellow Caesar. Ancient Rome, same time as *Cato,* so you've already got some of the dresses haven't you?'

Jemmy admitted that he had a few.

'We'll need more than a few. For the battles in Gaul, Philippi and such. Several armies means a lot of dresses. There's the mobs at the Forum as well. That will be a big scene, what? Then I've been wondering about bringing in the queen Cleopatra. Damned fine part for an actress. She'll take a bit of dressing, what? Perhaps the stage could be flooded for the Nile. . .'

Jemmy's curiosity was now sufficient for him to ask if he could read the text of Mr Plumptre's drama. Could he really have written it in less than a month since *Cato* had been staged?

'Ah well , there's the snag,' came the reply, 'tis not all got down. yet. Takes a deal of time,' But. . .' he pointed to his embroidered night-cap, 'it's all up here and when it's ready I promise, you'll be the first to act it.' Jemmy insisted that he looked forward to that event with the greatest impatience.

'Damned difficult writing a play you know. Needs thought. While we're at it, be sure my name is spelt proper on the bills. Pronounced plum tree but spelt P.L.U.M.P.T.R.E. An extra "P" and only one "E". You can always detect a good family, when the name's spelt differently from its pronunciation, what?'

Jemmy agreed to bear that in mind. He also bore in mind the fact that clearly Mr Plumptre's play would never be written. The woods were thick with rich dilettantes full of ideas and little else. He saw an opportunity of getting a donation from this wealthy fool.

'Your play will obviously need a great deal of preparation ahead of its performance,' he said. 'I would not want you to be disappointed if we were not completely ready. Perhaps If you were to make an advance. . .'

'An advance? Capital you mean. What have you in mind?'

'Shall we say. . . forty pounds?'

'Why not? Yes there's no difficulty there. Forty pounds it is.'

Mr Plumptre extended his arm to seal the bargain, once again almost upsetting the entire breakfast tray.

'You see everything still in position, ingenious what?'

They shook hands, after which Mr Plumptre wiped his vigourously on the bedclothes, ignoring his napkin. 'There we are then,' he continued, 'mind you I'm a very busy man and I can't promise the play will be ready until. . . well not just yet, what?'

Jemmy smiled, 'I shall be uncomplaining. . .' He stood up.

'You'll want the cash of course. Would you ring the bell?'

A man servant appeared. 'Rigby,' said Mr Plumptre handing a key from under his pillow, 'the money box from the dressing room.'

The man servant took the instructions with as little concern as if he'd been asked to fetch a candle. They waited until Rigby returned.

'Take the tray away first,' said Mr Plumptre. This done he opened the money box. 'Forty pounds, what?'

'That's correct,' replied Jemmy. Mr Plumptre took out a leather purse, emptied it onto the sheets and counted out forty pounds. The remainder he put back in the purse. Dropping the coins into his napkin, he twisted the top into a knot and handed the money to Jemmy.

'Let me have a receipt at your convenience,' said Mr Plumptre airily. He gave a deep sigh as if he had spent the day felling trees. 'I shan't be getting dressed yet Rigby. Plump up the pillows will you? Feeling a trifle flimsy this morning.' With a languid wave of his hand he dismissed Mr Whitley and slipped down in his bed in what seemed a state of complete exhaustion.

*

'I'm told Mr Handel's music is not nearly so popular these days,' said Lady Grandby, as she poured tea from her silver teapot. It was one of her monthly 'at homes' when she entertained close friends to plan forthcoming social events. As wives of the leading Tories in Nottingham, they were this day deciding on the entertainment for the coming Spring Assizes.

'Judge Woolley told me he was grown quite weary of his style,' she continued. 'Poor man, he had to attend three long operas at the Birmingham Assizes last December, so we must not inflict any more miseries upon him. No, we must seek a change, perhaps something that has ballads rather than arias.'

'You're not suggesting *The Beggar's Opera* ?' asked Mrs Greaves. A flurry of shock passed though the seated ladies.

'Indeed not,' replied the affronted Lady Grandby. 'There are much politer forms of ballad opera than that. And I'm told they are highly popular.'

'So is *The Beggar's Opera* with some who should know better. It is to my mind a monstrous attack on decency,' said Mrs Greaves, known for her acid tongue.

This was not helped by there being no sweetness in the tea at Lady Grandby's, who refused to support the slave trade by purchasing sugar, with the additional benefit of saving on household expenses.

'Thomas Arne, is much liked in Bath and Norwich.' remarked another lady, Mrs Pearson. 'His pieces are said to be full of delightful airs and totally proper they say.'

Mrs Greaves was not convinced. 'They have dialogue,' she said, 'and as we know there must be none of that.'

Lady Grandby made a point, 'I dare say that would not trouble Judge Woolley. Dialogue or not, he likes a good tune.'

It was Judge Woolley's custom to visit Lady Grandby during the Assizes and she felt it her duty to provide suitably gay entertainment for him during that grim time.

'In fact if the Judge approved a play, I imagine even Mr Fairlight would be powerless to prevent it.'

'We mustn't put him in that situation,' said Mrs Greaves. 'If we had two little pieces by Mr Arne they could be played together without any dialogue. Whether or not they make sense is of no matter.'

'There must not be any songs from the Whitley woman,' said Mrs Bentley. 'I know several who won't buy tickets if she appears. Her singing is appalling.'

'I've spoken to the Whitleys,' said Lady Grandby, 'and they're in the way of choosing good new singers. This may surprise you, but I've heard that Alderman Fairlight has suggested a fine tenor he knows personally. Of course normally the man only sings in sacred oratorios, but I believe he has a sweet voice for an English air.'

'Rule Britannia!' said Mrs King, an elderly lady prone to dozing off at these occasions, but now suddenly awake. Nobody was surprised by her utterance. 'It is wrote by Mr Arne,' Mrs King explained. 'I'm only coming if you can promise me that. It's loud you see.'

'Then we'll make certain it's included.' Lady Grandby raised her voice in reply, smiling tolerantly at the others.

'Well, ladies,' she finished happily, 'there it is, a ballad opera meets with our unanimous approval. I will tell the Whitley's in the morning what we require.'

She consulted her book of engagements. 'The Assizes begin on Monday week . That gives them more than eight days to prepare something.

'Plenty of time.' Everyone agreed.

*

Nine. *Love in a Loft.*

For an unknown time as he slowly returned to full consciousness, Thomas believed he was lying prostrate like some carved stone effigy. Above him in the gloomy light he stared at what he believed was a great cathedral roof. He studied the complex timbers which took on the form of trees arching over him, their branches dividing into boughs chasing each other in a lattice of purlins and rafters. From behind these, loomed a legion of gargoyles, green men and wood nymphs leering at him with obscene faces, mocking him as he lay helpless, drifting in and out of reality.

At other whiles his fancy took the roof to be the hull of a mighty up-turned ship where mariners descended from ropes as the vessel rose and fell in a storm. He wondered if he was in a craft that had capsized, or if he was in the belly of a whale or if he was back in the theatre with Bracer when the lighting wheels were swinging. He wondered where he was. Then he gradually realised. He was inside a barn where people were living with many animals. The din was constant as the farm creatures called in their own language creating a bestial Bedlam.

Sweeny's was the first voice he recognised, for of the two travellers his recovery had been the swifter. 'Well now,' said Sweeny, giving him some warm drink, 'you're back in the land of the living.'

'How long have I been here?' asked Thomas.

'Can't say for sure. I was laid low for some time myself. But I'd say it's been about a three night.' Thomas tried to look down towards his feet.

Sweeny laughed. 'You're all right, nothing gone. But you came nigh close to frost bite in your feet and legs.'

Thomas struggled to sit, but found himself bound in primitive swaddling.

'She's cared for us both like a mother,' said Sweeny, 'you wanted the greater nursing She has a remedy for everything, all her own making. Poultices, ointments, bandages. She's kept you clean an' all.'

Surprised, Thomas tried looking below the bedding he was wrapped in. 'Yes,' said Sweeny, 'the dead couldn't be washed better than you've been.'

'Don't fret,' he went on, 'she did the same for me. To her we're only littlings to be nursed and cleaned up.'

Sweeny began to explain where they were. 'It's called "Croft's Hearth." He's a blacksmith. They live here in the barn with an old farmhouse turned into his smithy. That goes to show his way of life; trade before comfort. He fashions all manner of ironwork, no time for owt else, least of all Rachel that's his wife. She has to do as she's bid. You'll not get a word from her.'

Moving to the lip of the shelf where they talked, Sweeny looked to the floor below. He could see Croft's wife preparing food whilst the animals also watched, their heads peering over the wattling.

'She never stops,' said Sweeny, 'he expects her to mind the animals as well as her other duties - cooking, mending, nursing. Don't know how she found time to care for us, but thank God she did.'

Thomas lay back looking once more at the roof. Without warning, the horror of the staring face underneath the ice returned.

Abruptly he asked, 'Have you told them about Wheeler?'

'Yes,' said Sweeny taken off guard.

'How you made no move to save him? Left him to perish.'

'Now look here,' said Sweeny, his voice darkening, 'if I'd come to the edge of the ice it would have given way, the three of us would have drowned.'

'You did nothing.'

'Nothing could be done. Even you weren't able to save him.'

'I tried.'

'Oh, that was valiant. The young hero. Listen here lad,' his voice harsh, 'we're lucky to be alive. It's a pity about Wheeler, but it couldn't be helped.'

'You didn't try.'

'Shut up about it! And don't you go on making I did nothing. You'll answer to me if you do.'

They reverted to silence, the noises from the animals sounding like murmurs of disapproval.

'And another thing,' said Sweeny. 'Don't let on we're actors.'

'Why not?'

'Because Croft is a dyed in the wool Puritan. He'd throw us out on our arses. Or have us burned for witchcraft. I've told him we're scribes seeking work. He doesn't set much store on scribes neither, but it's better than actors.'

'I'm not an actor,' said Thomas.

'But you've the ambition' said Sweeny. 'Oh yes, Bracer told me about that night when you thought you were alone on stage - the young barn stroller.' This surprised Thomas, for until then he had no knowledge that anyone had witnessed his secret manifesto in the empty theatre.

Sweeny stood. 'I've offered to give Croft a bit of a hand 'till we move on. While the weather's bad he's without help. At least I can work the bellows for him If you've any sense you'll remain here as long as you can. Get your strength back.' He climbed down the ladder handing back the bowl to Rachel before going outside. In the distance could be heard the sound of metal being hammered. Thomas tried to sit up but he felt weak and fell back onto the straw and sacking. He knew when he had his clothes returned he must be up and doing, not lying here helpless, wrapped in swaddling like a baby.

His recuperation was slow, for he had more to regain than Sweeny, but youth was his restorative. He had been drenched then frozen, bringing about the quaking chill. Rachel had brought him through the fever with her knowledge of country remedies. Vinegar and honey mixed with witch hazel and hops. These she had applied together with ointments of herbs and goose fat which she had worked into the damaged limbs of both men. At the same time she had washed Thomas's clothes, carefully dried his shirt and stockings, as well as mending the gashes and cuts in his breeches and jacket.

All this she had done with love, for he brought to mind her son, who at about this age had left home never to be heard from again. When the two lost walkers had been discovered, it had felt for a delirious moment as if might be him returned, bringing alive emotions she had long dismissed.

Was this how he might come back? Late one winter's night. Telling of how he had been press ganged or perhaps had made a fortune in the colonies? But no, this was not her son, this was an unknown wayfarer who brought no such wondrous news to relieve the severity of her life.

Croft was harsh in mind and nature. Sweeny found small common ground between them, which was hindered by the almost total silence of the countryman. Gradually Croft had revealed that it was his wife who had heard him calling in the night. She had gone out to bring in firewood and believed she heard cries from far away. Being mindful Christians they could not ignore the needs of a soul in peril, although Croft had been close to abandoning his search at the point when he had found them.

He told briefly of Pastor's Dyke the great drainage ditch where Wheeler had drowned. Covered in snow and ice it could easily be mistaken for a track by those not knowing the terrain. It would be the spring before Wheeler's body were found. Doubtless an inquest following, but Croft said he and his wife would say nothing of their knowing of the matter.

Croft worked for the Belvoir estate as a blacksmith. He had a journey man but the snows had kept him away. He accepted Sweeny's offer to help with no showing of gratitude, for he expected some return for the nursing and care that had been given.

Sweeny was intrigued by some great lengths of iron that Croft was twisting and welding into complex shapes. When he asked what he was making he got no reply, Croft simply taking him into what had once been one of the rooms of the farm house. There, on the floor, at least seven feet long, lay a complex mechanism between two long arms of metal. Sweeny moved closer but Croft held him back. Getting a short log of wood Croft threw it into the midst of the ironwork. With a terrible snap, iron teeth clamped cutting the wood in half. Sweeny who had never seen a mantrap before shook slightly.

'Well-liked by the duke and his gamekeepers, these,' Croft said. 'You had good luck not to stand on one in the snow.'

Days passed. At midday, Rachel took soup and bread out to the two men. One afternoon, she waited until she heard them resume work in the forge, then placing Thomas's repaired clothing by the fire to warm, she climbed the ladder to where he slept. She knelt and looked down at him and felt once more a pining within herself that she had not known for years. Thomas's hair lay spread wide which she longed to take in her hands and tend, to tie it neatly with the black ribbon she had ironed ready. She wanted to shave the light beard that he had grown. It was her intention to lead him down to the fireside where he could be washed and then properly dressed. By now she believed he was recovered enough to be about and walking; if not she knew her husband would be angry at the time taken with the caring of him.

She remained at his side, studying his peaceful face as he slept, trying to commit his features to a memory she could keep after he was away and gone. He opened his eyes. The shock was as great as if a corpse had woken. She sat back abruptly, feeling a sense of trespass, ashamed to think that he might believe she was spying on him.

Thomas smiled as sleep left him. He turned his head full towards her. 'Thank you,' he said, 'for all you've done. You've brought me back to life.'

Rachel looked away, wondering if he knew her thoughts. He was still encased in cloths and blankets tight enough to restrict him. She eased some of the swaddling from around his shoulders and sat him up trying to unwind the rest. He took the pieces of cloth from her as she removed them and placed them on the straw at his side, watching as she uncovered him.

When she took away the lower covers she saw that his cock was full erect. Her hand went to her mouth, and for the minute Thomas, only just woken, did not realise his state of arousal. He moved instinctively, taking the blanket to try and cover himself, but she prevented him. She looked at his young body, her eyes filling with tears, remembering her husband when they were new wed. Once this was how he had been, unlike the rough, coarse and unloving man he had now become. She remembered also how she had been in the years past, which was perhaps the true cause of her tears.

If only this boy could have known. Whilst realising it was a hazard, she placed her hand softly on his flat stomach. Perhaps he would push it aside. But he didn't; he covered it with his own hand grasping her firmly. Understanding his wishes she leaned over and kissed him. He opened his mouth desirously and returned her passion. By now she was ready. She took her lips away, lifted her skirts to be astride him and gently lowered herself. Still she was unsure, until he raised himself to help the entry. Snow slid off the barn roof with a roar. She felt she was a girl again, learning to ride as they rose and fell and he held her firmly putting his arms on her shoulders. Later, he made a little sound, a cross between a laugh and a moan as he came to his climax. She made no noise. As she returned to reason she wondered if this could have been the first time for him. She would have liked that. But she guessed that it was not.

One day later, Croft's labourer returned. He reported that the road to the Belvoir ridge was now clear. Sweeny was ready to move on, although Thomas was not yet so confident. His strength was near regained, but he was unsure of another long walk. More snow could come for it was still only early February, but he knew they had to leave.

Later that unique afternoon he had been fully dressed and come down by the fire allowing Rachel the luxury of brushing his hair. Croft had walked in unexpectedly. Showing her defiance she continued to brush Thomas's hair with the hard vigour of grooming a horse, as if challenging him to comment. A sense of guilt prevailed. At night, up on the ledge, she lay only inches away from the two visitors her husband snoring like a hog. So near, she and Thomas could have touched hands, even kissed. But they did not.

Thomas was astonished how calmly she behaved towards her husband, seeing to his needs as she must have done for years. Once or twice she caught Thomas's glance when the four of them were together. But she lowered her eyes, giving no more attention than if she was passing a total stranger in the street, One move too close and their intimacy would be revealed. At times he found himself loathing Croft for his cruel indifference towards her, bringing him near to a reckless urge to shout, 'You are a cuckold. I have topped your wife.'

He hated this thought. It was another reason why he had to leave.

Next morning early, Croft announced that the weather seemed set fair. He thought it would remain settled for a day or so. Clearly this implied they should be on their way. With their clothing as clean and fresh as possible, extra layers and good provisions prepared by Rachel, they set off. Croft nodded coldly as they took their leave. Rachel still without words shook Sweeny by the hand. She then hesitated, stood a tiptoe and kissed Thomas modestly on one cheek. He smiled at her and the two men walked away out of the farmstead.

As soon as they were out of sight, Croft walked up to his wife and struck her across the face with all his force.

He said nothing. Neither did she.

The weather did not stay fair. Within a few hours of their leaving, more snow began to fall, but they were now at Melton and were able to secure shelter. Thomas wondered if Croft had known the weather would turn bad, deliberately sending them into it. Melton was of sufficient size for them to find work that would earn their keep. They got chores with a timbersmith sawing logs into planks. Sweeny was strong enough to do more than his share on a two handled blade with Thomas below in the pit. They both noted how odd it was for the the sawdust to cover Thomas in the saw pit whilst snow covered Sweeny above in the yard. For this they were paid little but there was the needed addition of keep and lodgings. As the weather stayed bad they made no effort to move on. It was not until the month's end that they resumed their journey. Oakham was reached and overtaken, their next arrival being at Stamford. Here, the theatre was easy to find for strangely, like Nottingham, it was situated on a street dedicated to Saint Mary. That was the only similarity.

It's facade was of the local cream coloured stone which gave a gentle warm appearance. The street was broad. An air of prosperity embraced the whole town. Thomas and Sweeny looked at the building for a few minutes without comment. There were playbills neatly displayed on the front walls, well printed, smart.

'Plays,' said Sweeny, 'They're performing plays. No prosecutions here.' Together they read the programme, Sweeny excited by what he saw,

'*The Clandestine Marriage,* I've played that. Lovewell, good part. Who's got it? Mr Connor, don't know him. I'd like a crack at Ogelby one day. *Jane Shore!* I've played Hastings in that, another good'un. Who's got Jane? Mrs M'George! Bugger me, dear old Fanny, it has to be with such a name. There can't be another. And see - Mr Oldfield, that has to be Jimmy Oldfield. Well damn me. . .'

The words came so fast, Thomas was bemused, Sweeny was lost in a world he knew little of, but how exciting it sounded. Sweeny gave him a rough nudge in the ribs, 'Look at this, *The Maid of the Mill.* Will we ever get rid of it? Come let us make ourselves known.'

Laughing, they made for the stage door which necessitated going to the next street where down a jumble of alley ways they soon discovered the entrance. Sweeny opened the door eagerly.

'Ere 'ere just a minute, what's the 'urry?' A disgruntled man seated on a stool scowled at Sweeny who assumed rightly he was the doorkeeper.

'Fanny, Fanny M'George, I wish to see her.'

'You can't. She's re'earsing.'

'Can you get a message to her?'

'You'll 'ave to wait, 'till there's a break.'

'Whitley. Can I see Miss Whitley?'

'Not 'ere. And she's not Miss Whitley no more, it's Mrs Gosli.'

'She's not here? Where is she?'

'On the road, with 'er company.'

'Who's playing here then?'

'Can't you read? It's Mr Wilkinson's company.'

'What? Well sod me. A Whitley letting her theatre to Tate,' he turned to Thomas, 'Tate Wilkinson, the great enemy you know. Daggers drawn with Jemmy for years. I'll warrant Jemmy knows nothing of this.'

They were interrupted by a harassed man hurrying in from outside.

'I know, I know, I'll be fined,' he said to the doorman, 'but babies can't time their arrival. It's another girl,' he said rushing by. Sweeny shouted to him,

'Jimmy Oldfield you old devil. How are you?'

The man hesitated for a moment, then exclaimed 'Sweeny, well damn me. Look can't stop. . . horribly late. . . Betty's just given birth again. Another girl, makes four.' He tried to move on, but Sweeny held him by the arm.

'Tell Fanny I'm here. As soon as she has a break.'

'Trust me,' Jimmy freed his arm and ran into the direction of what had to be the stage.

Sweeny spoke eagerly. 'This is a bit of luck. Tate Wilkinson's comedians playing here. The finest company outside London. Based in York. If you can work with him, you're made. He truly cares for his people, a great promoter of talent. What an opportunity!'

Thomas was unsure. 'He might notice you, but not me.'

'That talk's no good. You must start puffing for yourself. If you don't do it who else will? You've got to . . . .'

'Sweeny, you old fart-follower!' A strident voice stopped him as a tall thin middle aged woman, her hair in a large mobcap and a face painted as thick as marzipan came towards him, her skirts flapping. She carried a roll of knitting on enormous needles which she waved as she threw her arms around Sweeny.

'Fanny, me ducky dew drop!' replied Sweeny as they spun in a circle, Fanny's ball of wool flying away. 'Well I never,' she said. 'How long has it been?

'Ipswich,' replied Sweeny. In unison they recited, *'Which switch is the switch for Ipswich?'* laughing at some private joke. Fanny broke off to find her ball of wool, which she tried winding as she retrieved it. 'What the devil are you doing here?' she asked.

'Seeking work,' replied Sweeny.

Fanny pulled a long face and sucked in her breath. 'There's nothing here darling. We've got fifteen in the company. There's no doubling with Tate you know. But he won't sign on any more. Fifteen's the most he can carry.'

Sweeny nodded at Thomas. 'Tom here wants to act.'

'Poor bastard, whatever for?' She stared at Thomas carefully, 'He's got the looks all right. What a life. . . Haven't you told him?'

Sweeny changed the topic. 'I see you're playing Jane Shore,'

'Yes, and Miss Sterling in the *Marriage*. We're rehearsing *Tom Thumb*. I'm Queen Dollallolla, no less,' she laughed at herself. 'Fancy me. After that it's the *Dream* . Titania, can you believe it?'

Thomas watched Sweeny seeing his look of envy as the actor listened to Mrs M'George. For she was in work, in a first class company, playing all those roles. He realised how painful it was for Sweeny not to be part of it.

Fanny M'George went on chattering. 'It's good here. The Burleigh estate you know. We were invited down to play there at Christmas,' she made a another funny face. 'Very grand. They come from the big house to see us here in Stamford. What about that then? Look deary I'll miss me cue. We break at four. Come back then.'

She ran away, dropping her wool, laughing as she picked it up.

'Not very promising,' said Sweeny, ' but who knows, there may be something, you never know.'

'I liked her. She seemed kind, and she's a real comic,' said Thomas.

'Fanny's the best. Always help a friend, damn fine actress too.'

Whilst waiting for Mrs M'George to break before the evening show, Thomas and Sweeny walked around Stamford which they found far more agreeable than Nottingham. There was a deal of traffic north and south on the Great North Road, with much activity centred at the George, the famous coaching house. On enquiry they found that temporary work might be had there, either in the sculleries or the stables helping load and unload the many coaches that passed through daily. Their spirits lifted. It was suggested that they came on a Wednesday when staff were sometimes hired.

Back at the theatre they also got into conversation with the door-keeper. From him they discovered that Tate Wilkinson rarely brought his company as far south as Stamford, but the invitation for them to appear at Burleigh House had proved irresistible Following negotiations with Mrs Gosli (née Whitley) they had 'swapped' seasons whilst she and her company had gone north to play a term in Sheffield. It was the doorkeeper's view, she should not have taken the backstage staff with her, especially the prompter's call boy, for he was expected to do the job himself which he thought unfair at his age.

Thomas thought quickly on hearing this, and immediately asked if he might offer his services as call boy to Mr Wilkinson.

'That's not for me to say,' said the doorkeeper. 'What with the gaffer being away, the only one who would take you on is Mr Trout, the manager.

'Can I see him?' asked Thomas.

'A difficult man to encounter. 'e won't see no-one outside theatre hours, and when 'e's 'on duty 'e won't see no-one neither.'

'Never was a man more hard to meet,' said Sweeny. 'You'd have a better chance young Thomas of seeking work at the George to tide us over.'

They walked away, Thomas following, thinking he must be right.

'I'll tell Mr Trout, what it is you seek,' shouted the doorkeeper as they left . 'Mebbe he'll take you on.'

'When Christmas falls in June,' muttered Sweeny.

*

Ten. *The Intrusion of Thornton Friars.*

From the start, Whitley had been opposed to the ballad operas. Unable to trace the celebrated Mr Saunders with his penny whistle and egg balancing, he continued to suggest an even more capable entertainer. This was the afore mentioned Mr Foote with his satirical *Lecture on Heads.* Using a number of busts to make witty comments on celebrities of the day, he avoided prosecution because there was no dialogue. Mr Foote had been an outstanding success in London and was now touring the provinces. True, his fee was enormous, but it would be nothing compared to the fortune that staging ballad operas would entail.

However, Whitley could not discourage Lady Grandby and her committee from their determination to have the ballad operas. There were to be two. *Love in a Village* and *Thomas and Sally,* each with fresh airs by Mr Arne, to a libretto by Mr Bickerstaffe. Now, a libretto meant dialogue and as dialogue would not do it must be converted into a musical mode or recitative. One thing was certain, it was necessary to have a continuo accompanying the recitative which required the employment of a keyboard.

Whitley watched in horror as the expenses mounted. He was obliged to hire a harpsichord which had to be transported from Derby at much cost. Someone had to be found to play it and also instruct the performers in the art of recitative. But what was recitative exactly? Clearly it was speech that had to be sung or intoned in some way. Early experiments resembled plainsong giving a sound more like Matins than a Matinée.

Mr Bracer had made it clear that eight days were not sufficient to design and paint the sets for two new pieces. It was impossible. He and the Whitleys looked to see what scenery was to hand. The Colosseum, it was agreed, could be adapted into the quarter deck of a man o' war without too much difficulty A familiar forest scene was again put to use, mainly as a village green and afterwards the quayside at Portsmouth, which was achieved with the addition of a pair of oars and a lobster pot in the foreground. Mr Whitley even thought wistfully that perhaps the music would be so sublime that audiences would close their eyes and create their own mental scenery. But he knew this had little currency. They were a literal lot that came to the theatre.

Costumes were not a concern for it was decided to mount the operas in the present day. The ladies were able to wear of their best. For the men, naval uniforms and sailor suits could be hired easily from the pawnbroker, it being a brief period of peace.

New singers were employed, some coming from as far as Leeds. Undoubtedly, though, it was with the arrival of Mr Thornton Friars that events began to take fire. Mr Friars was the tenor who had been recommended by Alderman Fairlight and he descended upon the small troop of performers with the subtlety of a ravenous wolf.

Mr Friars had a fine tenor voice. It was he who had sung the leads in Mr Handel's offerings in Birmingham of late. He was also a close friend of Mr Bickerstaffe, the librettist of the two ballad operas which fact he repeated many times so that everyone would make no mistake with whom they were dealing. Mr Friars brought with him a quartet of instrumentalists to augment the local trio of violin, cello and flute. Being sophisticated musicians, the newcomers' scathing criticism of the indigenous players did not make for harmony in the orchestra pit.

The discord amidst the musicians spread rapidly to the stage, when Mr Friars took it upon himself to be both lead singer and director of the entire enterprise. Before Mr Friar's arrival, Whitley had promised Miss Proctor the leading role of Sally in *Thomas and Sally.*

This opportunity had thrilled the young lady who, for the duration of the run, cancelled all her other engagements, at great monetary loss. However, Mr Friars, after his first rehearsal with Miss Proctor of the duet, *Oh tell me if thy love be true,* dismissed the poor lady, saying he had heard sweeter sounds from a herring gull.

A distraught Miss Proctor was led from the stage in a state of fury and near collapse.

At this point Mr Friars revealed the true depths of his subterfuge by declaring that the role of Sally was to be given to a Mrs Mountain who had sung it many times in Birmingham. It happened that she was a close friend and companion of his and happened fortuitously to be sharing lodgings with him here in Nottingham. That very afternoon, Mrs Mountain was installed as leading soprano in both the ballad operas. Her physical proportions belied her name, for she was not a big woman, but it was soon discovered that her self regard was of alpine dimensions. The scene, it could be said, was set for high drama.

For the Whitleys their theatre had become a foreign country. They felt (quite rightly) that their domain had been invaded. If they were not careful they could be overthrown, even evicted. What could be done? Like any occupying force, Mr Friars and Mrs Mountain wanted immediate changes following their invasion. They were totally dissatisfied with backstage conditions which were, they said, the worst they had ever known even when touring in Wales. They demanded a private dressing room each to be equipped with wax candles, new looking glasses and separate day beds. If this meant that the rest of the cast had to change in the corridors that could not be helped. Mutiny within Whitley's own cast became a strong possibility.

Earlier discord was forgotten as plans were discussed of how to be rid of the new enemy. Extremes, such as leaving trapdoors open, waxing the stairs could not be countenanced. Yet what else was there? Leading singers such as these were never known to miss a performance, so any likelihood of indisposition was improbable. A deputation approached the Whitleys to convey the seriousness of the backstage unrest. Subsequently the Whitleys agreed that a meeting with Lady Grandby was required urgently.

Lady Grandby did not provide tea at the conference. When it was suggested that an alternative to the ballad operas be found, she was adamant.

'I won't hear of it,' she declared, 'neither will any of my committee. We have toiled long and hard to find a suitable amusement for Judge Woolley and we expect you to provide it. That is your business is it not?'

When Mr Whitley complained of the enormous cost of mounting the pieces, Lady Grandby's hostility increased.

'My friends and I have subscribed considerable sums of money to Mr Pennell's playhouse. I am certain there is enough in the funds to pay for one or two simple evenings of musical entertainment. Why only last week Mrs Bentley herself devised a charming afternoon, for which she charged no admission and yet was able to give ten pounds to the new infirmary.'

Here Mrs Whitley tried to explain that the tensions arising were because of the impossible behaviour of the two newly imported singers.

'Now, that I cannot allow ,' said Lady Grandby. 'Only last night we met both artistes at a delightful welcoming reception organised by Alderman Fairlight Don't forget they are his friends Everyone was captivated by their modesty. It was remarked upon. Also it was agreed how lucky we are to have them with us. Recall, this is for Judge Woolley's amusement. He will expect only the best.'

The appeal was fruitless, the Whitleys left in defeat.

Mr Friars and Mrs Mountain's outrageous demands continued. Only one moment of relief was enjoyed, when a rat ran over Mrs Mountain's slipper. Those who heard her scream declared it was an octave higher than her usual top C. Otherwise all seemed to be lost. Ironically, with the first night only days away, the box office was doing excellent business. Anticipation was high. Two ballad operas with new top rank singers supported by fine musicians and chorus. Who could ask for more? The Whitleys could - and did.

That evening, as Mrs Whitley sought diversion with the latest London news sheet, she noticed an item. 'Listen to this,' she said.

'My dear,'answered Jemmy with glee, 'if that were known here it would be explosive. A sure means of ridding ourselves of Mr Friars.'

'Precisely. But wait. We must be constructive. If Friars were to be removed we'd need to suggest an alternative,' said Cassy.

'True. I believe Mr Foote is in the area. Tomorrow I'll enquire if he is to be had. If he is then we can start a calumny to our advantage.'

The two went to bed that night in a merrier frame of mind than for some time. A plan was emerging. Fire would be fought with fire.

Next morning, Mrs Whitley called upon Lady Grandby's friend Mrs Bentley. That lady was slightly taken aback, for it will be recalled it was she who had been so scathing about Mrs Whitley's singing. For a moment Mrs Bentley feared that her condemnation may have reached her visitor's ears, but as soon as she learned the true purpose of Mrs Whitley's social call she welcomed her cordially.

'My husband and I were with Lady Grandby yesterday,' Mrs Whitley explained, 'she mentioned that you had recently held a musical afternoon in aid of the infirmary.'

'That is so,' said Mrs Bentley, ' It was given by my daughter, a most accomplished singer. A recital of English folk songs. Only the seemly ones of course' she laughed lightly. 'Lavinia accompanied herself on the harp. We have a fine new harp, made in Germany, which she plays to perfection. It was very well received. Almost ten pounds raised for the infirmary.'

'You are on the board of the infirmary?' enquired Mrs Whitley.

'Indeed, yes,' Mrs Bentley allowed herself a tiny sigh of fatigue. 'So very demanding, but such rewarding work. We meet once every month to ensure that the staff are guided spiritually in their endeavours.'

'How very commendable. Which brings me to the purpose of my calling. Mr Whitley and I were thinking that perhaps one performance of the ballad operas might see the profits donated to the infirmary itself.'

The idea was greeted with enthusiasm by Mrs Bentley. 'How kind, and what a splendid concept. I am quite certain the board will be delighted. We next meet at the end of the month.'

'Forgive my impatience,' said Mrs Whitley, 'but by then the performances will be over. The opportunity gone. Arrangements have to be made at once. Playbills printed, dispositions made . . . . Could you not make the decision today of behalf of the committee?'

'Oh no. That would be most improper.'

'Alderman Fairlight is your chairman I believe? If you could gain his approval, would that not be sufficient? Possibly with Lady Grandby's support? It is most urgent if we are to proceed.'

Mrs Bentley was far from sure. It so happened that she was seeing Lady Grandby later that morning together with some of the other ladies on the committee. They could perhaps approach the Alderman . . . 'That would constitute a quorum if the idea is liked?' asked Mrs Whitley.

'I suppose it would. I will see what can be done.'

As she left Cassandra asked, 'Perhaps a message could be sent by hand. By about three o'clock shall we say? For there is so much work to be done if the idea is approved.'

A message did come and by half past two, with the news that the committee happily accepted the proposal. Alderman Fairlight had hesitated at first, for he was not by any means happy that the new infirmary, a place of unsullied merit, should be sponsored by a theatre. But finally he concurred when faced with the enthusiasm shown by Mrs Bentley and Lady Grandby, combined with the eagerness of the other ladies. Plans were announced for a grand charity performance.

Mrs Whitley was well suited with her achievements. She awaited her husband's return following his enquiries that day, it was not until late that he was back in Nottingham.

'Is Mr Foote available?' she asked.

'Yes he is.'

'So we may proceed?'

'Yes, I think we can.'

They hugged each other. (Another infrequency.)

Two mornings later, Lady Grandby was puzzled to receive a letter in a hand she did not recognise. It contained a small cutting from a London news sheet carefully pasted on a larger piece of writing paper. At first she did not read the printed extract, only the alarming words which were put alongside in menacing black ink, *'Do you associate with the likes of this?'*

Which led her to examine the report. Here the newspaper disclosed that Mr Isaac Bickerstaffe, the lyricist of Mr Arne's theatre works had been accused of the most gross and unnatural misdeeds known to society. So serious were these unspeakable crimes that Mr Bickerstaffe had fled to France to escape prosecution. Had he remained in England his crime would have be punishable by hanging.

This dreadful intelligence ended: 'Mr Bickerstaffe is celebrated as the author of several ballad operas including *Love in a Village* and *Thomas and Sally*. In addition to this he is a close friend of the well known impresario Mr Thornton Friars.'

Lady Grandby was made quite ill by the tidings. When Alderman Fairlight (who had received a similar missive) arrived, he found her in a darkened room, the curtains drawn by a thoughtful maidservant.

'Is it true?' asked Lady Grandby anxiously.

'I fear so. My wife has seen the same London news sheet and found the item for herself.'

'Oh how dreadful!'

'Indeed. It is doubly bad. For not only are we supporting the work of Bickerstaffe, but Mr Thornton Friars has frequently declared himself to be a close friend of the bugg. . . '

Lady Grandby gave a tiny involuntary scream. Recovering she asked, 'But Alderman, was it not you who recommended Mr Friars?'

'In all innocence,' thundered the Alderman. 'That's what's so damnable. I cannot afford to be associated with him, or promoting the work of a sodo . . . .'

Lady Grandby covered her ears, to avoid the Alderman's words.

'People might think. . . . well people might think. And we cannot be seen raising funds from such a . . . Suppose the news becomes common knowledge that Mr Friars associates with the likes of. . .!'

'Quite, quite,' said Lady Grandby who by now was listening again. She asked. 'But what are we to do?'

'Cancel. We cannot support such an undertaking. We can have nothing to do with ballad operas penned by a. . . Remember it's to be sung before Judge Woolley. And where would that put us?'

Entirely against his principles Alderman Fairlight went at once to speak to the Whitleys. They told him they too had been told of the scandal and were as dismayed by the revelation as was he. They wondered if those who had spread the rumours had done so to damage the theatre, for they realised the performances could not now possibly take place.

'Mind you ,' said Mr Whitley guardedly, 'only a select few in Nottingham read the London news sheets. The disgrace may not be common knowledge.'

'We cannot take the chance,' said the Alderman. 'For someone in my situation it is unthinkable. Can't have the new infirmary taking tainted money.'

The Whitley's both agreed and offered sympathy. Yet many tickets had been sold. The judiciary at the forthcoming assizes would expect the provision of some distraction from their grim committals. If none were supplied, what would they think of Nottingham and its corporation?

(Here it might be said that earlier, Mrs Whitley had suggested that *The Maid of the Mill* might be substituted, until Mr Whitley told her that that too was wrote by Mr Bickerstaffe.)

Alderman Fairlight was firm that something quite different must be found. At this point Mr Whitley said that he had heard recently that the well-known Mr Foote was in the locality and was, he believed, available to give his celebrated lecture on heads. This entertainment, he assured the Alderman, was reputed to be quite without blemish and totally above he law.

'If you are certain of that,' said the Alderman, 'we'll have him.'

There followed alarming rows and confrontations when it was suddenly and unexpectedly announced that the ballad operas were cancelled 'due to unforeseen difficulties.' Threats of law suits and damages, actions for libel filled the air, but Alderman Fairlight used his role as magistrate to impose his wishes with no argument.

Mr Whitley confirmed that following his enquiries Mr Foote was available to perform at the theatre throughout the assize period. Although there was initially some disappointment, people came out of curiosity and found he provided an evening of great amusement and continual mirth. Within two nights, Mr Foote's every appearance was sold out. It was also noticed that Judge Woolley came to all of the performances and was as much diverted as anyone. After the assizes, he thanked both Lady Grandby and Alderman Fairlight for the entertainment they had arranged.

'Enjoyed it thoroughly,' he said, 'not laughed so much in years. How clever of you to think of something so original. Thank God you didn't choose any of those damnable ballad operas. Can't stand 'em.'

*

Eleven. *Notes in an Interval.*

It would be hard for those only acquainted with Mrs Whitley of the present day, who invoked respectability above all, to learn that in her young days she had been a wild and headstrong Irish girl.

At the age of sixteen, Cassy O'Shea, as she was then, had run away from a decent home in Dublin with an actor from the Smock Alley Theatre, one William Parker. To be fair to Mr Parker, he had stood little chance of resisting her assault, for Cassy being confoundedly bit, had laid siege to him with a militant fervour. Having convinced him that she came from a well-to-do family, William Parker finally decided to abscond with her, in the hopes that her parents might pay him handsomely for her safe return.

Quite the opposite, for Cassy's parents were relieved to be rid of her. Being humble shopkeepers with little capital, they had three other daughters each in need of dowries before matrimony. When Cassy convinced them that Parker loved her to such an extent he sought no marriage settlement they readily agreed to the match. But the match was never struck. Cassy journeyed with Parker until he learned the truth and then quit her to go to sea, leaving the poor girl stranded, pregnant and without a penny.

Although never a beauty, she had a natural singing voice and a talent for comedy. This was just sufficient for a minor theatre company to offer her small roles which she accepted under the name of Mrs Parker, pregnancy being no problem as long as she was billed as 'Mrs.' Many in her condition continued to play until their waters broke on stage, as was the case with Cassy whose daughter was born, if not in a trunk, but in the scene dock of the Yard Theatre in Kilkenny.

By now Cassandra was known as 'widow' Parker and as such became fiercely ambitious for her small daughter's success. Realising her own limitations, she convinced herself that wee Eileen (for so the child was named) was a natural born prodigy destined to dazzle audiences in Ireland and beyond. True, the child had a natural talent which her mother saw as a better source of income than from her own acting career. Wee Eileen was reared to dance before she could walk, to sing before she could speak, and to display these abilities at the drop of a hat. Within four years she was appearing on stage as the Fairy Shamrock where she performed step dances, reels and jigs, curiously clad in dainty tinselled dresses, gossamer wings and traditional black clogs. For more than half a decade this amazing child remained no more than three years of age and managed to celebrate at least four birthdays every twelve months, the which were celebrated with benefit performances in place of birthday parties.

Many mothers watched Eileen's progress with envy, hoping their own small daughters might also succeed. Cassandra, ever mindful of lucrative ventures, recruited three of these mites to appear with Fairy Shamrock as a supporting chorus, named the Moonbeams of Mourne. In a rapid space of time the enterprise received bookings, including several from unexpected circles.

For the Fairy and her Moonbeams proved highly popular with gentlemen's clubs and bachelor supper parties, until the church authorities put an end to the venture by bundling the children into the nearest orphanage.

Cassandra managed narrowly to avoid criminal proceedings but by now, the Fairy Shamrock, after years of being forced like a stick of rhubarb, began to resemble the same. Audiences lost interest, as did Fairy Shamrock herself, who, with a monumental - 'SHAN'T!' refused to appear on stage in any guise; returning instead to her grandparents, where she took to working in the family shop with noticeable relief.

This arrangement left Cassandra desperate to find a new child prodigy who might profit from her experience as a manager. But her plans changed completely the night she first saw James Augustus Whitley on stage. For as with Parker before him, Cassandra on seeing the young actor was once more confoundedly bit and 'Jemmy' Whitley stood no chance of withstanding her advances.

Jemmy had been apprenticed to a lawyer who had taught him to read and write, for he had little formal schooling. He ran many errands which included trips backstage to the Smock Alley Theatre where he became friends with the prompter and several actors. This enabled him to see most of the productions from the wings, where in no time his ambition to be an actor took hold.

His personable looks, combined with a good voice, led to the management offering him supporting roles and in time secondary leads though not any major parts. It was at this moment in his career that Cassandra decided to prepare him for bigger things and lured him with several other breakaway actors to form a group in Capel Street where, with her modest savings, an old shop had been converted into a small theatre.

Their first presentation was *A Cure for a Scold* taken from Shakespeare's *Taming of the Shrew,* with Jemmy as Petruchio and Cassandra as the Shrew. The juxtaposition of the smaller younger man mastering the larger older woman pleased audiences greatly. They had their first success. It was realised by both that they could never play romantic leads, but this did not prevent their love from blossoming offstage. Once Cassandra had explained the circumstances of her being 'Mrs Parker' and Jemmy had made the acquaintance of Eileen, the two set forth on the path of matrimony. Cassandra even joked that she could provide her own dowry, but Jemmy refused this insisting that all funds should go into the assets of their troupe.

For a while the company of comedians fared well. By and by, Mr and Mrs Whitley followed their early triumph with an adaptation (penned by themselves) of *Much Ado* in which they played Beatrice and Benedick. Sadly, few customers came. Those that did found the Whitleys closer to Punch and Judy than Shakespeare's 'merry warriors' with the result that most of the nascent company deserted them to find work elsewhere. This left the Whitleys spending their days on bread and buttermilk until they decided that Ireland was not for them and sought their fortune across the water in Liverpool.

Here their luck changed. Liverpool was an enlightened city where dramatic entertainment was supported and encouraged by both the authorities and the public. Jemmy Whitley, although he had not yet obtained his majority, soon gained the patronage of a Mrs Tasker, the widow of a tallow chandler. With his Irish charm he was able to persuade her to construct a new playhouse for him, which she did by raising private subscriptions from her many friends. The Whitleys were always ready to perform the plays that Mrs Tasker and her circle asked to see. With Liverpool already a magnet for actors, when word broke out that a new company was being formed Jemmy was, as they say, spoilt for choice. The theatre gained favour both in artistic and financial spheres and with his patron's blessing after two seasons Jemmy took his company on a tour of several towns including Leeds and Manchester. In these and other locations he swiftly established what was to become known as the Whitley circuit.

It was as actor manager that he was most happy and it was said by his rivals that he had the complaisant ability to get other people to build theatres for him. A resourcefulness much envied, until quarrels and disputes caused the Whitley's to sever their associations with the north and accept Marmaduke Pennell's offer to manage his new theatre in Nottingham and create a fresh circuit in this virgin territory.

History repeated itself when Cassy's daughter Eileen, now a young woman, formed an alliance with Mr Gosli, an actor with a small theatrical company of his own . But, unlike her mother's experience with Parker, this partnership was a happy one and Mr and Mrs Gosli enjoyed a modest but successful life with their enterprise, which as far as the Whitley's knew, still flourished in Stamford.

*

Twelve. *Prompter's Devil.*

'So young whippersnapper, your want to be a prompter's devil?'

The doorkeeper had kept his word and spoken to Mrs M'George who had spoken to Mr Trout, the manager, who now spoke to Thomas.

'Yes sir.'

'You're quick in the mind and swift on your feet?'

'Yes sir.'

'Prompter's devil' was Mr Trout's term for a prompter's call boy. Whereas in Nottingham, Mrs Whitley had acted unofficially as prompt, here in Stamford it was Mr Trout who worked 'on the book.' As Tate Wilkinson was not expected in Stamford for several days Mr Trout had to decide whether or not to try out Thomas for the task.

'Ever done it before?' he asked.

'I worked back stage for Mr Whitley.' This was greeted with a derisive grunt from Mr Trout which implied that such experience did not impress him.

'Running in and out the green room I'll warrant?'

'Yes sometimes.'

'You don't go in the green room here, that's for the actors and not for tom-tits like you. Just knock at the door and call the name, understand?'

'Yes.' Thomas had been given a cast list for the night's main play *The Clandestine Marriage.* Every character had a number. Thomas was to wait by the prompter's side until an actor was due to make an entrance. From the text Mr Trout would call 'Four ' which required Thomas to consult his list, run to the green room and call 'Mr Lovewell,' or in the case of Mrs M'George who was 'Twelve' - 'Miss Sterling.' From then it was the actor's responsibility. A late, or a missed entrance meant a fine. When this occurred, inevitably there were disputes as to whether the call boy had been audible or the actor had not been listening. Inebriation was the commonest cause of missed cues and never excused

'Very well,' said Mr Trout. 'Tonight we open with the *Marriage,* that's followed by interval dancing and singing, then the afterpiece *The Trip to Scotland.'* Have you got your cast list numbered for that?'

'No,' said Thomas.

'Why not?'

'You've not yet given me the job, that's why not.'

'I'll take no lip from you, young whippersnapper. Find a cast list and get it numbered right away.'

'Are you're giving me the job?'

'You'll be tried out tonight. See you're on your toes.'

'How much am I paid?'

'Threepence a night, for a start. If there's any mishaps you'll be paying me. Five o'clock, on the dot. Now get out.'

Thomas left and walked into Mrs M'George.

'Have you got it?' she asked.

'Looks like it.'

'Good lad. We need someone fast on his feet, so see you prove your worth,' said Fanny patting him on the shoulder. 'Watch from the wings young man. Learn everything you can,'

Here it was. Thomas had a foothold; an advantage over Sweeny, for as Fanny M'George had said there was no work there as an actor.

Sweeny had been offered a job as a stage hand which he had refused saying he was a player of repute and had no intention of shifting scenery. This he soon regretted as little else was forthcoming. He was later taken on as a coach porter at the George Inn, earning very little and relying on tips to supplement his small wage. This was not to his liking and soon his mood worsened. Because of their differing hours of work, the times when he and Thomas could meet were few. On the occasions when it was achieved, Sweeny showed his resentment at Thomas's good fortune and refused to hear of life backstage which his young friend longed to talk about.

Once or twice Fanny M'George gave Sweeny a free seat for the play, but he abused the kindness, criticising the players saying how much better he would be in their roles. Fanny realising his situation, tried cheering him up further with occasional meals which he accepted showing little grace, his ill will towards the theatre growing.

But Thomas thrived as prompter's devil. After a week's trial Mr Trout and the actors were satisfied with his probation and he was given the job at the rate of six pence a night. Backstage conditions in Stamford was far better organised than in Nottingham. There was no clutter with the corridors kept clear and well lit. Mr Trout gave exact instructions allowing Thomas good time to call the actors' cues. Some even thanked him on receiving them. He found it exciting to stand in the wings as the actors brushed past in their stage gear, allowing him to feel part of the whole performance. He longed to make the move from the dark obscurity of the wings into that glowing sphere of the stage. He could think of nowhere better to be than with this band of players, trusting that before long he would be one of them.

Jimmy Oldfield, Sweeny's friend, gave him the most trouble. He was always late, cutting every entrance to the last second. When called, he ran frantically down the passage frequently putting on part of his costume as he reached the wings. Despite this, Thomas admired his ability to walk on stage after such haste, giving the impression he had strolled on at his leisure.

Mr Holland, the oldest member in the company played Lord Ogleby in the *Marriage,* a part Garrick had written for himself. It was a great comic role and there were scenes in the play where Thomas noticed the cunning with which Mr Holland timed his laughs. When the audience was laughing the old actor made a strange noise to himself, a cross between a hum and a warble in his throat which could not be heard out front, but was a sign to the other actors not to speak until the laughter ended. 'Never talk through the laughs,' was one of the first rules he learned.

Mr Holland was a favourite with audiences something he accepted with modesty but made it clear that as a leading actor he expected small signs of respect. He took it as his privilege to be the first to walk off stage after the curtain call, which his fellow actors allowed as his right. Thomas was told that he appreciated a glass of cordial at the end of each act and the supplying of this became a regular duty. 'Thank you dear boy,' said Mr Holland slipping him a ha'penny with a smile at the end of the evening.

He noticed the habits of others. Mrs M'George, before she went on stage seemed to wipe her feet as if on a door mat. This, he discovered harked back to her time as a dancer, when she trod in the resin tray before an entrance. Some made the sign of the cross before appearing and he decided they must be either Catholics or merely superstitious. One or two actors touched the prompt copy held by Mr Trout which he seemed not to mind. Perhaps they thought they would better remember their lines. Everyone tried to cough silently and appreciated a jug of water held by Thomas should it be needed. A spare handkerchief was often required and he saw he had one always at the ready.

It was not long before he became known as Mercury, running between the stage and the green room. He learned quickly the content and moves of the plays performed. He became able to judge by the sound of a voice when an exit was imminent even if the speaker wasn't visible. When not in the prompt corner he could run round to the other proscenium door and open it to give a smooth withdrawal. An egress was more impressive when the actor did not have to feel for a door knob. Sometimes they had a candlestick, a lantern to carry off. Whenever possible Thomas was there at the door relieving them of their props, which most actors appreciated.

This earned him a number of friends, easing his entry into the fellowship of the company. He thought of asking if he could 'dress the stage,' but knew this was not possible with his call boy's duties. All he could do was wait until there was a chance. Perhaps when Mr Wilkinson arrived. . . .

At quiet times, even though it was out of bounds, he went into the green room Here there was a small bookcase of plays which he went through carefully seeking a possible role for himself. If the time ever came to audition he wanted to have some speeches ready prepared. The choice was hard for most of the titles were unknown to him. Most of the volumes were of Shakespeare of which he knew nothing. There were versions of the *Marriage* as everyone called it, but he thought he would only be mimicking what he saw here on stage. Then he found the part of George Barnwell in *The London Merchant* which seemed ideal. Here was a young apprentice his own age in prison a few hours before his execution.

This was perfect and he learned the touching speech beginning,

If any youth, like you, in future times,
Shall mourn my fate, though he abhor my crimes;
Or tender maid, like you, my tale shall hear,
And to my sorrow give a pitying tear. . . .

It couldn't fail. Pathos and tragedy, this would melt the hearts of any onlooker. But there must have a contrast. There was a copy of Othello, but he knew he was too young and anyway wasn't he black? There was another role, (what was it, Jago?) which he liked better, for he thought it the best part in the play, so that became his second choice. Had he still been friendly with Mr Sweeny he could have discussed the choice with him, but these days they rarely saw each other. Thomas was now lodging with Mrs M'George whom he liked but she always seemed busy learning lines herself, rehearsing or looking after the needs of everyone in the lodging house. Mr Holland might advise him, but he was far too grand to be approached.

Thomas arrived one evening to find an excited atmosphere in the theatre. It was hard to explain. It was as if the entire place had been given a jolt of electricity that new and wonderful substance he had heard talk about.

It reminded him of his days in Colonel Hayter's Regiment when there was to be an inspection by the commanding officer. Everyone was affected and moved more swiftly and carefully. No-one dallied or chatted in corners, everyone had 'purpose.' As he was about to ask what was happening, he encountered Mr Trout backstage who grimaced suggesting he should not be there and tried to push him aside. Puzzled he suddenly found himself facing a small portly man who looked like a prosperous farmer. Trout coughed and announced,

'This sir, is Thomas. In your absence I employed him as a new prompter's boy.'

The prosperous farmer asked, 'Has he proved satisfactory?'

'Quits sufficient, yes.'

'Good.' The prosperous farmer regarded Thomas. 'Do you know who I am, young fella-me-lad?' he asked.

'I would be so bold as to say Mr Tate Wilkinson, sir.'

'And you are right to be so bold,' said Mr Wilkinson. Thomas was about to offer his hand but realised that Mr Wilkinson made no such advance. 'Are your duties here to your liking?'

'They are sir.'

'And so they should be, it is a goodly company. We do not say we are the best, but we are certainly the most distinguished.'

He paused briefly.

'A general call for tomorrow morning at ten,' he said to Mr Trout. 'I shall be announcing the new programme and posting the cast list, as well as notes after I see how they do to-night.'

Quite unexpectedly he concluded by proclaiming, 'Hallelujah. Praise the Lord,' and walked away with Mr Trout in pursuit.

It was noticeable that Mr Wilkinson's demeanour was more refined than that of Mr Whitley. Another difference being that had a full head of curly red hair. It could not be imagined that he would parade through the streets in anything as vulgar as a pink satin suit. Moreover, parading was unlikely as Mr Wilkinson walked with a heavy limp. The part he played was that of a gentleman. If he was mistaken as such - all to the good. Much of this attitude may have been due to his being the son of a clergyman who had vigorously disapproved of his chosen career.

The fear of 'notes' may have spurred a good performance that night, which Thomas had thought to be excellent. He was not sure if the general call for the next morning applied to him, but decided he must attend.

Even Jimmy Oldfeild was on time, sitting with the company in the pit promptly at ten o'clock when Mr Wilkinson walked on stage.

'Last night's performances was. . .' he paused, '. . . adequate. For me however, adequate is not sufficient. I expect excellence, and so do my audiences.' A ripple of discomfort was felt in the pit.

'Why is it after I am away for a few days I return to find bad habits so rife? All is slovenliness. I should sack all of you.'

'These are harsh words, Mr Wilkinson,' came a voice which was that of Mr Holland, who knew he did not deserve such criticism.

'Indeed they are, Mr Holland. Unfortunately harsh words and the threat of dismissal appear to be the only means of putting resolve into the lot of you.'

The ripple of discomfort at this point became audible.

'I tell you, I could go into Stamford market this very morning and find stall holders whose vocal projections would put all of you to shame. Last night I heard about one word in five. I wondered if it was a mime to avoid prosecution. Please remember there is no law here against the use of speech. . . ' Another pause, 'so. . .USE IT!'

By now there was a clear mumble of annoyance from everyone.

'You see,' said Mr Wilkinson, 'you continue at it. Muttering. I cannot hear a word you're saying down there.'

Mrs M'George was brave enough to speak out. 'We would be obliged if we could be told which parts were so poor.'

'All of 'em! I'm having a complete run-through as soon as I've finished. If it lasts until curtain-up that's your misfortune.' Sighs of dismay were heard as Mr Wilkinson brought out a sheet of paper from his pocket.

'You will be wanting to hear the programme for the remainder of our time here in Stamford. Next week will be added to our repertory the celebrated tragedy of *The Rival Queens* by Mr Lee, to be followed by a new farce, *The Capricious Lovers*. This contains music, so be prepared for extra rehearsal time. Our last week will begin with *The Unhappy Favourite* and a new afterpiece *Midsummer Night's Dream* by Shakespeare of course. In this you'll be pleased to know I'm cutting out the lovers so we shall only be playing the scenes with the rustics and the fairies. This is what the public likes the most. You will find your casting on the call board. That's all for the moment. Ten minutes and I want a complete run through of *Marriage* and *The Trip*. Out of costume, as I am feeling benevolent. Hallelujah. Praise the Lord!'

The cast stood and started gradually to move. Thomas found himself standing near Mr Oldfield. 'Why was he so angry?' he asked.

'I thought the performance last night was good.'

'Mmmm?' said Mr Oldfield airily, 'Oh that's nothing. We always get this after he's been away a few days. Thinks we won't come up to scratch unless he rants and raves. It's his way, that's all it is.'

'You mean he wasn't angry?

'Not a bit of it, he's a showman. Case in point.' Mr Oldfield moved to join the others.

Thomas was about to do the same when he noticed Mr Wilkinson was still alone on stage. If Mr Oldfield was right and he was not really in a bad mood, now was perhaps an opportunity to approach him. Gathering his courage, he stood at the foot of the stage and cleared his throat.

'Sir. May I speak to you?'

Mr Wilkinson turned. 'What is it young fella-me-lad?'
Thomas wondered why he was called 'young-feller-me lad' when he had a perfectly good name. However, now was not a time to question such things, so he continued,

'I would like to ask you for a role.'

'Would you now?' replied Mr Wilkinson, 'I'm told you already have a role, that of prompter's boy and that you do it well.'

'Thank you sir, but I would like to act. . . upon the stage. I would like to perform a speech for your consideration.'

'An audition you mean?'

'Yes. If you can allow me a few minutes of your time.'

'A few minutes? That can seem a lifetime at a bad audition. Have you something at the ready?'

'Yes, I have sir.'

'Very well, but let it be brief.' Mr Wilkinson noticed some members of the cast were still in the auditorium. He called to them, 'Hold there. We have a new actor at the day spring. Here he is.' He indicated Thomas.

'But sir . . .' Thomas was embarrassed at this turn. 'I wanted to do something just for you alone.'

'Never decline an audience young fella-me-lad. If you desire to be an actor you must lust after one. Pray begin.'

With Mr Wilkinson onstage and one or two scattered in the pit this was not how Thomas wanted things to be.

'Sir,' he called.

'Yes? Mr . . .? I don't recall fully your name as yet. Though doubtless the world will know it soon.' Amused laughter came from the benches.

'My name is Hammond, sir, Thomas Hammond.'

'Very well. Display to us your skills Mr Hammond. . .'

'May I request, that I be on the stage, and you be seated here?'

Mr Wilkinson frowned at him. ' I'll give it to you lad, the scene must be set to your liking. Have it your own way. We will change places.'

He came down to the pit and Thomas with a shy smile went on the stage, standing to one side.

'Sir, I would like to present to you . . .'

'Centre stage, Mr Hammond, centre stage. You have it now, it may not always be yours'. Thomas took his direction.

'Sir, I give to you the final speech from *The London Merchant. . .*'

Mr Wilkinson smiling turned to the others, '*The Tradesman's Tragedy,'* he whispered. There were subdued laughs from those long in the profession.

'What was that sir?'

'An aside young fella-me-lad that is all. Forgive my discourtesy.'

Thomas stood firm and began. He was nervous but able to conceal it. He felt confidence, he felt sure he could do justice to himself, he began,

'*If any youth, like you, in future times. . .'*

Giving all the emotion he could summon, Thomas used every gesture and vocal trick he had seen, until he reached the tragic conclusion. . .

'*. . . Since you nor weep, nor I shall die in vain.'*

Not until he ended his speech did Thomas allow himself the luxury of regarding his audience. What he saw pleased him greatly, for each one of them had handkerchiefs to their eyes, clearly moved beyond words to tears. He waited a few seconds before announcing'

'Next, in contrast may I offer you . . .'

Mr Wilkinson on the front bench raised an arm,

'No more, no more, Mr Hammond, I beseech you. I can say in all honesty I have never seen anyone die so convincingly. . .' at which point the laughter broke out from everyone. Mopping his tears Mr Wilkinson came to Thomas on stage, trying hard to contain his laughter he said,

'Thank you for that. . . for that. . . remarkable airing of your faculties.'

Mr Wilkinson smiled at the few still in the pit, '*Yet I do not perceive here a divided duty.'* Sounds of laughter continued. 'Our profession is not yet ready for such intensity of feeling No audience would be proof against your blazing sincerity. In all honesty, young feller-me-lad, you do better to devote yourself to the respectable business of prompter's boy. Indeed you do.' He blew his nose. 'Rehearsal in five minutes. Hallelujah. Praise the Lord!'

Still laughing he walked away leaving Thomas centre stage for the first, and it would appear, the only time in his career.

*

Part Three.

Thirteen. *Encumbered with Help.*

There had been few moments of merriment during the Nottingham assizes. A total of three hangings, sixteen transportations had left Judge Woolley and his arbiters much fatigued. Rare evenings of recreation had brought visits by Mr Pennell to the Judge's lodgings; here over brandy and pipes of best Virginian tobacco many issues had been discussed into the night. Amongst these were the activities of Alderman Fairlight and his condemnation of all convivial pleasures. The Judge was angered to learn how the Alderman was all but misusing the law to impose his restrictive views.

'What is required,' said the Judge, 'is to get the new oligarchy behind you. For example, their support of racing is so powerful that narrow minded opponents are left helpless. Look to the rising merchants, those with the means to buy what only the nobility could once afford: fine houses, furniture, silver. . . . and diversion. With their patronage you'll defeat Alderman Fairlight and his kind. Yes, woo those who want to be entertained and will pay for it. When it suits them they'll spread money like horse muck on marigolds.'

Mr Pennell passed this message on to the Whitleys. Together they drew up a list of the well-to-do in the vicinity who, if approached, might bestow their bounty in the direction of the theatre. Before long, a letter of introduction was devised and sent to new and prosperous houses. Lady Grandby and her circle were not approached, for after the ballad opera fracas their power and influence was much diminished.
A carefully worded note sent to Lord and Lady Simpkin at their newly built mansion, Bulwell Hall, was typical of their tender.

'*Mr and Mrs Whitley present their most humble respects to Lord & Lady Simpkin and beg leave to request their future patronage at the*

Theatre Royal, St Mary's Gate. In their desire to present that which will delight their benefactors, Mr and Mrs Whitley have used every effort to procure the finest performers and plays and will continue to exert themselves in providing entertainments that are both agreeable and instructive.

Should Lord and Lady Simpkin wish to suggest any pieces that they would require to see at the theatre and be so gracious as to offer the great privilege of hospitality, Mr and Mrs Whitley will be honoured to call and be informed of their wishes at a time convenient.'

Lord and Lady Simpkin having recently acquired their wealth, were still a crumb unsure of their social footing. When a request arrived for them to act in a patronal capacity they sensed a role of influence they had of late been seeking.

A reply was quickly despatched to the Whitleys inviting them to take afternoon tea at Bulwell Hall. This grand and costly new house being several miles outside Nottingham, it was out of the question that the Whitleys should journey there on foot. For them both to ride on Gunpy was also not to be considered. 'My dear friends,' said Mr Pennell generously, 'you must borrow my landau, no question. Stebbings my coachman he'll drive you. What day is it you are invited. . .?'

It was decided that the Whitleys' apparel should be sober. Mrs Whitley settled for a new dress to be made by Mrs Stirrup, the late Mr Wheeler's landlady. She agreed upon a French style gown in pale blue satin, with matching embroidered slippers and bonnet. This required rigid corseting but the effect achieved was judged to be elegant if an upright position could be maintained. By her side, Mr Whitley, was dressed with a sobriety of attire that would not have been out of place at a Methodist funeral.

After a journey of some half hour, in Mr Pennell's resplendent landau, Mr and Mrs Whitley arrived at Bulwell Hall and examined the two and a half storeys of the majestic new house.

'Where's he made his money?' enquired Mrs Whitley. 'Nails,' replied her husband, 'and screws as well no doubt.'

They drew up before a white columned porch where, almost before the vehicle had halted, two footmen in cherry coloured livery descended the steps. One opened the door of the carriage and the other pulled down the short flight of steps enabling the visitors to alight with dignity. At the same time a butler appeared at the great front door and watched their ascent.

'Good afternoon madam, good afternoon sir,' intoned the butler in a cheerless voice indicating that they should follow him across a massive hall, its marble floor so highly polished that Cassandra's feet almost shot from under her. She grasped Jemmy's arm, to which he muttered, 'Hold tight, old fruit,' all of which the butler ignored, walking ahead like an automaton.

They came to a pair of elegant doors which were opened ceremoniously. 'His Lordship and Lady Simpkin will be joining you,' the butler announced. The door was closed without a sound, although in the distance could be heard raised voices and the unmistakable barking of large dogs.

The salon in which they found themselves was manifestly created to impress. It was dominated by a gigantic fireplace of red and black marble. Over this, in a gilt and tortoiseshell frame, was a near life-size painting of a young woman on horseback vaulting over a five bar gate. On either side were black marble pedestals each supporting an ormolu candelabra of at least twenty holders. Around were tables together with chaises-longues, sofas, side chairs and footstools, all upholstered in multicoloured shades of floral damask. Before the Whitleys had time to absorb these wonders, the doors opened wide and Lord and Lady Simpkin made their entrance.

'Aahdeedoo?' Lord Simpkin extended a large welcoming hand.

He was a big man of capacious girth and redness of face. He wore a scarlet hunting coat in conjunction with buckskin breeches and riding boots, complete with spurs. He had a powdered wig and a tricorne hat which he did not remove. In his left hand was a riding crop. Behind him came Lady Simpkin. She wore a high wig surmounted with flowers and artificial fruit. Her dress of orange silk carried an abundance of lace bows. She wielded a silk fan, much as her husband held his riding crop.

'Charmed. . . charmed I'm sure. . .' she said to both her visitors. 'Please be set down. We don't stand on ceremony 'ere. You'll 'ave to take us as you find us 'cos that's the way we are.'

Mr and Mrs Whitley attempted to sit together.'

'No, no, no, not there! We can't 'ave married couples set together. It's bad luck.' At length the four found themselves seated with vast distances between them. Semaphore would have been easier than conversation.

Minutes passed until Lady Simpkin said, ' 'In't it about time we 'ad a cuppa tea 'usband?' Husband obliged by pulling a silken rope so that in some faraway part of the house a bell sounded giving rise to more barking of dogs.

Still, nobody spoke. Finally, pointing to the equestrian painting with his riding crop, Lord Simpkin asked, 'What d'you make o' that then?'

Mr Whitley replied that it was very fine.

'Stubbs,' said Lord Simpkin.

Jemmy, who regretfully had never heard of the artist asked, 'Is that the name of the horse?'

This gave rise to loud laughter from their hosts. 'e don't know who Stubbs is,' came the rebuke.

When the gaiety had ceased, Lord Simpkin said, 'Stubbs, 'e's the oil painter. Did it all by 'and he did. Two 'undred guineas we paid. And the frame was extra on top o' that,'

The Whitleys both agreed that it was most impressive. They went on to enquire who was the young lady depicted on horseback.

'oo is it? 'oo is it?' This time the Simpkins were affronted, 'It's our Lydia, our oldest, that' 'oo it is. She's a norse rider, can't you tell?'

Here the doors opened once more and one of the footmen entered, carefully placing a table next to Lady Simpkin on which the butler set a tray of silverware, fully equipped for the serving of afternoon tea. Salvers of cakes and sweet meats were also produced and placed on individual stands.

As the butler withdrew and the footman was closing the door, two large hounds bounded into the room. With deafening barks the excited dogs skidded around the salon, their tails thrashing like a flogger's rope. Claws skidded and tore at covers. Tables and chairs went pell mell and rugs were crumpled.

'Who let them bloody dogs in 'ere?' demanded Lord Simpkin as a cake stand toppled and the contents were greedily attacked by the animals. The butler without losing composure pleaded that it was none of his doing. One of the dogs leaped upon Jemmy, joyfully licking his face, while the other, not caring for cake, turned instead to Cassandra and attacked one of her embroidered slippers.

With remarkable calm Lady Simpkin insisted, 'Don't fret, they're only being friendly, they're just in the way of getting to know you.' The dog, that was so involved with Cassandra's foot, began exploring regions about her ankle until that lady stood up with a cry of alarm.

'Sit! Sit!' commanded Lord Simpkin. It was not clear if this was directed at Cassandra or at the dog. Neither obeyed.

Lady Simpkin, ignoring the uproar, arranged her tea cups. The hound, having removed Cassandra's slipper, worried it as it would a dead rabbit.

'Bad dog, bad dog,' said Lady Simpkin almost to herself.

When Jemmy tried to remove the other dog's paws from his shoulders, it snarled and barked at him.

'Geddown yer boggers!' bellowed Lord Simpkin but to no avail. Only by the use of his riding crop did he stop the hound from further harassing Jemmy. Possibly to show its indifference. the dog walked away, sniffed at one of the marble pillars and cocked its leg. This example was swiftly followed by the other animal, until Lord Simpkin beating them with both his hat and riding crop kicked the dogs away.

Suddenly and as quickly as they had appeared, the animals departed into the hall, his lordship and the butler in pursuit. The remaining footman, unused to such incidents, paused and then closed the door quietly as if nothing had happened. Somewhere beyond, a great deal of swearing combined with barking continued to be heard.

Jemmy tried brushing off the dog hairs and saliva from his black coat, whilst Cassandra replaced her damaged slipper onto a badly bleeding foot.

'Milk and sugar?' asked Lady Simpkin.

*

'Mr and Mrs Whitley present their most humble respects to Colonel and Mrs Padley and beg leave to request their future patronage. . .'

After the disappointments with the Simpkins, a visit to the Padleys seemed to offer better prospects. Marmaduke Pennell assured them that the colonel and his lady were great lovers of the drama and he was certain they would bestow some beneficence should they be petitioned. Colonel Padley had been happily involved with the East India Company, to the extent that he had taken early retirement from his regiment and built a fine house on Castle Gate. It was to that residence that a week later the Whitleys called (on foot) to take another afternoon tea, hopefully resulting in sponsorship.

The house on Castle Gate was imposing, but reticent in style after the vulgarities of Bulwell Hall. The front door was opened by a neat maid servant and after their outdoor garments were removed, Mrs Padley greeted them quietly and led them to a modest parlour. All that was noticeable was a fine long-case clock which ticked comfortingly and chimed politely at every quarter. In here, Colonel Padley joined them and engaged in pleasantries until the housemaid served tea.

'Yes, we're most interested in the drama,' said the Colonel. 'A lot of it to be found in India. The English out there you know. Mostly amateur of course, but of a very high standard, isn't that so m'dear?'

'Very high indeed,' agreed Mrs Padley. 'In fact,' she blushed delicately, 'I myself, took a part in one or two of the dramatics.'

The Whitleys asked what roles Mrs Padley had played.

'Oh, I can't remember now, it was such a long time ago. Before the babies came.'

'You were very good, m'dear.. She could have done it as a proper calling if she'd wished.'

Mr Whitley after mourning this loss to the stage enquired, 'You must have seen many plays when you were in India?'

'A great number, yes, we did,' replied the Colonel.

'Are there any you would like us to stage here? "By particular desire," as the phrase goes.'

The colonel thought. 'Ah, yes. Mmm. There was one we liked, wasn't there m'dear?'

'Yes, there was one we liked especially' agreed Mrs Padley.

'What play was that?' asked Mr Whitley.

'Yeeees,' pondered the colonel, 'we enjoyed it very much. Saw it more than once, didn't we m'dear?

'Yes I think we did, yes.'

Mrs Whitley, equally anxious for details asked, 'Can you remember the title of the play?' The Padleys both thought carefully.

'Ummm, There you have me,' admitted the colonel with a sigh 'Damned, if I can recollect it after all this time. Can you m'dear?'

'I don't think I can, no. It was so long ago. Well before the babies came. . .'

Mr Whitley asked what was the subject of the play.

'Ah yes. Let's see now,' the colonel thought, 'it was about a king. Yes that's right, a king. And wasn't there a queen in it as well m'dear?'

'Yes, there was a queen in it, you're quite right.'

Mr Whitley now on to the track of something positive asked,

'Was there perhaps a prince in it?'

'A prince? A prince. . .? Yes. . .well. . .' the colonel paused, 'No I don't recall a prince. There wasn't a prince was there m'dear?'

'I don't think there was, no. Not a prince. Only the king and queen.' said Mrs Padley.

Clearly the trail had gone cold. Mr Whitley beginning to face defeat, tried another approach. 'That aside, are there any other plays you'd like "by particular desire"?'

Here Mrs Padley appeared to have a suggestion, 'There was another play,' she said, ' that was very good, but you know I can't remember what it was called.'

'Which one was that m'dear?' asked her husband.

'You'll know. About a girl who was extremely poor. Yes, that's it, a poor girl and she married well and became extremely rich. It was very good. I'd like to see that again. Indeed I think we both would.'

'There you are,' enthused the colonel. 'Gives you a start, eh? Let us know when you're doing them and we'll come along, won't we m'dear?

'Most certainly.' said m'dear.

*

With lessening enthusiasm the Whitleys again consulted Marmaduke Pennell. Disappointments were shared, but Mr Pennell was positive that patronage was out there be found. 'It only requires one big name to give support, after that the flock will follow. I'm sure of it.'

The Whitleys were not.

'I'm not going through any more humiliations,' said Cassandra, 'my foot is still not healed and acutely painful.'

Mr Pennell insisted there would be no such privations in future.

'Let me see that list again,.' He ran his finger down the names of those who had not yet been visited. 'The Gartons - no, don't bother with them, Hancock - no, John Renshaw the attorney - well possibly. Wait - we haven't included the Sedleys. How foolish. Charles Sedley MP, knows everyone. You must call on Sedley.'

'He may know everyone, but what's his attitude to the theatre?' asked Jemmy.

'Very favourable, I'd say. Naturally, he spends much time in London. Sees a lot at plays in town. Get his support and you're made.'

Sir Charles Sedley lived in a fine new Palladian House at Nuthall, a small village a little further away than Bulwell. Once more Mr Pennell's landau was employed and the Whitleys arrived this time to make a morning call by appointment. The house, aptly named the Temple, was approached by a double flight of steps leading to a portico of Doric columns supporting a pediment. Here, was to be seen the family crest which consisted mainly of an enormous goat's head.

'This Englishman's castle appears to be his home,' said Jemmy as they climbed the steps.

'I don't care for the way that animal looks at us,' said Cassandra,

The obligatory butler admitted them to an octagonal hall, lit by a dome at great height above floor level. Beneath this on the first floor ran a gallery with four frescos depicting the finest pursuits of mankind, namely music, sport, science and warfare.

'But not theatre,' remarked Cassandra as they were shown into the music room.

After little delay, Sir Charles and Lady Sedley and a young man came into the room. 'How very good of you to call,' said her ladyship warmly. 'I hope you will allow our son, Edmund, to join us. He is mad keen on theatre.'

'Now then,' began Sir Charles in a business like manner, 'about your theatre. I understand you're not able to put it to use at the moment.'

'No, we are not,' said Jemmy.

'For what reason?'

'Strong opposition by the nonconformists.'

'Yes.' Sir Charles considered this. 'I think it's time for some resistance and I'll tell you why. We and our friends enjoy a play and intend to support you. What's more we're not having a bunch of hypocrites tell us what we can or cannot see. I take it you've nothing in rehearsal at the moment?'

'Nothing,'Jemmy replied lamely, 'there seems little purpose. . .'

'What was that play Edmund?' Sir Charles turned to his son.

'*The School for Rakes,* father. I thought it excellent.'

'D'you know it?' asked Sir Charles.

Jemmy replied that he did, but could not recall the author's name.

Sir Charles turned to his son, 'Who wrote it, Edmund?'

'A Mrs Griffith, father. Mrs Elizabeth Griffith.'

'Can you get hold of it?' asked Sir Charles. Jemmy said he was sure he could. Here Lady Sedley joined the conversation.

'I saw a play some time ago at the Lane called *The Author*. That was by a Mr Foote I believe. Most amusing. I'm sure it would also be well worth your time.'

Jemmy said he knew the play and agreed it could be popular.

'Good,' said Sir Charles. 'Have you got sufficient actors in your company to offer these pieces?

'Not with our present number,' said Jemmy.

'Pity. Very well. If I can guarantee a stipend of two hundred pounds for the next quarter, will that enable you to recruit more?'

The Whitleys almost swooned with astonishment.

'That would be exceeding generous, Sir Charles,' they agreed.

Sir Charles continued, 'Good, we'll get that drawn up. Now then. I'm going to suggest we arrange a performance here in advance to introduce your plays to a private audience. That way we can create an interest. I can't guarantee this, but it may be within my power to invite someone of standing to attend your theatre when it reopens. If that person were to come, I can assure you that many of your difficulties would diminish.'

'I imagine they would,' said Jemmy.

'Good. Now I suggest you go away, form a workable company and start rehearsals. When you have a piece ready, bring some of your players here and give us a foretaste of your goods. We'll invite some friends and do our utmost to get support for your venture. Does that sound reasonable?'

Jemmy was only able to nod his head.

'Capital,' said Sir Charles. He shook hands with both Jemmy and Cassandra, as did Lady Sedley and their son, Edmund. 'Forgive me for being so brief, time is too finite I fear. We look forward greatly to another visit before long, with your new company of course.'

Less than thirty minutes after arriving, the Whitleys left the Temple. They said nothing to each other until the journey home was well underway.

It was then that Jemmy said, 'We couldn't have asked for more, could we?

'I'd have liked a cup of tea,' his wife replied.

*

Fourteen. *Speculations. . .*

Letter from Tate Wilkinson to Jane his wife at Goosegate in York.
My Dear Wife,

To inform you of my safe arrival in Stamford. The journey was tolerable, the stay over night in Lincoln agreeable. The Moon Cow Inn providing good comfort and food. We were delayed at Newark as the change of horse was not ready. A long wait was wasteful of time.

Here, in Stamford, the theatre has survived during my absence without collapse. We play on the whole to good houses, doubtless the Burleigh affiliation brings that about. Would that we could bring it up with us when we return north. Trout has sustained the rule of order to my satisfaction.

We have two benefit nights before our season ends. Mrs M'George has chose *The Double Gallant* with *Midas,* which I think a strange preference but Mr Oldfield should do well with *The Good Natured Man* and *The Deuce in Him.*

I may have discovered a new talent. Trout took on a prompter's boy in my absence, who has ambitions to become an actor. Before you sigh with dismay at yet another ambitious youngling let me tell you that I think he has ability.

He asked to give an audition and played the last scene of the *Tradesman's Tragedy* so badly it was almost inventive. All who saw it were much enlivened. It happened, the following day by chance, I came upon him sweeping out the yard. Believing himself to be alone, he sang *Let us take the road,* in a pleasing voice and danced more than capable with the broom. 'Bravo' I said asking him why he did not enact that instead of the bad tragedy.

He replied that he did not think a dance and a song was of sufficient seriousness. I told him how rare that capability was, which pleased him.

We begin tomorrow rehearsing the Shakespeare and I have decided to let him read for it. If he does well I might try him out in Newark. If not, it is no great matter and he shall go back to being prompter's boy.

My health remains good Deo Gratias, and I ask that you keep good care of your dear self and not to take cold in this variable weather.

I remain, I trust, your one true love, Tate Wilkinson.

*

'Puck? It sounds rude.'

'Well it's not. It's a fairy.'

'A fairy?'

'Robin Goodfellow. A sprite, a mischievous imp.'

'It's not my fancy to play a fairy.'

'Not your fancy? Look here young fella-me-lad, If you want to act, you take what's offered. "Play as cast," the infallible rule and beggars can't be choosers. Shall you read it or not?'

'Can I speak it to myself first, in preparation?' Thomas asked,

Tate Wilkinson had expected gratitude if not delight at the prospect of a second audition. Instead of which Thomas's prevarication irritated him.

'I'll give you five minutes,' he said, 'I'll hear you after that.' He handed the text, 'last speech in the play,' he said indicating the concluding page.

Thomas left his room and examined the text. He saw quickly that it was marked as an epilogue. Aware of Mr Wilkinson's annoyance, if he delivered the text emphasising its harmonious temper he might gain approval. After reading it through twice, he knocked and returned. Mr Wilkinson sat in his chair regarding him. 'Proceed. . .'

If we shadows have offended,
Think but this, and all is mended . . . .

Give me your hands, if we be friends,
And Robin shall restore amends.

He read the words in his normal voice standing still, hoping his speaking of the text conveyed its meaning. Only when he concluded did he lower the book to regard his adjudicator. Mr Wilkinson viewed hm austerely, cracking his knuckles as he considered. The lad was raw, but perhaps he possessed an ingrained talent, an instinct that could be nourished.

'Where d'you come from?

'Lincolnshire, as far as I know.'

'It sounds in your voice. Have you read that speech before?'

'No sir, never seen it 'till now.'

'You come to if fresh?'

'Yes sir.'

'Aye,' said Wilkinson, 'full of faults. Indeed full of faults. Right young fella-me-lad, come back tomorrow with that speech known by heart. Learn also, *The king doth keep his revels. . .* and *My mistress with a monster is in love.* Not a lot. If you ever join the trade I'll expect three times that to be learned over night. I'll see you sharp at nine thirty tomorrow morning and mind, say nothing of this. Not a word. Right young fella-me-lad, cut along and praise the Lord.'

Thomas went into the yard. He found the two new speeches in the text and placed straws to keep the places. His excitement was tempered by fear that he would not have time to learn the lines. There was a whole evening of work ahead, already it was late afternoon with the light fading. It would require staying up all night. He longed to ask for advice, but 'say nothing' were his instructions. He wished the evening's performance over so he could start his memorising.

Strict conditions were imposed at the lodging house concerning candles. After midnight they were forbidden. He had to ask Mrs M'George for a handful of candle ends to light him through the night.

'What for? You know my rules,' she said.

'Mr Wilkinson has given me some work.'

'What sort of work?'

'He told me not to say.'

'He's said nothing to me.'

'It's my task . He will be angry if I don't get it done. Especially if I tell him you wouldn't give me light.'

Mrs M'George paused. 'I suppose you tell the truth. Very well, you may stay in the scullery, not so dangerous there and I want the candles kept standing in dishes of water.'

The scullery was an outside building containing little apart from a stone sink and a copper, lit only on wash days or for the boiling of puddings. He knew that there would be no warmth apart from the candles, but he knew also that no-one would see him working through the night. After the performance he got settled as quickly as he could Given an allowance of ten candle ends, he seated himself with a slice of pease pudding and a jug of ale.

He began.

The king doth keep his revels here tonight. The lines were in rhymed couplets which made the learning easier. Three nearby churches chimed throughout the night, never in unison. Walking round the scullery the meaning and delivery slowly became fixed and with this the excitement of becoming a character. The clocks between them struck fifteen times. That made it five. The last candle gutted into a pool of wax, the dead wick lying in the black shape of a question mark.

'D'you work while you sleep?' asked Mrs M'George, 'if so give me the trick.' She woke him from his slumbers on the stone floor, the text nearby. 'Why the secrecy? She looked around until she saw the play text. 'What's this? Have you been learning a role? What d'you mean by telling me Mr Wilkinson had important work?'

'He told me to say nothing.'

She looked at the book. 'Puck is it?'

'He's asked me to learn three speeches. Will you hear my lines?'

'Wait on. First there's a fire to be lit under that copper.'

'I'll do that.' Excitedly, Thomas went out to the fuel store bringing in dry grass and faggots. Once the fire was underway he fetched more wood. Putting it near the copper he brought out his text.

'I start with this,' he said, showing her the speech. '*The king doth keep his revels here tonight . . . .*'

'Very well,' said Fanny, 'let's be having you.'

He was confident until he reached *'And now they never meet in grove or green. . . . By fountain clear . . .* He stopped.

'Or spangled. . .' said Mrs M'George.

'Yes. "*or spangled starlight sheen,*" ' There were few such stumbles until he came to end of the last speech, '. . . *And Robin shall restore amends.'*

With relief Thomas stood still and looked at her. 'Well. . .?'

'You might get away with it. You're almost stable on your lines.'

'What else?'

'That's for Mr Wilkinson to say. . .'

'Well you rattled through it me lad,' said Tate. 'Fairly well acquainted with the author. Your accent's strong, yet that could be in character. There's much work to do on your movements. But I'm going to give you a trial. Attend rehearsals from tomorrow, learn the part by Thursday. I'm going to try you out in Newark, mid April. Not here in Stamford, for the audiences are too knowing, but in Newark 'tis no great matter if you're unhorsed.

'That means you'll be wanting me to come to Newark?'

'Where else? And I've spoken to Mr Holland. He'll give you some tuition while you're on the road. There's none better than he. Acted with Betterton. Till then you're still the prompter's devil, which you're good at by the way. Cut along and praise the Lord.'

He was part elated and part baffled. He was to play a role, even if it was in Newark. He'd heard there was no proper theatre, merely an inn with a galleried yard. Could he do it? Yes, he thought he could. But it would have to be in his own say. He couldn't be doing those arty farty voices like some of them in the company. He wanted to be natural. To speak like a human being, a real person. But hold on . . . he was going to be a fairy. That wasn't a real person was it? No, he'd be Robin Goodfellow the lord of misrule. He'd use his tumbling skills. That's it. He'd come on with a broom, perhaps a hobby horse if they had one.

From the next day Thomas attended rehearsals with the company who slowly began to treat him as one of their own, even if he was not yet allowed in the green room. He could sit out front and watch everything from the audience viewpoint, far better than sidelong glimpses from the wings. He got to absorb every actor's performance. What to use and what to avoid.

Tate Wilkinson had said Mr Holland will give him tuition. Would that mean having to do things in his manner? If only he could discuss it with someone. But there was nobody. Fanny M'George was kindly but he wasn't sure if he could yet trust her. Mr Oldfield? No he was unreliable. Certainly not Mr Holland - far too grand. Sweeny might have helped but where was he to be found?

At the George they said he had left after the first two weeks. One of the grooms thought he might be working for a solicitor who had an office on Maiden Lane. 'Try there.' Thomas did. 'No,' said the solicitor's clerk, 'I think someone of that name came asking for copying work, but we had nothing. An actor by trade is he not?'

Stamford was not a large place, he must be somewhere, unless he'd left the town completely. It had been several weeks since anyone had seen Mr Sweeny.

He was aware of a tension in both Mrs M'George and Mr Oldfield as their benefit nights approached. Both complained that they had had no time to visit their supporters in the town to ensure tickets were being sold. For Mr Oldfield his evening was vital. What he earned that night would mean prosperity or poverty for months to come. Now, with four daughters he had to make a good return. He asked for assurance that his choice of play was the right one. Everyone told him the plays he'd picked were always popular and he must not worry but put his mind to his performance on the night.

'By then it's too late,' he insisted, 'Suppose nobody comes? The public may not want me.' Everyone told him there was no actor more favoured than he and his benefit night was sure to be a financial success.

Sadly for Mrs M'George, her benefit night proved a failure. Heavy rain all day and evening had cut severely the numbers paying 'on the door,' and the poor lady raised less than ten pounds.

'Ah well, the worse luck now the better next time,' she said philosophically. 'At least I've no-one dependant on me. All the same, bugger the lot of 'em.'

Came the benefit night for Mr Oldfield and his disquiet was sad to see. 'Have no more, Jim,' said his friends as he knocked back the brandy, some believing he had secret supplies hidden in the dressing room. Half an hour before curtain-up he peered fearfully through the tabs at the auditorium.

'Don't worry,' they said, it's a good house. 'Listen to the noise, they've come to enjoy themselves. This was true, for a rowdy crowd waiting out front, invariably meant an audience ready to delight in whatever was played before them.

But Jimmy Oldfield wouldn't be cheered. 'They might have come to give me a bad time,' he complained after being sick just as Thomas called 'beginners please.' By the time the 'five minutes' was heard he was cold with fright. But as Thomas had seen before, Mr Oldfield could run to the wings like a demented hare and then walk calmly on stage as if taking the evening air in a garden.

At his first appearance the house gave him a welcoming round of approval, usual for an actor on his benefit night, which sobered him as swiftly as a slap in the face. With this assurance his anxieties fled; he proceeded to give a performance that was much liked by everyone. The audience increased in number for the after piece *The Deuce in Him,* a farce in which Mr Oldfield excelled. The final curtain brought cheers and a sense of solid achievement, with everyone happy and well pleased.

'Praise the Lord,' beamed Tate Wilkinson later. 'You've done well, Just over forty pounds.' Most of the cast applauded as he later handed the money to Jimmy, saying, 'a good performance, deservedly earned,' shaking him by the hand as the actor wiped away tears at what he had accomplished.

Most of the cast changed quickly with shouts of 'good night' sounding into the dark of the streets. The uproar and delirium of the play was ended, the event passed, the atmosphere back stage sinking once again to normality and a quiet slumber cradled the building. Thomas too was leaving when he heard excited talk coming from the green room. He was surprised when the door opened and Fanny M'George called him.

'Thomas, come and see who's here.' Going cautiously into the room he saw Mr. Sweeny, his sought after friend, engaged in spirited talk with Jimmy Oldfield. But before him was a very different Sweeny.

Well dressed, smart and full of gaiety and confidence. 'Thomas,' he smiled brightly, casting a silver cane from right to left as he moved forward shaking his hand with a confident grip.

'What are you doing here?' asked Thomas.

'Need you ask?' 'D'you think I would not support my old friend Jimmy Oldfield on his benefit night?' he laughed. 'And what a night of triumph it has been.'

Thomas regarded Sweeny, astonished by his fine clothes. 'You look prosperous,' he said 'Are you playing Drury Lane?'

Sweeny laughed, 'No more acting for me. I'm for "All Change Alley." Canals, that's the future my friends! That's where prosperity lies.'

'Canals?'

'That's just what I said,' laughed Fanny, ' I thought he was digging 'em.'

'Not dressed like that, he isn't,' said Jimmy Oldfield.

'Certainly not. No my friends I am investing in them. Canals the new means of transport that will change everything in this country.'

'Barley straws,' said Fanny, 'change everything? No barge can travel faster than a stagecoach.'

'It is not about speed,' said Sweeny, 'it is the amount of freight that can be moved. By road it takes six horses to haul a ton. With barges up to thirty tons can be moved with only one horse pulling them. That's the modern way to shift coal.'

'Who wants coal? Dirty, filthy stuff, when there's plenty of wood.'

'But there isn't. We're fast running out of wood and our country needs all the coal that can be got. It will be wanted everywhere, which means moving it in big quantities and cheaply. That's what canals can do. Think, soon we'll be able to transport goods from Hull to Manchester in days, not weeks.'

'Why should we?' asked Jimmy.

'Because things are changing. Goods are being made in this country that will be sold world wide. There are fortunes to be made, with investment.'

'How's this come about all of a sudden?' asked Jimmy.

Sweeny almost preened himself. 'This comes from working at the George. You get to meet every class of people. It's there I met Mr Bellows. He's an eminent broker.'

'What's he broken?'

'A broker deals in stocks and shares. When a company is formed to build a canal, the capital is raised by selling shares. Usually at a pound a piece. These shareholders then get a dividend, a percentage of the profits.'

'What if there's no profit?'

'No profit in canals! I tell you chum, you can earn your money back in the first six months and be making a good gain within a year. But that's too slow for me. I buy up shares as soon as they're issued and with the help of a broker like Bellow I can sell them at ten time the cost within a few days.'

'If you don't mind my asking,' said Fanny, 'where did you get your money in the first place?'

'A bank loan naturally, I went back to Nottingham. Smith's bank, the first outside London. I got a loan of fifty pounds,'

'Fifty pounds!' the others said in unison.

'Most certainly. And what's more I paid it back within a month with the interest, and made a profit of nearly five hundred pounds. I bought fifty shares at a pound a piece and sold them at ten. As easy as that.'

'Get away,' said Fanny.

'Can't you tell?' asked Sweeny showing off his fashionable clothes, 'I'll have you know there's real money to be made old girl.'

'Five hundred pounds,' said Jimmy Oldfield sadly. 'And here's me, overjoyed at a forty pounds benefit.'

'You've every right to be proud,' said Fanny. 'You've worked hard and you've earned your benefit That's come by honest toil.'

'Honest toil!' said Sweeny. 'Sweated labour more like! Get a loan, Jim, speculate! You'll be a hundred times better off than staying in this business.'

Thomas spoke quietly. 'I like this business,' he said.

'There's a wise head on young shoulders,' said Fanny. 'And as for you Jimmy Oldfield, you've got a good many mouths to feed.

This spectaculating or whatever you call it isn't for folks like us.'

'Not so,'said Sweeny, 'It is for everybody. Why the selling of stocks and shares is becoming commonplace - open to all. But enough of this. To show my goodwill I'll take you out to dine. Fanny you've treated me often enough, now this is my turn.'

Such an invitation could not be declined. Although Sweeny's generosity did not rise to taking them to the George, instead they supped at a chop house in Broad Street until the early hours. Sweeny dominated the table recounting his passion for trading in canal securities and how his partnership with Mr Bellow would make not only his fortune but that of anyone who had the vision (and the money) to become an investor. It was hard not to believe him.

After the success of Mr Oldfield's benefit, the last night of the run at Stamford seemed an anticlimax as preparations were made for moving on to Newark. Costumes, sets and props all had to be struck prior to departure on Sunday morning. They had to be ready to perform by the coming Tuesday which meant two days walk and no time for observance of the Sabbath.

Fanny M'George had not enjoyed the celebrations with Sweeny. Although she thought it proper for him to buy her food and drink after so many meals at her expense, she felt disquiet at Sweeny's sudden prosperity. She did not trust him and was uneasy with the admiration shown by Thomas and Jimmy Oldfield. Returning to the lodgings she took Thomas aside,

'Be warned against that man,' she said. 'I've known him some time and he's a shake-bag if ever there was one. All this talk about quick fortunes. It's nothing but flummery. Have no part of it.'

'What part can I have? Me with no money,' asked Thomas, ' He won't be bothered with me.'

'See that he isn't. And, as I'm of age to be your mother I tell you this also. You beware of your drinking as well. Look at you, hardly able to stand.'

Thomas laughed. 'After just one night's rowdy dow? What about Mr Oldfield? He was well tippled even before the performance began. After all he downed he'll be regretful on the morrow for sure.'

But Mr Oldfield was not regretful. The next day he was as brisk as a biscuit, arriving at the theatre brim full of good cheer, smiling at all and sundry. Again he was congratulated on his successful benefit, which he accepted with goodwill.

'Yes,'he said, 'and before long I shall be even more prosperous. You see before you, an investor, one who will make a bundle in no time. For I have followed the advice of my good friend Sweeny and put my benefit money into canals. There it shall grow as does a meadow in May. By which time my fortune shall be made!'

*

Fifteen. *A Spot of Temperament.*

With the encouragement and financial support of the Sedleys, Cassy and Jemmy Whitley began the enterprise of re-forming their company. One or two of the old guard remained. Dora Proctor, after her ordeal with Mr Thornton Friars was set to be the leading soubrette in spite of Cassandra's disapproval. Mr and Mrs Willis accepted the renewal of their engagement, whereas Mr and Mrs Mitteer were nowhere to be found, greatly to the Whitley's relief. Bob Naylor had formed a profitable association with Jud Drinkwater at the Old Rose public house where nightly he led the company in rousing Scottish songs. His words remained as unfathomable as ever, but the gusto of his performance was much enjoyed. The death of Mr Wheeler had been met with dismay, for he had been one of the most dependable of actors, something which had not been thought of Mr Sweeny. The loss of two such men left a vacancy difficult to fill, as the finding of competent male actors was always hard to accomplish. London was without doubt the best centre of recruitment, but it was too distant. Second best was either Norwich or Birmingham and because it was nearer the latter was decided upon.

When Jemmy announced his intention to travel there, Cassandra was concerned. The roads were lonely and dangerous and after much debate it was agreed that their ancient steed Gunpy could not make the distance, certainly not to Birmingham and back. Eventually Jemmy travelled by the aptly named stage coach leaving Cassandra at home with the dependable Mr Bracer who had become as much a part of the company as the stage itself.

A week before he arrived in Birmingham, Jemmy placed an advertisement in the local newspaper letting it be known that he would be at the Peacock Inn for two days, where any actor seeking engagement would be welcome to meet and discuss the possibility.

His first morning of interviews was discouraging. Those auditioning had little aptitude and being mostly distant from the bloom of youth, presented neither pleasure to the eye, nor solace to the ears. It was sad for him to reject so many for he knew the only work they could expect was the sock and busking of the portable theatres. When possible he favoured married couples, experience proving them to be more dependable than single men and women. By the end of the day he had offered places to a Mr and Mrs Venables and a Mr and Mrs Kirk who seemed capable and whilst not raising high expectations might form an adequate core to his company.

The one bright talent revealed was that of a young woman named Belinda Armstrong. She came with a cuttings book of good reports, modest in size, for she was yet at the start of a career. Claiming to be eighteen, she had jet black hair, deep violet eyes, and a figure which might well become stout in time but at this, the spring of her life, was quite perfect.

In truth Belinda Armstrong was already a beauty. Her speaking voice was not strong, but Whitley felt her appearance would atone for that. So keen was Miss Armstrong to join Mr Whitley's company that she asked to travel back him with in the same stagecoach, insisting that she felt much safer in his company than on her own, especially if he paid the fare.

Yet he still lacked a good leading man. Although Mr Venables and Mr Kirk would be good in supporting roles, neither had the quality of playing major characters. On his second night he went to two theatres to see what the town had to offer, but there was nothing worth his poaching. In earlier days this would not have concerned him, for he would have simply played the leads himself. But his increased difficulty in learning lines revealed that he was getting older, with tiredness affecting his once unflagging powers.

In spite of the company of the charming Miss Armstrong, he returned home soberly with an air of defeat. Alighting with a beautiful young woman at his side, would be understood only in the acting profession. Even so he hastened to introduce Miss Armstrong to Cassy with the injunction that the one should take care of the other and he was sure that in no time they would be firm friends. It came as a surprise when Cassy took scant notice of Miss Belinda, instead her first question being,

'Have you found a leading man?'

When he told her 'no,' he was again surprised when she answered,

'What a relief.'

'Why so?' he asked.

'An old army colleague of Mr Bracer paid a visit whilst you were away. His name is Powell, he has left the army and taken up a stage career.'

'That is nothing unusual.'

'Ah, but wait. He has made a great success at York and by all accounts seems right for our company.'

'If he's at York, then he's one of Tate Wilkinson's men and unlikely to leave.'

'Not so. There have been 'differences' and he seeks another place. He was making his way to London, but Bracer and I prevailed upon him to stay until your return, for we are both convinced he is ideal.'

'Then I might as well have stayed home.'

'Don't be sour husband. When you meet Powell I am sure you will agree with our judgement.

'Doubtless he is handsome. Is that the attraction?'

'You know full well I have an eye for ability. As it happens he is not especially handsome, he has a quality overriding mere good looks.'

It was agreed that they would meet Mr Powell that night at the Blackamoor Inn where Bracer could introduce his former colleague.

'He was an officer when we were both in the King's Light Dragoons. I had great respect for him,' he told them.

'An officer? What rank?'

'Lieutenant. Since the peace he's been laid off and took up acting.'

'He's played several Shakespearean roles,' said Cassandra, 'including Antony and Tamburlaine'

Whitley, making the point that Tamburlaine was by Marlowe and not Shakespeare, said that he was impatient to meet the gentleman.

Indeed, patience was required on his part for although the meeting with Powell was arranged for eight o'clock, the actor did not arrive until one hour later. Whitley observed with barely concealed disfavour how Bracer at first greeted his old colleague with hearty hand shakes and some back slapping.

'Mr Whitley, may I acquaint you with Mr Brook Powell?' said Bracer. Powell took Whitley's hand and arm enthusiastically. 'This is indeed an honour sir,' he said. 'Your reputation is wide spread. I have heard much about your achievements.'

Brook Powell was a tall man. Cassandra was right, he was not handsome, but he had a face that drew attention. Dark brown hair, a large nose and heavy lips, but his eyes, which were big and black, were what was noticed. Whitley felt that if he knew how to use them, his eyes could pierce the back of the gallery, an asset many actors would give much to possess. He was well spoken, a little loud perhaps, and was carefully and neatly dressed. Still, his smile was too frequent and dazzling for Whitley's taste.

'How long have you been on the stage?' he asked.

'Two years past, since I resigned as Major in the Dragoons. Before that I had done some acting with amateur groups.'

'You look to be this side of thirty?'

'I shall be eight and twenty next year.'

The conversation continued amicably. Whitley was much annoyed by Powell's late arrival, a fact that continued to irritate him like a stone in the shoe. It had not escaped his notice that he had raised his rank in the army and he wondered what the 'differences' at York had been that had caused him to leave. The meeting ended with the agreement that Powell would be give an audition at the theatre next morning at ten o'clock.

'I like punctuality,' said Whitley.

'Indeed so do I!' Powell replied heartily. Whitley sniffed audibly.

Powell was on time the next morning, well prepared with pieces from Shakespeare and Colman which were impressive and led to his being hired for three months, by gentleman's agreement, at twenty two shillings a week, the paying of a salary an innovation Whitley disliked.

The company was still not up to the ideal number, which

necessitated Whitley playing in many of the pieces himself. For this reason he made sure that the plays he chose were those he knew already, with lines that might easily be recalled.

Spirits were raised when a letter arrived from Sir Charles Sedley reporting an enthusiasm amongst many of his friends for the reopening of the theatre. He hoped that shortly a private visit by some of the players to the Nuthall Temple could be arranged to give a view in advance of their work . This he felt, was sure to gain the sponsorship from several important names which would override any objections from the Fairlight fraternity. If it was agreeable to the Whitleys, his son Edmund, would like to call at the theatre during his vacation, to watch rehearsals and report progress to his father.

Late one night, Whitley with Mr Bracer were having a review of in the scene dock on what could or could not be used for the coming weeks. The theatre was mostly in darkness, no lighting at all in the auditorium, and only the minimum of candles on the stage. Both were tired and ready to leave when they were brought up sharply by a crash from the backstage regions which they had assumed to be empty. The two men stood still and listened. A cold draught passed over them. Candles flickered. Another crash was heard, followed by a shout. Neither man admitted his misgivings.

'Who's there?' called Whitley. There was no response,

'I'll see what it is,' said Bracer starting to move.

'Take care,' said Whitley, 'best take a stave or something.'

'I think we have an intruder,' said Whitley following a third crash.

Before any search could begin, a side cloth moved unusually, showing a movement from behind. Someone, or something, was there.

'Come out,' cried Bracer, 'whoever you are.'

A further series of bulges, obviated by the slashing of the canvas with a sword, revealed Mr Powell, his head covered in blood. With one arm he clutched his side and with the other waved his weapon as he staggered onto the stage, Bracer ran up to him and caught him before he could fall. Jemmy, relieved that it was nothing worse, was more angered by the damage to his scenery than that done to Powell.

'Forgive me my trespasses,' said Powell, 'I could think of no other place to go.' Bracer moved a stage chair for him.

'Mind that,' cried Whitley, 'it's newly upholstered. I want no blood on it. And I shall require compensation for the harm done to my property.'

Bracer laughed, and finding a sheet threw it over the seat before Powell collapsed into it. Bracer turned his attention to his injuries, taking the sword from his hand. 'A bruise and cut to the forehead,' he said, 'and what else?'

''Not serious,' said Powell. 'A small flesh wound at the side. If it could be bound, the bleeding will soon be stemmed,'

'Best get him to the green room,' said Whitley. 'There he can lie down.' They moved him away, not before Whitley had looked to see if his chair was unstained and inspect the tear in the backcloth. In the green room Powell's head was bandaged and his wounds bound.

'By Harry, this town's a dangerous place,' said Powell. 'Would you have it? There I was at the Weekday Cross I believe it is named, when with no warning this happened.'

'You were attacked?' asked Whitley.

'Aye, and for no other reason I suggest, than I was well dressed. Some rogue came at me with the sword. Placed it to my throat and demanded money. I turned round and was hit on the head behind by another rascal. But I grappled the cudgel from the rogue's hand and gave him twice times better. We don't serve in the dragoons without learning how to defend ourselves, eh Bracer? I must have seemed an easy picking. Next, the sword carrying villain thrust at me piercing my side but not deep. I put him out of combat quick and took the blade from him. With that both rascals fled.'

'You'd best fetch the sword,' Whitley said to Bracer.

'It must be stolen,' said Powell, 'it's a good piece as you'll see.' There was no more talk until Bracer returned. Powell looked at the weapon brought in by Bracer. 'Yes, gold filigree laid into the handle, probably French.'

'How did you get it from the fellow?' asked Whitley.

'By grasping the blade.'

'Without cutting your hand?' said Whitley.

'I wear stout gloves. But see the blade is triangular in section, it has no edge, yet the point is sharp enough. The sort used in duelling.'

'An ugly thing,' said Whitley, 'it must be put somewhere safe.'

In spite of assurances from Powell that he was sufficiently fit, Whitley and Powell saw him safely to his lodgings.

The new company was assembled for the first time. Some of them, Mr and Mrs Willis, and Miss Proctor, already knew each other, this giving them the superiority of senior school children regarding new pupils with scorn.

They chatted and laughed together as if they had been lifelong friends, which they had not. For the rest, the newly recruited Mr and Mrs Venables and Mr and Mrs Kirk had lately met each other, this new found fellowship providing a bulwark against being entirely fresh and unknown. There remained Mr Powell and Miss Armstrong who were drawn together simply because they knew no-one else. An odd pairing, the decade of difference in their ages allowing him to pontificate to the pretty girl who could only respond with giggles of embarrassment. Completely outside the circle of actors were Mr Bracer and Mrs Kenna who, with the other backstage staff, were ignored by everyone as being persons of a lesser race.

Mr and Mrs Whitley walked in promptly at ten o'clock. Out of politeness the hum of conversation ceased and the schoolroom atmosphere continued when, after being bid 'Good morning,' the company returned the greeting in unison. The Whitleys looked at the new group with experienced foreknowledge. They knew that the present atmosphere of goodwill would shortly be replaced with jealousies, feuds and temperaments. They had seen it all before.

It was announced that there was to be a repertory of plays to prepare. *Romeo and Juliet* was the first to be worked at.

'I believe you have played Romeo Mr Powell?' asked Whitley.

'Many times and to great acclaim,' replied the actor. His temerity noted by Jemmy with scorn.

'Miss Armstrong,' asked Whitley, 'you also have played Juliet?'

'Yes sir, once,' answered Belinda.

'To great acclaim?' asked Jemmy sarcastically.

'That's not for me to say,' said Belinda shyly. This was better liked. The Whitleys were anxious about the relationship between Miss Proctor and Miss Armstrong which could so easily led to friction if not . enmity. Such a course seemed possible until Miss Proctor quickly discovered that Miss Armstrong had no singing voice which left Dora's position as prima donna unassailable, upon which footing a cautious friendship was begun.

'My wife and I will be playing the Nurse and Friar Laurence. The other roles, be they Montague or Capulet are on the call board,' said Jemmy. The rehearsal pattern was soon underway. In the mornings the play was invariably a tragedy usually by Shakespeare, in the afternoon it was more likely to be frivolous, namely a farce, or a pantomime.

The amiability within the company lasted for a few days. It was with Mr Powell that problems began to surface. From the start he was found to be inattentive to Whitley's directives, spending time in racy conversation with both Miss Armstrong and Miss Proctor. He was late for rehearsals and in spite of fines did not reform the habit. Whitley was patient for a while, for he intended to give Mr Powell leading roles from Romeo to Macheath, but not until he was sure of his being trustworthy.

When it came, the confrontation between the actor and his employer was due to Powell's unreliability in learning his lines. He had assured the Whitleys that he was capable of committing three lengths a night, a guarantee swiftly exposed as false. After days of stumbling and clearly not knowing what he was about, tempers at last were lost. Jemmy accused him of not knowing his lines.

Mr Powell maintained that the real problem was that the script was unreadable and thus unlearnable. It will be recalled that these parts were previously hand copied by Cassandra, and admittedly had been used over many seasons. Still, for Jemmy this was insufficient.

'I'll not have that as an excuse sir,' he said.

Powell was not prepared to be reprimanded before his peers.

'It is a sign of a third rate company,' he replied, 'when it cannot afford proper printed texts. With Mr Wilkinson such a thing is unthinkable.'

'Then it is to be grieved you left Mr Wilkinson's company.'

'Entirely my sentiments sir.'

'I suggest sir,' continued Whitley, 'that it is your idleness and not my wife's fine handwriting that is at fault.'

'No sir. The handwriting is faded to invisibility and the paper so worn, it is like handling a dried lettuce leaf.'

'No-one in my company has ever complained before.'

'They dare not, that's why. I am man enough to say what they think.'

'Man enough? You are nothing of the kind sir, You are a fraud. You do not know your lines. You're no actor, you're a mere dabbler '

'What did you say?' asked Powell, his eyes narrowing in anger.

'You heard well enough,' said Whitley. 'I said you were a dabbler.'

After a moment's stillness charged with tension, Mr Powell tore his script in half, throwing the pieces to the floor.

'No man, not even in my army days, has so insulted me.'

'Then it seems I have more honesty than your fellow foot wobblers,' said Whitley, by now fuelled with anger.

'Foot wobblers! You know full well I was an officer.'

'I doubt sir, if you ever rose above the rank of fifer.'

'Fifer! If you were not such a slack-bellied, feeble old man, that would be grounds for me to fight you sir!' shouted Powell.

'My age is no barrier. I am at your service when e'er you wish!'

'You sir, at my service? Hah. I'd expect no more from a horsefly.'

'You shall have it,' said Whitley, 'here at this moment. I may be twice your age sir, but I'll give you satisfaction. . . .'

Whitley had never before lost his temper so completely and at such speed. He realised as the exchange continued how much he had grown to dislike Powell. For his own part he would never have engaged him. The man was here at his wife's behest, which added to his anger. It was she had hired the abominable lickspit. He hurried to the cupboard where he had kept the sword Powell had brought earlier.

'Choose your weapon sir. ' Whitley held the sword, taking a stance he had done many times onstage. Powell, believing he was in the stronger position, looked at Whitley and laughed,

'Then I'll have that,' he said pointing to the blade in Whitley's hand, 'You know full well 'tis mine.'

'As much mine as yours.' Whitley looked ridiculous.

Powell laughed,'What a performance! *Cry "havoc!" let slip the dogs of war!* I fear sir, you're not equipped to play the warrior.'

Some of the onlookers giggled at this, increasing Whitley's wrath. Even though his opponent was unarmed Whitley took a lunge at him, but Powell was able to grasp the shaft, easily twisting it from his hand. Whitley next tried to punch him, but as he swung forward his entire appearance changed. His face turned from red to purple, until clutching at his throat he fell, gasping for breath.

Cassandra gave a scream and ran to him . 'Jemmy, Jemmy!' she cried, kneeling beside her husband in an effort to help him. 'This is your doing sir,' she shouted at Powell whose mood remained defiant.

Everyone in the assembly offered help.

'He needs room, give him air,' his wife insisted and several hands lifted Whitley into a chair where he sat, his chest heaving, his head ominously fallen to one side with only the whites of eyes showing. Numerous remedies were suggested from burnt feathers to hot bricks at the feet.

A surgeon was sent for. Someone asked nervously if the rehearsal was to continue, but it being late in the afternoon, Cassy told everyone to go home and return at ten next morning by which time she was certain her husband would be better.

'*My lord is often thus. . . he will again be well.*' she smiled until realising she had quoted from the Scottish Play she turned cold with misgiving, Those who heard her and knew the reputation of Macbeth, left the room, spun round three times and spat on the floor.

*

Sixteen. *'Next to Godliness.'*

'Whenever Tate Wilkinson looked at his company about to take the road, he thought of the children of Israel and their exodus to the Promised Land. Whilst not seeing himself as Moses, he regarded them as his people - quarrelsome, temperamental, often infuriating and difficult, but nearly always loveable. He was frequently touched by the faith and trust they put in his guidance. Did they, he wondered, ever look upon him as a father or was he merely their master?

April brought early sunrises. As it was considered ungodly if not unlawful to travel on the Sabbath, it was tactful to be out of town before church services began for he had no wish to offend Christian folk. They were soon on the Great North Road. Tate rode ahead on horseback to be at Newark where a licence to play was required from magistrates or the mayor.

'Stay close together,' he told everybody. 'There are good places for halting on the way, but avoid Grantham, too far off your track, as well as costly. I will see you in two days time. Good fortune attend your endeavours. Hallelujah. Praise the Lord!' He departed waving like a general to his raggle taggle army of players.

Mrs M'George and Mr Holland were the only actors who Thomas had got to know. Sweeny was gone and with him the artless Jimmy Oldfield. There was much head shaking over Jimmy's belief that riches were soon to be his. At the same time there was relief that he and his family were not with them for small children slowed down the speed of walking.

A large cart carrying pieces of scenery and costumes had to be pushed in turn. Nobody enjoyed this but it was taken as part of the rigours of touring. At least it was better than carrying props on the back which was expected in the poorer companies. Tate Wilkinson was well organised enough to have basic scenery at his other theatres, so it was special items only that had to be moved from place to place. Occasionally a farmer with an empty wagon would offer lifts to the women but this was rare as most farmers took goods on their return journey from market for extra income.

Spring was a good time to be on the move. The snows and cold of winter were gone, the ground was neither muddy nor yet dusty. Throughout Sunday the walk was uneventful. Stagecoaches did not run on the Sabbath; only two light carriages driven by godless owners passed them perilously.

It was not usual to discuss theatre matters whilst on the road, the hours could be more enjoyably passed with the singing of songs or the telling of tales like their Canterbury predecessors. Those of a more solitary disposition used the while to learn their lines.

On Monday the traffic would increase with pack horses and wagons outnumbering those on foot. Passing travellers were met with caution or warnings of conditions ahead. Should they be gypsies it was thought best to be amiable, there being the fear of a curse if palms were not read or trinkets not bought. They passed a group of convicts trudging to transportation. Sadness fell upon those who saw them, for they knew how easy it was to fall foul of the law. Sympathy was expressed for the hapless underdogs as it was shocking to hear the crack of a whip urging the men forward like cattle.

'Poor souls,' they said as the shackled troop of men passed by. One or two wanted to offer food and drink, but their warders, walking along side, refused this.

'How can you take a whip to your fellow men?' shouted Fanny.

The guard smiled scornfully, 'The whip is no more used than a lady's fan in winter,' he said, 'and should it be, these scoundrels scarce feel it.'

'You have no heart,' was her reply but the warder shouted at his charge urging them onward to their fate.

Following this dismal sight, little was said until they reached a village where it was decided to camp overnight. The weather being dry they would put up makeshift tents and sleep in the open thus saving money by not renting a barn, for it was found that the only barn in the district was already occupied. Curiosity led one of the company to find out who was inhabiting the building. The actor came back, shaking his head as his colleagues enquired,

'Are they rogues and vagabonds?'

'Wesleyans,' came the reply. Doubtless come to save us.'

Morning began clear and bright but to the weather-wise it was apparent that rain was on the way. Between the field and the barn where the Wesleyans had slept, a horse trough boasted a pump and a welcome supply of fresh water.

Not long after cockcrow the barn door opened and a cautious female face surveyed the yard. Seeing it was deserted, the woman dressed in sombre grey approached the pump and filled a wooden bucket which she took back hurriedly to the barn. There followed a circumspect group of men who gathered around the trough for their communal wash. In their white shirt sleeves this amounted to the cleansing of hands and face apart from one man, acting as barber, who shaved those who wished to make use of his skill.

Upon this scene arrived Fanny M'George from the actors' camp also carrying a bucket. 'Good morning gentlemen,' she said as she approached the pump.

Her greeting was received in silence. One of the elders replied gruffly, 'Woman, you are not welcome. Wait until we are done.'

'Is not the water for the use of everyone?' she asked.

'You are unseemly. Can you not see we are at our ablutions?'

'Have no fear. I have seen men in far less state of undress,' she smiled.

'That I can believe, knowing your trade,' said the elder.

'That is unwarranted sir. You speak as if I were the whore of Babylon.'

'Your words ma'am, not mine.'

'I would prefer be likened to the woman of Samaria who, as I recall, also required water.'

The elder had not expected such Biblical awareness.

'It would seem that you know your scripture.'

'I do sir and I ask to be allowed to fill my bucket.' She looked at him humorously. 'Not that I expect to receive "living water" from you.'

'That is near to being blasphemy, woman.'

'Your words sir, not mine.'

She primed the pump energetically until one of the younger men came forward and took the task from her. After thanking him she asked, 'You also are on the road I believe. In what direction are you bound?'

The young man unsure whether to reply looked to the elder for help.

'We travel north to Newark,' said the elder solemnly.

'We too go in that direction. We might walk alongside. There is said to be safety in numbers.'

The elder was unsure. 'That must be decided by the majority. 'It is not our custom to walk with strange company.'

'You mean with the unhallowed? Perhaps this may be God's will and a opportunity for you to bring salvation upon us. Unless you fear we might persuade you to adopt our way of life.'

She said this with a smile as she took her bucket, now filled with water. The young man from the pump offered to carry it for her, a kindness she accepted gladly.

Once on the road it was hard for the two groups to keep apart, sharing as they did the same route. Gradually a muted camaraderie developed between some members of the rival parties. The majority of the Wesleyans strode with no side glance at the strangers, their dull garb separating them from the colourful dress of the comedians.

It was the children who, in spite of repeated warnings, ran alongside the actors looking in wonder at their motley attire and asking questions about their acting life. The young ones were forbidden to fraternise and when caught were boxed about the ears. Yet one lively girl about eleven years old attached herself to Thomas, rather to his annoyance for he was trying to learn his lines as Puck. His indifference did not in any way deter the girl who was content to walk admiringly at his side.

Perhaps because of his seniority, Mr Holland found himself engaged in conversation with brother Sterne one of the elder

Wesleyans. 'I once heard your founder preach,' said Mr Holland, 'although preach is hardly the correct word, for I have never seen a more theatrical display. He was a born actor, portraying as he did everyone from Abraham to King Herod. Had he chose, he could have been one of the best players in the land.'

'Had he done so it would have been for his own glory. Instead he used his gifts to bring the word of God to the multitudes.'

'By entertaining them, precisely as we do. Mr Wesley was an actor by nature. I would have given much to hear him speak Shakespeare.'

'John Wesley knows that such ornate words bring a corruption of the mind. That is why he bids us oppose them. Stage entertainments tempt the young to waste God's good time, as well as being hurtful to industry.'

'Ah,' said Mr Holland, 'I fancy I see through you sir. You endorse that which serves the needs of trade rather than the intellect. Which is the worse? For the young to see a play in which the mind can be fed by imagination, or to work for the profit of their masters?'

Sterne frowned. 'Imagination cannot be placed in the uncertain hands of actors. It should only be employed by those who serve God, not those who deceive by pulling faces to gain laughter.'

'That is unfair sir. True we may induce laughter which is no bad thing in this grievous world. But as the noble Hamlet said, "the purpose of playing is to show the very age and body of the time his form and pressure." I believe we are, "they who are the abstract and brief chronicles of the time." '

'Brief, you say?' asked brother Sterne. 'You substantiate my argument. We do not deal in passing values, we proclaim the everlasting truth. And so my good sir, we must remain in disparity. . . '

Here brother Sterne walked towards the girl who had attached herself to Thomas. 'Mary,' he said quietly, 'come away child, your place is with your brethren. It is not seemly for you to accompany this popinjay.'

The child knew she had to obey. She looked sadly at Thomas, then turned to walk with Sternc, her face troubled as she followed his command.

A second village was reached whilst daylight lasted. Here the comedians decided to rent a barn as rain was beginning to fall. The Wesleyans being expected by the people of the village had lodgings already prepared for them. It appeared the missionaries planned to stay there one or two days to conduct a series of prayer meetings.

The farmer loaning the barn to the actors, forbade the use of candles, offering instead two or three lanthorns for use during the evening, warning that he would remove them before they slept. Everyone found places in the barn in which to pass the night.

Mr Holland took the occasion to give Thomas some of the promised tuition suggested by Mr Wilkinson as he prepared to play Puck. Finding an empty stall before dark, the old actor looked hard at his pupil.

'I shall not concern myself about your words, anyone can do that. I am anxious to see your gestures. First, let me see you stand in repose.'

Thomas stood before him.

'No, no, no, that will never do. Do not stand with the weight equally on both legs. That is the bearing of a soldier.'

'Which I have been.'

'Then disregard all you have learned. On stage, one toe should point straight out front, that is to say at twelve o'clock, the other at ten past or ten to as the case may be. Let me see you take such a pose.'

'Ten to or ten past?'

'Either way.' Thomas readjusted his position as he thought best.

'No! Your feet are at ten to two. It is unbeautiful and will not do. One foot must always be a midday.'

'Or midnight?'

'Bend one knee. No not both - merely one.'

'Which one?'

'The one that is at ten to or ten past. Do no bend the knee. The secret of acting is in the feet! How the actor appears in the eye of the audience depends entirely upon the feet.' Thomas felt uncomfortable - and unnatural. 'Your hands. We must do something with your hands. Never let your hands hang down as if dead. That is very disagreeable to the eye. Show me an attitude with your hands.'

Thomas struck what he thought was a good stance.

'No, no, no. If an action has to be shown, it is only done by employing one hand, which has to be the right hand. It is indecent to make a gesture with the left. And the right hand must always be above the left.'

'Why?' asked Thomas.

'Why? It is the rule, by way of good manners. It is so easy to offend with bad movements. Now then, let me see you in repose with an attitude.'

Thomas's posture had no repose and was clearly the wrong attitude.

'How does that seem?' asked Mr Holland.

'As if I'd shit myself.'

'Which is precisely how it looks. Dear, oh dear,' Mr Holland shook his head in despair. He stared at Thomas searchingly,

'Can you move your head? No, not to the side. The face should rarely be in profile.' He leaned forward taking Thomas's head, his hands containing his cheeks.

'Look straight at me,' he said staring closely into his eyes. Thomas blinked uncomfortably as Mr Holland became pensive, looking hard into his face. Something odd was happening to Mr Holland for he began to breathe unsteadily. Mr Holland's hands ran from Thomas's face to caress his bare neck then to pull him forward clumsily.

'Perhaps if I could ask you to be a little closer. . . If possibly you could take hold of me. . .'

For the moment, puzzled at what was happening, Thomas stumbled unintentionally towards Mr Holland. Suddenly the old actor took his pupil passionately in his arms holding him tightly and pressing their bodies together.

'Thomas, Thomas . . .' he said, 'that is not what I meant. . . and yet,' he continued holding him, tightening his embrace, '. . .and yet, it is what I have longed for . . oh Thomas, do you have any notion how deep in love with you I am? From the first time ever I saw you, I have been overwhelmed, you must have seen. . .'

His agitation greatly increased as impulsively he kissed Thomas full on the lips, at the same time frantically trying to pull his shirt away from his breeches. After a moment of shock, Thomas entangled himself fiercely.

'So that's the way of it,' he said.

Mr Holland stood forlorn, his arms empty and desolate. Sadly he looked away and spoke, his voice choked with affliction.

'No, no, it isn't,' he began, 'Forgive me. I have been foolish. Please understand, it will never happen again.'

'No it will not. And if it does you'll get a fist in your face,' he wiped his mouth on his sleeve.

'Yes I believe you, and I would deserve it. Be assured, young sir, my true wish is to instruct you in the art of playing.'

'I'll do without it.' Thomas wondered if anyone else in the barn had seen the incident. As he looked around the stable he saw one who had. 'There has been a witness,' he said.

'What?' asked the anguished Mr Holland.

It was the girl who had been trailing him all day. Thomas moved and took her arm, gently drawing her from her place of hiding. The child looked at him nervously. 'You should not be here,' he said. Turning round he called, 'Mrs M'George, your help is needed.'

'Please, say nothing to anyone . . .' Mr Holland asked pathetically.

'My concern is for the girl, not you,' said Thomas as Fanny M'George answered his summon. 'It seems we have a stowaway,' he said placing the child's hand into hers. 'Can I put her into your care?'

'You bad girl,' said Fanny, 'there will be people searching for you.' The child shook her head. 'I'm sure there are. What is your name?'

Very softly the girl said, 'Molly.'

'I heard you called Mary this morning,' said Thomas.

'My mother named me Molly, but they won't allow me that. Here they say Molly is a wicked name and it should be Mary.'

'Is your mother here in the village?' asked Fanny.

Molly shook her head. 'She's left me. I am put with these people. Don't send me back. I want to be here with you.'

Fanny looked at Thomas. 'I'm surprised nobody's come for her. She asked Molly, 'Which house were you at?'

'I do not know. I hid before they gave me anywhere.'

'You'll have to go back as soon as it's light. You had better spend the night with me.' She looked at Thomas.

'You're like a magnet aren't you?'

In the dark of the night, once the lanthorns had been removed, Molly told Mrs M'George about her short life. The story was not unusual and it was clear that the company of comedians was unlike anything the child had ever known. It reminded Fanny of herself in many ways, so that she wondered what was the kindest way to tell Molly she must remain within the strict life of the Wesleyans.

There was no pump or horse trough at this barn but as rain had fallen in the night, the grass was wet in the early morning next day. Fanny woke the child and without speaking took her outside where they could be alone together.

'Molly,' she said, 'I was once like you. With no mother, I ran away. I've been running ever since. You must not waste your life as I have done.'

'But I want to be like you,' said Molly, 'to wear bright colours and bracelets. I'm put into drabs all the time.'

Fanny made no reply. She had brought with her a bundle of rags and a pot of grease which she began to smear over her face without speaking. Molly was shocked by this, which was Fanny's intent.

It took time, for it was not something she had done of late, but slowly she removed from her face the white lead, the carmine and the rouge. At the start, her countenance became one big smudge, like a water colour left in the rain, and as the grease took away the make-up she gave a cloth to Molly.

'I have no glass,' she said, 'I know my face looks like a piece of raw steak. I want you to take away all the colour until it is clean and you can see me as I am.'

Molly dampened the cloth in the wet grass and wiped gently until the last traces of paint had gone from the face before her. She did it with care as if she was cleansing the stone face of a saint, soothing away the stains from the ivory coloured skin, wringing out the cloth until she was done. Then she sat back and looked at Fanny. What she saw was a face, lined, pocked and worn.

The two regarded each other.

'All done?' asked Fanny. Molly nodded. ' Now you see the bare canvas, the picture of an old woman who ran away to go on the stage. She was never really happy. Now she is sad inside and paints her face like an old hussy pretending she is young and beautiful which she is not.'

Fanny paused. 'Once I was just as you are today, thinking I would give the world to be in the shoes of someone like me . But don't step into my shoes darling. They don't fit very well and they hurt a great deal.' She took Molly's hand, 'Shall we find the people who'll be wondering where you are?'

The girl was about to protest. 'No, Molly, you cannot stay with us. We are not bad people but we are no good for such as you. Come along, we must find where you should be. Because after that, I've got to come back here and paint my face afresh before my own people are to see me. For if I don't, they won't know who I am.'

*

Seventeen. *Up and Down, Up and Down.*

The surgeon attended Mr Whitley. Following his examination the patient was bled, it being decided that the attack was due to an excess of blood in his system. It was recommended that Mr Whitley be confined to his bed for two or three days because of what the surgeon established as a brain fever. Mrs Whitley said she had not seen any sign of a fever, rather it was a sudden passion that had caused the attack. Either way the surgeon insisted that rest was essential treatment. Rest and arrowroot.

'Rest! Rest! How can I rest with plays to be produced?' cried Whitley, throwing aside his bedclothes.

'Either you do that or die on stage,' said his wife, 'I know which is my preference,'tucking him tightly under the blankets.

'Nonsense I had a touch of apoplexy and now it is gone.'

'I shall take rehearsals myself for the next three days. You will stay here in bed. I shall hide your clothes if needs be.'

'Then I shall come down in yours. I have no shame.'

'And no sense. Mr Powell will assist me.'

'I'll not have that man take my place. D'you hear me wife?'

'He will not take your place. He will be your . . . lieutenant.'

'Drivel! It is his one purpose to depose me, to usurp my authority, he intends to take over my theatre . . .'

Cassandra left the room quickly and before he could prevent her, turned the key in the lock of the bedroom door, leaving her husband to exhaust his fury until, she hoped, he would fall asleep and rest.

She had told the cast to be in attendance as normal the next morning and loyal troupers that they were, she found them waiting for her. After saying that her husband was to convalesce for a few days she set about the work in hand with the vigour she had shown in her younger days. She read in for Whitley and decided she would even play his roles if needs be, though how she intended to double as

Friar Laurence and the nurse she did not say. 'Worse things happen at sea,' she pronounced and when in that mood few disagreed with her.

Edmund Sedley had chosen this unfortunate time to ride from Nuthall and watch one of the rehearsals. His presence had to be accepted as part of the financial agreement with his father Sir Charles, but it did not please Cassy to have him witness the disorder that was taking place. He was a sensible young man tolerably well versed in theatrical manners. Seeing the difficulties caused by Whitley's absence he offered to read in for him. Suspicious at first, Cassy accepted the proposal for it relieved her of the task and soon young Sedley's efforts as Friar Laurence showed an aptitude better than expected.

As the morning progressed, Cassy and some in the company almost wondered if the newcomer might actually play the part should Jemmy not be recovered. To Brook Powell this became a tangible threat for should Edmund Sedley gain a foothold in the company his own situation could soon be in jeopardy. Here was a serious rival of handsome appearance combined with a good natural diction. Such a threat must be removed.

In addition, young Sedley had been drawn to the charms of the lovely Belinda Armstrong. This Mr Powell had noted with concern, for with the advantage of playing Romeo he had hoped the role of lover might possibly become a reality off stage. When the midday break arrived Mr Powell decided to come to grips with the matter, seeing with alarm that Edmund Sedley had invited Miss Armstrong to a nearby tavern. Showing neither tact nor manners he joined the couple as they sat at a table.

'Well sir,' he said, 'your reading this morning has been remarkable. I dare say you are not a newcomer to acting.'

'I have performed as an amateur,' answered Edmund.

'And where was that?' asked Powell.

'At my university in Cambridge. For recreation only, you understand.' He smiled at Belinda, who looked admiringly into his eyes. Powell went on, 'You are sufficiently gifted to consider joining our company.'

'That is a fine compliment, but my studies will prevent that.'

Belinda and Mr Powell both expressed disappointment. She in all sincerity, he with relief.

'May one ask what it is you are reading?' said Mr Powell.

'I am studying the law. For I hope in time to follow my father into a political career.'

'Admirable,' said Mr Powell.

'Oh yes,' Belinda agreed.

It must be said that on this occasion young Mr Sedley took far more notice of that lady than of Mr Powell. He continued looking hard into her eyes, 'There is much inequality in our country to be redressed. I hope to continue with the reforms that my father has proposed until it is brought into a permanent statute of legislation.'

Belinda returned his gaze, with small understanding of his words.

'Shall you be reading in again this afternoon?' asked Powell.

'I fear not. For I must be at my studies.'

On being told how well Mr Sedley had read as Friar Laurence, Jemmy Whitley recovered with amazing rapidity. For like Powell he had a fear of his position being usurped. During his stay in bed he had decided to rearrange the new season. He would revive *Richard III* and *The Tempest* and perform two of his best roles, the villainous king and the magician Prospero.

Above all he was determined to keep Mr Powell in his place, resolving that after Romeo he would have no other major roles; Whitley would play the leads himself. He had also decided to promote the career of Belinda Armstrong. She showed promise as Juliet and would be ideal as Lady Anne and Miranda, two undemanding parts that would display her loveliness rather than her limited acting skills.

For his instinct had been right, her talent was small but onstage her charms were dazzling, a currency that has seen the start of many a stage career.

Having gained possession of the key to his bedroom, Jemmy ignored his wife's protests and was back at rehearsal the following day.

*

With concern on internal matters so strong, the company had failed to notice the unrest that was often occurring outside the theatre.

In Nottingham this had becoming a regular problem. It began with a riot over an unwelcome increase in the price of cheese. An angry crowd had attacked farmers and their market stalls, carrying off many of the cheeses, even rolling away those they could not carry. The mayor had been called for and whilst endeavouring to restore order was knocked down when a large stilton hit him in the chest.

The cavalry was brought in and quickly quelled the tumult, but not before a farmer guarding his pitch was mistakenly shot dead by one of the militia.

Theatre folk, never greatly interested in matters beyond the stage door, gave little thought to the event. After all, they said, rowdiness at elections and over rises in food prices were all part of life in any market town. Yet what they were not seeing was that Nottingham was changing from a market town into a place of industry. If they had cared to look outside their confines, they would have seen that hosiery frames were being installed into dozens of homes, to be rented and operated by former agricultural workers who had left the countryside to work in the over crowded town.

Though the Whitleys and their fellows may have been aware of these hosiery workers, quite likely passed them in the street, they paid them little heed. It was unfortunate such people were crammed into badly built houses they agreed, but it should be asked, 'Did they ever visit the theatre?' The answer was, 'No, they did not.' It was still the gentry who had to be wooed and their patronage sought, not these so-called framework knitters, who had never been known to buy a seat, not even for the gallery.

Only Jemmy believed that perhaps the theatre should try to help the hardship suffered by the many workers and their families. They were, he thought, as deserving of charity as any hospital and although it was self-serving, theatres often found that charity performances helped improve their standing. Although the previous venture into philanthropy at the time of Mr Thornton Friars had best been forgotten, he put the idea to his wife.

Cassy did not share his view,

'We are not a benevolent foundation,' she insisted, 'furthermore we would gain little support if we sided with such people. The knitters are not trusted by anyone, they are well paid everyone knows that. Why else would they come into the towns? They know where the money is, that's why.'

'They come because there is no work in the countryside.'

'Moonshine! Of course there's plenty of work there. Mr Powell was saying so only the other day. "You'll never see a poor farmer," said he.'

'Oh, Powell understands agricultural economics does he?'

'Yes I believe he does. He went so far as to say that the framework knitters are born trouble makers. Look what happened to him that night at Weekday Cross. In all likelihood it was knitters who attacked him.'

'He was attacked because he was flaunting himself. That's asking for trouble when many people are close to starving.'

'I've no patience with you,' Cassy complained. 'Whenever you can, you pour scorn on Powell, hip and thigh. One could take you to be a radical.'

'Perhaps I am. Times are changing.'

'Changing? We've no business to be changing. We've got a theatre to run, not a poor house. Our work is give the patrons what they want.'

But what did the patrons want? Even if the theatre reopened with Sir Charles Sedley's support, would it attract custom? People liked to be entertained, but their preference was for comedies and simple minded pastorals. They might enjoy seeing the downfall of a pantomime villain such as *Richard III,* but *Romeo and Juliet* was only acceptable if the lovers survived, as Garrick knew when he rewrote the play. What the public wanted were tragedies, but tragedies with happy endings.

*

There it was, all over Newark-upon-Trent for everyone to read.
A Midsummer Night's Dream.
And then the cast list, including
Bottom, the Weaver .... Mr Holland.
Titania, the Fairy Queen .... Mrs M'George.
Robin Goodfellow, a puck .... Mr Hammond.

Yes. It was only an after-piece, but THERE IT WAS.

Scores of posters had been printed, pasted up and handed out through the town; with his name for all to see. If only it had been at a proper theatre and not here in Newark. Still the yard of the ancient coaching house gave several advantages that could not be achieved on a common stage.

It had a gallery running above the acting area which Tate Wilkinson had decided to use as a level for the fairy world. It worked well. From here Puck and Oberon looked down on the confusions and follies of the mortals below.

Oberon rarely left the upper region, but Puck had to move up and down between the two. Once Thomas had shown his ability for rope climbing this problem was solved and he shot up and down with a dexterity that was sure to please the house. Though not without its problems At the start it had been proposed that he should have wings. Tiny wings, but wings in spite of Thomas's protestations, for they were tightly strapped and greatly restricting his movements. As the rehearsals progressed he introduced somersaults and leaps which soon saw an end to the wings, which flew away as if with a life of their own. In their place, pointed ears were made. Thomas disliked these almost as much and had plans to be rid of these also.

The first performance approached, so did his nerves.

'You'll be fine,' said Fanny M'George, 'just keep still when you're not speaking and listen to those who are. Above all,' she said, 'enjoy yourself.'

All very well, but throughout the day before the show, he discovered what it was to suffer the horrors of stage fright. The thought of being before an audience terrified him. Like so many, he discovered a remedy - strong ale. A great deal of strong ale, so that once his first cue arrived he was very, very, light headed. Until all at once it was his turn. He began. '*How now spirit, whither wander you?*'

By the time the evening ended, Thomas's life had changed forever. Many things went awry but he had the wit to use them as advantages.

His ears came off, so he picked them up and turned them into characters of their own. When overhearing others he held one ear at arm's length then put it to his own, as if it conveyed the message. He did handstands, somersaults and cart wheels. At one point he swung on the rope across the full stage, thumping the ass's head of Bottom as he passed.

He forgot everything about attitudes and how he should place his hands and feet. He stood in ungainly but comic positions. He clenched and unclenched his fists as if they were beating with a pulse which gave him a strange insect like aspect. He sniggered and hissed mischievously to himself - he was a malevolent spirit. This was a new Puck. And it was his.

The fairies, played by local children, joined in the romp with unaffected glee; they genuinely screamed with fright when Puck unexpectedly chased them off stage. Thomas enjoyed himself. And so did the audience.

When the play ended it was Puck the house called for. He stood in line with the cast, but Mrs M'George pushed him forward to take his bow. For the first time, Thomas knew the intoxication of a cheering audience. It was far more potent than strong ale, but as he was to discover, it came with a dangerous dependancy to feed upon it.

Everyone left the stage. They gathered together in an unused pantry which was acting as a dressing room.

'I think Puck is now welcome in our midst,' said Mr Holland.

There was general agreement and for the first time Thomas found himself surrounded by the cast offering their congratulations.

Until further away in the tavern a door slammed loudly. Heavy footsteps foretold that Tate Wilkinson was striding along the corridor.

'Where is he?' his voice harsh with anger. 'Thomas, I want you before me this minute.' Few had seen him so thunderous. Thomas was prepared for the retribution ahead, but he was too drunk with ale and applause to think of any immediate excuse.

'Thomas!' shouted Tate Wilkinson, storming into the room, 'you are undisciplined, inconsiderate of your fellow players and completely out of hand. You have turned a beautiful play into a vulgar pantomime. You have broken one of the cardinal rules of the theatre, which is to serve the play.'

Thomas and the cast stood, shocked by the intensity of his voice until the darkness flew from his face and his smile became boundless,

'And I have delighted in each minute of it.' He embraced Thomas which allowed the cast to laugh with relief, and clap their hands in agreement.

'You are a clown, my boy, a tumbler of great talent, perhaps genius. By rights I should sack you on the spot for the multiple sins of misbehaviour and disruption. Instead I shall offer you an agreement to play in York. I think they will like you there.'

Thomas smiled with pleasure, swaying slightly, for by now he was shivering and deathly pale. Then he threw up.

*

Eighteen. *Lightning Strikes Twice.*

On his return to York, for Tate Wilkinson the role of Moses had turned to that of Odysseus Here was his heartland, his Ithaca, the finest town he knew, where his own theatre was situated in Mint Yard, with his home nearby.

Compared to Covent Garden and Drury Lane it was for him superior. It was more compact requiring none of the coarse acting necessary to fill the huge London houses.

It was a pleasure to have the new six week season ahead which included the Spring Race week, always a high point of social life in York. But greatest of all was the happiness of a time with his wife Jane and the comfort of his own armchair and hearth after the vexation of lodgings.

Formerly an actress, Jane had retired from the stage, her involvement now being as advisor and helper. She had also written two plays, a unique achievement in provincial companies.

As spring was come, the actors who had elected not to go on tour would rejoin the company. Mr Cobb, whom Wilkinson considered a great actor, having rested through the winter months at his own expense, was welcomed back warmly. Aged well over fifty, Mr Cobb preferred his home during the cold and dark of the year but appeared again like a swallow in April. This pleased everyone apart from Mr Holland who knew full well that Mr Cobb was the finer actor and that he would be relegated to lesser roles when his rival chose to reappear.

Tate was glad also to have Mr and Mrs Treadgold and their two children with him once more. The Treadgolds were a dancing family and throughout the season performed during the evening intervals. Far from being idle during the winter, it was their busiest time for they ran a popular academy of dance, endeavouring to instruct the young and socially aspiring of York in deportment and formal dance. Their curriculum was broad and included the minuet, the courante and the cotillion. However, the popular taste was for English dance and the Treadgolds were equipped to instruct pupils in this as well as Scottish Reels, Irish Trots and the ever popular Sir Roger de Coverley.

Their children, Walter and Lucy, had been dancing all their lives. When little they were much alike but with the passing years this had changed, Walter being near six foot in height, way above his sister's stature. They shared the extended family face, Walter's fair hair hanging over his eyes in lank curves whereas Lucy's hair, long and blonde, was confined in class to a snood.

Now aged seventeen they were able to give a *pas de deux* which pleased all who saw it, to the extent that audiences sometimes hailed them in preference to their parents. Nonetheless the four family members graced the stage together, how else could a quadrille be presented? Lucy was beginning to claim the greater approbation for she had the advantage of a good singing voice, an ability her brother lacked. It was thought that soon she would be dancing and singing professionally on a wider stage. A great future was predicted.

After being on the road the company of comedians was increased in number. With extra men and women there was competition for major roles in the twenty plays that were soon to be given. Those like Fanny M'George, knew that they would be relegated from leads to the smaller roles of confidantes to the heroine or even maidservants. It was humbling, but Fanny was aware of her good fortune to be working in one of the best companies in the kingdom. Thomas, still with his success of Puck in mind, was also sensible enough to know he was very much the subordinate but the words of Wilkinson *'I think they will like you there,'* gave him the hope of new chances in York.

Before that, lodgings were to be found and he was offered a place with Mrs Abbott, a landlady who had a small attic room available in her house in Stonegate. It was up many flights of stairs, culminating in a ladder. The tiny space under the roof was no bigger than a cupboard, its one delight being a small dormer window in the sloping ceiling.

'No pissing onto the street,' Mrs Abbott requested, as from up there it was possible to look down on Stonegate far below. At the head of the street was the great central tower of the Minster, from where many believed God kept watch over His people. As he moved in Thomas listened to the noise of jostling crowds rising upwards, mixed with the smells of animals, refuse and cooking.

Although he had already been in York, today he was in the town, not as a beggar, but as a young actor with money to hand. From now he would be paid a salary, Tate Wilkinson being one of the enlightened managers who had abandoned the old system of sharing. In return he expected hard work for as soon as the group arrived they were called together and given the crowded new programme complete with cast list for the first plays.

It was disappointing for Thomas to find that *The Dream* was to be given as an after piece only in the second week and as far as he could tell was to be his one appearance. But it was Tate's custom to call each actor separately and explain what could be expected in the coming weeks. Thomas winced when the conversation began yet again with the jarring words, 'Well now, young fella-me-lad and what are we to do with you?'

He replied simply, 'That is not for me to say sir.'

'Truly.' Wilkinson paused. 'I asked Mr Holland to give you tuition in the art of gesture. He tells me you were not responsive.'

Thomas hesitated before answering by merely saying, 'No sir.'

'What is the reason for that?'

'I would prefer to keep my silence, sir.'

'Mr Holland is well equipped to help you learn your craft. Yet he says he found you indifferent to his efforts. Why was this?'

'It was my fault I fancy.'

'Come Thomas, if you reject my efforts to help you improve I shall lose patience. So. . .?'

Thomas considering his reply carefully. He had been angered by the actor's crude overture, even so he had no wish to condemn him. Finally he said, 'I fear he cannot keep himself to himself.'

Wilkinson took out a handkerchief and wiped his nose.

'Ah, I did wonder. I'd hoped he'd mended his ways.' Tate

paused, 'In that case we'll have to find another tutor. As I have said you show much promise but little idea of demeanour. Perhaps lessons in deportment might help. The Treadgolds would be best for that. I'm told they hold a morning class every three days. See that you attend next week. I suggest you go to all three classes. I shall cover the expenditure.'

'Thank you sir.'

'In two weeks I want you to repeat Puck. Three performances. You'll find dates on the forthcoming call sheet. You will find also that I've cast you as Blinks in *The Mistake* and Toby in *The Widow's Wish*. You'll be with Mr Cobb in both so you'd best be on your mettle. Word perfect before each rehearsal mark you, Mr Cobb expects nothing less. Admittedly they are small parts but you will learn much from acting with him. Right lad that's all, cut along. Hallelujah and Praise the Lord.'

Thomas left the room well pleased. To play Puck again and two new parts was good. He had no idea what Blinks and Toby were, probably only a cough and a spit, but it was a first step. He was now in three productions. Hallelujah, Praise the Lord indeed.

Treadgold's School of Dancing was on Swinegate. It was a basement room, lit by three windows at pavement level, which in the dance room below, were close to the ceiling. The windows had been lime washed to prevent curious passers-by from watching the choreographic activities within but this had cut out so much light that the glass was cleaned and the gaze of the inquisitive tolerated. That was until vulgar comments became too much, whereupon young Walter Treadgold was despatched to send away the miscreants.

Mr and Mrs Treadgold were tall and stately with faces to match. They would have been glad to be taken as 'gentry' but more often they were thought to resemble giraffes, all neck and forelegs. In spite of being laughed at secretly, pupils approached them with caution. Even those of the minor aristocracy were obliged to perform a *reverence* at the start of class and before any communication with the two teachers.

Mr Treadgold left all discourse to his wife. If asked a question, his answer was to walk away as if the inquirer did not exist.

In comparison, Mrs Treadgold was almost garrulous. Dressed without variation in black taffeta, her one form of decoration was a matching choker, the ribbon always pinned with a bright jewelled brooch at her throat. So intense was the shine from this, that it took on the character of a third eye which might explain why, in conversation, her own eyes were kept shut.

This gave the disdainful impression that either she could not bear to look at whoever she was talking to, or she had forgotten their name and her closed eyes might help her recall who it was. Mrs Treadgold was never without a silver capped baton which served as an authoritarian black rod, a walking stick or as it was rumoured, a billiard cue.

Thomas arrived for his first class unsure of himself and what he would be expected to know. He had been given suitable clothes from wardrobe which added to his discomfort when he found himself in the company of a group of young girls, all giggles and whispers, together with a smaller number of well-dressed youths who yawned and chewed their finger nails to convey their boredom. He was approached by Mrs Treadgold.

'You are . . .?' she asked imperiously, the two vowels sounding like some exotic foreign phrase.

'Tom Hammond, miss.' he replied.

Her eyes shut firmly, Mrs Treadgold said, 'Stand up straight, let me look at you and see how you are deported.' She placed the tip of her baton under his chin to examine him, her eyes opened a fraction.

'Yeeeees,' she said wearily, 'I'd say you have definite premises. But in future young man,' she continued disdainfully, 'be so kind as to refer to me only as "Madame." I respond to no other apparition.' She then walked away, with the wave of a scented silk scarf in her free hand.

'You're Hammond aren't you?' said the fair young man, 'I'm Walter Treadgold. I say, you can't dance in those heavy shoes.'

At once he took him away to a changing room. Thomas did not care to admit that these were the only shoes he possessed as Walter opened a drawer full of light black leather dancing slippers.

'Find what you can,' he said. 'We'll be starting in five minutes. Best get a move on.'

Thomas found slippers that more or less fitted, then hurried into the dance room where already the young boys and girls were standing in two lines opposite each other. Mrs Treadgold tapped her baton loudly upon the wooden floor as a mark of reprimand for Thomas's late entrance. She pointed to a space at the end of the row of boys. Thomas took his position, glad to find he was standing opposite Lucy Treadgold whose smile made him feel he was welcomed by at least one person there.

Mr Treadgold, now with a fiddle and bow in his hands, made a screech-like chord to command attention. As soon as he spoke it was clear why he kept silence whenever he could. His voice was as high as the strings on his violin and far less agreeable.

'Mesdames et Monsieurs. Prenez vos danseurs pour "My Lady Carey's Caper." ' Mrs Treadgold following her husband spoke in a voice at least two octaves lower as he struck up a tune on the fiddle.

'*Vis a vis*,' she ordered with her baton thumping the floor. Then with the aid of the violin the dance began. Rhythmically, Mrs Treadgold called,

'Fwun two, end beck to beck - Face your partners, forward paaaarss. Fwun two, and *Dose a Dose* - single turn to corner faaaawll.'

Or so it sounded to Thomas for the directions were senseless. He was aware that all the other pupils in the room seemed to know exactly what they were about and were able to create neat lines with some style. Without Lucy's guidance it would have been a disaster, but she helped him skilfully through the moves taking his hands and at times his waist or shoulders to show which way he should move. There was one anxious moment when she held his left hand and he felt the transient shock as she discovered he had two fingers missing. But he warmed to her because of the grace with which she ignored this, taking his hand as if there was nothing amiss.

'Fwun two, end - Fwun two, end . . .' it went on seemingly for ever until after some time Thomas realised he had grasped the sequence and was almost enjoying the dance. Finally the dance ended with Mr

Treadgold playing a final chord, at which point everyone bowed to each other, turned and gave a *reverence* to Madame and then to Mr Treadgold.

For the first time Lucy spoke directly to Thomas,

'You did well.'

'With your support.'

'I've known pupils take hours to learn that. You did it at one attempt.'

Thomas found he was blushing at the praise. 'I'm not sure why I'm here - learning to dance. I'm not likely to be going to any assembly balls.'

'Don't say that, a presentable young man like you.'

Thomas did not know how to take this compliment, if that was what it was. 'Are you laughing at me?' he asked.

'Why should I do that?' asked Lucy. 'Everyone looks a little foolish when they're learning something new. This is a good morning to be starting for next we begin to learn the quadrille, which is more taxing.'

Before the conversation could go further she was stopped by a second call for quiet from Mr Treadgold on his violin.

'*Attention, s'il vous plait. Maintenent nous avons "Randall's Quadrille"* ' he announced in high hesitant French which his wife heard with satisfaction.

'Can you dance the quadrille?' asked Lucy.

'I've never tried,' said Thomas noticing that Walter was joining them with one of the giggling girls on his arm.

'It's a bit more elaborate, but we'll get you through it, won't we?' Lucy smiled at her brother, who did not react. The four of them formed a square.

This time the outcome was less successful. There were several collisions and trips which Mrs Treadgold regarded with loud sighs of disapproval.

She said to him afterwards, 'There seems little *motif* in continuing *avec l'ensemble,* until you are more *conversant* with the basic *movements*. For this we shall divide *a deux groupes*. Lucy *ma petite* please take the group *ici* and Walter *mon fils* you will take *l'autre*.

The division meant that Thomas was parted from Lucy which he regretted, but found Walter a competent teacher. After an hour the whole room was moderately adept at the quadrille, the morning ending with a tolerable execution of the dance. This had given Thomas the pleasure of partnering Lucy within the dance patterns, when her smiles of encouragement were, he thought, the most beautiful he had ever seen. Before the dismissal of the class Mrs Treadgold announced that at the next session the mysteries of the *courante* would be revealed.

'Is that difficult?' Thomas asked Walter standing next to him.

'So difficult that it cannot be mastered without private tuition.' Walter winked at Thomas, 'Would you like some coaching?' he asked. 'Come on, I know the very best academy for education,' and shortly the two young men were seated in the Gun and Partridge with large tankards of ale between them. 'I do my best work in here,' he said, 'now the dance goes like this. . .'

Some jugs later, Walter believed he had taught Thomas the basic moves of the courante which he achieved by drawing with a finger dipped in beer and working on the slate table top, Much amusement was had by the two of them dancing their fingers through small puddles of ale until, with no warning, Walter became darker in tone.

'Tell you this Tom,' he said bitterly, 'I've had as much dancing as I can stomach. All my days I've been dancing. Dancing, I ask you. Ever since I was first put into breeches. What life is that for a man?'

'You're good at it,' Thomas said. 'You could start a school of your own.'

'What? Teaching spoilt brats how to besport themselves at an assembly? That will not do for me, I want something better. You look as if you've seen the world, am I right?'

'I am resolved to be an actor.'

'Like Lucy. God, how I detest the stage and all it carries. I tell you it does not suit me. What? End up like my ridiculous parents. You will agree they are grotesque?'

Thomas knew that it was unwise to abuse the parents of others, even if their progeny did so themselves. 'They are perhaps, unorthodox,' he said.

'They are preposterous.' Walter kicked the table savagely. 'All that posing and false French. My mother was born in Chatham, God knows where my father comes from. If he is my father, which I hope he is not. But I'll soon be gone. Lucy and I will shortly be eighteen, when I for myself will be off.'

' Where? And what will you do?'

'That's the devil of it. I'm fit for nothing. I fancy being an attorney, that's a sure way of success, but I'm too old to be articled. There's the army, but I have no money to buy a commission. Anyway that's a fruitless career now that the French are defeated and there will be no more wars.'

'Where will you go?'

'London. I'll maybe dance all the way there like Kemp. Abroad who knows? India, Jamaica, the moon I don't know. Does the man in the moon need dancing lessons? Not much room when it's just a sliver. . . '

Walter was drunk. Thomas guessed he had no head for ale for he himself felt quite sober. He thought it best to try and take him home if he could find where he lived, perhaps also discover Lucy's home. He rose, and offered to help him from the stool which annoyed Walter who knocked him away fiercely. His voice now slurred, his mood displeasing.

'I'll tell you this. Those Yankee fellers have the right idea. They know the need of independence. They'll get it soon, just you see. . .'

Unexpectedly, Lucy was standing beside them.

'Oh, Walter. Not again.' She looked at her brother, with a combination of patience and weariness, which told Thomas that this situation was not new.

Walter looked angrily at his sister, 'Don't come here with your odour of sanctity,' he said seizing her wrist.

Lucy replied quietly, 'I'm not reprimanding you.'

'Yes you are.' He mimicked her voice, '*Oh Walter. Not again,* but hark to me, you may be the good dutiful daughter . . .' he began twisting her arm, so that she gave a cry, 'but remember this . . .'

Thomas moved quickly and took Walter's arm, forcing it behind his back. He shouted with pain and let go of his sister's wrist.

'You don't do things like that,' said Thomas. 'Not to a sister as kind and gentle as yours.' He released Walter's arm.

'Come,' said Lucy, 'we'll go home.' She supported her brother and guided him out of the tavern, both walking awkwardly with none of their usual grace. Thomas watched, thinking that until a few hours ago these two had been unknown to him. What little time it had taken for him to discover how much he disliked the one and how much he loved the other.

*

Once rehearsals for *The Dream* began, it became apparent how important the upper gallery had been in Newark. There was no high level in York, yet Thomas was quick to demonstrate that he could achieve the same effects by climbing ropes up to the flies. Two were to be hung just out of sight, stage left and stage right, enabling him to appear unexpectedly at different heights. One minute he could be way up high, the next on the stage.

He could also swing from one side to the other as if in flight. The actor playing Oberon attempted the same feat. Two attempts by the portly fairy king to climb aloft left him dangling on the rope's end like a plumb line. From then the upper regions of the stage were entirely Thomas's domain.

With the new season underway the Treadgolds performed their dances at the theatre in the evening intervals. Thomas attempted to see them whenever he could, but found no chance of speaking to Lucy. As soon as their dancing was done, she was hurried away by her parents to help distribute cards to any member of the audience who might enrol at their dancing school. Once this was complete they disappeared into the night.

The first week began with good houses resulting in satisfactory returns at the box office. The company rehearsed all day from ten in the morning till six at night with few breaks. The short rest before performance was often forgone and some nights they went straight from rehearsal to performance. Meat pies and a great deal of beer were downed rapidly giving dreadful wind for those who gulped their food, or near fainting for those who did without.

As the first night of *The Dream* approached, Thomas found once more the terror of stage fright awaited him; lying in ambush was the monster with whom he must give battle. Whenever he could, he practised his climbing, his tricks, his lines but there was no dispelling the fear that lurked ahead. What was it? Why was it? He told Fanny M'George of his fears.

'Don't think it's just you,' she said, 'We're all have the shits. What's more it never leaves you, it gets worse. The more you know the worse it gets. You have to accept it. Remember If you don't have jitters you're not much good.'

But Thomas had found a way to be rid of the jitters. It was costly. It came in a bottle. And it worked.

The Dream cast was mostly unchanged. Fanny again played Titania and Mr Holland, Bottom. Tate Wilkinson was not prepared to spend much time on the play when there were new productions needing attention. One run-through and a dress were all he allowed. But the latter went well.

'Now young fella-me-lad,' he said, 'Audiences here in York are more particular than Newark. You'll have to work to get their approval. Do well in York and it gets to be heard about. So let's have a performance. Hallelujah. Praise the Lord.'

He meant well, but it added to Thomas's fears. It underlined how he must not fail. As he waited for his entrance the monster stood behind him.

'I can't even remember my first bloody line,' he said to Fanny.

'You will,' she said, 'as soon as you're out there. You'll know it.'

'But what the fuck is it? If I can't remember. I know your first line for God's sake, *"What jealous Oberon? Fairies skip, hence."* '

'Maybe we should swap parts.' Fanny laughed.

'It's not funny.'

'Yes it is. Stop worrying, only makes it worse.'

Stop worrying. Yes, he could stop worrying. There was a way. Easy. Just remove the cork . . .

As usual, the Treadgolds did their dances before the after piece. Lucy had yet to speak to him, other than give a smile as they passed.

In Puck's costume, he was able to stop her momentarily,

'I play Robin Goodfellow tonight,' he said.

'So I see,' she answered walking away.

The play had begun. Bottom and the rustics finally left the stage.

It was his cue. He was underway.

All went well with his two big speeches, then came the moment when Oberon and Titania entered. It was now he was to climb upwards and look down from on high at the courtly procedure below.

Thomas took the rope and began to hoist himself. Nothing happened. He could not get a grip. His hands were running with sweat. The rope slid through them. He remained stage bound.

So, here it was. The failure he knew must come. The monster was victorious, it rendered him helpless. He felt his legs turn to jelly, every muscle had dissolved. Unable to move, he was as heavy as stone.

A voice whispered from the wings. What? He tried to listen. It could not be a prompt, so what was it?

'Chalk. Here. Quickly.' It was Mr Holland. Thomas looked into the darkness of the wings. Holland was holding out a bag of white powder.

'Chalk. Rub it on your hands, you should have been told.'

White powder was put into the palms of his hands. He looked out front. They were watching him. He pulled a face, then made a mime of rubbing his hands together as if he meant business. Someone in the audience laughed. He acknowledged it. Were they on his side after all? That laugh showed him a way to use the audience. Matters were improving With hands now dry and strong he was able to climb; right to the upper region where he hung until. . .

'Come gentle puck, come hither,' said Oberon. He lowered himself to hang above the fairy king, listening to his instructions,

'Fetch me this herb and be thou here again.'

In a moment of inspiration he tied the rope round his waist and after a wild swing caught the other appearing to hover in mid-air.

'I'll put a girdle round about the earth In forty minutes.' and with this, Thomas managed to disappear from view as if by magic. The house approved and he heard laughter and a tiny smattering of applause.

Things were starting to work.

The foolery with his ears went well. Every tumble, every cartwheel every somersault got increasing laughs. He knew how to look out front and share his enjoyment with the audience. He won their approval. He was giving them a good time. It had little to do with Shakespeare. That did not matter. Once again he had done it. He had taken the house. It was his. Laughter and applause greeted him.

Lightning had struck twice.

*

Nineteen. *Command Performance.*

There was concern about the Sedley's offer of patronage. The two hundred pounds promised by Sir Charles had been deposited in a new account at Smith's bank, but no word had come about a date for the theatre to reopen. Cassy had read in her London news sheet that Parliament had been busy with an abnormal number of bills before the coming recess which may have meant Sir Charles was tied to business in the House. But still they waited, several plays ready for performance if ever the call should come.

Eventually patience was rewarded when Edmund Sedley brought an invitation from his parents to bring the players to their home, Nuthall Temple, the following Sunday and perform extracts from *Romeo and Juliet.* It was accepted with eagerness, later moderated when it was realised that only the two principals were requested to act, thus excluding the Whitleys themselves. It was tactfully suggested that as Friar Laurence and the Nurse were essential to the plot perhaps the invitation could be extended. This was acceptable as long as the presentation did not exceed one hour.

Dora Proctor was furious at not having been included in the party. Her anger was exacerbated on discovering she was passed over in favour of the inexperienced Belinda Armstrong.

'I don't mind her playing Juliet, she's a namby-pamby anyway, so is Miranda, but everyone knows I am the first lady of the company.'

Mrs Willis pointed out that if anyone had such a claim it would be Mrs Whitley.

'Very well then, so I am the second first lady.'

'Decency, madam, should prevent you from assuming such a role,' said Mrs Willis one of Whitley's original company, who had formed an alliance with newly recruited Mrs Kirk and Mrs Venebles.

'And pray what does that mean?' asked Dora, facing the trio.

'It means madam, that if you are a first lady, it is of the bed chamber and nought else.'

This exchange, taking place in the green room during a performance, was only curtailed by Miss Proctor's cue being called. In a rage she went onstage leaving her critics deep in debate.

'Serves her right,' said Mrs Willis, 'she should know her place.'

'Doubtless she thinks she's Lavinia Fenton,' said Mrs Kirk.

'Lavinia Fenton?'

'She played Polly in *Beggar's Opera*. The Duke of Bolton became infatuated with her.'

'That's true, it was the talk of the town.' Mrs Venebles joined in.

'Before my time,' suggested Mrs Willis.

'Every night he sat on the stage his eyes devouring her. A married man, needless to say.'

'Became his mistress, though he was thrice her age.'

'Set her up in a her own establishment.'

'Where she bore him three bastards.'

'And the Duchess, what of her?' asked Mrs Willis.

'It killed her, everyone said so.'

'Just what they wanted. So they could wed.'

'And there she is, Lavinia, the second duchess.'

"Lording it up at Bolton Abbey.'

'Her looks have gone. So has he.''

'Died at Christmas. Left a widow.'

'Filthy rich.'

'How fickle is fortune.' The three sighed as they waited their cues.

Not only did Dora choose to rise above such slanders, a friendship with Belinda Armstrong had blossomed, perhaps as means of defence. The two behaved sweetly towards each other with no sign of rivalry. When, shortly,before the visit to perform before the Sedleys, Miss Armstrong complained of feeling unwell, Miss Proctor's concern for her welfare was thought by many who saw it to be questionable.

'You have been working too hard,' Dora told Belinda, hoping Mr Whitley might hear her words. She added loudly, 'We have all been working too hard. It's a marvel we're not all in our sick beds.'

Uncharitable minds suspected Dora Proctor of bringing about Belinda's sickness, by what means could not be discerned. Although the word 'bane' had passed no-one's lips, suspicions were rife that Dora was causing mischief.

When Saturday came, the day before the visit to Nuthall, it was wondered if Miss Armstrong would be in sufficient good health to appear.

'I shall be well enough,' she insisted,'The playing is all, is it not?'

Happily the weather on the Sunday was fair and mild. A carriage was sent for the actors, with a dog cart for their properties. Throughout the journey Mr Whitley and Mr Powell ignored the presence of the other. On arrival at the Temple they were received by the butler who instructed two footmen to take their boxes. Once indoors they were greeted by young Edmund Sedley.

'How good of you to come,' he said, 'we are so much looking forward to your performance.' He explained that some ten or twelve of their friends and neighbours would be attending the play in the music room. The four were taken there to inspect the arrangements finding a space had been made ready with screens, candles and chairs providing a small acting area.

'We shall be dining at four,' said Mr Sedley. 'There will also be a light meal provided for you. So it is to be hoped we can hear the play at about six, which we trust is favourable to you. I will tell my father you are here for I'm sure he will want to add his welcome.'

After he left, Mr Powell and Miss Armstrong wandered around the room, admiring the various treasures and paintings. Miss Armstrong discovered a harp and ran her fingers over the strings. The sound was much more than she expected.

'Just fancy,' she said.

'Don't touch,' commanded Mrs Whitley, 'you might harm it.'

'No such danger,' said Sir Charles, who with his wife had come into the room unnoticed.

'Do you play the harp, young lady?' he asked Belinda, who made no answer but merely blushed.

Sir Charles smiled. 'It's good of you all to come. I wanted to add my welcome after that of my son. Have you everything you require?'

They had, of course. Crossing the room, Lady Sedley engaged Cassandra and Belinda in polite conversation, whilst her husband spoke to Mr Whitley and Mr Powell. 'How are conditions in Nottingham?' asked Sir Charles, 'I mean in the town itself.'

'They appear well enough,' replied Whitley, but Mr Powell, greatly to Jemmy's anger disagreed truculently.

'There are frequent signs of unrest amongst the lower orders.'

'You are right,' said Sir Charles, 'it concerns me greatly. The framework knitters badly need firm legislation to ensure a fundamental wage. I've seen their petition. But it is not easy to achieve. If we allow higher wages we shall lose out to competition from the French.'

'Yes and the damned knitters don't seem to realise that,' said Mr Powell. 'Trouble makers everyone of them.'

Whitley wished he would hold his tongue. If there was to be a political argument, the patronage and all they hoped to achieve could be jeopardised

'I'm sitting on the committee to inquire into the merits of their appeal,' said Sir Charles, 'certainly it appears wages are low and the rents for frames are unfairly high.'

Whitley saw Powell was about to continue, so that in desperation he said brightly, 'Let us pray that there is a happy issue out of all our afflictions.'

'Indeed,' said Sir Charles, 'that is what we all hope for.' He smiled at Mr Whitley in the way he must have smiled at hundreds of his constituents over the years.

'Come my dear' he said to his wife, 'we must leave the players to prepare and our guests will be arriving soon.' They left as quietly as they had arrived.

Shortly after this, a cold collation was brought in, which consisted of game pie, pressed beef with vegetables, followed by a gooseberry tart and a corn flour shape. No alcohol was evident.

Mr Powell complained, 'Don't they know actors never eat before a performance, only afterwards?' For this he was admonished by Jemmy who suggested gratitude should be shown for such generosity.

Miss Armstrong refused to take any of the food . 'No, truly I couldn't,' she said. By now the Whitleys were becoming concerned, for during the past few days she appeared to have eaten nothing and looked pale and fragile.

'I'm quite all right,' Belinda insisted, 'I eat very little. Pray do not worry.' But the Whitleys did, as Belinda seemed quite ill.

From the windows of the music room the four of them watched the guests arrive in their carriages, after which, time dragged by as the Sedleys dined their guests elsewhere. Sounds of high enjoyment could be heard from what must have been the dining room which added to the the tedium of their waiting.

Two footmen took away the remains of the meal, bringing in tea which soon went cold but still there was no sign of an audience.

'It's intolerable,' Mr Powell walked about the room, 'we should not have been called until six o'clock at the earliest.'

The Whitleys had to agree but explained that this was one of the hazards of seeking patronage. Eventually, well past eight o'clock, Edmund Sedley put his head round the door and asked if the players were ready to give their performance. Assured of this the candles were lit, followed by the guests sauntering into the room talking at the tops of their voices, which indicated that seeing a play was not the first thing they had in mind. Even when Edmund Sedley called for quiet, conversation increased in volume. It was not until Sir Charles clapped his hands and called loudly for order that the chatter finally ceased and reluctant attention was given to him.

'My friends,' he began, 'we are about to have an uncommon treat. Mr Whitley and his company are here to delight us with some scenes from their forthcoming repertoire. This is,' he referred to a slip of paper, *'The Most Excellent and Lamentable Tragedy of Romeo and Juliet.'* To a faint smattering of applause he took his seat on the front row.

Whitley began with the celebrated chorus which was followed by the equally celebrated balcony scene between the two lovers. There being no balcony the effect was achieved with Romeo and Juliet positioned at some distance apart. This was not entirely satisfactory for the audience looked first at one and then at the other as if watching a game of tennis.

All went well until the final scene acted in the sepulchre Here, with the newly devised happy ending, Friar Laurence was to come and prevent Romeo from drinking poison; Juliet was to awake from her sleep and finding her love yet alive, all would end happily.

Came the moment when the friar declared,*'The lady stirs,'* the lady did no such thing. Patting Juliet's hand warily the friar got no response.

'Alas,' he said his disquiet growing, *'she lies there still,'* he further noted, *'far too still,'* and then in desperation, *perchance she needs an apothecary.'*

It was at this point, when both he and Romeo found the heroine to be insensible, that the audience began at last to show real interest in the drama. For sure, Juliet was unconscious. Some were alarmed, some were amused.

Various remarks were heard. 'Perhaps she had forgot her lines,' said one spectator. 'Turned out to be a tragedy after all,' another said. 'Is that your drink or mine?' asked someone else.

When it was realised that there was no apothecary in the house, the services of a surgeon were sought. A bed in the Chinese room was hurriedly aired by a scorch of warming pans and Miss Armstrong installed where, to the relief of all, her eyes opened with the familiar words, 'Where am I?'

The locality explained, she was next asked if she knew what ailed her. At first Miss Armstrong refused to speak, shaking her head as if she had no idea. It was not until young Edmund Sedley, risking propriety by sitting on the bed beside her, asked what was amiss. Tears filling her eyes, Belinda replied softly, 'my tooth, my back tooth.' She went on to explain that she had been suffering from toothache for almost a week, the discomfort filling her with fear for she had heard such horrid reports from those who had been to the tooth puller.

'You silly darling,' declared Edmund, at last able to express his hidden feelings. 'We shall send for Mr Spence directly, he will put all to right.'

'But once the tooth is gone does not the hole have to be plugged with gold? And I am quite unable to afford that,' moaned Miss Armstrong pitifully.

'I never heard of such a thing,' said Edmund, 'and if that were to be the case, which I doubt, we shall pay for it.'

It was proclaimed that under no circumstances was the young lady to leave her bed until the morrow. These comforting words had an immediate effect upon Belinda and she was persuaded to end her fast with warm beef tea taken with egg in a little sherry. As always in such emergencies, various well wishers suggested remedies for the relief of the toothache. These varied from drops of creosote to moist camphor applied with a hot stick. Wisely Miss Armstrong chose to relieve her suffering by sucking a clove, which was what had been suggested by Edmund Sedley in the first place.

Miss Armstrong's extended stay at Nuthall drew mixed responses within the theatre company. That it was due to toothache drew suspicion away from Dora Proctor, who in a reversal of her previous amiability, declared Belinda to be a calculating hussy who, in all likelihood, manufactured her stay with the Sedleys. Conversely, it did leave vacant the roles of Juliet and Miranda with only herself as a replacement should Belinda continued to be indisposed.

Dora was further astonished when Miss Armstrong returned to the theatre on the Monday afternoon in a carriage accompanied by an affable Edmund Sedley. He assured the Whitleys that the young lady was fully recovered, the tooth having been removed to allow the emergence of a wisdom tooth.

Of far greater importance, however, was the news that the Duke of Newcastle would shortly to be visiting Nottingham. One night was to be spent with the banker, Mr Abel Smith, at his house in the town and the next with the Sedleys at Nuthall. Almost as a second thought, as he was about to take his leave, Mr Sedley asked the Whitleys,

'Ah yes. My father wondered if the theatre might be opened on Friday. This would enable the Duke to bring a party during his stay with Mr Smith. Something light and cheerful would be in order. His grace has asked for no special arrangements to be made. He will be happy to see a customary evening's entertainment. Most likely there will be twenty guests.'

Had Mr Sedley announced the second coming, he could not have provoked more consternation. The Whitleys had long been hoping that the theatre would reopen, but not at such short notice. For to entertain a personage as distinguished as the Duke of Newcastle would normally have taken weeks of preparation and they had but four days.

'Can it be done?' asked Cassy rhetorically.

'It has to be,' said Jemmy. 'Nothing's ready, apart from *Romeo* and we can't play that as most of them will have seen it already. We must offer *The Author* for the first half instead. Not fully rehearsed but Lady Sedley said it was a piece she liked. In any case they probably won't arrive until the after piece so it does not matter what precedes it.'

'They might well come at seven. We can't be certain.'

'We'll give "*Acis and Galatea,*"' said Jemmy decisively. 'Full of good tunes. It ends happily, that is if the hero turning into a tree can be deemed as happy. Yes it shall be that, Call the musicians. Summon the singers. It's all hands on deck, *as fearfully as doth a galled rock o'er hang and jutty his confounded base.*' It made little sense, but seemed appropriate.

Few slept over the next four days as *The Author* with *Acis and Galatea* were rehearsed in a frenzy. For the latter local musicians were rounded up, a chorus hastily assembled.

Bills were printed and distributed widely in the hope that the nobility and gentry would hear of the great reopening. Once it was noticed - *'By particular desire of Sir Charles Sedley and in the presence of His Grace the Duke of Newcastle. . .'* the rush for tickets was immediate and Mr Parr at the White Bull was besieged by potential customers.

There was disagreement about where the distinguished guests should be seated. Jemmy insisted that the side stage boxes would be suitable. This was opposed by Cassy whose devotion to London news sheets made her an authority on these occasions.

'At the Lane and the Garden, dignitaries always sit in the boxes facing the stage,' she said.

'But the candle smoke is thick from that far back.'

'We must have wax candles.'

'But the expense. . . ' Jemmy was shocked.

'Husband, we have a duke coming to our theatre. It is not a time for penny pinching.'

Jemmy conceded. However, when the boxes were inspected their state was found to be wanting. There was no time for them to be painted, in any case the smell would linger. Here again Cassandra had ideas. 'They must be draped. That will conceal the want of colour. Let's find what curtains we have.'

Black velvet tabs were uncovered and immediately hung out in the yard to be beaten mercilessly. Whilst everyone else endlessly rehearsed and sang, Cassandra's industry was phenomenal. Volunteers were found to help her hang the black velvet (by nailing it to the walls). When this was found to be too sombre, Cassandra's next move was to consult Mrs Stirrup, the dressmaker. From her was obtained several lengths of bright coloured silk and satin, which when draped in swathes over the black looked very stylish. The addition of twisted silk ropes and tassels was an inspired finishing touch.

It was next decided that the present chairs looked dingy and would certainly not do for the notables. Cassandra hurried to the New Exchange where after explaining her plight to Mr Pennell she obtained the loan of chairs from the council chamber. A carrier was found and the chairs placed in position only hours before the party arrived. Vases of flowers were positioned in strategic places, leaving Cassandra pleased with her labours but close to exhaustion. She and her equally weary husband, had then to prepare themselves for the performance.

Their enterprise was well rewarded. Such a glittering night the theatre had not known before. A crowd of onlookers gathered in the street to cheer the arrivals. The pit and the gallery filled as soon as the doors opened. For once the 'fashionables' were seated in good time for everyone wanted to be there to see the entrance of the ducal party.

Only fifteen minutes after nine o'clock, the Duke of Newcastle and his guests arrived, to be welcomed on behalf of the management by Mr Pennell. Among the visitors was Mr Abel Smith, the banker and his wife, Sir Charles and Lady Sedley and their son Edmund with twenty other friends making up a most genteel and polite faction.

As they took their places in the auditorium the applause and cheers confirmed that the theatre had finally gained full social approval.

It was as well that the visitors were fashionably late for. *The Author* was under rehearsed and not a good start to the gala. However, the old war horse *Acis and Galatea* was given a fitting performance with which the Duke and his retinue expressed itself well pleased when they paid a short visit backstage. Congratulating everyone for their efforts, the duke himself described the evening as 'most commendable.'

A little after eleven o'clock carriages drew away from the narrow moonlit street as the audience departed into the night. An impromptu celebration was held onstage where thanks were given and toasts drunk to the prospect of success and recognition that must certainly lie ahead.

Next day, the decorations were removed and the furniture returned to the council chamber. The theatre returned to normality for the second evening performance. This was billed as *Romeo and Juliet,* with Miss Armstrong sufficiently recovered to play Juliet, to be followed by *The Author,* a little better it was hoped. As the afternoon rehearsal was nearing its end a letter came by hand from Sir Charles Sedley saying how greatly the duke and his friends had enjoyed their visit. So much so that they desired to come again that very night. They would be dining later than before which meant that they would only wish to see the first piece of the evening. Protocol was unnecessary for they would expect to enjoy a workaday performance and to be treated as ordinary theatregoers.

The Whitleys regarded each other. It was high praise of course, but what could they do? This time the theatre would be seen as it was in reality, far from clean and the auditorium thick with smoke, for all the wax candles had been used the night before. And the decoration of the main boxes was dismantled. After an anxious meeting it was decided that the special party would be best accommodated seated directly on the stage. The old custom of important visitors sitting alongside the actors although discouraged in London theatres was still practised in the provinces.

The programme could not be changed. *Romeo* had been clearly advertised as opening the first half. 'Perhaps they won't realise most of them will have seen that already,' said Jemmy.

'I'm not concerned about that,' said Cassy, 'It's when they arrive bothers me. They're sure to be late and we can't hold the curtain, Duke or no, the house wouldn't stand for it.'

With little time to hand, it was now gone six o'clock, the gallery was filling and the house expected the curtain up at seven. *Romeo* would have to begin on the hour.

'*Two houses, both alike in dignity . . .*' Whitley commenced with the famous lines. Almost at once there was a commotion in the audience. A murmur of excitement, all but drowned his words as the Duke of Newcastle with his guests appeared on the stage led by Cassandra already in costume. After a brief confusion the Duke and his party took their places on hurriedly provided chairs, carefully sitting at the sides not to spoil the sight lines of others. Once settled a round of applause broke out from the almost vacant boxes, although the Whitleys were shocked to hear several boos and hisses from the gallery. However, the Duke took all with good humour bowing politely to those applauding as he then settled to concentrate upon the play.

The tragedy (with its happy ending) was well received, the duke's party showing fully its appreciation. It was then found that, as they had said, the ducal visitors planned to leave after seeing only the Shakes-peare. This was highly unusual and a reversal of the normal custom.

After taking the curtain, the cast stood in line as the duke thanked them for their efforts. He explained that he had been told about the charms of the remarkable young actress playing Juliet and he had desired to see her for himself; so it was that Miss Armstrong was brought forward to be presented to the duke personally. Fortunately she was left speechless by the honour, for who knows what she might have said? The duke looked at her closely, smiled, and shook her hand.

'Most commendable,' he was heard to say as he and his guests made their withdrawal from the theatre.

*

Part Four.

Twenty. *Dance ti thy Daddy.*

Thomas did not wake to find himself famous but he did wake to find that among the theatregoers of York he was being talked about. People were examining playbills to find when next the *Dream* was to be performed and such was the call to see the new young comedian that Tate Wilkinson was obliged to amend his programme. He had planned to have the *Dream* as an afterpiece for three nights only. These were sold out as soon as announced, leaving him to recall that there was nothing that stimulated the sale of tickets so much as the rumour that none were to be had. Tickets for an additional three nights were bought within hours, indicating that it could have been a regular part of the repertoire for weeks ahead.

At first, Thomas found as he walked in town one or two people looked at him, sometimes smiling as if they were unsure whether they knew him or not. This quickly turned to individuals nudging each other saying, ‘There’s Puck,’ as they spotted him. Within a fortnight it happened regularly that passers by stopped him to say, ‘We liked you, Puck.’ ‘Very good.’

Complete strangers gave friendly waves. It was intoxicating. Before long he was greeted with, ‘We saw you last night Puck, it was well done.’

Tate gave an increase in salary to match his new status, at the same time warning him of the dangers that could lie ahead. ‘Enjoy it,’ he said, ‘but remember it’s fairy gold, it can disappear as quickly as it comes. And see that your hat size gets no bigger.’

Almost everyone in the company welcomed his success, knowing that it would benefit them all. Overnight, Thomas was admitted to the green room; the previous awe this honour had held, fast fading with familiarity. Mr Holland had added his congratulations. Following the clumsy revelation of his infatuation the old actor had kept a distance but Thomas was grateful for his help when he had been near to disaster.

That kindly act deserved his thanks, bringing a reconciliation between the two. Fanny M'George told everyone that obviously she had known all along that Thomas would become a name. She had been one of the first to be captivated by his charms, charms that audiences were eagerly prepared to pay money to enjoy. From the second night onwards a shout of recognition greeted his appearance on stage, an approbation he was soon to take for granted and quickly expect.

Yet the brighter the sun, the darker the shadow and inevitably this achievement gave rise to envy. Some said between themselves that he might just be a one part success. The acrobatics were all well and fine, but what would he be like in part where real acting skills were called for? This telling criticism was soon to be manifest when rehearsals started for *The Mistake* in which Thomas found himself up against Mr Cobb, an actor with a lifetime's experience on the stage.

Mr Cobb was polite but detached at their first meeting.

'Personally trust you know your lines?' he asked in a voice like a bored barn owl. Thomas had been warned of this air of superiority and replied,

'Yes, Mr Cobb.' Another member of cast whispered, 'You don't call him Mister, you call him "Sir." '

'In your case,' continued Mr Cobb, 'your memory will not have been over taxed. A mere cameo one might call it? Mmmm?'

'Yes . . . sir,' Thomas felt he was being appraised and so restrained himself, for it was true his was only a minor role. Moreover *The Mistake* was indeed a minor play and Thomas's role one of several that supported the central character Sir Swiftly Rich, a traditional comic squire which the veteran actor took as if by divine right.

Wisely, Tate Wilkinson left Mr Cobb to deal with his own production, being grateful that at least one play did not require his supervision. When it was said that Mr Cobb directed his own plays, it might be more accurate to say Mr Cobb sometimes attended rehearsals; when he did he gave no direction, leaving the cast to orbit around him like minor satellites circling a planet.

'Personally never move from centre stage,' he told them, 'You must find whatever positions best suit yourselves. Mmm?'

Thomas soon found that it was left to everyone to remember what they had done in rehearsal, for they would get no help from Mr Cobb. At one point Thomas asked if his move was correct, only to be told, 'Personally cannot recall. Not my concern. Mmm?'

Enthusiasm for his Puck continued, yet one who had said nothing about his performance was Lucy. It was the Treadgold's practice to perform their dances immediately before the *Dream*. This done, the four members of the family left the theatre promptly, showing no interest in what followed. One night Thomas saw Lucy hesitate as if she might stay and watch him. As he approached to speak she caught his glance, disappearing immediately. The next night, when he was not called, he stood in the wings to view the Treadgold's' turn. As the four dancers left the stage he was able to delay Lucy as she tried to hurry past.

'Lucy don't go. It's so long since we spoke together,' he said taking her arm carefully so she was not alarmed. Her skin was moist from the exertion of dancing. She looked at his hand holding hers, her head lowered so that he was staring down on her bare neck beneath the pinned up blonde hair. Several strands waved from side to side as she tried to remove his grasp. When he saw this was her wish, he let go his grip so that she moved slightly away.

'What do you want?' she asked

'To speak to you. To ask why you avoid me.'

'You want my praise more like. "How good you are," that's what you want me to say is it not?'

'Only if you think so.'

At this, she raised her head and looked into his eyes.

'You're very good, but you know that already don't you?'

'Are you laughing at me?' His question seemed paltry for he knew she was right, he was seeking her praise; it mattered to him that she more than anyone recognised his success. Realising this, he despised himself for his fatuous need of her approval.

Their brief exchange was ended by her brother calling, 'Lucy, we are waiting.' She turned to join Walter who abruptly propelled her away, leaving Thomas feeling disquiet and he knew not why.

Two nights later came the opening of *The Mistake* and with it, once more, his foreboding. In spite of nights of applause, there was his smouldering fear that the acclaim could easily turn to rejection. Tate had talked of 'fairy gold.' He knew this also applied to reputation. Going on stage was thrilling when shouts and calls came from the gallery with easy readiness.

Until now the shouts were friendly, even encouraging, but each call broke his concentration, causing him to wonder how it would be if they became hostile. Perhaps the whispers were true, he was only a one part player and it was now as Blinks in *The Mistake* he would be found wanting. Blinks was a small part, a friend to the hero, one of the plotters in the story to get the better of Sir Swiftly Rich. He would hardly be noticed, why then as the evening approached were his nerves heightened? Here again was the call for means of support, the need for a drink; after that the fears decreased - a little.

The Mistake began. Mr Cobb made his entrance five minutes within the play. He was a favourite with polite audiences, which was shown by gentle clapping from gloved hands in the boxes - the patter of gentility. Thomas came on stage with two others in the cast. As soon as the gallery spotted him a shout of approval was given which briefly stopped the play.

Mr Cobb concealed his annoyance his style being suited to the better seats and not to the gallery. Up there, they were getting fitful that Thomas was hardly in evidence. After some ten minutes of quietly watching the genteel comedy without him, someone in the gods shouted, 'Where's Puck?' The call was good natured but there was an edge to it that threatened.

Further calls for Puck caused the players to stumble. It was common enough to have comments from the gods, even on some nights missiles were thrown to show disapproval and it looked as if *The Mistake* was indeed becoming a truism. When Thomas was not on stage, signs of impatience in the gallery increased. A chant for Puck began with the paradox that although he was wanted, it was as if the call was for his blood. Mr Cobb continued with his part, ignoring the noise until after some time Thomas and the other characters re-entered. There was a shout of approval making it clear that the gallery wanted to see Puck with his acrobatics and not Mr Cobb. Judiciously, Thomas stayed in character as Blink, until the end of the play which was received with a barrage of complaints and grumbling. The gallery had not got what it wanted.

The curtain fell, rising again for the cast to take their call; Mr Cobb centre stage, Thomas modestly at the end of the line trying not to draw attention to himself. When the gallery continued shouting for Puck he smiled, until he found it impossible not to resist the calls and stepping forward he bowed modestly. On hearing the cheer that followed he impetuously bowed again, then encouraged by the applause he turned a cartwheel which ended with him standing directly in front of Mr Cobb. The house liked this. Mr Cobb did not.

At once, the enraged actor complained to Tate Wilkinson about Thomas's behaviour, demanding his immediate dismissal. It being a first night Tate had seen the performance and shared Mr Cobb's disapproval of the incident for he was angered by what had happened to the old actor.

Rather than admonish him in front of the cast, Tate ordered Thomas to come to his room.

'You know as well as I do,' he said, 'that you have a talent. You also have the gift of gaining the public's approval which is rare, but you lack discipline which is the first quality I demand from my comedians.'

Knowing this was true Thomas was unable to reply. He wondered what was coming. By now he reckoned he was an asset to the company so a sacking was unlikely. A fine perhaps, a rebuke for certain, but he was puzzled by his situation. Here he was, popular with audiences yet this popularity was the cause of his reprimand.

'What excuse do you have for turning a somersault and then masking Mr Cobb's curtain call?'

'The audience seemed to want it.'

'Who are you to decide what the audience wants? You are a very new and minor member of my company. I give the instructions, including who takes bows and when. You have insulted an old member of the profession; that is unforgivable.'

'I didn't realise I'd got in front of him.'

'You will express your regrets to Mr Cobb in person. Do that before he leaves the theatre tonight. And you will get no payment for this evening. Bad manners are not rewarded in my company.'

'But what shall I do if the audience wants me?'

'You will stay in character, that's what you will do. Any more crass behaviour and your future here will be under question. *The Mistake* has been billed for the next two weeks and will remain in the repertoire. You will enjoy the discipline of playing a straight role. By so doing, you might even grow up a little.'

'Personally find your behaviour insupportable,' said Mr Cobb when Thomas apologised, offering his regrets in the presence of his colleagues for the criticism had come from others as well as the old actor. His contrition was thought by everyone to be sincere, with the belief that he had learned his lesson and should now be forgiven. Not so Mr Cobb. The next night as the company assembled he continued to display his outrage to anyone who would listen.

'Disgraceful behaviour,' he complained. 'Totally unprofessional. In my day he would have been dismissed on the spot.'

Mrs M'George overhearing the remark, made herself plain, 'Oh for God's sake let it rest. It's a young man's mistake. Weren't you ever young yourself?

'Not him,' came an anonymous voice from behind a newsheet.

At the next playing of *The Mistake* the audience was less boisterous. Perhaps word had spread amidst the patrons in the gallery that they were not to get Puck. The play received one or two shouts of disapproval and generally was acknowledged coldly, with Thomas playing his role modestly and taking his curtain call unobtrusively at the end of the line.

Before long the season settled down to a normal run. *The Dream* being by far the most liked, it was consequently revived regularly to the satisfaction of both the company and the public. Soon they would be on tour for the summer with new offerings. For this Tate Wilkinson relied upon sensible advice from his wife, Jane. Naturally, *The Dream* would be a big attraction, word of its success having spread widely but the problem still remained: what else could Thomas do to show off his unique qualities? Tate had considered *The Tempest* with Thomas as Ariel, but Thomas, by now aware of his sway, had said he didn't want to play bloody fairies for the rest of his life. When it was pointed out that Ariel was not a bloody fairy but an imprisoned spirit seeking freedom, this did nothing to dispel his attitude, leaving Tate agreeing that it might be thought repetitious.

Thomas was by now popular with the company (Mr Cobb excepted) and did his share of the additional work demanded. The cleaning of the entire building was done weekly, the men dealing with the stage and auditorium and the women, the green room and the dressing rooms. All were expected to do this and there were strong complaints that the Treadgold family took no part in the practice, coming only to perform and then leaving without any offer of help.

Until it was noticed that one night Mr and Mrs Treadgold had appeared to dance on their own. Nothing was said but when after two nights their son and daughter were again absent, questions were asked. 'Walter and Lucy, are both disposed,' declared Mrs Treadgold. 'Quite unable to dance, as they are confirmed to their beds.'

This was believed and it was hoped that Mr and Mrs Treadgold would not also be affected by the ailment whatever it was. On the third night Lucy came with her parents looking far from well, but able to dance her solo.

She passed Thomas as he waited to make his entrance, still disregarding him. From the pallor of her skin and the sadness in her eyes he was convinced that she was not ill, but troubled. For an instant she seemed about to speak to him, but her parents called brusquely, 'Come child,' and she followed them without question.

'It's not your concern,' Fanny M'George said. 'They've always kept themselves apart. Like to think they're superior, "danseuses" you know, not rag tag and bob tails like the rest of us.'

But Thomas found this hard to uphold. He remembered the kindness and sweetness of Lucy that first day at the dancing school. He believed that Walter and her parents were preventing her from making contact and now he was convinced that there were other factors causing her unhappiness.

He knew it was out of the question to call at the dancing school, so how else to find if she was in need of help? He went to the Gun and Partridge in the possibility that Walter might be there, but he was not to be found, leaving Thomas to decide that he had probably carried out his threat to abscond. Yes, that must be the answer. The next night he took his place in the wings as the Treadgold's left the stage. After their bows, he stood in Lucy's path so that she had to stop.

'That was very well done.' he said, managing to pass a note into her palm in the moment before she moved away. He feared she would not take it, or drop it, but he saw that she had held it firmly in her grasp. In the message, he gave his address in Stonegate, saying *'If you need help, come to me here.'*

For the following two nights they glimpsed each other off stage, but there was no contact and she passed by quickly with her parents staring ahead as if he was not there. He had decided that she had chosen to ignore him, until three nights later she stumbled and as she regained herself, dropped a ball of paper at his feet. It was done with skill and the Treadgold's, he was sure, did not see what had happened. As soon as possible he unrolled it, finding the sphere made up of crumpled newsprint, until in the core he found a message on a tiny scrap of paper.

'I will be at the west door of the Minster at three this morning.'

The sense of mystery attracted him. Was she truly in distress? Or was it some sort of folly, an enticement he did not understand?

He had to meet her, of that he was certain. Yet it was not easy to know when the hour of three would be reached for he had no clock and would have to listen to the chiming of the hours. By one o'clock he fell asleep in his room, but the urgency of purpose prevented his falling into too deep a slumber.

He had been dozing until with a sharp recoil he was wide awake. Looking out of the attic window gave no indication of the time. Angry with himself at his carelessness he thought of Lucy perhaps already waiting. The back door to Mrs Abbott's house had no lock, relying for security on a wooden latch, which he lifted and left hanging, pulling the door shut behind him. A clock chimed, an unidentified quarter. There was no moon, but the walk to the Minster was achieved up to High

Petergate and thence to the west end. No clocks on the way gave the hour for it was deep night and he might not be too late. He reached the west end. It was deserted. In the distance he heard the watchman, 'Three o'clock of a fine night. . . .' the rest of his call was lost in the great chiming of the Minster.

It was the appointed time. The mighty towers rose above him, their fair stone keen against the night sky, stars so tightly clustered they formed a filigree of light. The cold was cutting and he was angry that in his haste he had come with no coat. He waited in the forecourt, alone but for the silent loping of a cat.

Soon it was a quarter past three. He resolved to wait until half past the hour after that he would return to his lodgings. Time passed. He beat his arms to keep warm, he looked at the sky and wished he knew more about stars to be able to identify them. Without warning, he saw a figure running silently across the close from the north. For one fearful moment he thought it was Mrs Treadgold when he recognised the black and silver cloak, but rapidly he saw it was Lucy her fair hair streaming behind as she ran to him.

'I didn't think you'd be here,' she said, trying to regain her breath, taking his hands in hers.

'Of course I am,' said Thomas. By now he was totally familiarised with the dark which enabled him to see her face closely, as if for the the first time. Yet what colour were her eyes? Still he could not tell. Tiny pinheads of sweat clung on her forehead below the hair line. Until now her hair had been restricted by pins and nets, but here in her haste she had left it free and he saw how plenteous it was, falling in fair curves over her eyes just like her brother. She swept it back and pulled up a hood to help keep it in place.

'Why did you come?' she asked.

'A strange question. I came because you asked,' said Thomas.'

'I can only see you at night. All day they keep me occupied. Teaching at school, dancing at the theatre. No chance to escape.'

'They don't know you're here?'

She laughed but with no humour. 'What do you think?'

'Will there be trouble if they found out?'

'Especially now that Walter's gone, you know that don't you?'

'I thought as much.'

'He wanted me to go with him, but I have no means. He can probably find work, but there is nothing I can do. I had to stay.'

She seemed about to cry. Thomas wanted to comfort her, but it was not easy, wrapped as she was in the voluminous velvet. Comically he could not get his arms fully around her, instead he tried stroking her hair under the hood with his left hand. She gently took it away.

'Your poor hand,' she asked for the first time. 'What happened?'

'Time enough for that. You want to leave them, don't you?'

She nodded, 'Yes.'

'Why?'

'I can't tell you. But things have worsened now Walter's gone.'

'Did he - look after you?'

'Sometimes. You see he always said we should leave when we were eighteen. "Once we're eighteen," he'd say, "we can be independent." But that's under the old law. Now we have to be twenty one. And that seems so far away. . . when you're seventeen.'

'You can be independent at any age.'

'If you're a man. And I'm not brave enough to be on my own. I earn nothing, just my keep. I'm only trained to dance, nothing more. A woman alone can only do one thing . . .' The warmth she had generated was diminishing. 'I must get back. If they find out. . .'

'But I must know more. I want to help,' said Thomas.

'Perhaps we could meet in there,' she pointed to the Minster. 'I could say I was attending service on Sunday morning. It wouldn't be entirely untrue. It's so vast, we could find somewhere to talk.'

'You mean next Sunday?'

'Yes. at the back of the nave. Matins is at eleven I think. I'll do my best to be with you. If not, say a prayer for me.' She gave a fragile smile. 'You're kind to come. Leaving your bed.'

She gave him a fleeting kiss on the cheek, immediately running from sight into the dark as the Minster clock struck the next quarter. . . .

*

'It's unlikely we can find a play for him, not with his peculiar talents ,' said Tate Wilkinson to his wife. 'Could you write one?'

'Not in time for this season,' said Jane, 'but the choice is obvious.'

'I wonder? Is it the one I have in mind myself?'

They both spoke the name together, 'Harlequin!' then laughed.

'When did you think of it?' asked Tate.

'Ever since I saw him as Puck that first night,' replied Jane.

'So did I. But why have you said nothing?'

'I know how much you dislike pantomime.'

'Not if it brings custom . . .'

'And it would with Tom as Harlequin.'

'I believe it would,' Tate paused. 'But have we got a Pantaloon? A Scaramouche? Most important, have we got a Columbine?'

'It's so obvious - Lucy Treadgold.'

'They won't let her do it,' said Tate. 'They need her in their act, and to teach at the school. Now more than ever since Walter ran off.'

For a moment they considered the prospect.

'That apart, what manner of Harlequin should it be?' asked Tate.

"Harlequin Sailor," Jane answered immediately. 'The Navy's always popular. We might partner him with Black Eyed Susan.'

'Have you begun it?' asked Tate.

'Not yet, but already I can see the finale. The quarter deck of a man o' war. Flags across the stage, with the entire company singing "Hearts of Oak." Garrick used it in his "Harlequin's Invasion." If not that, "Rule Britannia," that might be even better.'

'My dear,' said Tate, 'you are a genius.' He kissed her heartily. 'Get it written as soon as you can.'

'Lucy a comedian? Out of the question,' said Mrs Treadgold. 'She is a dancer, a trained artiste. The idea is an insult.'

Tate had expected such opposition. 'Madam,' he said 'surely you will not stand in the way of your daughter's career. Until now she is displaying only half her talents. Her sweet singing voice should be revealed for all to hear and admire.'

'The singing of vulgar songs is not for my daughter.'

'But now that your son has left. . . .' said Tate.

At this remark Mrs Treadgold's glare took on a Medusa like intensity. 'Yes. . .?' she asked.

'Lucy should not be restricted to dancing solo. As Columbine she could be in a new model partnership. . .'

'Whom with?' demanded Mrs Treadgold.

'With Harlequin. . .'

'Played by a tumbler, an acrobat, fit only for a circus? I am astonished at your resumption.'

Throughout the exchange, Lucy had been moving away, unwilling to be involved. Mr Treadgold had stood silently by his wife.

'But you sir,' Tate asked,'what are your thoughts?'

'Ummm. . .' Mr Treadgold began.

'My husband and I are in complete accord. Our unity is magnanimous. Good night Mr Wilkinson.'

Thomas had rarely been in a church before and never in a cathedral or minster. The immensity of the nave astonished him. He had walked around the outside of the building many times staring up at the towers and buttresses, unthinkingly accepting them as a natural phenomenon such as a high cliff or the edge of a forest. But inside! Once through the west door, he was confounded by the sense of height which seemed far greater than the exterior. The arches, flanking the huge empty space, were like a tide of frozen waves rolling towards a shore. Opposing this, the stone screen with its alcoved figures looked to him like an unyielding breakwater, a barrier that excluded him from the altar, the holy core of the place. He had no idea what happened beyond this point, yet its power filled him with an awe as great as that of any medieval mind before him.

In the overall silence were many smaller sounds, clicks and bangs that grew strangely in volume as they echoed. Footsteps, whispers, but other noises impossible to identify, perhaps sighs and groans as if the minster itself shuddered and breathed on its foundations.

A verger or warden, he had no idea which, came to him and said in a hushed voice. 'The service of Matins begins at eleven. There are places in both transepts.' He might have said there were thrones in the kingdom of heaven for all it meant to him. The threat of the Minster increased. God was in here for certain, watching and judging him. He could not stay and so retraced his steps back to the great west door.

Through it came a group of people, prayer books in hand, gravely entering the house of worship. Lucy was not with them. As eleven o'clock approached, a deep tolling of bells in the tower called the faithful to devotion. The authority of sound increased his sense of exclusion, he was a trespasser foreign to the rituals about to begin.

He stood in isolation at the back of the empty nave. The bells ceased, within the resultant quiet a distant high-toned voice proclaimed,

'When the wicked man turneth away from his wickedness . . .'

He left to stand outside. Lucy was nowhere to be seen.

She was waiting in Stonegate, not far from his lodgings. They saw each other from a distance but whereas he felt a jolt of recognition, she looked at him with no emotion, allowing him to walk up to her whilst remaining still.

'I've been to the Minster,' he said. She made no reply. 'You said you would be there,' he added.

'Yes, I did.' Looking around she gave the feeling of disquiet. She asked, 'Can we go somewhere?'

'My lodgings are close by. It's an attic with a steep climb.'

'That will do.'

Thomas opened the door to the house. Leading the way, he slowly climbed the stairs. Reaching the ladder he turned back offering his hand as she ascended. Both were weary by the time they reached his room.

Apologetically he said, 'I'm sorry it's not better.'

Her eyes looked around. The small space was dominated by the dormer window, the only point where it was possible to stand upright. It had no curtains and was wide open. There was a three legged chair and where the ceiling was at it lowest, a mattress on the bare plaster floor with bedding of sorts. On a shelf were several bottles and a few books which were most likely plays. From a row of pegs hung items of clothing; the remaining sum of his possessions, such as they were, lay strewn on the floor. Overall there was the familiar smell of poverty - and of him.

'At least it's yours,' she said, 'and safe.'

He offered her the wooden chair. Without knowing what was to come, he sat below her on the mattress. This gave her a dominant position above him which she seemed not to like.

'You're my first guest.' His remark seemed idiotic. She looked downwards, staring at her lap. At a loss he said, 'You got away then?'

She nodded, but in doing so slumped forth from the chair into a parody of kneeling to pray, until huddled on the floor she wept incautiously. He tried comforting her, pushing the chair away violently to make space to hold her, both of them ambushed by her anguish. As he gripped her, he felt for the first time the shape of her body, realising how slender she was.

Eventually she stopped, her passion gone, now she was shamed by her behaviour. He put the chair back on its legs, seating her on it.

'I have some brandy,' he said, 'no glass, just a cup if you'd like that.' She shook her head. He found the silence between them worse than her distress. Until now, they had hardly spoken together, their meetings scant of words. As she slowly recovered her calm, he asked,

'How can I help?'

Lucy said. 'Things once said, cannot be unsaid. They cannot be retrieved, they are known for ever. Do you understand?'

'I think so.' He paused. 'That sounds as if you can't trust me.'

She turned sharply. 'I do trust you, but it's too much to ask.
I must deal with things alone, as I have always done.'

They were close together. No words could convey his feelings. Kneeling, he embraced her, silently hoping she understood, that in no other way could he show his love and concern for her apart from kissing her as he did, on her lips.

For a moment she offered no response, until her arms rising above him, stretched in a wave of confusion. Then her hands were on his chest, furiously pushing him away, her head turned aside escaping his mouth, everything in her movements repelling him. He tried containing her, but she struggled, determined to be free. They moved apart, observing each other. He, with no understanding as her mood turned to anger.

'You see, you see. I cannot believe you. You are no different.'

'Whatever you think, that's not so,' he said. 'I love you, that is why it is different.' Again he tried to hold her until she prevented him, appearing to gain a new strength, the kind of composure she showed when she danced on the stage.

'You shall know then,' she said. 'About my apprenticeship and the master I serve and what it is you think you love.'

With a certainty she had not shown before, she was now become the performer, with a reckless scorn in her voice she said,

'I dance to my Daddy. That sounds charming doesn't it? *Dance ti thy Daddy*. At bedtime. Instead of a story. After supper. I am the sweetmeat that ends the evening meal. The morsel, the treat. . .

My mother? Oh no, she has no part of it. Like as not she's fast asleep at the supper table. Laudanum and brandy - very potent. Walter? He's never there, always out drinking that is until he left us. Before that he was packed off to bed first, the door locked 'cos he's a bad boy. Just Daddy and me. Lots of games. *Hunt the night-dress*. Why can't it be found? Daddy's hidden it. Where's Daddy's night-shirt? Why can't that be found? Such fun. So many different games. *Playing the flute,* do you know that one? That's his favourite. Daddy says I'm so good at it. A born flautist.'

She laughed at him. 'Now it's done. "Things once said cannot be unsaid." You've made a wrong choice Thomas. Sad to say you have chosen to love a little jade, a slut. Does that shock you? Yes, that's what I am . A little whore who dances to her Daddy.'

*

Twenty One. *The Riot Act.*

Two consecutive visits by the Duke of Newcastle established the social standing of the Nottingham theatre. If it met with favour from the duke, one of the most powerful men in the kingdom, even Alderman Fairlight could not challenge such privileged approbation. Audiences flocked in his stead and the Whitleys felt securely established as theatrical promoters. The season was extended. Other towns in the circuit, who were impatient to see the newly established company, would have to wait their turn.

Every night tragedies, farces, and pastorals delighted all parts of the house. The pit offered strong criticism, its vocal approval or dislike given freely. From the gallery came shouts and calls, adverse opinions manifested by the hurling of abuse and missiles. Midway, in the boxes, sat the fashionables; studying each other as if before a looking glass with only casual attention to the stage. In the corridors outside the boxes, maidservants and footmen drank, played dice and flirted whilst their betters were entertained. For those attending, this was thought to be part of an ordinary night out but for the fierce opponents of the theatre it remained a sink of corruption, a pestilence they waited patiently to stamp out.

Jemmy Whitley worked harder than ever, much to Cassandra's disquiet. Encouraged by full houses and acclaim he continued to play many of the leads himself, Prospero, Falstaff, and Macheath. Brook Powell simmered with resentment for Whitley allowed him only minor roles, usually young lovers which Jemmy reluctantly admitted were no longer in his compass. With the support of Marmaduke Pennell, Whitley was also planning to build an entirely new theatre in Derby as an addition to the circuit of his successful empire.

Spare time was rare. After performances, most in the company went straight to their beds, others spent time in the alehouse before retiring. Brook Powell was always to be found in the tavern, drinking or at cards where he sometimes won and more often lost. Never knowing when to retire he was soon owing large amounts that he was unable to honour, turning next to the cock pit in the hope that good fortune would salvage his liabilities. This was not to be and Mr Powell found himself swiftly falling into debt with imprisonment an ever present possibility if repayment was unmade.

Belinda Armstrong fared better. Her admirer, Edmund Sedley, was to be seen most nights in a box as close to the stage as decency would allow. He followed her appearances diligently and one time, when he found that she was not playing on the Monday, suggested she might enjoy a stay at Nuthall Temple from the Saturday night to the Tuesday morning. He believed she would find this a pleasing diversion as an Italian painter, Giuseppe Ceraccio, was in residence at the house decorating the ceilings of the reception rooms.

Edmund had seen and admired Signor Ceraccio's work whilst on an Italian visit and had persuaded his parents that his was the genius they sought to adorn the bare ceilings at their new house. With designs submitted, covering subjects from the *Judgement of Paris* to *Susanna at her Bath* (after Tintoretto), the Sedleys agreed to commission him in the hope that their new painted ceilings would be the envy of the county, perhaps even the entire Midlands.

Edmund Sedley advised Belinda not to make known her staying with him for fear, he said, of arousing envy in others such as Dora Proctor. With this, Belinda fully co-operated enjoying the secrecy and excitement of finding a private carriage awaiting her at a discreet distance from the theatre. After the Saturday night performance, accompanied by Edmund, she found herself racing through the night with a delicious sense of adventure. Thoughtfully, he had provided wine and ratafia cakes for the journey and they laughed together as they recalled her previous visit to the Temple when she had fainted by reason of the toothache.

'I trust you have no such discomfort tonight?' he asked.

'Oh no,' she told him, 'the puller removed the tooth so skilfully that the pain has quite gone.'

'Have you kept the miscreant ivory?' asked Edmund, 'for if you have I would love to have it as a part of you that can be mine for ever.'

Belinda found this a foolish idea. 'D'you mean my tooth? I don't know what happened to it,' she said, 'perhaps the puller kept it.'

'I must make enquiries,' said Edmund, kissing her at the moment when the carriage lurched over a hole in the road causing Belinda to spill wine onto his waistcoat. 'What a careless wench I am,' she said. But Edmund insisted that it mattered not a hang, even though the wine was red and his waistcoat white embroidered silk.

They arrived at the Temple, avoiding the front entrance, driving instead to a modest door at the rear. No footmen or butler greeted them, Edmund guided Miss Armstrong through a confusing series of corridors and chambers into one of the smaller reception rooms. Here there was a light supper laid in readiness and once Belinda's cloak was removed Edmund opened a new bottle of wine, this time one that sparkled with vivacity.

'I trust you will not object to a cold table,' said Edmund. 'It is more fun to serve ourselves that to be interrupted by the servants.'

'Are not you father and mother joining us?' asked Belinda.

'Oh, did I not tell you? They are in town,' he replied. 'My father is often required in the House, divisions you know, so much so that my mother stays with him whenever she can. Otherwise she says she will become a parliamentary widow. Your health, my dear.'

Combined with light enjoyable conversation, the supper proved agreeable until Belinda declared herself to be more than a little weary.

'Of course,' said Edmund. 'Let me show you to your room. This time we have put you in the blue chamber. We thought the Chinese room might bring back unsettling memories.'

Belinda was touched by such mindful consideration.

'I shall leave you now,' said Edmund. 'Pray do not rise early, for 'tis Sunday tomorrow. That is unless you wish to attend divine service.' Belinda replied that it was not her custom, so that after the exchange of wishes for a good night's rest she was left to delight in the luxury of Egyptian cotton sheets, pillows stuffed with swan feathers scented by camomile and lavender.

Sunday morning, being bright and warm, she was woken by Edmund, who after knocking at her door came into her room attired in a long crimson and gold braided dressing gown with his feet in exotic Turkish slippers.

'Here is some hot chocolate for you,' he said handing her a cup and saucer. 'When you are ready we will have some breakfast then we shall watch Signor Ceraccio at work.'

'First I must get dressed and comb my hair.'

'It is not the fashion to dress early. Regard myself,' he said. Crossing to a wardrobe he took out a light garment and laid it on the bed. 'Put this on, you will be quite at ease, for it is a mild morning.'

'What is it?' she asked.

'A *peignoir,* worn in the mornings by ladies of fashion. You'll find satin slippers in the wardrobe. When you're ready, come to my dressing room to break your fast, then we'll inspect the painting.'

Belinda was disappointed to find that breakfast amounted to finishing off the remaining cold chicken and ham from the previous night. To this was added another bottle of sparkling wine, something she had never taken before at so early an hour. Still in their night apparel they walked down to a large salon filled with scaffolding and ladders, revealing the painter, Signor Ceraccio, at work on the ceiling above.

'Buon giorno signor,' called Edmund.

A cry of recognition came from regions overhead and directly the great painter descended. He was a small man of indeterminate age, his long unruly hair turning grey. He wore a smock colourfully flecked with paint, with a bundle of brushes in one hand, the fingers noticeably affected by arthritis.

'This is Signor Ceraccio,' said Edmund.

The signor in his own tongue asked forgiveness for being so unkempt as he kissed Belinda's hand. Unable to understand him, she merely smiled.

'This is to be the "Psyche" room,' said Edmund. 'My father is very fond of the legend of Cupid and Psyche which will be depicted on the ceiling. You know the legend of course?'

Belinda shook her head. 'I must recount it - later.' Turning to the painter, Edmund asked, 'Hai fatto dipingere la tua Psyche?' explaining to Belinda, 'I have asked if he has a model for his Psyche.'

Cleaning his bespattered spectacles, the painter shook his head, lamenting how hard it was to devise beauty without a true subject to inspire him. He had tried the services of several servant girls in the house, but with no success.

''Questa e la vostra "Psyche," ' said Edmund, indicating that Belinda was the answer. Ceraccio's face turned to a smile as he looked afresh at Belinda through newly cleared glasses, before rushing into a excess of Italian which neither could grasp, but which seemed to express his approval.

'Vorresti far degli semizzi?' asked Edmund, 'Si, Si,' was the reply.

'He wishes to make some sketches,' said Edmund. 'I suggest we go back to my dressing room, it is far more comfortable. The painter picked up his sketching materials as the three returned upstairs.

'You have often posed I imagine?' asked Edmund. Belinda said that no she had not, this new situation puzzling her. She had understood rather hazily that she might see a painter at work, now she discovered that she was to be the focus of his inspiration. She appeared to have little choice.

'You are quite perfect for it. Now Signor what would you like?'

Ceraccio carefully led Belinda to a chaise-longue, indicating that she reclined upon it. He studied her carefully, squinting and evaluating her person as his Psyche began to take form before his eyes.

'Is this correct for you?' Edmund asked. The painter faltered briefly, then said, 'Se la signorina. . . ' His hand waved airily.

'Of course,' said Edmund, as with nonchalance he continued, 'now if you could remove the peignoir my dear.'

'What?' asked Belinda.

'Take off the gown dear. As you must know a model is unclad,'

'Not likely,' Belinda drew the flimsy garb more closely to herself, 'what d'you take me for - a wheedle?'

'No of course not. We take you to be a might pretty creature.'

'I'm not getting undressed.' Belinda stood up, this was not what she had bargained for, as with decorum intact she made for the door.

'Come, come madam, don't be so provincial. Here is an opportunity to further your career. Why all the famous actresses have posed. Recall Mistress Gwynn no less. It is a guarantee of immortality. You will be admired for years to come, long after your looks have left.' He offered a further glass of wine, which she took cautiously.

'I never said I was no model,' she said without conviction.

'Don't be a torment,' said Edmund. 'Why else do you think I have invited you here? This could be very much to your advantage.'

'If he paints my likeness, shall I be up there on the ceiling?'

'Yes, a goddess above us all. A vision for centuries hereafter. Think what a tease it could be. Who posed as the legendary Psyche?'

'Well, perhaps. If it's kept a secret. . .'

'Now you're being sensible,' he said taking her empty glass, as she modestly removed her covering.

'Not for long, mind you. I don't want to catch me death. . .'

'Of course not. You are a very wise young woman.'

'What do I do now?'

Signor Ceraccio positioned her on the chaise-longue. Both he and Edmund looked with admiration at the beauty of her nakedness. Her skin had the sweetness of a fresh cut apple, heartbreaking in the knowledge it must soon spoil. Onto this whiteness her black hair fell in lovely disorder. In return, Belinda observed the two onlookers' admiration, beginning to enjoy their high regard.

'You are exquisite my dear,' said Edmund, bending over to kiss her on each breast. 'Exquisite.' Belinda thought it best to keep still - for the moment. Matters were perhaps moving to her advantage.

'Signor?' Edmund turned to the painter, who in a dispassionate manner settled Belinda into an attitude which he began sketching. For almost half an hour Ceraccio worked on the young lady setting her in different poses, which he rapidly transposed into pastel images. He found her a good model for when placed in a position she remained still without wavering. Edmund watched intently from over the artist's shoulder at the resulting work.

In time Belinda grew tired. 'I'm beginning to get cold,' she said. Edmund poured her a fresh glass of wine.

'You are superb my dear and deserve a reward.'

'Have we done?' she asked as the two men examined the

sketches, revealing them to her with enthusiasm.

'Is that what I look like?' she asked curiously, having not seen her likeness before. 'You are far lovelier,' said Edmund. 'Perhaps when the signor does the final art work your true beauty will be captured.'

'Can I get dressed now?' she asked.

Edmund looked at Ceraccio. The painter returned his glance, then with knowing discretion withdrew. The click of the door as it closed acted almost as a signal to the young man who moved eagerly towards Belinda. So eagerly that the belt on his dressing gown became untied and failed in its purpose of concealing his person.

'Well,' he said, 'I hope that was a pleasurable experience.'

'At least no lines to learn,' she giggled, stretching as she rose from the chaise-longue

'The signor may well ask you to return to make further studies.'

'Pray, where is my peign. . . whatever you call it?' She asked casually, observing that under his dressing gown he wore nothing, not even drawers

'Of course.' Edmund picked up the flimsy garment. As he was about to help her into it he hesitated. 'Of course,' he repeated thoughtfully to himself.

'What is it?' the girl asked.

'It has just dawned upon me. My father in his fancy has called this house the Temple. Now I see how apt that name is. You have consecrated it as it were.'

'Me?'

'A temple should house a goddess. Until now, that has been lacking. Today Psyche has appeared. Our temple has its goddess.'

'I don't know about that, but I'm getting goose pimples.'

Edmund laughed. 'How thoughtless I am.' Belinda's proximity emphasised the intense violet of her eyes. Never before had he seen such ocular fire.

'Poor dear, you are shivering, Come, here is room enough for two.' He stepped towards her, discarding his Turkish slippers as, at the same time, enfolding his dressing gown around her.

'Until this moment I never held a goddess in my arms.'

Belinda needed his warmth. First things first. She placed her arms around his agreeably slim waist, for he was very warm.

'You are taking advantage of me sir, are you not?' she said.

'I don't deny it. For rarely does a man have the opportunity to play Cupid to a Psyche as lovely as you. The prospect is one of delightful excitement for me. . .'

'That is evident sir,' said Belinda. 'So evident,' she said, 'that you could hang your hat on it.'

*

When Belinda returned to the theatre on the Tuesday morning she found the company in a turmoil.

'And where may I ask have you been?' asked an indignant Dora Proctor. 'You were called for rehearsal Sunday as well as yesterday morning. You'll be fined for not being here madam.'

'I wasn't called 'till this morning,' said Belinda.

'That's before Powell was sacked on Saturday night, after you'd been and gone. There's big cast changes. We've been at it for days.'

It was the business of Mr Kirk's make-up box that began the upset. Brook Powell was accused by Mr Kirk of using his make-up because he had none of his own. This led to a fight in which Mr Kirk was badly beaten by Mr Powell, suffering a black eye and a possible broken nose.

At once, Jemmy had summoned Powell demanding an accurate account of the incident. Mr Powell said yes, he'd been using Kirk's make-up, but only because he could not afford to buy his own on the pittance he was paid.

To this Jemmy said his wage was more than adequate for the quality of work he offered. A violent row followed, with Powell accusing Jemmy of hogging all the lead parts himself and giving him only minor supporting roles. Jemmy agreed, saying that this was because Powell was but a third rate comedian and not fit for much else. The deep animosity between the two men erupted into furious shouting, and ended with Powell being paid off after the Saturday night performance and told to leave forthwith.

This sudden change had necessitated extra rehearsals all day Sunday and Monday to deal with the recasting, about which Belinda had been innocently unaware. Powell was thought generally to be a bad lot and it was feared he could cause further trouble; leaving Cassandra deeply troubled, knowing as she did that Jemmy blamed her for introducing Powell into the company in the first place.

. Following his dismissal and with a small amount of cash to hand, Brook Powell again made his way to the cock fight in the hope that his luck would improve. There he met several out of work men, formerly framework knitters, with similar hopes of making a winning. Powell, who had previously scorned such artisans, now discovered their malcontent to be very like his own. Their belief that all masters were grasping and unjust concurred with his own feelings. For not only had Powell been cashiered from the army, he had also been dismissed by two theatre managers, all of which fuelled his resentment.

In the cockpit he heard much talk of Parliamentary reforms which it was hoped would improve the hosiery workers' lot; without new laws it was believed unrest would follow. This growing mood of discontent was a comfort to Powell, deciding him to support their grievances in the belief that should rebellion break out, his army experience could benefit their cause.

His sense of injury was further inflamed by a notice Whitley unwisely placed in the local press:

'Mr Whitley finding that POWELL, a previous fifer in the Dragoons has broke his article through all the Rules of this Community, has engaged Mr PERRY from Covent Garden Theatre as a better Performer . . . .'

To be humiliated by the announcement was sufficient, but to be described as a fifer in the infantry was the ultimate indignity, giving Powell more thirst for revenge. He told his new companions that of all the villains in Nottingham, Whitley was the foremost. Recounting that it was Whitley who had sought patronage from Sedley the MP whom he declared was firmly against all framework knitters. Worse than that, Whitley had been favoured by the infamous Duke of Newcastle who was known to be the most unyielding opponent of reform. He proclaimed that the proper target for retribution was the source of Whitley's livelihood, namely the theatre in St Mary's Gate.

News of the success or failure of the Parliamentary reform bill was expected on the tenth of June, a day declared a holiday for the many Tories in the town to celebrate the birthday of the Old Pretender. All day the London coach was awaited. When it arrived it brought the grievous tidings that the bill had been defeated by a large majority. An outlook of gloom and discontent appeared on every countenance and most hearers retired to the nearest tavern for solace and discussion. With this, rebellion slowly fermented until several hours later, ignited by liquor, the commotions began.

As water runs downhill, so trouble makers poured into the market square bringing a torrent of mischief. A malign prelude was sounded by scores of sticks rattling along railings as the crowd hastened forward. Anger filled the night with shouts and roars from drunken agitators culminating into a river of rage.

The mutinous sound had a life of its own, a toxic vapour infecting all who breathed it. Soon the miasma filled the streets and alleys with mobs seeking out the properties of their detested masters. Weapons appeared as if by sorcery. Bill hooks, daggers and staves might have been expected, but shortly swords, pistols and pikes were in the hands of the insurgents. Blacksmiths and butchers were plundered so that cleavers, saws and a forests of iron bars were added to the armoury.

A number of rioters, including many woman and boys, ran up the alleyways from the square to the misnamed street of Back Side where some of the wealthiest were known to live. Mr Joyner, a hated manufacturer was the first to have his house attacked. With triumphant shouts, ground floor windows had their shutters torn away, roars of approval followed as every pane of glass was smashed. Ladders were used to enter the first floor. Furniture was flung to the ground below and pillaged for jewellery and clothing, after which the costly pieces were chopped up and turned into bonfires of rejoicing.

Powell found himself in the midst of the mob. Earlier in the taverns, a muddled list of targets had been made, which was soon forgotten in the frenzy of destruction. If the name of a street was called by some drunken voice the mob swerved like a shoal of fish in that direction. Low Pavement drew the largest crowd, for here were the residences of many of the wealthy.

Terrified householders offered money for their properties to be spared, but it was not long before several dwellings regardless of ownership were ransacked and set alight. Directly, the sky was filled with flames and fountains of sparks shimmered upwards as roofs collapsed into the burning shells of the ruined houses. Powell tried to urge the crowd towards the theatre which was nearby, but such was the uproar his voice was unheard in the horrid cacophony.

Unaware of these disturbances, the magistrates and officers of the Royal Horse Guards were attending a masked ball in the new stand at the race course. This was situated a mile away from the town, separated by a hill which prevented the revellers from seeing the fires burning in Nottingham. It was not until the deputy mayor received a message telling of the riots that the alarm was raised. Being called to arms the officers, most of them in full dress uniform, rode directly to the market place. By this time the crowd had moved to the outer streets leaving the square eerily empty and quiet.

Law decreed that the riot act be read, which was done by a magistrate, the wording *'all persons to disperse themselves peaceably,'* seeming ridiculous when delivered to an almost deserted square littered with debris like excrement from the mob. With the final words 'God Save the King' the officers saluted. Commands were given to divide the guards into two detachments, one to ride to the crowd known to be on Low Pavement, with another up to High Pavement via Stoney Street from where it was hoped the mob could be contained. Bugles sounded the summons to engage, followed by a cold silence, in which was heard only the threatening trample of horses hooves on cobbled streets.

The main body of protesters having tired of the havoc on Low Pavement surged up the hill to find new victims. It was known that Turner a wealthy hosier lived in St Mary's Gate and chants of his name began like some vicious call to judgement. This development well suited Mr Powell's purpose. Get the mob to move into St Mary's Gate, he thought, and soon the theatre would be under attack for by now the horde was delirious with destruction.

That was until the bugles were heard, sending a tremor through the multitude. In seconds the mood swung from reckless purpose to uncertainty. The shouting faded as the realisation came that mounted cavalry was at the ready. People listened. Harsh sounding commands confirmed the presence of mounted troops. Images of charging horses with flying sabres came into the minds of many. Confusion took power as the crowd broke into separate individuals, each indecisive of what to do. Stay and fight, or run for shelter.

'The theatre, the theatre, we march on the theatre,' called Powell despairingly as he sensed failure ahead of him. 'The theatre must be burned.'

This had no effect apart from murmurs of dismissal, until the harsh clatter of the advancing cavalry was apparent, scores of hooves striking on hard stone sets, accompanied by the threatening jingle of harness and spurs. Alarmed people ran in different directions and it was hard not to be carried into whatever course the frightened crowd took flight. Powell tried vainly to continue his progress towards the theatre knocked this way and that by rank and file running to safety. He became aware of a terrified woman's voice, 'Mr Powell, Mr Powell!'

He had no idea who it was and at first there was no indication where the cry came from. He was angered by the distraction. Who was this bloody woman? He tried ignoring her, but her voice persisted, frantically calling his name. He looked to see who it was.

'Here,' shouted the woman, 'by the railings,' and he saw a distraught figure holding onto the wrought ironwork in front of the Guild Hall. Her clothing badly torn, her hair fallen about her shoulders as if she had been molested, it was Mrs Kirk, the wife of the actor he had quarrelled with.

'Thank God,' said Mrs Kirk, 'I have been near trampled to death. I thought it was your voice that called. I need your help.'

Powell did nothing until he found her clinging onto him for security. At any moment he realised she might collapse.

'Can we get to the theatre?' she asked. 'Anything to get away from these savages.'

By now most of the crowd had gone, disappearing into the labyrinth of alleys like water through a colander, as the military advanced down the almost empty street. Slowly it progressed forward, a fearful line of force, ready to clear everything before it.

‘We must get to the theatre,’ pleaded Mrs Kirk, ‘there’s nowhere else.’ Powell said nothing, knowing she was right and the two rapidly took a circuitous route from Weekday Cross through narrow lanes and passages until they gained the back yard of the theatre.

They knocked on the door. It seemed at first as if the building was deserted. Further knockings eventually brought a voice from within which they both recognised as Mr Bracer. ‘Let us in, Mr Bracer for God’s sake,’ called Mrs Kirk. The door was opened a few inches showing the familiar face.

‘We need shelter,’ said Mrs Kirk, pushing to gain entrance. Mr Bracer allowed her to pass, then on seeing Mr Powell he said, ‘Didn’t expect you to show your face ‘ere.’

‘Don’t be hard on him,’ said Mrs Kirk, ‘he helped me in the crowd. I was trying to get home with my husband. We were in the square in the midst of the trouble, where we got separated. I was carried with the crush to Low Pavement. There was no resisting it. I’ve never been so afeared in my life. Pray God my husband is safe.’

‘You’d best stay here ‘till the morning. Then we’ll get you home,’ said Bracer. He looked at Powell, ‘I’m not giving you no welcome.’

‘Don’t worry. As soon as things are quiet, I’ll be gone.’

‘I shall tell my husband how you helped me,’ said Mrs Kirk.

‘You needn’t bother,’ said Powell, ‘I doubt he’d believe you.’ He looked at Mr Bracer whose glare was sufficient for him to leave. He stood in the yard alone as a pale dawn was competing with the dying flames of burning buildings. For the time being, Powell’s hatred of the theatre had cooled, but it had not gone. There were still scores to settle.

To prevent further anarchy it was immediately decreed that all those in the town should, wherever possible, give quarters to military personnel. Until the new barracks could be occupied, officers and men must be billeted within the town to be readily on hand if unrest continued. Thus, out of the chaos of the riots, one person at least had gained. This was Dora Proctor, whose small dwelling having a spare room was thought by the authorities to be suitable accommodation for an officer.

223.

It was a Captain Kern of the Oxford Blues who was billeted upon her, 'He's such a fine gentleman,' she said, 'so handsome in his scarlet uniform. With such shoulders and moustachios. And bless my soul, I am paid to keep him with me! Tenpence a day for the subsistence, with twopence a day given for small beer when regularly quartered. There is an additional allowance of ten pence ha'penny for his horse but alas I am unable to accommodate his steed.'

*

Twenty Two. *Travelling Players.*

'Never say that.'

'Why not? For it's what I am.'

'You are not a whore, don't use that word. It is your father who is the pander, not you.'

Lucy took hold of Thomas's hands. After the rebuffs, he thought this might be a gesture of trust, perhaps more. He returned her grasp.

'I have told you something that is my secret,' she said. 'And I have revealed things that must stay hidden.'

'It is too much for you to carry.'

'I have kept it secret for so long.'

'No more. You must speak out.'

'It would do nothing but bring misfortune on everyone.'

She picked up her cloak, draped it around her shoulders and began fastening the ribbon at her throat.

'If you will not let me help, who else is there?' asked Thomas.

'No-one.' Lucy leaned forward and kissed him on the cheek. She left his room so hastily that he faltered until it was too late to prevent her departure.

He heard her foot steps pattering down the stairs as church clocks began striking midday. Failure filled him with disgust. How could he have let her return to that situation? All he could do was look down from the window at the street below and watch as she ran away from him, her cloak billowing in her wake.

She did not look back.

'Recall. We are all His Majesty's Servants,' Tate Wilkinson told his company on Monday morning. 'I expect a standard of behaviour from each and every one as if the king himself were present. This is Race Week when we shall be on display more than ever. There will be no drunkenness within or without the theatre. Any form of lewd conduct will be fined on the spot. This is the busiest week of the season, with great rewards artistically and financially, so let us begin. Hallelujah, Praise the Lord.'

It being Race Week, the town was abundant with visitors. Houses and rooms were let specially for the event, with hotels and taverns full as herrings in a barrel. Street stalls sprung up everywhere. The Minster rode above it all with solemn jurisdiction for beneath its towers the town was in a merry mood not least the theatre. A total of twelve plays would be given during the six nights, a prospect the actors approached with excitement and apprehension. More would be demanded of them than at any other time, yet houses were likely to be full, which could mean largess for everyone. All the plays were comic for at such times audiences liked to laugh. So dominant were the races that performances could be delayed until the last contest had been run, meaning that curtain-up was held until then, only coming down in the small hours.

It was planned that Thomas was to play Puck every other night, for such was the demand for *The Dream* that Tate made it one of his main productions. As he said, 'he knew what made his windows rattle,' for Thomas's fame was spreading beyond York to other towns, where his arrival was anticipated with excitement. Once this season was finished, the company would be starting the summer circuit, visiting Tate Wilkinson's other theatres in Hull, Wakefield and Doncaster. Older actors like Mr Cobb did not tour, allowing Mr Holland and Mrs M'George to regain their leads, which required daily rehearsals as roles were rediscovered and newly burnished.

Beyond this, preparations were underway for *Harlequin Sailor* which was planned as the main attraction in the coming year. Tate's wife, Jane, was completing the text in collaboration with scenic painters, joiners, wardrobe and musicians, for it was to be a lavish offering with elaborate settings and machinery. Tate and his wife were aware that they were taking a risk, as the pantomime relied heavily on the talents of Mr Hammond (as Thomas was now billed) their new star performer, who had yet to be fully tested. He was firmly cast as Harlequin but a Columbine was still to be decided. Lucy Treadgold would have been ideal, but without her parents' agreement that was impossible. Meanwhile, the Wilkinsons wondered if any other girl might be considered for the role. Unaware of this, work dominated Thomas's days for he had devised one or two new pieces of business for Puck, which took time, finding moments when he could rehearse on his own.

This proved worthwhile, the Race Week audiences showed their approval with loud laughter and applause. There was no doubt that he had become an important asset to the theatre, which he recognised with good will and modesty, at the same time enjoying the acclaim. Thoughts of Lucy were with him constantly with no hour passing but he reflected on her circumstances. Every night at the end of her dance she continued to leave with her parents as he waited in the wings. Each time she paid him no heed and knowing her dilemma, he thought it best to assume the same indifference. Shortly he would be on tour and they would not see each other for weeks. Regularly, he waited and watched as she gave her dance, thinking how much he loved her and how near impossible it was to conceal his feelings.

Until one night when she had taken her curtain call and walking past him with her parents, she hesitated for a second, her parents being ahead of her. She was about to speak but her father, probably sensing this, turned and pulled her away roughly. Her head jerked clumsily from the force as she looked back in distress. At once anger took command of Thomas.

'You don't do that,' he said defiantly to Treadgold.

'Mind what you are about,' he answered in his strange high voice.

'I do mind. And you won't mistreat Lucy.'

Lucy looked at Thomas as if to say 'No,' but Treadgold continued to make his departure, dragging her with him.

'Leave her be,' said Thomas.

Treadgold ignored him, making for the door with Lucy. Thomas ran and stepped in front blocking his way.

'Leave her be,' he repeated. Treadgold tried forcing Thomas aside to make his exit.

Time slipped a beat.

With a flash of pain, Thomas found his hand was hurting. Treadgold was lying at his feet, groaning. Why was that, what had happened? He had no memory of it.

All this chanced in his mind as a fumbled silence, as if swimming underwater. Then, as his head felt to be breaking above the surface, he heard the uproar around him. with company members looking in astonishment. He saw Lucy weeping. Mr Treadgold was there on the floor. Mrs Treadgold was screaming abuse at him, vaguely trying to assist her husband, who whined in his weird falsetto, After helping her husband to a chair, Mrs Treadgold directed her fury upon Thomas.

'You will be punished, mark what I say! We have witnesses. This is a clear case of assault and battlement. . . .'

Tate Wilkinson pushed his way through the assembly. 'Let me attend to this. Hammond, go to my room. . .'

'I'm due onstage. . .' said Thomas.

'Go to my bloody room. Now! Thomas hesitated, then did as he was bid. Tate looked at Mr Treadgold, who was regaining his breath.

'He's been winded, no more,' he said to Mrs Treadgold. 'Take him home in a chair. I'll cover the expense.'

'That scoundrel must be comprehended,' demanded a vehement Mrs Treadgold.

'I'll deal with this ma'am,' said Tate. 'This is my business. Now get you home, all three of you.'

'Not until that young bully . . .'

'Get home woman!' shouted Tate. 'I'll see you both on the morrow.' By now, the start of *The Dream* was overdue; from the auditorium came shouts and calls from an impatient house. For the moment, Tate ignored this and followed Thomas into his room violently slamming the door.

'You may think you're cock o' the walk, you young devil, but I have rules. You've been drinking.'

'I have not. . .'

'Don't lie to me lad. You drink every night. Your breath could start a bonfire. That's your business. But not when it turns to assault. I won't have it. You'll get no salary for tonight and you'll pay a fine

'Then I'll not go on,' said Thomas.

'You will go on. If not you can get out for good. I've sacked better men than you.'

'There'll soon be a riot. Listen to that . . .' Thomas opened the door so that the tumult in the theatre could be heard. Tate in turn slammed it shut again.

'Now hark to me. I warned at the start of the week about bad behaviour. Get out there or I'll sue you for breach of contract. You'll be in such debt you'll be gaoled for months. I'll not tolerate behaviour of this kind, you young whippersnapper. . .'

An anxious prompter knocked at the door. 'We can wait no longer sir.'

'He's coming,' shouted Tate. He threw open the door. In the corridor could be seen the cast, waiting for Thomas. In his Puck costume he looked foolish as he stared indignantly at everyone. Fanny M'George looking equally bizarre in her Titania dress left the others and approached Thomas.

'This won't do Tommy,' she said. 'You'r not only failing yourself. You're failing all of us.'

His bad temper still showing, Thomas walked out of Wilkinson's room and took his place in the wings. The prompt opened his book, nodding to the musicians. As they began to play, a cheer went up from the gallery. Thomas went onstage to give by far his best performance, fired it would seem by his inner anger.

'Temperament,' said Tate to his wife. 'Already. What is he, eighteen, nineteen? And still behaving like an unbroken colt. He's as dangerous as lightning. Tell me I'm mad giving him a major role when he's so unreliable.'

Jane Wilkinson said calmly, 'We've dealt with the like before.'

'Not with one of his age. If he was older, it might be excusable, but not when he's a beginner, still wet behind the ears.'

'Do you know why he hit Treadgold?'

'He won't say. It involves Lucy I don't doubt. Whatever the cause, I shall fine him, he's got to learn.'

'What if he leaves?'

'He won't. He needs our patronage.'

'We also have need of him.'

'Yes, dammit it we have. And it's all my doing!'

By the week following, the company was ready for their late summer tour. The first town was Hull, a distance of just over thirty four miles from York. With fair weather and a dawn start, Tate expected his troupe to cover the journey in a day. He hired a wagon for the costumes and scenery which might take longer to shift, but this would not hamper rehearsals once the Hull theatre was reopened.

'From Hull and High Water, Good Lord Deliver Us,' grumbled Fanny M'George as they set off early in the morning. For most of its way the road was turnpiked, but this did not mean that it was an easy walk. Road conditions varied from parish to parish. Some stretches were covered in layers of loose stones which easily caused sprained ankles. At other parts there were deep ruts equally hazardous for the unwary. Arguments occurred at nearly every toll house over the charges for the scenery cart. Dues were expected for horse drawn vehicles but this being pushed by hand caused disagreements. Some toll keepers let it through with no fee, but others demanded payment.

Memories of Dick Turpin survived amongst the more nervous. Some of the women took precautions against footpads by carrying two purses. One, readily available, contained a few coins to be surrendered easily if they were waylaid, the other, carefully hidden, contained their real treasures.

Tate had given them written road directions, for fingerposts were few. The first destination was Market Weighton, known locally as Wicstun. Here it was anticipated there would be rest and food. Tall pine trees ahead signified a coaching house, the Briggs Inn, a handsome hostelry with a porticoed entrance which was approached by the company. But the landlord refused to serve them, declaring them to be rogues and vagabonds to whom he would not extend the civility of his house.

'Sir,' declared Mr Holland, acting as their senior, 'I would have you know that we are His Majesty's Servants.'

'And so are we all,' answered the innkeeper.

'We are under a patent from the king himself.'

'You're comedians, and I'll not have you at my table. I know your kind. Too much drink, then disruption often without payment. Clear off, you're worse than the gypsies.'

To argue was useless and the indignant actors found welcome at one of the lesser alehouses. After they had moved on, Tate caught up with them on horseback. There was no resentment at his superior form of travel, after all he was the master and his lameness was also remembered with understanding.

After encouraging words and suitable indignation over the reception at the Briggs Inn, Tate rode ahead to Hull. Late in the evening the tired troupe arrived at the theatre, where he awaited them and escorted them to a local inn for supper and ale.

*

Seaport theatres were always different. Old timers shook their heads saying that at such localities you had to work hardest of all. So it seemed with Hull. Furnishings discovered in the theatre underlined this; a row of spikes along the footlights was in place to repulse any invasion by the audience. Before rehearsals could begin, the building had to be cleaned. Even in early September the place was cold and damp, a biting east wind from the sea mostly contributing to the chill, so that 'fires were well kept' as a priority.

Handbills had to be distributed, a chore taken with resignation by the entire company. These wearisome tasks were accepted by the troupe as part of the travelling life, play acting being almost less of the whole. Plans were to open on Friday (pay day for most in Hull) with Thursday and Friday mornings occupied with a pumping through the town to proclaim widely the arrival of the company. Thursday arrived a dull, cold morning and the prospect of taking the town was daunting. Tate Wilkinson and the cast waited for a junior member to return from the printers with the paper work. When the boy ran into the green room, his arms filled with playbills, he brought unwelcome news.

'The Brewsters are here,' he announced breathlessly.

Had he said that the plague had come, the news could not have been more disturbing.

'The Brewsters?' asked Tate.

'Yes sir. The printer's done their bills. Got 'ere before us. Playing

The Beggar's Opera an' all.' He handed a playbill to Tate, who sighed as he read it, 'The Brewsters. . . this is not welcome.'

The Brewsters, let it be explained, were a family of travelling players, considered by the likes of Tate Wilkinson to be the dregs of the acting world. They owned no theatres and they traversed the north of England with little more than props and a few costumes. Acting talent was equally scarce. They were a large family with each member employed in some capacity.

Mr and Mrs Brewster, both septuagenarians, played the leads in every play, portraying dashing heroes and maidens with a lack of plausibility that was almost praiseworthy. Should duels or other physical activities be required, plays were rewritten so that younger members of the family could deal with the exertions. Romeo and Juliet they never attempted for the simple reason that Shakespeare was beyond their comprehension and also that of their public.

Their repertoire was stolen or pirated from other companies with no thought of payment and consisted of lurid melodramas or romances of more than usual sickly sentimentality. In short they were the theatrical equivalent of the rag and bone trade. But they were cheap, their bench prices no more than tuppence and for that reason they had a loyal following in the docks area.

Wilkinson examined the playbill. 'Where are they appearing? Ah. the old whaling shed on the quayside. A suitable choice. It should be the county gaol for their crimes against Thespis.' He put the bill aside. 'Well, praise the Lord, we must live and let live.'

Regardless of the arrival of the Brewsters, the handbills were divided amongst the company which split into pairs for their distribution. Thomas and Fanny M'George elected to be together and were deputised to cover the seagoing district.

Sadly, the weather had turned horrid, the seaward wind increasing in strength with broadsides of rain beating upon them. In no time the streets and docks became unpopulated, making the handing out of playbills impossible. The temptation to forgo the task was great, but both understood that announcements of the plays were vital if an audience was to be found.

'It could well be fine tomorrow,' said the ever optimistic Fanny, hardly convincing herself or Thomas. They were close to the harbour and agreed that a nearby inn could act as a refuge for half an hour, by which time the rain might have eased. The Scrimshaw Arms was not an inviting establishment on this gloomy day, having an interior almost totally dark until a small shabby tap room was discovered. As they entered, it was empty apart from three large young men playing at dominoes, who looked up and then resumed their game in silence.

Their orders placed with the saturnine landlord, Fanny and Thomas took their handbills from under the protective sacking to see how much damage the rain had caused. Fanny offered one to the landlord as he brought their drinks,

'Perhaps you would be kind enough to display this for your customers,' she said. 'Or it might interest you and your friends.'

The landlord looked at the paper, saying nothing.

'What you got there?' asked one of the three young men.

'See for yourself Charlie,' replied the landlord passing the playbill to him.

Charlie examined it at arms length until, with a hard grin, he asked the largest of the three, 'What would you say this is about 'arry? Would you like if I was to read it to you?' He looked to Fanny, 'My brother 'asn't got the reading yet, 'ave you 'arry?'

'Stow it,' replied 'arry. 'What's it say?'

'Now this will be of interest to us all, it being a playbill no less. Well, well, well, 'ark to this 'Tis a playbill sent by Mr Tate Wilkinson 'imself. We are honoured.' He read with difficulty, *'Mr Wilkinson's Company of Comedians acknowledged to be the best in this Part of the Kingdom, intend to entertain the Nobility and Gentry. .'*

He stopped, looking at his brothers, 'Don't that sound a bit hoity-toity? *"The best in this part of the kingdom."* '

'*"To entertain the nobility and gentry,"* oh my word!' said the third.

'Tut, tut,' said Charlie, 'we can't be 'aving that. We being in the same line of calling so to speak. 'ow is that you're distributing these 'ere?' he asked.

'We are members of Mr Wilkinson's company,' replied Fanny.

'Oh, Mr Wilkinson's company,' Charlie smiled sarcastically.

'And me and my brothers are members of Mr Brewster's company.'

By now the triumvirate saw some sport in the offing. Charlie, who seemed to be their spokesman asked, 'My brother 'ere,' he indicated the now menacing Goliath, 'would like a copy for 'imself. As a keepsake as it were. Could you oblige?'

Fanny did as he asked. 'We'd better humour them,' she muttered.

Charlie asked caustically, 'I think we'd all like one each, if you'd be so kind. . .' Fanny handed another.

The three regarded the bills with exaggerated interest.

Charlie regarded Thomas with mock politeness. 'And may I be so bold as to ask 'oo you are? You bein' one of the *Hactors* per'aps?'

'I'm Hammond,' replied Thomas, 'this is Mrs M'George.'

' 'ammond.' He looked at the bill. 'My oh my. *"the celebrated Mr 'ammond."* Could that really be you ?'

'It might be,' replied Thomas carefully.

'So Mr 'ammond, you entertain the nobility and gentry, do you?' As he asked this, Charlie held the paper in the flame of a candle and slowly watched it burn. When done, he scrunched the blackened paper to ash.

'Oh dear. 'ow careless of me. My copy has gone up in flames. Could I 'ave another . . . if you please?

Thomas paused. Fanny sensing his suppressed anger whispered,

'Keep your temper for God's sake.'

The young Goliath who had said little so far, chose this moment to stand and reveal fully his size.

'Give 'im another one,' he mumbled.' He left the table to approach Thomas and Fanny, looking down at them directly. Without shifting his gaze, with his large hands he took a wad of the playbills from the pack, scornfully tearing them in half with ease.

'And I'll 'ave these to wipe my arse with,' he growled.

Thomas stood up, but the huge youth towered above him. The other two by now were on their feet moved towards Thomas. Saying nothing, the three picked up the remaining handbills.

Charlie spoke, 'it's not very friendly of you, Mister celebrated 'ammond, to come 'ere takin' business away from us poor acting folk.'

Fanny her drink finished stood saying to Thomas, 'Come along.'

''ang on,' said Charlie. 'We don't take kindly to poachers, for that's what you are, trespassing on our territ'ry and taking our livelihood from us.'

Fanny, by now wishing to leave quickly attempted to pick up what remained of the bills before leaving. They were knocked out of her hands.

'Poachers are 'anged in this part of the world,' Charlie said.

For an instant Thomas sought to protect Fanny, but with no warning Charlie's ruffian brother punched him full in the face. At once blood poured forth. Unable to see, Thomas tried hitting back, but the three youths surrounded him, punching and kicking him to the floor. All this the work of a minute.

'Stop it!' shouted Fanny. 'He means you no harm.' Seeing the landlord, she called to him, 'Can't you help? Look what they're doing.'

The landlord, himself a big man moved quickly saying,

'Get 'im out of 'ere.' He opened the door to the street. Thomas managing to stand, staggered outside with Fanny's help to avoid any further injury. They found themselves in the wet, empty street.

'You forgot these,' shouted Charlie. And he threw the remaining bills after them, where they flew upwards in the rain before fluttering into the many puddles on the cold wet pavement. Of no use to anyone.

The Hull Gazette reported,'*We have heard much in advance of the astonishing qualities of young Mr Hammond, a new and rising member of Mr Wilkinson's Company. It has come, therefore as a disappointment to witness his feeble playing at our theatre last night. In fairness to the young gentleman we are told he has suffered a mishap, which may account for our frustration. In that case we hope after his recuperation we may have another opportunity to reassess his performance. Meanwhile those who are seeking a louder laugh might be better advised to visit Mr Brewster's Company, where a number of hilarious dramas are pleasing packed houses.' ~*

After the skirmish at the Scrimshaw Arms, Fanny had helped

Thomas back to the theatre, where he was cared for and his injuries tended. A black eye, several bruises and perhaps a cracked rib were discovered, painful but not debilitating, given time to recovery. Tate was angry when he first heard of the fight, until Fanny explained it was not due to any recklessness on the part of Thomas.

'Why did you not call for a constable?' asked Tate.

'A constable rarely improves the situation,' replied Fanny tartly. 'And where was I to find a constable in that God forsaken place?'

Tate's company had opened on the Friday night as planned. The audience was small and the evening far from a success. Heavy rain and cold winds had prevailed, discouraging many from going out of doors. Thomas had insisted on appearing, which saddened everyone seeing him only able to give a diminished performance due to his injuries. His playing was limited to the stage level, climbing and tumbling both beyond his ability, leaving a house who had anticipated fireworks, unable to understand this lacklustre showing.

No-one could adequately replace Thomas as Puck, so after the one sad performance, Tate withdrew the piece, insisting that he rested for the remainder of the Hull run. He had admired Thomas for his attempt to appear, a quality he told himself he must remember in the future. Perhaps he was turning out to be a young trouper after all.

In place of *The Dream,* Tate had substituted an old favourite *Miss in Her Teens,* but disappointed audiences who had waited weeks to see *The Dream* stayed away.

'Ah well,' said Fanny as she removed her stage make-up. Never short of a platitude she added, 'it's an ill wind blows nobody good, even in Hull.' Her role in *Miss in Her Teens* was more substantial than Titania, leaving her well suited, perhaps with an extra payment at the week's end.

Thomas, officially 'resting,' spent most evenings with Fanny reporting on his day's activities, which amounted mostly to walking around Hull. This gave him time to meditate upon the vagaries of success, for having become used to recognition in York, here he was once more an ordinary citizen. Even his black eye drew no attention, for among the many dock workers and sailors it was a common sight.

One evening, without letting it be known, he decided to attend a performance by the Brewster's company. He knew it was foolhardy, but he wanted to know how good or bad they were. He chose a night when they were giving the *Beggar's Opera* and slipped late into the rowdy, stinkardly whaling shed.

The playing was as bad as he had hoped it would be. Mr and Mrs Brewster played Macheath and Polly at a rheumatic pace. The music was provided by a superannuated fiddler who tortured the tunes on his one stringed instrument. This mattered little to the audience, who knew the old songs well and sang the original words, unaware of Mr Gay's new lyrics.

All this he reported to Fanny, giving an impersonation of the Brewsters that reduced her to helpless laughter. 'You ought to go on the stage,' she told him, at the same time admonishing him for the dangerous risk he had taken.

In the course of their conversation Thomas said,

'I saw something today that has set me thinking.'

'That must be to the good,' said Fanny, 'as long as it's not about feeling sorry for yourself.'

'No. I saw a bill posted in the town, several of them, regarding Freight and Haulage. It was headed *"James Sweeny, Oxford Canal Navigation Company- ."* Do you think it could be . .?'

Fanny stopped and looked at him in the mirror. 'If it is, he owes me twenty quid the mean bastard. Was there any address?'

'Nothing apart other than Stamford.'

'It has to be him. Try and find out more. I could do with the money.'

Here, their conjecture was interrupted by the young call boy, coming into the room without a by-your-leave.

'What is it?' asked Fanny, sharply.

'Beg pardon miss, it's not for you. It's for Mr Hammond. Someone at the stage door.'

It was Lucy Treadgold. Thomas was confounded by her arrival. Why she was here? For what reason? It could not be because he'd been injured, she would never have heard about that. Had she walked all the way to Hull from York - alone?

He ran out to the corridor, where he found her, dishevelled and exhausted. Straightway he led her into Fanny's dressing room where they both attempted to help her to a chair. She refused to sit, appearing so near to exhaustion that even to bend was impossible.

'Tom,' said Lucy, her voice so quiet it could scarce be heard, 'Hold me. Do but hold me. That's all I ask.'

Saying this, she fainted.

*

Twenty Three. *Caesar, Cleopatra, ... and Jemima.*

After the riots the talk was the same - in the Club Rooms, the Assembly Rooms, the Billiard Rooms - 'Hang the lot of 'em.' In the Card Rooms, the Tea Rooms, the Ball Rooms, again the same - 'Hang the lot of 'em.'

'That it should come to this.'

'Things have reached a pretty pass.'

'Never thought I'd see the like of it.'

'And what are the authorities doing?'

Indeed, what were the authorities doing? The militia had been caught completely off guard. When the riots broke out, most were attending a ball on the Forest race course, if you please. The worst damage was done long before they even reached the trouble spots. Scandalous! True, barracks were being built for permanent soldiery, but it would be months before that was effective. Meanwhile, in several villages lace mills had been destroyed, something the army had failed to prevent. However, it must be asked, even if troops were employed, could they be in more than one place at a time?

Those eminent citizens who had seen their properties destroyed said they were leaving town and who could blame them? Moving to the new outskirts; fashionable areas certainly, but too distant for evening visits to the play.

'It's all very well building a new theatre in Derby,' complained Cassandra, 'But what use will it be if people are too alarmed to go out at night?'

'They'll be frightened for a week or so, but they'll soon want entertainment again my dear,' Whitley replied. 'And we might be getting a new quality of patron, have you thought of that?'

'What sort of - quality?'

'The officers in the militia. They need amusement as much as anyone. Stationed away from home, they'll be bored and seeking diversion. Make no mistake, they'll soon be coming to us. And think of it, they've got their own bands. The theatre will be ideal for concerts. That will surely be to our advantage.'

Cassy was not convinced. In her view Nottingham was changing for the worse. Those who'd formerly lived in the town centre were selling off the land for the building of warehouses.

'Yes, warehouses in St Mary's Gate. And that's not all. They say people were putting their orchards and enclosures on the market for building upon and we know what that means. Those lovely little private parks will be covered with horrible back to backs. Cheap houses for more framework knitters who never come near a theatre. This used to be called the "garden city" but no more I fear.'

After the riots the talk was the same, but it was different - in the Alehouses, Spinning Rooms and Back Yards, - 'ang the lot of 'em.'

'Less and less pay for our work.'

'Rents for the knitting machines sky high.'

'Price of yarn risen again.'

'All reforms thrown out.'

This was heard repeatedly in the cock pit under the Feathers Inn, where Brook Powell spent most of his evenings Many of those crammed together in the fetid cave had taken part in the riots, giving rise to arguments about future plans for further disruption. Although the destruction of more than fifty knitting machines was considered a triumph, there was no avoiding the reality that there followed no work for those who rented them. In desperation many had turned to gambling as a means of raising funds. Bare-knuckle fighting for the aggressive sometimes made fortunes; matches between game cocks could bring in as much as five guineas a fight should the bird be a champion.

A young out-of-work machinist, John Galpin, was telling Powell of his trials. He had stolen several cockerels in the hope of training them as game cocks. This was a perilous undertaking, for he knew that even for this minor crime of poaching he could face seven years transportation.

'I got ' old of the last bird from a farm in Burton Leys. Nearly came to grief, farmer fired two volleys at me afore I got away. But the bird was no good, even with spurs it was killed in its first fight. At least we 'ad it in the pot for a meal. I've lot of mouths to fill. We've got the wife's old father living with us, 'im a cripple bringin' in nowt, but eats 'earty enough. And we've got the giant to feed an' all.'

'Giant?' Powell began to show interest. 'What's that?' he asked

'Our youngest. Summut wrong wi' 'er. She's a monster. Not yet two year old, but she's a giant. Folks always wantin' to see 'er, she's that big.'

'What sort of folks?'

'All sorts. They've heard we've got a giant baby and they want to come and gawp at 'er. 'orrible if you ask me.'

'Not if you put it to your advantage.'

'Advantage?' She's no use is our Jemima.'

'You are mistaken,' said Mr Powell, 'If there are people asking to see her, why not let them, for a payment?'

''ow d'you mean?'

'What if I was able to arrange somewhere for your Jemima to be seen, where people paid to visit, would you agree to our forming a partnership?'

'Partnership?' John Galpin feared he was sailing into ticklish waters.

'We become sharesmen,' explained Powell. 'I find a room where she could be seen, for a small charge, which shall profit us both on a fifty-fifty basis.'

'I dunno . . .'

'She could become famous. "The celebrated Joanna . . ." '

'Jemima. . .'

'I apologise. "The celebrated Jemima Galpin." The public will flock. You will make a fortune.'

'It don't seem right. . .'

'Not right? To turn a millstone into a gold mine? Give me a day to make enquiries and we'll meet tomorrow to make a compact.'

'I'm not signin' nothin'.'

'Of course not. A gentlemen's agreement, that's what it shall be. Shall I call round and see Jemima for myself? Midday tomorrow?'

By that time, Brook Powell had been in conversation with the landlord of the Feathers, and had arranged for a private room to be used for the exhibiting of Jemima. He had called on the Galpins, housed in wretched quarters in Blossom Street, once the site of an orchard. Expecting to find a horror, he was pleased to discover that although the baby was of massive proportions, she had a quite amiable countenance. He was also glad to find that the family agreed to the project, with John Galpin and he shaking hands on the deal, placing Mr Powell in charge of the advertising and of all arrangements for the attraction.

That Friday In the *Weekly Journal* it was announced -

'JUST ARRIVED IN THIS TOWN. And to be seen only at the FEATHERS in the Market Place, for a Few Days only. A Most wonderful and Surprising FEMALE CHILD. Only 13 months old, yet measures a YARD round the waist,

22 Inches around the thigh, and is in Proportion every way. She is Very Healthy and lovely to behold: and allowed by the Faculty to be the finest Child nature ever produced. Ladies and Gentlemen 1/-, Tradesmen 6d, Servants 3d each.'

At the same time Powell had arranged for a board with similar tidings to be displayed outside the Feathers Inn on Long Row.

Cassandra Whitley noticed this when walking with Mrs Kirk, now recovered from her ordeal during the riot. She did not approve. 'They say it is promoted by Mr Powell,' Cassandra observed. 'It is the sort of horror one would expect of him. There's no harm in his setting up in opposition, but upon my word, a freak show! So squalid.'

'I believe you misjudge Mr Powell,' said Mrs Kirk. 'I have an abiding debt of gratitude that he rescued me that dreadful night.'

'Even after he assaulted your husband?' asked Cassandra.

'My husband is often hot headed and intemperate. He might have been as much to blame as Mr Powell.'

'What ever the case, you do well to be wary of him,'

With Jemmy away making final arrangements for the opening of the new Derby theatre, Cassy had been left in charge of the Nottingham premises. As she and Mrs Kirk returned to the stage door of the theatre, sounds of raised female voices made it apparent that something was amiss. Almost at once, Mrs Kenna the wardrobe mistress as before them. Hot and heaving with anger, she made the situation known,

'I spend more time patching quarrels between these addle headed hussies than I do making and repairing costumes. I'd throw a bucket of water over 'em, if it didn't mean ruining the dress they're tearing to pieces.'

'Bless my eyesight, what has happened?' asked Cassy.

'Just 'ark at them. Bruisin' like vixens they are.''

From the ladies' dressing room came shouts and crashes so violent and disturbing that Cassy hastened to find what was the trouble. There, with hair awry, clothing torn, scratches to arms and glaring at each other like spitfires, stood Dora Proctor and Belinda Armstrong. At the moment, Dora seemed to be in the ascendence, holding as she did a silk gown at arms length to prevent Belinda from gaining it. Animosity between the two young women had finally erupted.

'Stop this at once,' said Cassy, 'What are you about?'

'Ask her, the slut,' cried Dora. 'Filching what isn't hers.'

'Nor is it yours neither, it's mine by rights.' shouted Belinda.

'Be finished, both of you, You bring disgrace upon yourselves and the company. You will be fined for this, depend upon it!'

The two women, seeming to have spent most of their energy, glared at each other with hostility. Neither spoke.

'Do you know the cause of this Mrs Kenna?' asked Cassandra.

'They're both wanting a dress, that don't belong to neither of them. I made it months back for *The Wrangling Lovers*. Now they're saying they're both in need of it.

'I wore it last week as Juliet,' said Belinda.

'And I wore it first in *The Grecian Daughter,'* replied Dora.

'Nobody's wearing it after what you've both done to it,' said Mrs Kenna. 'Only fit for a scallywag.'

'Why do you need it?' asked Cassy.

'She wants to impress her precious Captain,' said Belinda.

'And you, madam, want to show off to young Sedley,' retorted Dora. 'I saw you sneaking away with it.'

Sadly, this was true, for Belinda had once more been invited to spend time with young Mr Sedley. Her purse did not allow for new apparel and she had indeed been hoping to wear her Juliet costume.

'You would not have minded, madam,' replied Belinda, 'had you not needed it yourself.' Again this was true, for Dora's lodger, Captain Kern, had invited her to partner him at a forthcoming military ball and she had no suitable gown in which to accompany him.

'Bitch,' taunted Dora.

'Harpy,' retorted Belinda.

'Slut.'

'Whore.' Thus ended the delicate equipoise between the two former friends. Yet the reprimand given by Cassandra because of its severity, almost drew them together again.

'Silence, both of you!' she commanded. 'And show respect for the civility of this house. You shall neither of you have the dress and you will both pay for the damage. Furthermore, as penitence, you will spend this coming Sunday assisting Mrs Kenna with repairs and mending in the wardrobe. If you value your places with this company, look to your behaviour.'

As she left the dressing room with as much seemliness as she could, Cassy was dismayed to find herself facing a liveried footman.

'I 'ave a message for Mester Whitley,' pronounced the footman.

'I am Mrs Whitley. You may leave it with me. I will see he gets it, on his return from Derby.'

'Might hay enquire when that might be?'

'Any day now. Who is the message from?'

'It is from Mr Plumptre who wishes to remain hanonymous.'

With this, the footman handed a folded and elaborately sealed letter. Cassy placed it with several other documents awaiting her husband's return, knowing he would probably ignore it. In truth, Whitley had found himself longer in Derby than expected. He was fortunate to be on good terms with the mayor and aldermen of that town, all of whom had to be dined and entertained to assure the granting of a licence for his new theatre

On his return to Nottingham there was much to be done. The missive from Mr Plumptre he neglected to read until a second letter. arrived. This demanded that Mr Whitley visited Plumptre House, without fail, which he felt obliged to do the following morning.

Once more he was shown into Mr Plumptre's bedchamber, where that gentleman again received him. Jemmy wondered if he had ever left his bed since their previous encounter. This time Mr Plumptre was not breaking his fast. Instead, his enormous counterpane was covered with stacks of paper, some bound with ribbon, but many tumbling in disarray onto the floor.

Mr Whitley realised with misgivings why he had been called.

'Finished!' declared Mr Plumptre triumphantly, 'at last, what?'

Feigning ignorance Jemmy asked, 'What is?'

'My play,' replied Plumptre with sharp annoyance. 'What else?'

'Of course.' Jemmy played for time as he felt the rush of chickens coming home to roost.

'All ready for you to act. My God, I anticipate seeing it with great excitement. It will be unlike anything previously beheld. Of that I am entirely persuaded.'

Jemmy, cleared his throat. 'What have you called the play?'

Mr Plumptre, took a page close to his hand and read,

'The Most Tragical and Lamentable History of the Lives and Loves betwixt Cleopatra, Queen of the Egyptian Nile, with firstly Julius Caesar, Ruler and Emperor of the Ancient Roman Empire. Next with Mark Antony, Consul of the Same. I think that explains it, what?'

'Indeed it does,' said Jemmy, thinking to himself how little space would remain on the playbill if the title were printed in full.

'Thought so,' replied the playwright. 'Some of it may require extensive ingenuity in bringing it into being. The barge on the Nile is an instance. That will want the stage flooded, as I mentioned before, what? The same water can again be re-used for the sea fight at Antium, so it won't be wasted. You see I've thought about these things. Naturally the land battles require horses. I have wondered about camels for Cleopatra's army, but they may be hard to come by, so horses will have to suffice. . .'

Jemmy steadied himself for what was to come.

'You do realise, Mr Plumptre, that Shakespeare has already wrote one play about Caesar, with another about Cleopatra and Antony, as also has Dryden. Handel an opera. . .'

'Of course I realise that. D'you take me for a fool? But they only wrote part of the tale. I have written the full history from start to finish. It's all there!'

'But the staging. You talk of battles on land and sea. Shakespeare had the wit to have them appear off stage.'

'Wit you say? He flunked it. That was in the old days. No stage machinery then. Not like today when people will want to see these things, what?' With enthusiasm Mr Plumptre began consulting a calendar. 'Now then, arrangements. You will require time to make preparations, I'm aware of that, but I'm impatient to see how it comes across. What about October . . .?

'Forgive me,' interrupted Jemmy, 'but how many pages are there in your drama?'

'No idea. An author does not count pages when he is writing, that would stop the flow of creation, what?'

'It is important to get some idea of the playing time.'

With an aggravated shrug Mr Plumptre turned his attention to the many piles of paper . Picking up one thick bundle he consulted the title page. 'This is Act the First. In which Caesar's early career is portrayed.'

'How many pages?'

Regardless of the time he was taking, Mr Plumptre painstakingly counted the leaves moving them from one pile to another. Jemmy wondering if he could charge for the hour that was being wasted. At last it was done.

'One hundred and thirty four.'

Jemmy sighed, 'How many acts are there?' he asked.

'One, two, three. . .' Mr Plumptre slowly considered the total. 'About ten or eleven. Shall we say a round dozen?'

'Are they of a similar length as "Act the First"?'

'Most certainly.'

'Mr Plumptre,' Jemmy took a small volume from his pocket. 'this is my copy of *Marriage a la Mode,* by the aforementioned Mr Dryden. It has one and forty pages. Even at that extent we shall have to reduce it before it is of the right duration for performance. It would seem your play would amount to at least . . . .' he calculated, 'about one and a half thousand pages.'

Mr Plumptre glowed at his achievement. 'Yes,'tis well done. I will admit is is a great play.'

'It would run for days.'

Mr Plumptre's glow increased, 'Yes, doubtless several nights, I have known from the start, a masterpiece has no bounds.'

Jemmy stood. 'It is impossible! Nobody, not even the Sun King and the entire Comedie Francaise have the facilities to produce anything of such monumental extravagance that . . .'

'Monumental extravagance? Be damned to the expense sir. . .'

'Mr Plumptre, it cannot be staged.'

'Be watchful what you say, when you have not even read it.'

'I have no need to. Your demands are absurd, and impossible.'

'Sir,' Mr Plumptre's glow was fading. For a moment it appeared that he might even leave the security of his bed. 'You have already received from me forty pounds in advance to act my play at your theatre.' he said. 'It is a matter of honour sir, that you keep your word, what?'

Desperately, Jemmy sought a way out of the situation. In a placatory tone he said. 'Mr Plumptre, my apologies if you are misled.' He waved his edition of Dryden. 'This, sir, is the fabric and size of an acting playscript. Each actor in the piece requires one copy to learn and study his role. That brings a total of twelve to fifteen copies. In addition there are required others for the prompt and the stage staff.' (As he said this, he recalled how miserly he was with hand copied play-scripts and wondered if he'd be damned in perpetuity for his falsehood).

'You will appreciate,' he pointed to the mass of paper on the bed, 'that in this unruly form, it would be impossible for the actors to learn their roles.'

'Oh! Is that the only cause of your disquiet?' asked Plumptre. 'Then sir, the remedy is to hand. The play is indeed to be published. I have already consulted with Mr Derry, the stationer, whose presses wait at the ready.'

'To print all of this?' Jemmy was confounded.

'Certainly. I fully understand your needs. One copy for each actor, and how many a' top of that for the. . . underlings?'

'It would want at least thirty, possibly more.' Jemmy said quietly.

'It shall be done. Let us us decide upon fifty.' Mr Plumptre leaned back wearily on his pillows. 'Would you ring for my man to show you out? I'll inform you when the printing is realised. After that we must confer as to dates. Well now. I am exceeding glad our difference is resolved. Good day to you sir.'

'And you permitted him to threaten you thus?'

'It was not a threat my dear,'

'Pardon me, but it was.' Cassandra did not care to hear Jemmy's account of his experience at Plumptre House. 'He has used threats to ensure his stupid rigmarole will to be acted here.'

'Either that or we return his forty pound advancement.'

Cassy was alarmed. 'You didn't suggest that?'

'No, my dear.'

'Because we do not have it. Husband, we are in sizeable debt. With your insistence on building a theatre in Derby we shall be repaying loans beyond the grave, so let there be no more talk of returning his money.'

'Tis thought genteel to be in debt,' Jemmy suggested meekly.

'Then we are at the very pinnacle of fashion. Nobody throws himself into the expenses of life with a freer spirit than you.'

'That is harsh my dear.'

'And so is the debtors' cell. Pray, end this talk of returning money. This sorry venture could be the very ruin of us, we must find some escape from your folly. God alone knows how.'

*

Twenty Four. *Just Cause or Impediment.*

A winged dragon, or a sun chariot? Which should it be?

Both required flame effects and both had to be flown, which was almost more than the stage machinery could provide on limited finances. In the end a sun chariot was favoured, with the logic that winged dragons were rarely encountered at sea, even by the Royal Navy. Indeed neither were sun chariots, but she felt that the solar symbolism would be appreciated by audiences in these troubled times.

Such problems confronted Jane Wilkinson daily as she wrote the text for *Harlequin Sailor*. Her imagination was boundless but not her budget. The task was complicated during her husband's absence on tour. By now he and the company would have left Hull to be in Doncaster, which was too far away for easy consultation. Instead she conferred with Mr Watson and Mr Weaver the stage carpenter and painter, who were able to confine her flights of fancy to a sensible level of stage bound reality.

The two craftsmen were keen that York should keep apace with new stage techniques and took delight in devising fresh wonders. The painter, Mr Weaver, had installed rolling canvases which would drop from the flies and astonish audiences with their swiftness of scene change. Until then, shuttered flats had been pushed in grooves from the wings which were clumsy and noisy and always left a join down the middle. They would still be used at times, for Mr Watson had cleverly put doors in some of them, hidden in the settings which could be opened to sudden and dramatic effect.

When playing Puck, Thomas's tricks and antics were mostly enacted behind the proscenium arch, where ropes and pulleys achieved the magic. By the time he came to play Harlequin the reliance on scenic effects would be even greater which Jane knew would not be popular with the actors. The apron stage was the acting area where they felt comfortably at home. They disliked having to act behind the proscenium arch, complaining that they would be either inaudible or invisible so far away from the audience, with the added danger of tripping on the grooves in the stage floor.

However, it was with stage lighting that innovative ideas would achieve new and dazzling effects. Cross battens of lights would be employed which could be shifted backwards and forwards overhead. With some of the scenes painted on transparent gauze, when the lights moved from front to back, a location could change in seconds before an astonished audience. Also there were vertical stands of six or more lamps in the wings to be swivelled giving gradations of light. With these, the stage could turn from night to day almost in seconds, an ingenious trick which delighted everyone. It was hoped that with these new devices *Harlequin Sailor* would be a creative success.

*

After arriving in Hull, Lucy Treadgold had not spoken for twenty four hours. She was put to bed at Fanny M'George's lodgings in River Street, where she slept for more than two days refusing both drink and nourishment. Thomas, still recovering from the Brewsters' attack, sat by her bedside waiting for her to wake and recount what had happened. As she gradually became sensible she murmured once or twice, 'It was because you hit him.'

Thomas took this to mean her father, for Lucy said no more. Once recovered she described slowly her walk from York to Hull, which it appeared had taken a week. More than once she had lost her way, eventually finding herself in Beverley. By the time she arrived there she was exhausted and confused, mistaking the Minster for the one at York. She was fortunate in being helped by a carrier who took pity on her and saw that she travelled safely on the last part of her journey. It was he who had also found the theatre at Hull and so restored her to the shelter of her friends.

'It was because you hit him,' Lucy said again.

'Did he maltreat you?'

'He guessed I had told you of the secret between us. He'd made me swear to silence. Oh, I know he seems harmless and he's often taken for a molly, but he can be cruel, very cruel. I had to leave.'

The reserve Lucy had shown towards Thomas was now gone and she accepted the comfort he gave her. She was able to return the affection he had for her and he felt that from this time he could protect her from her father and any other evils.

Tate Wilkinson welcomed her back in the company realising his Columbine was possibly to hand. He gave them both time to recover for he badly needed his young players to be fit enough for his new production in York.

The run at Hull was almost complete with the move to Doncaster imminent. Even though Lucy was not well enough to walk the twenty miles between the towns Wilkinson always a kindly man, arranged for her to ride with him on horseback.

Many in the company were puzzled by her dramatic arrival, even though Tate made light of this saying,'She could not bear to be parted from us,' As yet he refrained from suggesting that Lucy and Thomas were to be stage partners, believing that until it was settled that would be tempting Providence.

Once arrived in Doncaster, Thomas slowly regained strength and was able to perform during the first week with the encouraging approval of audiences bolstering his recovery. A further season lay ahead in Wakefield before the return to York, by which time he felt he would be able to play as normal.

Lucy's youthful constitution also helped her revival, with Tate arranging for her to have singing lessons before she resumed her dance practice. Yet Lucy showed increasing fears abut returning to York.

'Why have they not come after me?' she asked.

'Perhaps they believe you will return,' said Thomas.

'I'd rather kill myself.'

'Never say that, even though you do not mean it.'

'I mean it I would rather die than return.'

Thomas sought Tate's advice when the season began at the Doncaster theatre.

'What is it young feller-me-lad?' asked the busy manager.

'To begin, I ask you to stop calling me that. It aggrieves me.'

'Well strain my sinews, "It aggrieves me," he says. What then would you have? "Your lordship?" "Your altitude?"

'Just Thomas, will suit.'

'Well then Just Thomas what is it?'

Thomas tried describing Lucy's situation without revealing secrets about her father. He said simply that she was unhappy with her parents and wished to be free of them. But neither she nor Thomas knew what to do next.

'Easy,' replied Tate. 'Marry the girl.' He smiled. 'Only don't get her with child if you do.' He asked anxiously, 'She's not with child already is she?'

'No sir, she is not.' Thomas was resentful. 'But how can we be wed? We are both under age and her parents will never agree.'

'Now listen to me young feller-me . . . .' Tate stopped himself. 'Listen Thomas. Get you both to a church and hear the banns read. Three consecutive Sundays. Once that's cleared, you can be wed, before we leave here. As for your parents, say they're dead, which at least is likely in your case. Once you are married you cannot be unwed by parents or anyone.'

'You would truly have us married?' asked Thomas.

'You love the wench don't you? She loves you. That's the stamp we've put on you both. And the public will like that. Always good for trade newlyweds in the company.'

This was not the direction Thomas had expected, although he knew above all it was what he wanted.

'How do I set about it? Which church should I go to?'

'Find the parish church where you're boarding. As long as you leave a bag at your lodgings, it passes as being resident. Waste no time, get the banns up this coming Sunday. Now cut along, I've no more time today for wedding arrangements. Hallelujah, praise the Lord.'

There was a vigour in Thomas's walk as he returned to Lucy. 'I put it to Wilkinson that we should marry and he fully agreed with my idea.'

Lucy said, 'It will seem I have I have left home only for you to marry me.'

'Why else have you left home?'

'I had to leave my parents, you know that full well. But that is no reason to marry you.'

Thomas kissed her. She returned his affection As he embraced her there was none of the previous rigidity. Her body yielded softly against his and in spite of her words, he felt she was already part of him.

'I have loved you since that first day at the school,' he said, 'when you helped me with the dance and I thought you were laughing at me.'

This time Lucy did laugh, 'If every young man felt like that, I would have suitors from here to Huddersfield.'

'To hell with Huddersfield. I would crawl there to be with you.'

'Now you are being ridiculous.'

'Perhaps that is the only way I could get your answer. You have never said you love me, but I know full well you do.'

Lucy kissed him, 'I do. And have longed to tell you so, Robin Goodfellow. Yes, I have fallen in love with you, as have your audiences. It will be hard having to share you with so many admirers.'

'Audiences aren't people. They're a wall of noise. A sea of eyes.'

'Suppose some jade may attract your eye.'

'I swear that will never happen,' he paused, 'but what if it did?'

'She'd best be on her guard, for I shall swiftly deal with her.'

For a while they traded kisses in blissful silence. Lucy sighed as she looked at him. 'All the way here I wished for a map. Now I have arrived, I wish I had another map. To show me where I go next.'

'No need for a map when you have a lodestar,' said Thomas.

As soon as she heard the news, Fanny M'George took it upon herself to be both the mother of the bride and planner of the wedding. The tidings delighted the whole company for none could remember a marriage taking place in their midst before. Liaisons certainly, but marriages, no.

'What shall she wear?' was Fanny's first concern. it was the custom that the bride wore her best clothes. Being a theatrical marriage this meant finding something from the wardrobe where many fine dresses had been given by wealthy patrons with no further use for them. Anything connected with a tragic character was unthinkable, yet it was hard to find something that was not connected with a sad story.

Mrs Kenna's help was called upon.

'Oh I like this,' enthused Lucy,' as they sorted through the wardrobe.

'From *The Distressed Mother* that will never do.'

'What about this? It's very pretty.'

The Fallen Wife. No.'

'This?'

''Quite unsuitable.'

'Why so?'

'Tis Pity She's a Whore. Now this is a possibility. . . No I had forgot, *The Mourning Bride*. How difficult it is. . .'

'Now this has to be my choice,' Lucy brought forth an ivory silk gown.

'Let me see,' said Fanny. '*The Constant Lovers*. Yes, that will suit. It moves nicely and must be taken in, there's so very little of you.'

'Then this is the one,' said Lucy. And so it was decided.

When they approached the church to have their banns read, they were fortunate in finding a curate new to the district. He did not yet know many in the parish and so accepted their residency as authentic. Also he believed them when they said their parents were no longer living and they were both aged eighteen. The fee was paid with the promise that the banns would be read for the next three Sundays.

'They will be published at Matins,' the curate told them,' and it is usual for you to be here.' The wedding date was fixed for the Wednesday following the last reading, Lucy having been told by Fanny that according to old custom Wednesday was the luckiest day of the week for a marriage.

'I publish the banns of marriage. . .' that Sunday they held each other's hands in a grip of anxiety. There were many names,until they heard,

'. . . between Thomas Hammond, bachelor and Lucy Treadgold, spinster, both of this parish.' The clergyman closed the register and continued, 'This is for the first time of asking. If any of you know just cause or impediment why these persons should not be joined in Holy Matrimony, ye are to declare it. . .'

Perhaps it was their imagination, but both Thomas and Lucy felt a whisper within the church at the announcement of their names. In a parish where everyone knew each other, the question 'Who's that?' seemed to be heard as their unfamiliar names were announced. They sat together at the rear of the nave, feeling to be impostors in this gathering of churchgoing families. Knowing that they were false in their request, increased their unease. As soon as the service ended they attempted to leave by the south door, but with astonishing speed the vicar was already there to greet the departing congregation. He looked at them with a relentless smile and an extended hand, 'You are both most welcome,' he said adeptly, 'Your names are . .?

'Mr Hammond and Miss Treadgold,' said Thomas quickly.

'Ah yes We have not seen you here before. Not regular worshippers. Pray, where do you live? I would like to call on you for some short deliberation prior to the ceremony. It is my usual custom.'

'I live at River Street,' said Lucy.

'River Street? I know it well. Which house is that?'

'I live with Mrs Strickland. . .'

'Ah yes, Mrs Strickland. Is not that a lodging house?'

'I live there,' said Lucy uncomfortably.

The vicar continued to smile, but as his parishioners were building up behind in the porch, they moved on.

'He's suspicious,' said Lucy as they walked away.

'We're not criminals,' answered Thomas.

'We shall be if he marries us wrongly.'

Thomas knew she was right and wondered why they were risking a felony and why it seemed so important to be married. Most of the couples in the company were unwed for it was said that some ladies liked a variety of husbands, whereas gentlemen frequently favoured a plurality of wives.

The week passed by. Thomas appeared as Puck with audiences as enthusiastic as in York This meant he was being recognised in the streets once more, which might be an added complication if he appeared again at the church. He took comfort from the belief that churchgoers did not frequent the theatre.

Lucy was now recovered enough to be practising her dancing daily and also finding her singing voice. Tate regarded them both benevolently, convinced that he had two foremost performers emerging. So pleased was he, that he announced a holiday from rehearsals on the Wednesday when they would be wed, with a party for the entire company to be held after the ceremony.

Fanny M'George hugely enjoyed herself making arrangements for the nuptials. Lucy's dress was fitted lovingly, remembering that it was good luck that the last stitch must be left unfinished.

'Don't forget, you must make a shirt for the groom,' she told Lucy. 'For the bride must always do that.'

'But I am little use with a needle,' said Lucy.

'No matter as long as the shirt is newly worn. You can sew on buttons can't you? That will suffice. And be sure it has a button hole, for a flower from your bouquet.'

Fanny remembered many old superstitions telling Lucy that under no circumstance must she look in a glass on the special day.

'Don't worry for I shall be there to see you appear well. Oh, and by the by, I have arranged for the fiddler to play you back here from the church. It will be a fine procession with the company following all dressed up to the nines. Oh, and you must have a spare garter for the bridegroom to throw to the men.'

Beneath all the laughter and making ready, Lucy continued to be uneasy. Every night she returned to her lodgings on River Street, fearing that the vicar might call for his deliberation. The approaching Sunday troubled her. She and Thomas not being versed in church matters, believed that they had to be present at each reading of the banns. This would mean another encounter with the clergyman and possibly more questions. Again they sat as far away from the east end as possible, hoping not to be noticed. They held hands as the second publication drew near. he vicar's words sounded louder and more stern than before. After reading the names, he closed the register.

'This is for the second time of asking. If any of you know just cause or impediment why these persons should not be joined in Holy Matrimony, ye are to declare it. . .'

There was a moment of quiet in the church following the familiar words. Coughs and a low buzz of polite comment as to be heard when from somewhere a strange high pitched voice broke forth,

'I forbid this marriage. The girl is under age and has not her parents' consent. . .'

Immediately a concert of conversation filled the church. Heads were raised, turning to see from where the voice had come. The vicar looking as if he had been struck by a missive, hesitated in his pulpit, adjusted his brocaded stole, cleared his throat noisily and declared,

'As several names have been published, I know not which you refer to.' He was at a loss. 'See me afterwards. . .' he said like a ineffectual teacher.

Lucy knew Treadgld's voice immediately and ran from the church. Thomas pursued her into the church yard where he found her sheltering amidst the gravestones, alone and frightened.

*

Twenty Five. *This man's art and that man's scope.*

The Feathers was one of the many ale houses and taverns to be found on Nottingham's Long Row. It was not of the first quality, possibly because it hid its presence from the common gaze by being situated up Easton's yard. Like many others, Easton's yard gave access for pedestrians between the north of Nottingham down to the square. This narrow passage was used on Wednesdays and Saturdays for the driving of cattle, sheep and pigs to market, with the resultant underfoot perils which often remained all week.

The Feathers was a converted house which may once have been a proud abode but was no more. Its frontage had become a tailor's shop, leaving only a common doorway up the alley, off which the various gloomy tap rooms and drinking parlours were to be found. The hostelry's main attraction was the cock pit in its cellars. Here sales of intoxicants were prodigious, especially on fight nights.

Powell had booked a private room for the exhibiting of *Jemima, the surprising female child.* This was for six days from Monday to Saturday, with an option for a further week should the attraction prove a financial success. The deal was for John Galpin alone with the child to be 'in situ' from eleven in the mornings onward. Space being limited, the attendance of Mrs Galpin had not been considered.

But Jemima did not wish to be parted from her mother. For the first hour of her being on exhibition the infant screamed lustily at the lack of maternal care. Mr Galpin tried unsuccessfully to assuage the child's full-throated protestations but to no avail. Quite rightly, the landlord insisted that although it gained attention, such noise would not attract any custom to view. It was then agreed that the mother should be brought to console her daughter. However, this gave rise to further difficulties, for Mrs Galpin was obliged to bring with her two other siblings aged three and four who also would not be estranged from their mother. Although by now the din was diminished, before the doors were re-opened to admit the public, the hired room being modest in size, seemed crowded.

The public response was lack lustre. Inevitably, it was not long before the two older children grew bored with the enterprise and in whining tones asked to go home. This was answered with cuffs to the ear, leading to screams of protest which were taken up in full volume by the wondrous child of nature, all resulting in an uproar greater than that endured in the first place. So loud was the noise that few approaching the exhibition chose to proceed further.

Tiredness and temper took their toll. Jemima, usually swaddled, grew hot and had to be displayed with less covering than usual so that by the afternoon she was in urgent need of cleansing. When the Galpins, in despair, decided to return home the landlord declared angrily that the best time for business was just approaching. So it was settled that on the morrow they would start later and try to be available into the evening time.

The next day Powell and the landlord were further aggravated when the Galpins appeared with the addition of an ancient father. It was explained that he would be able to keep the older children amused for they still refused to be parted from their mother.

Business was little better. From five o'clock when drinkers began their evening revelries, a small number were curious to see the unusual display. But dissatisfaction grew. Those who visited the room, saw not a marvel but a family much like their own. This was not worth a shilling of anyone's money and the venture was variously described as trickery or an outright humbug. At the close of day, less than two pounds were banked for safekeeping with the landlord. Reluctantly Powell admitted that the project appeared to be a failure. Nevertheless on the Wednesday, being market day, he hoped for better things.

Powell returned that day to be met by the landlord,

'Didn't expect to see you,' he said.

'I want to see the room is clean and ready for business,' said Powell.

'What business? Galpin said you'd agreed.'

'Agreed what?

''e came back last night. Told me you'd chucked in your cap.'

'Are you telling me he's piked?' asked Powell.

'Looks like it.'

'In that case I'll have my deposit back.'

'You won't. 'e took it last night along with the takings.'

'You gave it him?'

'Said you'd quit the venture.'

'The thieving bloody gutterfly! Wait till I get to the bastard.'

'Won't do you no good. Last night was a fight night.'

At once, Powell understood the meaning.

'He gambled it?'

'And lost the lot. Couldn't 'elp but feel sorry for 'im, poor sod.'

Black with anger, Powell took off his hat and threw it to the floor. It was a pointless gesture, but the only immediate way of relieving the rage within himself. To have been so trusting, not to have realised that an inept idiot like Galpin could get the better of him. He had been duped. He'd paid for everything, the hire of the room, the newspaper advertisement and the display board and here he was - penny cramped.

He went at once to the Galpin's lodgings where his furious banging on their door obtained no response until a weary voice called, 'Who is it?' The door was opened by Mrs Galpin. Tired and tear stained her face told everything. Looking into their wretched room he saw the old father and the children staring emptily at him. John Galpin was not there.

'I know not where he is,' wept his wife. 'I fear he is obliged to skulk and keep out the way for fear of arrest. He's done it many times before, plunged everything away on a wager and left us with nothing.'

It was pointless wasting time trying to find him. The takings had gone and he had no way of retrieving any part of them.

Yet in spite of his anger, his real wrath was still directed at Whitley. Whitley, the third rate manager. It was he who had brought him down to this. For sure, Whitley was to blame. Yes, and Whitley would pay for his misfortunes. Depend upon it.

*

The Commons rose for the summer recess meaning that Sir Charles Sedley was able to spend more time with his family at Nuthall Temple. He had hurried home from London, eager to see the ceiling by Signor Ceraccio which was now completed. As the scaffolding was removed the legend of Cupid and Psyche was revealed in gentle shades of the softest hues providing an overhead visual delight. Sir Charles was thrilled with what he saw. The choice of painter had proved to be inspired and he commended his son for his adroit discovery.

'Very fine, very fine,' said Sir Charles to Edmond. 'The Psyche is a wonder. So very lovely and yet she almost puts me in mind of some-one I am acquainted with.'

'Indeed it should father,' replied Edmund. 'For the model is none other than Miss Armstrong.'

'Miss Armstrong?'

'From Whitley's company. She played Juliet.'

'To be sure. What a beauty she has proved. But how did the painter find her? Did he go to the theatre?'

'No father, I brought her here. She seemed to be the perfect model for Psyche.'

'How true. And ingenious of you to devise it.'

With Signor Ceraccio's task complete and his parents at home, there was no further occasion for Edmund to invite Belinda to Nuthall. He continued to see her every performance at the theatre for their liaison had become intense; how this was to be be maintained was something that occupied him throughout the vacation. Whereas Sir Charles and Lady Sedley were delighted to have Belinda adorning their ceiling, to have her as a daughter-in-law or even their son's mistress could not be countenanced. Presently, Edmund managed to rent rooms in St James's Street, on the far side of Nottingham where *incognito* he hoped they might spend many joyous hours in the weeks ahead.

An evening arrived when a private reception was held for the revelation of the masterpiece at Nuthall. Neighbouring gentry and their friends were invited to admire and, it was hoped, be envious of the fine painted ceiling.

As usual with the English, the cultural event promoted the

exchange of gossip, rather than appreciation of the art on display. It had not been realised by Sir Charles that the examination of a ceiling was almost impossible without giddiness or dislocated necks. Indeed the best way to regard the work was to lie flat on the floor, an attitude few were prepared to adopt.

Signor Ceraccio was almost totally ignored. Only one or two when told he spoke a little English, said loudly 'Very nice!' or even 'Bella, bella,' at which the signor bowed modestly.

Only Edmund engaged him in conversation, being able to converse in clumsy Italian and also out of gratitude for his secrecy concerning his intrigue with Miss Armstrong.

'You will now be returning to Milan, signor?'

'Alas no. I have been advised not to.'

'Why so? Is there cholera there?'

'There is a pestilence, yes, but it is called the Hapsburgs. Their Austrian rule contaminates the freedom of my homeland. Soon we will rise against them. In the past I have painted posters denouncing their oppression. My style of politics is well known so that if I return I am in danger of persecution.'

Edmund thought for a while. He asked, 'You paint portraits of course?

'Ah, un ritratto! Yes, of course I paint portraits.'

'If you were to paint some of the gentry here in this country, your reputation would be made. Of course you would require a studio.'

'Ah yes. But that requires finance. In spite of your father's generous payment I have no means.'

Edmund had a fresh idea. 'Would you paint theatrical scenery?'

'If it was required,' said the signor. 'It is not unlike poster work.'

'Let me consider this. I may be able to help you.'

That night when Edmund took his seat at the theatre, he decided to approach Mr Whitley about the possibility of employing Ceraccio as a scene painter.

Jemmy Whitley liked the idea, especially when Edmund was prepared to meet any expenditure. Bracer complained constantly about his burden of work, so that Whitley was sure he would be glad of some skilled assistance.

'Not from no Frenchie,' said Bracer.

'He is not a French,' said Whitley. 'He's an Italian.'

'All foreigners are Frenchies,' insisted Mr Bracer.

'You will have to overcome your objections. For I have said we shall have him.' With reluctance Bracer agreed to give the signor a time of trial.

At the start the collaboration was tense. Whitley asked the signor to design and paint a new settings for *Oroonoko* or *The Regal Slave*. This was an ambitious enterprise, requiring scenes on board a slave ship and in tropical forests. Bracer was scathing when, from the beginning, Ceraccio insisted in making miniatures of the sets which he dismissed as 'farting about' and wasting time. Yet once the main painting was embarked upon, Bracer had to admit the signor achieved some original effects.

The two men tried to discuss the mixing and choice of colours, which with no common tongue was difficult. There were conflicting shouts of *nero* and *black, rosso* and *red, green* and *verde*. But gradually the two learned that they were both 'artista'. All his life Bracer had mixed his paints with water and applied then with a large brush in the manner of white wash. He was mystified by the Italian's use of oils and waxes both as thinners and driers.

Ceraccio's use of coloured chalks was new and effective, being quick and accurate in outlining and defining objects with a clarity Bracer had never seen. The Italian was generous sometimes and used costly materials of his own if he felt an effect needed it. Soon, a palette of colour appeared that was fresh and remarkable. Bracer admired this whole heartedly and was also glad to have a partner with whom to share his craft. One that he could admire and learn from, even though he was still a Frenchie.

Whitley, working incessantly, was showing signs of fatigue. The forthcoming opening in Derby and the heavy acting load he was carrying gave Cassandra disturbed and worrying nights.

'We must get a replacement for Powell,' she said. 'We must find a new leading man. You cannot continue playing leads with so many other burdens to carry.'

'I had hoped that either Mr Kirk or Mr Venables would prove useable but they will never be any more than supporting actors.'

News of the new theatre about to open in Derby, had brought an array of letters from unemployed comedians craving auditions. Eventually three applicants were thought worth sending for, which included a Mr Oldfield and a Mr Grist. A date was arranged for interviews, which required the reading of a Shakespearean soliloquy with an additional speech from a modern play.

At the appointed time the Whitleys sat in the auditorium awaiting the candidates. The first two contenders offered *'Now is the winter of our discontent. . .'* causing Jemmy to think he would be a rich man if he had a penny for every time he had heard the familiar words. For their modern pieces they both offered sentimental monologues which Jemmy found of small interest.

However, with the newcomer Mr Grist he sat forward in his seat excitedly. Leonard Grist chose unfamiliar ground with *Titus Andronicus* and the terrifying speech, *'Come, come Lavinia. Look thy foes are bound. . .'* He portrayed the tormented hero avenging his enemies, so convincingly that the previous two actors still on stage drew back in alarm.

'Very good,' said Jemmy who hardly knew the play, but Cassandra disagreed. That Mr Grist had chosen a speech containing throat cutting and cannibalism she found unpalatable.

'I think his choice is shocking,' she said. 'What sort of a man would select something so offensive?'

'Wait my dear. He takes a chance which is commendable. Let us see what he offers as a contemporary piece.' To Mr Grist he asked, 'You have something more modern prepared for us?'

'Indeed,' replied Mr Grist. 'I wish to put before you the love scene from *The Tragedy of Tragedies* by Mr Fielding. 'I shall play both roles.'

'By Jove, he takes a risk,' whispered Jemmy to his wife.

Mr Grist continued, 'I shall perform the personages of Lord Grizzle and the Princess Huncamunca.' He proceeded to portray the two parts in the burlesque love scene with such skill and sense of the ridiculous that Jemmy and Cassandra were shaking with silent mirth, for it would not have done to encourage him by laughing out loud. Sharing a handkerchief they both wiped the tears from their cheeks and without further thought, Mr Grist was engaged.

The two rejected comedians commiserated with each other in a nearby tavern. Of the stories exchanged, Mr Oldfield's was the saddest.

'Have you come far?' he was asked by the other.

'Stamford,' said Mr Oldfield. 'I was with Wilkinson's company.'

'Why ever did you leave? That's the best outside London.'

'How right you are. It was foolishness and nothing else. I was persuaded to enter a business partnership with an actor turned haulier, name of Sweeny. I believe he used to be here with Jemmy Whitley.'

'Perhaps you should have mentioned that.'

'Not so, for I know Sweeny has a bad name He persuaded me to invest my benefit money into the canal projects. At first I was paid some good dividends then without warning they stopped. I asked Sweeny - why? "My dear fellow," he said, "Some companies thrive, others do not. I fear the company you invested in has failed." '

'"But you said it was good," I told him, when he put my money in it. "Yes, it seemed sound, at first," he said "I too have lost money you know." "But not everything as I have," I said.'

' "True," he said, "stocks are a gamble. Much to gain but much to lose." I could have struck him, he behaved so heartlessly. I have a family to keep. He has none. When I reminded him of this he offered me a job as a copyist in his office. But I am not able to write with any skill. Besides, I have been a comedian all my life. I am not suited to other trades.'

'Is your family still in Stamford?'

'Where I must return. My wife has some work at the George and I too might find something there.' Sadly he added, 'Had I'd known Grist was auditioning I wouldn't have come. There's no holding a button to the likes of him. In a rank of his own, is Mr Grist.'

Which was true. Within a fortnight, Mr Gist was playing Dr Faustus and Orlando as well as comic roles which pleased every house. Clearly he had played them before, being word perfect and it was wondered why he was still in the provinces, such was his ability. Surely he should be in London?

A born *dilettante* with no formal training, he performed by instinct. His talent was God-given as was his sonorous voice, which together with charm and politeness of ease, gained him the grace to entertain on and off stage.

For ten years in Chester, he had followed his father's trade as a bookbinder. He was married to a dull woman who disapproved of his amateur acting fearing, quite rightly, the tempting proximity of pretty young actresses. This jealousy, together with her refusal ever to see him act, kept them apart. Ultimately, she and her family were scandalised when he paid all of fifteen shillings to act the role of Othello for one night only with a professional company. The idea of paying money to appear in public was shame enough, but blacking himself up was unforgivable and it finally separated them. This proved to be ideal, for his debut was triumphant with Mr Grist receiving a ten minute ovation, setting him free to make a new career on the stage.

Soon Whitley was planning for him to include Macbeth and even Hamlet in his repertoire, as Grist claimed to know all four of the great Shakespearian tragedies. But Whitley would not allow him to have Lear. That was not to be considered. For it was still Jemmy's ambition to play the king himself.

*

Twenty Six. *Let it be tenable in your silence still.*

Jane Wilkinson was preparing for bed. It was midsummer, that balmy time of year when it was light well beyond ten in the evening. She had closed the shutters to the street windows, bolted the front door and moved into the parlour at the rear to enjoy the paling day. Even at this hour there was a mistle thrush singing high in a hawthorn tree and she stood by the open door to the garden delighting in its musicality. As the evening was warm she had already changed into her night-dress over which she was wearing a light negligée. A mob cap, soft embroidered slippers comforted her head and feet. Before going upstairs she would take a glass of porter and write her journal by the oil lamp already lit on her table. This evening she felt content because she had finished the *Harlequinade* her husband had asked from her. She took up her writing things,

Sunday June 19th,

This day I have completed the main draft of 'Harlequin Sailor.' Or so it will seem until my dear husband shall examine it. The task has been considerable for I had not realised that Harlequin was less of the comic figure and more of Columbine's romantic lover. From what I can foregather in the original 'tis Pantaloon who is the true comic character.

However, I have made Harlequin the knave and changed Pantaloon's revenge into the reason for his going to sea. This may not be true to the original 'commedia dell'arté' but will not trouble our audience here in York.

The opening scene is intended for . . .

For some reason she stopped. Looking up from the table, a rush of alarm ran through her body. This was unusual, being alone never before held fears for her. Tate was more often away than at home and she prided herself on never being anxious. But at this moment there was something just beyond her knowing that caused her to worry.

She took a sip from the glass, intending to continue writing, but disquiet prevented her. The thrush had stopped singing and the door to the garden was still open. All seemed silent apart from distant sounds of the street on the other side of the house. She was aware that the parlour curtains were undrawn and with the lamp alight beside her, knew she was clearly visible from outside. But the garden was walled and the only other access was from her neighbour, an old lady who kept her gates firmly locked at all times.

'It is my fancy,' she said aloud to herself, ashamed at her anxiety. She dipped her pen in the ink well, but her thoughts would not return to the page. 'What was it that was wrong?' A mixture of anger with herself and a sense of forewarning took control.

Yes, there it was again. Nothing that could be seen, yet she felt a presence in the garden. The deep blue of the gloaming which lingered in the sky held the trees in silhouette but it was not sufficient to illuminate the ground which had turned velvet black.

'A cat, yes of course.' Again she spoke aloud to herself, which was unseemly She must be more rational. On the other hand, it was said rats were as plentiful as kittens and having no wish to be invaded by either, she rose to draw the curtains and shut the garden door.

It was then that a blackbird gave a flittering cry of warning which was unexpected in the twilight and the sound unnerved her. To lock the garden door had become urgent and with her body beginning to tremble she moved, carefully walking the short distance. She would not rush; if she was being spied on that would not do. When she reached the door, she realised with dismay the key was left on the table. No, she would not go back. She would shut the door, draw the curtains and then fetch the key to secure herself.

Putting her hand on the latch she began gently to close the door, until a heavy boot stamped on the threshold and prevented her. The shock made her scream. She tried forcing the door closed, but was prevented by a strength greater than hers. . .

'Let me in,' a man's voice spoke hoarsely. She had no choice.

'What do you want?' she asked. As she did she realised her voice was indignant, not the right tone for dealing with a marauder. It might exacerbate his mood.

'I want to talk to you,' said the man.

Because she had screamed she was at a disadvantage for it revealed that she was frightened. The man was now in the room enabling her to look at him. His clothing was unkempt. Even though it was a warm night he had on a heavy woollen coat, much soiled. His fair hair was long and he had a beard that had not been tended for weeks.

'Do you not know me?' he asked.

'No I don't. How did you get in here?

'With determination.'

'I have nothing of value,' she insisted, 'if that's what you seek.'

'What I seek is news. News that you can give me.'

'No, you're wrong. You must think me to be someone else.'

'I ask for news of my sister Lucy. Now do you know me?'

Jane's mind was in turmoil. The mixture of shock and outrage had made her shatter-brained. She knew that what was happening was real yet it had no truth. All she wanted was for it to stop, to go away, until she realised that she knew who it was confronting her. Once understood, she gained an authority which changed the situation in a trice. Her voice became steadier.

'I think I recognise you but you had better tell me.'

'Walter Treadgold. Much altered I know,' he said.

Annoyance now composed her as she sat in her chair by the table. 'Why have you forced your way in? Like a thief.'

'Because I'm wanted by the law. I can move about only after dark. If I'd knocked at your door, would you have let me in?'

'If I had known it was you, yes.' She waited. 'Why are you wanted by the law?'

'Best you not know.'

Jane sighed, her mood changing to weariness. 'Oh you foolish boy. Whatever it is, you have brought it on yourself. You had good steady work with your parents.'

'My parents! That is one reason I am here.'

Her passions were changing by the minute. Now pity overcame her. She saw before her, not a thief but a young man in peril. He needed help whatever he had done.

'Sit down,' she said, 'you look finished.' He slumped into an armchair by the empty hearth. It was Tate's own chair. This would not have happened, she thought, if he had been here at home with her.

'How long since you ate?' she asked.

'A long while.'

'I will get you something.'

At last she drew the window curtains, but left the door unlocked, for she might need to depart hurriedly. She had known Walter Treadgold for years, but who was this man in the armchair? She went to the kitchen where there was remaining some cold potatoes and a piece of beef. She sliced some of the meat, placing it onto a plate. There was no ale in the house, so she poured him a glass of wine and put this together with the food onto a board, returning to the parlour.

'You know it is quite wrong for me to be serving you, dressed as I am,' She spoke deliberately lightly as she set the board on the table. However, conversation was unnecessary, Walter was deep asleep.

She looked at the unconscious man knowing some sort of watch must be kept over him. She was now so alert she would never sleep that night, for there could be no repose with an intruder in the house. No longer was he the dancing boy she had known. Now he was a trespasser, a danger.

He said he was wanted by the law and she believed him. He looked like a fugitive. What had he done? He said he would not tell her, that he had come to ask about Lucy, but there was nothing she could say about his sister.

Removing the board of food she returned it to the kitchen, but she could not stay there. She had to be with him when he woke, for there was no knowing what he would do. For the present his breathing was low and soft, a rhythm balanced against the genial ticking of the mantelpiece clock, as if he was some honest labourer resting after a day's toil. Well, for the time being she must sit and keep guard. Her journal remained open, the entry unfinished.

And so it must stay. What would she be writing tomorrow, assuming she reached another day with safety? Before that there was this night to be lived through.

She had some mending and there was a novel she was reading.

Best occupy herself, even if she was not sure that the oil in the lamp was sufficient. It was grown totally dark outside and possibly it would last, the night being only six hours long this time of year.

In the street the watchman passed by, 'Eleven of a fine night and all's well.' 'All's well!' if he did but know. She found the novel to be dull, or perhaps she was not giving it her proper attention. . .

'I've had the food.' Walter was standing over her. She woke, for a moment not recalling the situation, aware only of an ache in her side from sleeping clumsily at the table. It was almost light outside and the bird was beginning to sing once more. How long had he been awake? Long enough to go into the kitchen, and perhaps other parts of the house? It was hateful to be suspicious, but after what he had said. . . She looked at the clock. It was nearly four.

'I must leave, before the day starts,' he said. 'I have come to ask you, where is my sister?'

'I don't know. All I know is that like you she has not been at the theatre for some time. Your parents said she was unwell.'

'My parents! Do you believe their lies?'

'Lies, what else should I think ?'

'They are deceivers. He is not our father, you must know that.'

'I've no reason to think otherwise.'

'I will give you reason. He is foul. First it was me he corrupted, then when I prevented him, it was her.'

'What was?' She did not understand.

'Did you not know? No, nobody knew, that was his craftiness. Lady, our home, was nothing but a private brothel. Run alone for his benefit. Lucy and I were his drabs. For years it was me, for he's a molly by nature. But then I grew able to refuse him, so he turned to Lucy to satisfy him.'

Jane was disturbed. She was shocked but not entirely surprised by this malignant news, for there had always been something unsound about the Treadgold's. Now it was made apparent, she was confused. Feelings of guilt arose; should she and Tate have realised and perhaps prevented the misdeeds?

'Why have you left Lucy? Does she not need your protection?'

'I gave her the chance to come with me, but she refused. I could do no more.' he said/

'What lies ahead for you ? Where will you go?'

'Away, out of York. I cannot stay here.' He stood up. He had not removed his coat, having slept in it, possibly lived in it for weeks. If anything he looked more dishevelled now than when he had broken in.

'If you intend to report me, give me an hour first,' he said.

'Walter. Would I do such a thing?'

'If they know you've sheltered me they will be hard on you.'

'I shall tell no-one.' For the only time a distant smile lit her face.

'What about that?' He nodded towards her journal. She realised that he must have looked at it, perhaps read it, whilst she slept.

'Nobody, not even my husband has means to that.' She hoped he would believe her. 'You'll need vittles for your journey. Oranges and ginger bread are all I have.' She offered them to him carefully wrapped in a cloth and winced as she saw him stuff the bundle roughly into his coat pocket. Realising that he was now about to leave, she walked towards the street door, expecting him to follow.

'No, I'll not go onto the street.'

'There can be nobody about at this hour,' she said.

'Can't be certain of that. No, I must leave the way I came in. Otherwise 'tis bad luck, isn't it?'

Without warning he departed as swiftly as he arrived.

*

It was Lucy who recovered firstly from the refusal of the banns. She appeared almost relieved that the wedding was not to take place, as if she had been rescued from some dangerous endeavour. Thomas was far more troubled, refusing to discuss her father's intervention.

Not so the members of the company, for everyone had a theory of how Treadgold had found out about the wedding. Had some malicious person informed him? If so, who could that person be? Was it a member of the company? Such thoughts gave rise to an uncomfortable atmosphere. Whilst there was broad sympathy for Thomas and Lucy, their confounded situation gave them an air of contagion, as if they might infect others with a fatal mishap. To many backstage they were tainted with bad luck. Like Jonahs onboard a ship.

News spread through the town that the couple whose banns had been refused were comedians at the theatre which boosted audience attendance. Notoriety was always good for business but, then as now, it added to the strain of the performer. Thomas realised how much was expected from him. Success was entangling him. There was no escaping its embrace.

The hour before a show, sickness and fear almost paralysed him, so that ahead of each performance he was in the alehouse until the last minute, dashing into his dressing room always with a bottle to sustain him throughout the evening.

'This is what happened with Walter,' Lucy said to him angrily. 'Very soon it will be impossible for you to be without it. If you want me by your side, there is no place for the bottle.'

Thomas knew she was right, but her words had no effect. Like most in the company he needed *a line of the old author* before and during a performance. Brandy enabled him to go on stage with the confidence to enjoy himself. To give what the audience wanted.

There were the other times also. In the night, when he could not sleep, his mind racing with distortions of dialogue and songs turning over and over, until only a drink gave respite. Yes, he knew the dangers. There were actors like old Mitteer back in Nottingham, whose memory had been dissolved by alcohol. But he was different, no such thing would ever happen to him.

Late one afternoon, when Lucy returned to the River Street lodgings, she was met by her landlady Mrs Strickland. There had been a visit from the vicar asking to see Lucy for a pastoral talk. Mrs Strickland, who had no time for clergymen, took the visit to be a bad omen. She believed it was the premonition of something awful, perhaps a death in the house. The parson, on finding Lucy was not there, said he would call again. Mrs Strickland was adamant that Lucy would instead call on him; another visit from a priest was more than she could tolerate.

Lucy called next day and was shown into the vicar's study, a cold school-like room. The reverend came directly to the matter, saying,

'The refusal of banns is very rare, I myself have only experienced it once before, but it does mean that your wedding cannot take place,'

Lucy said she understood this.

'With the new marriage laws if you are under age there must be consent from your parents.'

Again Lucy said she knew this but told the vicar that the man who had objected to the banns might not be her true father.

'Indeed!' said the vicar. 'You surprise me. He came to me greatly troubled as only a father can be. He insisted that both he and your mother were totally opposed to your marriage with Mr Hammond.'

Lucy said that she and her brother had long thought Treadgold was not their father. What's more they were convinced that their mother had taken his name without being wed to him. This news concerned the vicar .

'If your parents are not married,' he said, 'that puts a new bearing on the situation. You and your brother would then be. . .'

'. . . bastards,' said Lucy.

'Quite,' said the vicar. 'In that case Mr Treadgold has no true jurisdiction. But, young lady, If he is your legal father and I married you knowingly without his consent, then I would be committing a felony. You see my predicament. I cannot take that chance. It would leave me liable to a prosecution.'

On that unhappy thought, the meeting concluded.

'It's a wicked shame. And when all the arrangements have been made.' Fanny M'George was highly indignant. She was berating Tate Wilkinson as if the matter was his own doing.

'Who does this vicar think he is?' she asked. 'Is it not his business to marry people? Who's he to pick and choose? If you ask me he should do his job properly and marry them.'

'It would be breaking the law,' said Tate.

'Does he not know the dress has been made specially? Altered at any rate. And what of all those in the company who will be greatly disappointed?

'How can a marriage that has not taken place be celebrated?'

'Then they should marry by common consent. They could do so

in the theatre itself, that would seem fitting. It would be a delightful ceremony, would it not? To be married on stage. Then when they are both fully of age, they may be wed in church if they so wish.'

'No, it will not do.'

Fanny had another idea. 'They could be wed in the Fleet prison. As happens in *Clandestine Marriage*. I should know, I've played it often enough.'

'And go to London in the middle of a tour? No, Fanny, you must give up this matchmaking. The theatre comes first, even before weddings.'

However Tate began to wonder about his stance the following day, after receiving a letter from his wife.

My dear husband.

I have neither time nor paper for half I would say. Sufficient to tell you that last night I had a visit from Walter Treadgold, the full circumstances of which must wait until we next meet. He has revealed to me the reason for his sister Lucy running away from home. Unhappy girl! If what he told me is precise, her reasons for flight are most shocking being due to unforgivable malpractices by her father. So villainous that I think you may not want to continue with the employment of him in our company.

Young Walter was in a pitiable state and asked if I knew the whereabouts of his sister. I think he suspects she may have joined you and Thomas in Doncaster, but I gave him no indication this was so. Do not, therefore be surprised if he should appear . . .

Walter did not appear. As planned, the season reached its last week in Doncaster. Wilkinson decided to leave early for York, primarily to study the text of *'Harlequin Sailor'* which must shortly go into rehearsal, also to learn more from his wife of Treadgold's transgressions. He was annoyed by recent developments. Why, he asked, did actors have such disordered lives? They were always creating problems with their loves, their hates and their debts. Far better it would be to have marionettes. They could be kept packed in boxes and only removed when required.

He thought seriously of talking to Lucy about her father but had little notion how to open such a subject. Anyway, as yet he had no firm evidence, only hearsay. Slander could easily arise. Jane was better suited to approach Lucy than he, if what she had written was true.

Above all the role of Columbine was still uncast with Lucy the only contender. He knew how well she could dance and her singing was coming along beautifully, but her acting ability had yet to be evaluated. He was convinced she could do it, but all must wait until they were back in York.

'Very well, I'll go to York,' said Lucy, 'but I will not work at the theatre. Not if they are there.'

'Your father ruined your past,' answered Thomas, 'will you allow him to wreck your future? Our future ?'

'Nothing will prevent your success. It's your career that matters, not mine.'

'We are to work together. It's all set, you are to be my partner. We must tell Tate Wilkinson how it is. He knows you've run away from home. He should know the reason why and the true nature of your father.'

'No! I will not turn evidence against Treadgold. He would be imprisoned. What then about my mother ?'

'She will still have the school.'

'The school? Do you imagine the genteel and polite people of York would send their children after those revelations?'

'That's the price that must be paid, for what he has done to you.'

'Hark to me, Thomas. A few years past, there was a man convicted for what he had done to two little girls. He was sentenced to be imprisoned, but part of his punishment was a public disgrace in the pillory. Even though it was driving with rain that day, there was a huge crowd to lambaste him. You've seen the pillory. He climbed the steps before they locked his head and arms afore him. He was a big man and he was stooped by the chocks. The jeering and shouting was horrible, yet he showed no contrition or shame. He was undaunted as he stood captive, with people throwing filth and rubbish at him. Some hurled bricks which cut open his head and blooded his face, but he still he showed no shame. After, when he was led away, he bowed to the crowd fully playing martyr.

You can guess who took me to see this. Yes, he enjoyed it, telling me that's what happened to bad people. That was how the wicked were punished. he told me. That is what would happen to me if I ever divulged our secrets.'

'It is how he should be punished,' said Thomas.

'As maybe. But I will not bring it about.'

'Then I shall make known his crimes.'

'If you do,' said Lucy with a clarity and resolve he had not seen before, 'you will play the traitor. What I have told you has the sanctity of a confession. Break that and you break our accord for ever.'

*

Twenty Seven. *Cat calls, Curtain calls.*

With Bold Street in Derby seeming a suitable address for his new theatre, Jemmy Whitley believed that in this new town there would be none of the antagonism he had encountered in Nottingham. In truth, the prejudice against playhouses was appearing to fade throughout the country and the enjoyment of plays and players was predisposed to many.

In the local newspaper he had begged leave to acquaint the Nobility, Gentry and Populace in general, that he had spared no pains nor expense in making the theatre commodious and elegant for their reception. He believed that all parts of the house could not fail to be advantageously pleasing to every spectator. The premier offering was the same as that recently desired by the Duke of Newcastle in Nottingham, namely the farce of *The Author,* to be followed by *Acis and Galatea*. The scenes and decoration were entirely new which, with an additional band of music and vocal performances, he humbly hoped would give general satisfaction. Invitations to the official opening had been forthcoming for the carriage trade, civic leaders, eminent Masons and, as a sign of goodwill, Tate Wilkinson. Whitley reckoned his rival would come at one time or another and he'd rather have him on hand when he could keep an eye on him.

The opening night brought all the usual advantages and drawbacks. The gallery and pit were filled an hour before curtain up, with Derby audiences proving to be as rowdy and rumbustious as any other. Those in the private boxes, having paid most, kept up the tradition of arriving as late as possible. Local dignitaries, aldermen and magistrates, were acclaimed when taking their places long after the start, holding up proceedings as they accepted applause from their supporters and boos from their detractors.

From the front of house to the tastefully decorated auditorium, the new theatre was admired for its light, bright welcoming atmosphere.

Newcomer Mr Leonard Grist, was declared to be the great success of the evening. Not only did his comic talents shine in *The Author,* he captivated everyone in the role of Polyphemus with his fine bass singing of *Oh Ruddier than the Cherry* receiving three encores, no less. Whitley was delighted to have him in the company, but at the same time wondered ruefully how long he would stay, for surely with such talent he would soon be lured to London.

After only a few hours' sleep, the Whitleys were at the theatre prompt for ten o'clock the next morning. There were rehearsals ahead for the coming performances and it would not be long before they left Derby to be on the road. Four new plays were in preparation and it was a weary and disgruntled cast that set about blocking *The Troubled Captain,* a farce that would be offered in the forthcoming week.

Just before noon, as the rehearsal was nearing its conclusion, a message was delivered to Whitley from four gentlemen requesting the pleasure of his company at a nearby hostelry.

Fully expecting some flattering comments on the opening performance, Jemmy called an early break with a resumption at one o'clock. He then walked briskly to keep the appointment.

It was a disappointment that no-one in the busy tap room seemed to recognise him. Not knowing the appearance of those who had invited him, he waited to see if anyone approached him, when a touch on the shoulder and the words, 'Mr Whitley?' caused him to turn.

He found himself looking into the face of a thin young man in a startling pale blue jacket, full length matching waistcoat, a wig tied at the back with ribbon that also wound round his neck.

'Quite right,' said Mr Whitley, with a friendly smile. 'Whom do I have the honour of addressing?'

'Allow me to introduce myself,' said the thin young man, 'my name is Griffiths, Joseph Griffiths.'

With a polite wave of his lace frilled hand, he indicated a direction that Mr Whitley might care to follow. He found himself approaching a small circular table around which sat two heavy set young men with their own hair, together with a much older man who bore the appearance of a clerk - with no hair.

'This is my advisor, Mr Deeds.'

Whitley shook his hand, wondering why it was he had not been introduced to the two other men. Seating himself at the table, he was asked to share a bottle of wine that had already been well sampled.

'Your health, Mr Whitley,' said Joseph Griffiths. Glasses were raised and Whitley sat back, ready to receive compliments upon either himself, his theatre or his company when Mr Griffiths said,

'We were at the play last night.'

Mr Whitley smiled, sure that his intuition had been correct. 'I hope sir, it proved to your liking.'

'No sir, it did not,' replied Mr Griffiths. Whitley was nonplussed.

'I regret to hear that. Pray, what was it displeased you?' he asked.

'It was the farce sir, that displeased us.'

'*The Author?* Why sir, that is one of the most appreciated of all our plays. Was it the performance disappointed you? Tell me what was wrong and we will amend it at our next rehearsal.'

'No need. For there will be no further rehearsing, nor further acting of the farce.'

Whitley was without words. Why did Mr Griffiths speak so? What could be amiss? He believed the fees had been paid. The Lord Chamberlain had long since given approval. What could be wrong? Mr Griffiths continued,

'I beg you to understand you are guilty of a serious offence, by a flagrant breach of the law, thus flying in the face of authority. This impudent libel called *The Author* written by that scoundrel Foote, was stopped from any future performance six years ago and has not been permitted since.'

'This is astonishing,' Whitley replied after a moment of misgiving, '*The Author* is a much favoured piece. I have known it played often.'

'Not of late,' said Griffiths, 'I have seen to that.' He paused. Whitley noticed him looking at his fellows as if seeking approval of what he was saying. He continued, 'The character of Cadwallader is an affront to the memory of my late father . As his son, by God, I will not suffer such insolence to pass either unnoticed or unpunished.'

The previously silent Mr Deeds then spoke. Leaning forward with a finger quietly tapping on the table he said, 'If on any night you dare attempt or presume to play that farce, I have instructions from Mr Griffiths and his friends, one and all, to leave not a solitary bench, lamp, nor any piece of property untouched within your brand new theatre.'

The four men stared hard at Whitley. After a pause Mr Griffiths spoke, 'Come now, Whitley, what have you to say?'

Whitley stood to gain advantage. All the men were taller than he, and for the moment he could look down upon them. 'Gentlemen,' he said, ' you are threatening me. I have a mind to inform the magistrates of this.'

The four men looked at each other and smiled mockingly.

'No sir, ' said Mr Deeds. 'We are not threatening. We are advising you not to continue breaking the law, which we are well within. We merely request there be no more airings of *The Author*. I hope the meaning is clear.'

Still standing, Whitley knew that the seated men had the better of him. He turned away, feeling there was no course for him but to submit. It was like facing a displeased house and in such circumstances he knew all he could do was capitulate to avoid disaster.

'Very well gentlemen. I appear to have no choice. We shall replace it with another piece this evening.'

'That is all I request,' smiled Mr Griffiths. We shall attend the theatre tonight, where we expect no infringement to be made on our treaty, either by secret or offensive means.' With a dry scraping of chairs on the stone floor, the four stood and solemnly walked away.

Whitley was left standing angry and humiliated. What was he to do? Could he resume the rehearsal by saying 'A party of gentlemen would not suffer *The Author* to be acted; for if it was, they threatened a serious riot? ' Furthermore, at such short notice he could not give out handbills and inform the public of a change in the programme

He sought immediate council with Cassy and they agreed nothing could be done but substitute *The Author with Mayor of Garratt* which would have to be given without apology or notice of change.

This proved unwise. The Derby audience had heard of the remarkable new actor, Mr Grist, and was agog to see him in the farce of *The Author*. Alas, there was no part for Grist in the substituted *Mayor of Garratt*. He would not appear until the afterpiece *Acis and*

Galatea. That evening when the curtain rose, a baffled house found not the farce about an author, but a comedy about a knavish politician. For a while this was received in puzzled silence, until Whitley appeared in the main role of the mayor and the spectators realised it had been given an inferior product. Hisses turned to shouts and in little time uproar drowned out anything the actors could say. A demand for 'Grist, Grist, Grist' surmounted everything, yet Whitley and his fellows took no notice but went on with the play. The disapprobation continued. Great jumps were made in the text, noticed by no-one until mercifully *The Mayor of Garratt* ended, having played but half its usual time.

Those providing the *entr'actes* fared no better and it was not until the merry overture to Handel's opera was heard that order was restored with the appearance of Mr Grist. As before, he received encores as Polyphemus and in an inspired decision after the conclusion of the opera, he sang a couple of comic songs which sent the audience home in a far sweeter frame of mind.

For Whitley though, the evening ended in near exhaustion. The strain of getting the new theatre prepared for opening and the subsequent events left him close to a collapse. Cassy, recalling the nervous prostration she had seen earlier, ordered him to bed with bread and milk laced with brandy.

Her husband did not resist and capitulated for the second time that day. 'What a business we are in,' he observed getting into bed. 'When we opened in Nottingham we were prosecuted by the law, now it is the same in Derby. Perhaps we should take up a greengrocery.'

'You must be mindful of your health,' said Cassandra firmly. 'Unless you rest I fear for the future. I will take rehearsals tomorrow,'

Jemmy had not the energy to argue and realised that his wife was correct. He must conserve his strength for the months ahead.

Mr Grist, aware of a chance to further his career, insisted that given twenty four hours he could memorise the *Mayor of Garratt,* and be ready to act it. Cassy agreed to the suggestion for it enabled her husband to have two further days of bed rest. Handbills were produced announcing that 'at very short notice' Mr Grist would assume the role of the Mayor of Garratt, and after one night of having to perform with the book he was soon delighting the Derby audiences with yet another sparkling performance. Of Mr Griffiths and his cohorts, nothing more was heard.

Tate Wilkinson had not been at the opening night. He was aware of Whitley's tactics and preferred to be anonymous and attend an ordinary performance where he could decide if anything was worth his poaching without his presence being known.

Word of the brilliance of Leonard Grist had reached him and he was desirous of seeing this rising player for himself. True, on seeing him Tate was impressed, but at present he was not in the market for that particular type of lead. He was, after all, building up his own luminary in the shape of Tom Hammond, ramshackled though that construction might prove to be.

Like every man who saw her, he was greatly taken with Belinda Armstrong. Such beauty was rare and he was surprised how little Whitley appeared to be employing her. Apart from Juliet, she had no major role, which seemed to him a waste of a potential asset.

What he did not know was that Belinda was much of the same mind. Unable to match her beauty with a singing voice, the dominance of musical offerings found her either in the chorus or placed as a mere decoration.

'I only play Juliet once every three weeks,' she complained, 'The rest of the time I do no more than audition for a monument.'

In addition to this dissatisfaction, Belinda's love for Edmund Sedley had waned. Realising that marriage was unlikely, the prospect of continuing as his mistress had become tedious. What was more surprising was the attachment Belinda had formed with Signor Ceraccio. The painter had taken Edmund's advice and in addition to creating some fine theatrical decor, he was also establishing himself as a painter of portraits.

Belinda was his constant muse and posed in numerous guises, usually in a state of near or complete undress which by now, held no restraints for her. Originals of her likeness not only fetched handsome prices, but were quickly and cheaply made into engravings. These being eminently saleable produced a highly satisfactory return shared between both painter and subject.

Tate Wilkinson knew none of this, instead it was the Ceraccio's new and exhilarating stage designs made him sit forward in his seat with excitement. Here was just what was needed for his own *Harlequin Sailor*. So certain of this was he, that he sent a note to the signor requesting a meeting after the show. Waiting in the suggested locality, he saw the lovely features of Belinda Armstrong searching for someone. Taking a chance Wilkinson approached her.

'Madam, excuse me,' he said, 'could you tell me if Signor Ceraccio is to be seen?'

'You're Mr Wilkinson?' she asked. 'He's not at the theatre tonight, so your message came to me and I took the liberty of seeking you out. You wish to meet him?'

'Very much.'

'He's not here in Derby. He's back in Nottingham where he does most of his work. Could you come to his rooms there tomorrow?' Belinda looked upwards, her violet eyes knowingly framed by her dark hair. 'I plan to walk to Nottingham early tomorrow,' she said hesitantly. 'Your company would be most welcome, for I do not care to walk alone. Because of the many dangers.'

'Would it not be safer if you travelled by coach?'

Belinda looked shyly aside. 'Alas sir, I do not have the fare.'

'If I were to pay for you, we could be there in two hours which would allow me to travel back to York later in the day.'

'You are too kind, sir. I could then take you direct to his studio.'

'Always assuming we can get a place on the coach.'

Only outside places were available on the coach. But with the weather being dry and not too cold, the journey was tolerable. Conversation between the two was almost impossible, which prevented Wilkinson from asking Belinda, how it was she could take leave from the theatre company so easily. Once arrived in Nottingham, as they walked to Ceraccio's rooms, he put the question to her.

'Oh, I'm not bothered about the stage sir. Truth is, I'm not much of an actress. I am of a mind to seek something else for I am told there are many opportunities in other form of art.'

They arrived at a terrace house. Tate was led into a small room where all the confusion and paraphernalia of the painter's craft filled every stretch. Amidst canvasses, easels, sketches and paints, Ceraccio was discovered. The small undistinguished man, his unruly hair and clothing bespattered with colours smiled happily at Belinda. She embraced him warmly, kissing whatever part of his face was to hand, causing Wilkinson to turn away and examine the many canvasses piled one against the other.

'Mr Wilkinson is ever so keen to see your pictures,' said Belinda, at last separating herself from the painter.

The painter bowed and extended a paint stained hand in greeting.

'I admire your stage work greatly,' said Tate.

Ceraccio shrugged his shoulders in modest acknowledgement. Wilkinson walked round the room climbing over the jumble and avoiding the many obstructions muttering, 'Beautiful,' and 'Excellent,' from time to time. But this was not what he was seeking.

Spotting a set design in miniature, he kneeled down to examine it and was able to say with complete sincerity, 'This is very very handsome.' Turning to Belinda he asked what play it was for.

'I do not think it is for any play especially. Just some ideas he's had. Perhaps something like *Sinbad the Sailor*.'

'Is it for one of Mr Whitley's future productions?'

Ceraccio following the remark, laughed, 'Whitlee? No.'

'You mean you make up designs merely for the pleasure of it?'

'He does an' all,' said Belinda. 'Never stops. A lot of them are settings for me.' She rummaged through a pile of heavy paper until finding a rough sketch of a sylvan forest, held it up alongside an incomplete portrait, 'That's going to be for me. That's me as Diana the huntress,'

'No, no, no,' said Ceraccio, '"Andromeda." '

'To be sure. There's no bow and arrow is there?' She laughed, squeezing the painter affectionately.

So the conversation continued. Wilkinson was much taken by the contrast between the earnest little artist and the beautiful girl, who appeared not fully aware of the quality of the work she had inspired.

Before long, other stage designs in model form had been found, each tiny design a detailed working model. In addition to the exotic sailing ship, there were ideas for temples, jungles and sea shores, each one seemingly perfect for his forthcoming pantomime in York.

Tate was hardly able to disguise his excitement. What he was discovering made his visit well worth the while. 'I want to be clear,' he said, 'these are not commissions for Whitley. You have not been paid by him. They are your own, private work.'

Ceraccio was not entirely sure of the meaning, so that Tate had to rely upon Belinda to clarify matters between them.

'Oh yes, he does them for himself,' she said. 'Crafty isn't he? He has shown them to Whitley, but he says they're too extravagant. Bracer says the same. Says he can't make out how they'd work.'

'In that case, would the signor let me purchase them?'

Ceraccio was surprised at the interest in his models. 'Purchase? Purchase?' the puzzled Italian looked for help.

'Acquisto,' said Belinda.

'Ah yeees, you want to buy?' He spread his hands inviting an offer. Tate thought quickly. 'I will give you ten pounds for the five models.'

The artist was not impressed. Tate held up his ten fingers saying,

'Ten pounds for the five sets.' Belinda's Italian was still limited, but she had learned to count to one hundred. She explained, 'Dieci.'

'Oh no, no, no,' replied Ceraccio shaking his head, which made Tate realise that being a foreigner he would expect to bargain. From somewhere at the back of his memory he remembered,

'Quanta costa?'

'Venti,' said the artist opening and closing his hands twice.

Tate shook his head, pretending to lose interest. He started as if to move out of the room. The trick worked.

'Diciotto,' suggested Ceraccio in a change of tone.

Wilkinson, hesitated. He looked at the designs, which in reality he wanted badly. He asked Belinda, 'How much is that?'

'Eighteen,' she said.

'Tell him, fifteen,'

'Quindici,' she told the signor. There was a silence.

'Mmmm,' a strange sound from the signor. 'Ci, quindici,' he said.

Smiles broke out. The two men shook hands. Wilkinson

produced his purse from a jacket pocket and the money was counted. A small cardboard box was found and after cautiously dismantling the tiny pieces, they were laid into it with reverence until the whole was carefully secured with string.

Wilkinson was well satisfied. He had come looking for talent, never expecting anything as original as these thrilling stage designs. He anticipated showing them to his wife Jane with pleasure. For sure, she had completed her text for *Harlequin Sailor* and these new ideas would likely require major changes to incorporate the signor's spectacular scenic ideas. No matter. With such designs as these, he knew they would have something new and different. Unlike anything seen on any stage before.

With a light heart he boarded the return coach to York, clutching his small cardboard box and thankful he had not encountered Whitley.

*

Twenty Eight. *For the First Time on Any Stage.*

Harlequin Sailor

or

The Press Gang Outwitted.

A Comical Pantomime

by

Mrs Wilkinson.

With additional scenes and speeches by Tate Wilkinson.

Scene the First.

The Little Village of Long Suffering.

A high street of shops: T. and H. Bone, Butchers. Jack Boot, Shoemaker. B.Troot Greengrocer and Herr Cutt, Barber, &c.

In front of her father's tavern 'The Wet Blanket,' Columbine dances as she cleans the windows. and whitens the front doorstep. She is joyful, for she expects her lover, Harlequin, to come courting. Her father, Lord Luvverduck, warns her against seeing him and reminds her that she is betrothed to the local squire, Baron Wasteland. Harlequin appears. They declare their undying love. This is overheard by Lord Luvverduck, who arranges for the Press Gang to kidnap Harlequin and send him to sea.

Scene the Second.

On board the British Man o' War, 'HMS Repulsive.'

Poor Harlequin is forced to swab the decks by a cruel bosun. He bemoans his fate in a sad song. . .

'No, that won't do,' said Tate.

'And why not?' asked his wife.

'Because I want the second scene to be on an exotic ship. All silken sails and colour. The one Ceraccio's designed. A complete transformation.'

'But the British man o' war scene is already made and painted. It can't go to waste.'

'It won't go to waste. It will be the used for the finale. The closing patriotic scene at Plymouth Ho.'

'But, how do you explain the press gang putting Harlequin onto an exotic silken sailed ship?'

'We must forget the press gang. Let it be a band of Moroccans who sell him into slavery on a Mediterranean felucca. . .'

'They'll mishear that in the gallery.'

'Ah yes. I have it! Best make the exotic ship, a dhow.'

'You don't get dhows in the Channel. How do we explain a band of Moroccans pirates appearing in an English village?

'There have been several instances in Cornwall, only recently.'

'If you say so.'

Scene the Second.

~~On board the British man o' war 'HMS Repulsive.'~~

On board an exotic Moroccan Dhow.

Poor Harlequin is forced to swab the decks by a cruel ~~bosun~~ caliph. He bemoans his fate in a sad song. He finds a bottle of rum, takes a few sips from it and becomes drunk (always popular with the gallery).

'No,' said Tate. 'I have a better idea. He finds a bottle, which seems to be empty. He removes the stopper and a genie appears. A great fantastic figure, a flibbertigibbet.'

'Who's going to play that? I can't see Mr Holland in the part.'

'We'll settle that later. It'll be a splendid effect though.'

'For what reason?'

'It will give us a flying scene over the mountains as the genie takes Harlequin to a temple in the jungle.'

'Why a temple in the jungle?'

'Because Ceraccio has designed a magnificent tropical temple.'

'Ridiculous! Where's the logic.? The whole point of my pantomime is that Harlequin defeats the French. He can't do that in a tropical temple.'

'He will at the end. Meanwhile we have . . . are you making a note of this?'

Scene the Third.

A Magnificent Temple in the Jungle.

Harlequin wakes to find himself asleep on the altar stone of the Temple. Before he knows it, savage natives tie him up and prepare him as a human sacrifice. A chorus of dusky maidens perform a tempting dance before the hapless Harlequin. A procession of native witch doctors in terrifying masks appears and surround Harlequin. . .

'Now really this is too much.' said Jane Wilkinson. 'I have written a sweet little scene for the second act where Columbine arrives in a rowing boat and effects an escape for Harlequin, from Plymouth Harbour.'

'Too tame. People want excitement, spectacle. . .'

'They also want to see Columbine.'

'Later. Here I want a war dance. Something that threatens Harlequin.'

'It was easier to have him escape with Columbine by boat.'

'I have it! The savages are just about to sacrifice Harlequin, when he warns them if they do, he'll make the moon disappear.'

'How can he do that?'

'He has an almanac with him and he knows there will be an eclipse of the full moon that very night. So when the moon disappears, the savages bow down before him and make him their king. That'll be a good scene'

'But where is Columbine?'

'Now she can arrive in her rowing boat.'

'All the way from England?'

'Not on her own perhaps. Yes, of course. She's been assisted by mermaids. Ceraccio has a splendid scene of an underwater palace.'

Scene the Fourth.

A Palace under the Sea.

Comprised of coral reefs, grottos, shells and sea weed. At the back of the stage is a rocky cavern where a chorus of mermaids are singing and dancing as they look into mirrors and comb their tresses.

'Mermaids can't dance.'

'No but they can sing.'

Harlequin and Columbine can be seen in the foreground arriving on the sea shore. King Neptune appears in his shell-like chariot, drawn by sea horses.

'I've specified a sun chariot, it's already made.'

'It will have to be changed to suit Neptune.'

'You forget the French have to be defeated. So far they haven't come into the plot at all.'

'They will now. Are you ready . .?'

Scene the Fifth.

The French Warship: 'Tete de Merdre'

The French warship has arrived at the tropical island. The full moon having reappeared, the savages, are angry at the way they have been tricked. They tell the French Captain (Sailor Guerre) about Harlequin's deception and he promises to recapture him and Columbine. After a rollicking sea shanty,

(Le French Horn Pipe) the French sail for the Submarine Palace.

Scene the Sixth.

A Ruined Abbey by Moonlight.

'I give up.'

'We always have a ruined abbey by moonlight.'

'Whatever for?'

'It's traditional. Complete with Fairy Nuff and her attendant elfs. You'll find audiences expect it. And it gives us time to set the finale.'

'Have it your own way.'

Scene the Seventh.

Aboard HMS. 'Cock o' Hoop' in Plymouth Harbour.

Harlequin and Columbine are to be married by the ship's captain, when the genie appears to warn that the French are about to attack. Harlequin calls for the aid of King Neptune, who from his submarine palace pierces the hull of the French ship with his trident. It sinks spectacularly. General rejoicing.

Finale

'Heart of Oak are our ships, jolly tars are out men,
We always are ready- steady boys steady.'

All is forgiven. Harlequin and Columbine are finally married. The bride given away by her father, Lord Luvverduck with Baron Wasteland the best man. King Neptune rises from the sea in his chariot to be greeted by Britannia sailing from the dockside. Final Tableau with the entire company as well as the genie, mermaids, fairies, sailors and reformed witch doctors and savages.

Final Curtain.

'It's nothing at all like my original text.'

'Perhaps not my dear. But then we didn't have Ceraccio's ideas.'

'It will mean starting all over again.'

'You can do it my dear. I have every confidence in you. And remember we start rehearsals next week.'

Harlequin Sailor, which had been conceived as an neat little folly for the Races Week slowly turned into an elephantine production with a gestation period almost as long as that of the huge mammal itself.

Jane Wilkinson attempted to rewrite her original pantomime to conform with her husband's ideas. In the interest of matrimonial harmony she had subdued her true feelings, but this did not stop her grieving for the original text she had written. Her husband's vaulting ambition meant that the piece required such intricate preparation that it was unlikely to be ready for presentation until Christmas.

'That's no good,' said Jane. 'At Yuletide people want something like *The Jealous Wife* or *The Suspicious Husband.* Not a pantomime.'

'You never know my dear,' said her husband. 'we might be setting a precedent But all the same we'll aim to have it ready for the October races.'

Everyone backstage at York quietly cursed the day that Tate had met Signor Ceraccio. Mr Weaver and Mr Watson the regular painter and joiner took exception to the foreigner's designs. As with Mr Bracer in Nottingham their first reaction was, 'It can't be done. We haven't got the apparatus.'

Yes, they agreed the ideas were new and different, but they were near unworkable. It would require far more elaborate machinery than they had at present. New devices were needed to achieve many of the effects. The Transformations could be not be achieved without more constructions and lighting effects than ever before. As for the Temple scene, it would fill the stage meaning that the dusky maidens and witch doctors could only appear on the apron. So how on earth could Columbine rescue Harlequin in a rowing boat on the fore-stage?

Tate pointed out to the indignant workmen that Ceraccio had written full instructions on how everything was to be achieved.

'In Italian,' came the answer. Their point was made.

Wilkinson was a reasonable man, believing that resistance to new ideas was part of the English character. After listening to every complaint he smiled at his workmen.

'Astonish me,' he said and left them to work it out for themselves.

More pressing, perhaps, was the fact that he did not yet have his Columbine firmly cast. Lucy Treadgold had always been the first choice, but after the marriage debacle and her refusal to enter the theatre it became impossible to rely upon her.

On his return to York, his wife had told him in detail about her encounter with Walter Treadgold and the revelations concerning their father.

'I don't think we should have such a wicked man here with us,' Jane told her husband. 'His place is in the stocks, not on our stage.'

'We cannot dismiss a man on rumour,' said Tate.

'Then enquire as to the truth. Speak to Lucy. Ask if this is the reason she will not come in the theatre.'

'That is not my concern. It is a matter for a woman. You can perhaps make enquiries.'

'It is too delicate a matter for me.'

'Then the business is best left alone.'

*

On their return to York, Thomas and Lucy had taken a room with the ever hospitable Fanny M'George. For a long time Lucy held to her vow not to go into the theatre but being alone in the house every day began to bore her. Fanny had tried to assist by bringing costume work home for her to help occupy her time but Lucy's talent was not with the needle. The longing to dance was strong and the sewing was mostly put aside as she zealously practised her steps alone.

The Treadgold's' order of work never altered. They arrived a few minutes before going on stage, refusing to speak to anyone. When their performance was ended, they took their bows and departed. In time this tight routine made it possible for Lucy to return to the theatre tentatively, provided she kept hidden during the her parents' act.

Thomas continued to practice his dancing under her guidance. She was a natural teacher and Thomas responded effectively. Tate, when he had time, watched their efforts and with other members of the company, enjoyed seeing the young couple laugh and argue as they worked out movements. In addition to his Puck, which was still hugely popular, Thomas was being given bigger and more responsible roles. Wilkinson called *The Dream* his 'golden egg' knowing it would be madness to drop it for the time being.

As the new season began to shape, Tate decided it was time to try out Lucy in a speaking role. He chose Garrick's one-act farce *Miss in her Teens,* in which he had already cast Thomas as the young lead Captain Rob.

To Lucy he gave the minor role of Tag, a maidservant, believing it would reveal what ability she had. When he offered her the part he told her, 'You will see your name on the playbill at last. Think how it will look, "Miss Treadgold."'

'No. I will not use that name.'

For a moment, Tate wondered if he should mention her father. Here could be the perfect opportunity. Yet Lucy seemed so delighted, so excited to be gaining her first small role, he left those waters unmuddied. Instead he asked,

'How then would you like your name to be billed?'

Lucy thought. 'I think I should like. . . Miss Hammond.' she answered.

'Miss Hammond? Is not that rather demure? My dear, we look upon you and Thomas as a couple. In this situation perhaps Mrs Hammond would not be incorrect?'

'I would like that of course,' said Lucy, 'if it is not too brazen.'

'I think it would be just right,' said Tate. I'm sure everyone will agree.'

And they did. None more than Fanny M'George. Running into

Lucy as soon as she had heard about the role and the new name chosen chosen, she threw her arms around her,

'At last!' she cried kissing her. Turning, she found Thomas. Jubilantly she pulled Lucy towards him, and embraced them, with hugs and kisses.

The excitement quickly involved several others who formed a bundle of laughing, happy people.

'Mr and Mrs Hammond,' said Fanny, beaming benevolently.

'For the billing only,' insisted Lucy, 'tis only a convenience.'

'No such thing,' said Fanny, 'Mr and Mrs Hammond it shall be. After all we can't have falsehoods on our play bills can we? It must be settled good and proper.'

Lucy and Thomas all of a sudden looked very young and vulnerable. 'How can it be?' asked Lucy. You know full well we cannot be married.'

But Fanny was not to be cheated of her wedding. Here was her opportunity and she was not to be denied.

'Not within some mean old church perhaps but that does not prevent you exchanging vows. Come now. I have you under my roof abed together And I can't have my house gaining a bad name.'

Fanny's enthusiasm was increasing.

'You love him, don't you?' she asked Lucy, daring her to deny it. Lucy standing apart from the noise, gave an assuring smile to Thomas,

'I do.'

Thomas was quietly delighted that she had said this aloud before these people. Two words that she had hardly spoken to him in private had been heard before witnesses. As if they were completely alone he kissed her to endorse the utterance.

'So now we must have it done genuinely,' said Fanny, plans filling her head. 'A celebration with a full exchange of vows as befits. It happens all the time in the colonies, so we'll have a settlers' wedding of our own.'

'Wait a minute,' said Jane Wilkinson entering the scene. 'This is all very well, but it is not within the law. You know that Fanny.'

Fanny regarded the company, 'Love is above the law is it not? It requires no ceremony to be justified. And we have our own customs, our own ways do we not? They may be unwritten, but we hold to them as strict as does any notary.' Heads nodded in agreement.

'I never had no luxury of a church ceremony with Mr M'George. Yet we had four children and can you be more married than that? Book or no book, with your permission, my dear Mrs Wilkinson, it can be done after we open next week .'

'It's not for me to say,' said Jane, 'First I must speak to my husband. . .' but everyone knew that this meant with her persuasion agreement would be forthcoming. Fanny raised her voice,

'That's settled. Monday week. All of you bring something, food and wine with a present for the happy couple.'

As quickly as it had begun, the outburst of happiness subsided. Everyone left, leaving Lucy and Thomas together in the dark back stage area. As if in the aftermath of an explosion, they regarded each other.

'Do you want this?' asked Thomas.

'We can hardly stop it, can we?' said Lucy.

'We shan't really be wed, shall we?'

'We shall as far as my belief,' said Lucy.

'That's so,' said Thomas.

The moment of commitment was come.

Past obstacles were dismissed. Promises would be undertaken that could not be truer, nor more sincere, were they exchanged before the highest authority with the utmost benefice.

'In my acting days within our noble profession,' said Tate Wilkinson,'I have brought together many young lovers. . .'

He was speaking on stage after the evening performance, standing at the head of a linen covered trestle table, full laid for the wedding feast. No matter that the hour was late for this was not a wedding breakfast but a wedding supper. At the centre of the table sat Thomas and Lucy, around them the full company and on the table itself a fine improvised array of food, drink and flowers brought to celebrate the occasion culminating in a Bride's Pie which had been cut and distributed. They were indeed *The Constant Lovers,* for her dress and his costume both from that play proclaimed it fully.

'. . .usually at the end of the last act,' continued Tate. 'I have made many brief appearances as a priest, a curate, a provost, a friar, even a druid. *(Laughter).* I once appeared as Hymen, the god of marriage no less. *(More laughter).* And on one memorable occasion, there was my materialisation as the Abbess of Ephesus herself.' *(Much laughter and thumping of the table.)*

'Of course the lovers were all play acting as was I. But this is not our province this evening. For Lucy and Thomas highly gifted actors though they be upon this stage make no pretence when it comes to their love for each other.' *(Cries of 'Hear, Hear.').*

'Tonight we have heard them declare their constancy, here within our own theatre, and dare I say it? Our home, our fraternity and our family.' *(Cries of assent).*

'We all bear witness to their declaration of fidelity in their years ahead. We band of brothers and sisters here tonight declare that within our sight they are truly man and wife. As such we welcome them both, into our midst whatever the world outside may say.' *('Well said.' etc.)*

'My friends, please raise your glasses as we toast Lucy and Thomas. May blessings on you fall. Hallelujah and Praise the Lord!' *(Shouts of 'Lucy and Thomas' from all assembled.)*

Earlier that evening before these celebrations, there had been a tense moment when the Treadgold's had come to the theatre to perform their act.

The couple functioned together as always, with Lucy and Thomas keeping out of their way. But it was wondered, had they not read the newly posted bills outside? Did they not realise it was Lucy who was named as Mrs Hammond? Had they thought, perhaps just once, to stay and see her successful debut as an actress?

Who knows? As ever, Mr and Mrs Treadgold performed and then departed. But this night it was to be for the last time.

For the following morning, Mr Treadgold was found dead in his dance room. He lay on the floor, a deep wound to his left temple from which had formed a pool of his blood. Mr Treadgold had been murdered.

*

Part Five.

Twenty Nine. *The Rivals.*

Whitley's weariness had become a fever. Having capitulated to his anxieties he was soon overwhelmed by them, being restricted to his bed for more than a week. To start, he slept for two days; a dreamless debilitation without time or region, the kind of weariness that was close to the final repose. After this, he became cloudily aware of his being in a full degree of exhaustion.

' 'twill not do. There is work to done,' he mumbled as the fierce ague took control of his body. Several times he pushed upon his elbows striving to rise, but each time he came close to a swoon as the bed swayed beneath him and he could swear his brains swivelled within his skull. At these moments he was aware of a girl coming to his aid. When he fell back on his pillows she tried to correct the muddle of his bedding and tucked the blankets tight at his side. Later it was Cassy who looked down upon him.

'High time we had you on the jordan,' she insisted. With the girl's assistance, they sat him on the chamber pot held within a nursing chair to do as he was bid. After which, with much lifting and groaning, he was shifted back once more into his bed.

Taking advantage of his dazed state, Cassy sat him up and spooned sack-whey into his complaining mouth but for him this was not right. What he wanted was ale.

'I have a damnable thirst, woman, and you offer me dew drops,' he protested, but she merely wiped his brow with a worrisome sponge.

'Don't fuss. All in good time,' she said. 'You dampen the bed sufficient with sweat, without making more moisture.' He was too weak to argue. Months of stress and physical neglect had done him damage which would take long to repair. Being pent up in their Derby lodgings worsened the plight, with Cassy making arrangements for their return home to Nottingham. Shortly the actors must leave Derby and move on to Retford, then to Chesterfield for the seasons there. Cassandra had so far overseen rehearsals with useful help from Leonard Grist. But now it was her husband who needed her caring and there was no alternative but to place Mr Grist in charge of the company with the assistance of the dependable Mr Bracer. Conscious of the error she had made in favouring Brook Powell with that task, she was unsure of entrusting Grist with the selfsame authority.

It was then that she thought of her daughter Eileen and her husband Gosli whose small company had been based in Stamford. It was likely they were now in the West Riding of Yorkshire, possibly without employment. Rumour had it that their troupe was disbanded and their acting careers forsaken. She hesitated before making contact, recalling their past turbulent associations.

Yet Cassandra thought this was perhaps the time for a family reunion and who knows, some welcome filial support. She wrote a conciliatory letter asking if Eileen, with or without her husband, would like to pay a visit and perhaps assist in the nursing of her father.

A week later, she received a curt reply declaring that it was characteristic of her mother only to make contact when she was in need of help. No, the invitation would not be accepted for contrary to what she had heard, the Gosli Theatre Company was touring with great advantage. In any case Whitley was not her father, as Cassandra well knew, and there the matter should rest.

*

All the while, Nottingham was growing rapidly and with this came a heightening of public unruliness. The number of framework knitters increased daily. Overcrowding and shortages of food, combined with poor wages were leading to a frequency of riots. To keep the peace, a permanent military presence was housed at the newly built barracks, where officers and men were stationed. Consequently, inn keepers and those such as Dora Proctor were rid of their enforced paying guests. In Dora's case the handsome Captain Kern had long been gone, only to be replaced by a dyspeptic major waiting to sell his commission, whom she disliked thoroughly.

Changes and upheavals affected most people in the town, the Whitleys not excepted. Once nature's restorative capacity, combined with Cassandra's nursing, had gradually returned Jemmy to health they took stock of the future.

'I read here,' he told his wife by the fire one night, 'that there are no less than two hundred persons at the new barracks.'

'Certainly,' replied Cassy, looking up from the dress she was repairing, 'I too have been told there is such a number.'

'Eight officers, five of them married,' read Jemmy from the local newspaper. 'Twenty three non commissioned officers and close to one hundred and forty privates.'

'In addition to that,' said Cassy, her needle darting in the candle light, 'I hear there is much civilian staff. They say it is near impossible to find servants anywhere at present. Wages paid by the soldiery are far higher than ordinary decent folk can afford.'

'All this would indicate, my dear,' said Jemmy, 'that the officers will be glad to be quit of the place, particularly of an evening. As I've said all along, they will require diversion. And who better to provide that, than ourselves?'

'Quite right,' said Cassy, biting off her cotton. 'And what do you suggest we are to do about it?'

'Make ourselves and our theatre known to them' said Jemmy.

In due course, the Whitleys left their card with the commanding officer at the new Park Barracks and as a consequence were invited to take sherry with that gentleman, a Colonel Mundy of the King's Own Troop of Light Horse.

On the appointed morning, the colonel and his lady welcomed the Whitley's who were by and by conducted on a tour of the officers' mess, stables and other brand new buildings. They were suitably dazzled by the regimental silver, assured by the weaponry and roused by the instruments of the band, which they immediately invited to be played at the theatre. It was foreseen that the band could delight audiences by providing incidental music to plays, in addition to special concerts by desire of the officers of the regiment. The prospect seemed bright for all parties.

By now, under the direction of Mr Grist and Mr Bracer, the company of comedians had completed their tour of Retford and Chesterfield, with reports of good fortune, both artistic and monetary. The Whitleys were relieved by this, yet there was annoyance that everyone had seemed to manage very well without their supervision.

Mr Grist and Mr Bracer gave a full report of the tour starting with the essential comparison of rainfall in the various districts compared with that of Nottingham. Next, Mr Grist reported that he had given two benefits from which he had gained handsomely. Receipts were then closely examined, the tolls and taxes noted, damage to costume and scenery disclosed, and the excellence or otherwise of lodgings described. Finally came the enjoyable recounting of amusing incidents, the main being the antics of a pet monkey which had been taken to the play and got loose only to run on stage, eventually toppling Mrs Kirk's wig in the midst of *The Provoked Wife.*

Amidst the many letters that had accumulated during his illness, one addressed to Whitley stood out as if from Nemesis herself. It was on the heaviest ivory coloured writing paper, bearing the dreadful seal of 'P' and had been hand delivered.

Unable to bring himself to open it, finally Cassandra found what was within. It announced that Mr Plumptre's play was printed complete in three volumes and as instructed Mr Plumptre had thirty sets now ready. He desired that Mr Whitley could arrange for these to be collected from Plumptre House and he further trusted that rehearsals would start immediately. This news re-ignited Cassandra's wrath,

'We cannot be having them,' she scolded. 'We have no room for thirty sets. Why 'tis more than. . . three hundred volumes,'

'Tis but ninety.' corrected her husband.

'One hundred, three hundred, I say it will not do! Husband, this is your folly,' Cassandra was now in full torrent. 'You should never have agreed to perform his abominable play. Did I not say so? It would not surprise me were he to charge us for the printing. It's ill enough owing forty pound, but to have this in addition.'

'Calm yourself, my dear,' said Jemmy.

'Calm myself! Why he may summons us for breach of contract.'

'There was no contract, Nothing was consigned to paper.'

'Never mind. It may well be be the ruin of us! We could be sued. Debt, sir, debt! It might be a prisoning matter. And all because you dare not tell him that his play was terrible in the first place.'

She fell into noisy weeping, mostly for dramatic effect. 'I wonder now why I have nursed you back to health only to have this come upon me. Fool that I am,' she continued. 'if you had not lived, I would at least be free of this obligation.'

'I'm certain you do not mean that, my dear.'

'Do I not? You have always acted as if we were plump in the pocket. My mother said we would end up in the sponging house. She knew well enough and I should have marked her warning.'

'Come now, drink this,' he offered her a glass of her favourite cordial. Blowing her nose and wiping her eyes, Cassy swallowed the drink in one bolt. Jemmy gave her another immediately.

'Here, my love. You require double when you are so out of order. Your nursing labours have left you near exhausted. I tell you wife, you have been a wonder. I grant you I have done a rash thing, but there will be found a way out of it.' He bent to kiss her, at the very moment when Mr Grist came into the room.

'Forgive me,' he said and made as if to leave.

'That's quite all right sir,' said Jemmy. We have just mended a small domestic difficulty,'

'Mended!' Cassandra looked angrily at her husband, 'If only it were so.' Looking tearfully at Mr Grist she moaned, 'Oh Leonard, we are in such dire trouble.'

Jemmy was indignant that his wife was prepared to divulge their problem which he considered to be a private matter. He further noted that his wife referred to Mr Grist by his Christian name, a small but distasteful item he noted for a future reprimand.

'May I ask what is the problem?' asked Mr Gist.

'No sir, you may not,' Jemmy answered.

'The world will know of it soon enough, so Leonard may hear it now. I fear Whitley has bound us to a wretched play,' his wife continued, 'which he is entrusted to perform. It will be the undoing of us.'

'A play? What manner of play?' Grist asked.

Jemmy reluctantly recounted the content of the Plumptre play. In defending his own misjudgement, he did not dwell fully on its absurdities, describing the piece as far more rational than the abomination he was burdened with.

Grist listened with curiosity. 'I have played Antony in both the Shakespeare versions,' he said. 'How would it seem, if I were to visit Mr Plumptre to tell him that you have me in mind for his play?'

'No sir you must not. It would but encourage him,' Whitley said.

'It might purchase a little time,' said Cassandra.

Grist continued. 'I could request a personal copy, to study the role for myself.'

'But do not have the rest delivered,' said Cassy urgently.

'Perhaps if I ask for but two copies of the text.' Grist smiled at the Whitleys. 'A copy to read and a copy to spare, for I think there may be a device that will see you out of the predicament. Let me explain. I recall a situation not dissimilar. It would require the support of an esteemed and influential individual in this town. Do you have the confidence of such a person?'

'Esteemed and influential?' Cassy looking at her husband. At once they both said together, 'Marmaduke Pennell!'

'Good,' said Grist. 'When I have a copy of the play, if it is as bad as you say, we will need to enlist the aid of Mr Pennell, if he is to be trusted. . .'

As described by Mr Grist, it would take time for the plan to work. In the meantime, the new season at the theatre was to be arranged. Once more a prospectus of plays was planned that it was hoped would appeal to subscribers. True, the number had fallen of late and this was thought due to the riots. But now the militia were here on a permanent footing, audiences would surely have more confidence to go abroad of an evening.

Yet there were other perils - challenges in fact. For the Whitleys were soon to find that the mayor, no less, had perpetrated an act that seemed little short of treachery. That Friday when they opened their Weekly Journal the following thunderclap was read: -

THEATRICAL REPRESENTATIONS.

By Permission of the Right Worshipful the Mayor of Nottingham. Mr HAMILTON and Family, with the utmost respect, beg leave to inform the Ladies and Gentlemen of Nottingham and its Vicinity, that he has fitted up a genteel Room in a neat, commodious, and Theatrical Manner, and purposes to open it, on Tuesday next the 17th inst. with DRAMATIC ABSTRACTS: and he humbly hopes for the patronage of the Public in general during his short stay.

'Despicable!' declared Jemmy, for now it was his turn to 'take it upon him,' which he did with relish. 'Such ignominy. *'Oh! villain, viper, damn'd without redemption!'* He took care to air his spleen, not only in front of his wife, but before Mr Grist. 'That the mayor, Alderman Fairlight's close ally who did his best to imprison us should now support the enemy.'

'Do you know these people the Hamiltons?' asked Mr Grist.

'Know them? Nobody knows them. They are below the salt, *the lowest and most dejected things of fortune.'*

'You don't like them?'

' "Dramatic abstracts" indeed! Scraps that's all they give. Bits, played before curtains. Like the clatter of dishes before a good meal.'

'You don't like them.'

'That they could be given permission, when they should be driven out of town for the tricksters that they are. And look, they are performing at the Old Rose, sponsored by Jud or should I say Judas Drinkwater. See he gets no more free places.' he said to his wife.

'Surely you do not fear competition?' said Grist.

'Compete with them?' Whitley stopped. He looked at Cassy. 'Yes, we'll do that very thing. We'll act the dogs off the stage,with our best season yet.'

Intrigued to find what the Hamiltons were offering, a boy was sent to obtain a playbill which was later read with scorn.

'Scenes from *As You Like It,'* pointed out Jemmy in derision. 'When there are but five of them. The Hamiltons with their three woeful daughters. Oh, the beggary of it - we must fight back!'

Grist, sensing an opportunity said modestly, 'I have of course played Orlando, whereas Othello has always been considered my finest role and my best puller. Perhaps now is the time for me to air it once more.'

'If you are prepared to have the trouble of it. All that burnt corking of yourself.'

'Tis no great bother. I shall only colour face, hands and arms.'

'That was not how I played it,' said Jemmy. 'For I covered my entire person. How else is one to know how the moor feels?'

Whitley understood that allowing Mr Grist to play Othello would be to place him as the main attraction of the new season. Once again the yearning to play Lear rose within him. Cassy was most disquieted when he proposed it once again.

'You are not well enough and far too old. . . ' she began.

'I am the proper age,' insisted her husband.

'I repeat you are too ill and too advanced in years.'

'But it would be an ideal spoiler for the Hamiltons. Consider. If we offered both the great tragedies in one season.'

'Husband, you have ever lacked subtlety. You are as the old stag being challenged by the new buck. I won't allow it. Mr Grist as Othello is sure to be our crowning attraction. You must allow that.'

Nothing she said could have furthered more Jemmy's desire to play Lear. He realised his health was not sturdy, but he had been learning the part for years and at last he knew it. Now was the moment, or at no time would he ever achieve his desire.

'Why not play Iago opposite Othello?' suggested Cassandra, disguising her sarcasm. 'You have always said it is the better role.'

'It is,' agreed Jemmy. 'A fine suggestion, my dear. . .'

Cassandra smiled as she felt herself unbend with relief.

'. . . but I shall play Lear also.'

'Fie on you for an old fool!' cried Cassy. Throwing her apron over her head she walked angrily from the room, narrowly missing the door.

*

Thirty. *Old Scores, New Starts.*

They called it 'spoons.' After love making they lay asleep, Lucy on her side with her arms crossed and her legs drawn up. Behind her, Thomas matching her shape. His arms around her, their hands firm together and his legs fitting behind hers - like spoons.

He was asleep, snoring a little and she could feel his breath on her neck, the warmth forming a patch of moisture on her cool skin. Here they were, together in new rooms entirely their own. Slowly, outside, daybreak was bringing into view the pattern of the leaded lights in the casement. She watched the criss cross lines grow black and solid against the pale yellow sky. A bluebottle crawled across the window and she half wondered how it was able to pass under the leads as it moved from one pane of glass to another.

At that moment her mind was serene, until with a punch it came back - Treadgold was dead. Treadgold was murdered.

All other thought was dismissed. Everything was spoiled now she remembered. Tate Wilkinson had come to them at once on hearing the news, greatly sympathetic. He had recently served his year as constable and told her of the the legal procedures that were ahead. Her mother, Amelia Treadgold, (how strange to think of her name used formally) would be obliged to answer enquiries from the parish constable and make a statement.

'*About three o' the clock on Monday morning last, I had been awoken by a sound from below in the dance parlour. Mr Treadgold my husband and I do not share the same room. After lighting my candle I had called to him asking if all was well. On rising I discovered his bed to be empty hence I had divined that he had gone downstairs.*

Again I called for him and after receiving no reply descended carefully to the basement where the dancing parlour is.

At first I could see nothing amiss but on entering the room saw my husband lying on the floor. His head had been struck and he lay face downwards in his own blood. I examined the wound and found it to be a mortal one. I felt the vessels of sensation and tried every way to see if I could discern any life, but perceived him to be dead.

I raised the alarm and my neighbour came forthwith. We next found that the drawer where his money was kept had been opened and the contents and some other valuables removed. The outside door to the street had not been forced open, neither had the drawer been harmed. It could thus be reasoned that Mr Treadgold had willingly admitted the intruder who had then committed the theft and killed him.'

Mrs Treadgold spoke slowly, scarcely hiding her disdain for the constable, as she watched his sad efforts at handwriting John Wright had only lately begun his year as constable and although he worked as a clerk, he wrote slowly and laboriously as she narrated her statement. Until that time he had dealt only with two minor crimes of robbery. Murder he had not foreseen.

Watching him struggle, his tongue protruding from the left of his mouth irritated Mrs Treadgold and she angrily removed the barbs from a feather before sharpening her quill with a pen knife.

'Where shall I sign?' she asked when eventually he concluded.

Wright pointed to the bottom of the page. She wrote her name boldly; *Amelia Treadgold.* Fine sand was scattered on the page.

'Thank you,' said Wright. 'This will be taken to the magistrate.'

'I know the magistrate. His daughter is one of my pupils.'

Constable Wright coughed tensely. In spite of having a role of authority he knew it was Mrs Treadgold who dominated the situation.

'Doubtless the magistrate will discuss the evidence with you, before it goes to the grand jury,' he said.

'I don't imagine it will come to that,' said Mrs Treadgold.

'But, ma'am, it is required by law. There has been a murder.'

'That sir, is quite oblivious. If that is all you require I have matters to attend to. I bid you good day.' She indicated the door to the street, giving the constable no option but to depart with his papers.

He opened the front door with the smallest gap to allow his leaving, yet in that slanted moment she saw there was a crowd gathered outside on Swinegate. It mattered little to her if these curious onlookers had seen her, yet nonetheless she was glad her apparel was habitually black, and would be seen suitable for the situation.

Her late husband's corpse had been removed. She would now set about the enterprise of cleaning the dancing parlour in preparation for the class which she intended would be held the day after his funeral.

*

Thomas woke. Yawning, he moved slightly away from Lucy who turned and looked closely into his face. They smiled like conspirators, their faces only a kiss apart. He took a lock of her hair and twined it round a finger.

'It is like spun gold,' he said softly.

'I hope not,' she replied. 'Spun gold must feel much like wire.'

'And as fine as the web of a spider.'

'Again I hope not. That would be a trap for the unwary and it would likewise be sticky would it not?'

'You're as clever as cutlery.' He kissed her.

Pulling a handful of his hair she said, 'Hemp, that's what yours feels like, and it is longer than mine I'll swear. I must cut it e're long.'

'You mean cut it e'er short,' they laughed and kissed once more.

In a loving tumble she took his damaged hand in hers. He tried to withdraw it but she held tight. 'You've never told me how this happened,' she said. Shifting in the bed she moved to look at him. 'There's so little I know about you.'

'That's because I know so little myself. I've told you - I'm a bastard. A bastard from Baston,'

'You're making it up. I do not believe there is such a place.'

'God's truth. Near Deeping.'

'How was it you were born there ?'

'I was found in the church porch. Brought up on the parish by a couple name of Hammond. No children, that's why they took me.'

'That was kind,' Lucy smiled.

Thomas laughed. 'Kind? Not so. They saw a chance to get labour with no wages. Stockingers. Wanted little hands to thread the machines, pick up scraps, oil the joints.' He looked at the gap in his hand. 'Cost me two fingers didn't it?'

'Poor lost fingers,' she said and kissed him.

Thomas shifted and spoke lightly. 'Soon as I was old enough Hammond had me apprenticed to him. That's why they learned me reading and writing, so I could help keep his books, his ledgers. I got no wages, just my keep. Little better than a slave. He saw to it I learned the words of my indenture: "*Taverns, Inns, or Theatres he shall not haunt; at Cards, Dice Tables, or any unlawful Games he shall not play. From the Service of his Master day or night he shall not absent himself*". So I escaped.' He smiled at her.

'You ran off? Where?' she asked as if listening to a story.

'Straight up the North Road. Best track to get away fast. Ended up here in York. It was all right to start with, no-one asked questions. Then folks began to guess I'd absconded. Not so keen on giving me work after that, for fear of the harbouring fine.'

'How old were you?'

'Dunno. About fifteen I fancy. Not long into my apprenticeship That's when I suppose you'd say I went to the bad.'

'In what way?'

'Never you mind.'

'But I do mind. I want to know.'

'I'll tell you only this. I fell in with a gang. Little better than footpads we were. It didn't last long. We soon got caught. Yes, my love, I've done my time in York castle. But I was lucky. The other two sinners being older than me, stepped up to the string. But I managed to escape 'cause of my youth, and the goods I had on me being worth below a shilling,' he stopped.

'I'm glad of that,' she said. 'What then?'

'They told me I'd do better in the army and so I joined the Lancashires. Only they was down south because of the feared new war. When that come to nothing, there was talk of me going to the American colonies. I might have liked that, but that didn't come to nothing neither. And that's all I'm telling you. . .'

'So much sadness,' she said. 'Why is there so much?'

He forced her gently back as if he intended another loving, but she pushed his bare shoulders away.

'No,' her voice was strong. 'Not now.'

He realised her mood had changed. 'I shouldn't have told you,' he said.

'No, for I want to know all about you.' She sat upright looking down where he lay until without warning she said, 'I have to see her.'

For a second he was puzzled, then he realised what she meant.

'Why?' he asked.

'She may need me.'

'When did she ever need you?'

'Perhaps now.'

'I say you should not go.'

'Tom I am bound to, let it be with your favour.'

'Only if I accompany you.'

'No. It befits I see her alone. And on this day. My mind is set.'

He knew he could not prevent her.

Lucy had not bargained for the people gathered in the road. As she entered from Church Street the sight of the crowd almost turned her back. She would be identified. All eyes were upon her. It was distressing but it must be borne. The morning was cold and she was tempted to raise her hood, but no, she would allow them see her. There were nudges and murmurs as she was recognised. Passing the prying faces she bowed her head slightly to prevent her nervousness from being apparent. She knocked at the door.

'It is Lucy,' she called. Long minutes passed before the door opened allowing her admittance.

'I trust you have not come as one of Jove's comforters,' said Mrs Treadgold, shutting the door steadfastly behind her.

'No I have not.'

'Then what is your reason?'

'I am truly sorry for what has happened,' said Lucy.

'That is difficult to believe. I know how you disliked your father.'

Lucy looked directly at her, 'If he was my father?'

'Most assuredly he was. What a barbarous question. It is clear, my girl, you have come to chide me, when I am most vulnerable.'

'That is not my intent. Yet I believe you are aware how ill your husband used me.'

'I know no such thing. Your father was a man of great qualities. Ever heedful of the welfare of others. . .'

'If that is what you choose to believe,' said Lucy.

'It is the truth. I will not have his memory subtracted. If that is your purpose you can leave.'

'Will you allow me to help you with things that must be done?'

'I have seen to everything. The funeral is ready fixed. It shall be at Holy Trinity, Tuesday this seven day, at ten o'clock, should you choose to attend.'

'I shall, but are there not other matters?'

'There is nothing more to be done.'

'But the enquiry into events. . . Matters that are at your behest.'

Mrs Treadgold stared ahead coldly, impassive as a ship's figure-head. Lucy knew well this sudden turning to stone when confronted with things unwelcome. The mind curled tight like a hedgehog, prickles outermost. Recalling her talk with Wilkinson, she knew of the legal needs.

'It must be found who did it. . .who inflicted the blow.'

The silence was uneasy. Lucy continued, 'Mr Wilkinson tells me that an inquest must be lodged by the magistrates and then passed to a grand jury. Thomas and I thought that. . .'

'How dare you mention that villain! He who nearly killed your father.'

'Thomas struck him once, when he was ill-treating me. . .'

'You were never ill-treated. I won't hear of it madam!'

Mrs Treadgold's voice reared to a shout. 'After all our striving, the years of careful training and then what? Nothing but reproaches, with you and your brother absconding like criminals.'

For the first time Lucy raised her voice. 'And you know why. Walter and I both ran away because of the evil, here in this house.'

The slap on the face from her mother was not unexpected, but it shocked in spite of that. From that moment both knew there could be no accord.

Patently following the blow, all energy departed from her mother and Lucy watched as she seemed to dwindle before her, crying silently and coddling her hand as if it was wounded. Lucy felt a force grow within her, absorbing the power as if it bled away from her mother. Gaining strength she asked,

'Have you given a statement?'

'I have.'

'You know there could be a trial?'

'So I have been told,' said her mother now apparently calm. 'I know that such things have to be promoted by the victim. Combined with a reward which I must offer myself. And unless the reward is sizeable, it seldom bears fruit. It will be repaid they say if there is a conviction, but that is rare. You see I do understand.'

'But the murderer has to be caught. And it is true the finding of him is your undertaking.'

'Don't tell me my duties, young woman. It is for me to decide.'

Lucy asked with care. 'You do not want there to be a trial?'

'No, I do not. I shall make no moves towards a prosecution.'

'Because of what would be revealed if Walter was to be tried for murder?'

Mrs Treadgold could no longer stand. Artfully, Lucy had returned her mother's blow by these few words. The score was settled. She felt no triumph as this woman, suddenly old and defeated lowered herself into a chair.

'Whatever else, I shall not prosecute my own son,'

'And I shall not betray my brother.'

Lucy could do no more. She let herself out into Swinegate where the crowd waited still.

Going back to the theatre was troubling, for there in addition she found herself to be a gazing stock, assaulted with questions and dubious sympathy. Not surprisingly it was Fanny M'George who first descended upon her.

'My poor darling. Oh what a terrible mishap. How brave you are to come here. Now tell me. . .' she drew Lucy to one side, 'are there any hints as to who it was? The murderer that is. Do tell me, for you know I shall keep all matters to myself. You can trust me as I'm sure you appreciate.'

'No, there is nothing new,' said Lucy impassively.

'How dreadful for you, not knowing. But they'll find the wretch, God save our souls. 'tis said that Treadgold knew who it was. Opening the door as it seems without question. And the money box, not forced but unlocked with no protest. What a warning for us all, for sure. My door has both lock, bolts and a bar. Even then I would not open it after nightfall whoever came knocking. Oh, but hark to me. How unthinking I am. Here is your poor father but one day departed and I chatter so. We'll take some tea in the dressing room. You can tell me all there is. By the by, what sum was taken? Some say a hundred pound. . .'

Lucy smiled wearily at Fanny and left her to search for Thomas.

The night following the killing, the house had been fuller than usual - sensation was always good for business. Serious debate had been given on how to replace the Treadgold's interval dancing. If the audience had expected the widow to dance a *pas de seul* it was to be disappointed. Instead, one of the company filled the space by singing *Oh the Golden Days We Now Possess* and other suitably respectful songs. Few references was made of Mr Treadgold's death. Mortality in the theatre was rarely if ever mentioned. It brought bad luck.

Truth was, the Treadgolds had not been liked. Their superior manner had made them unpopular and was the cause of much hidden ridicule. It was generally agreed that they resembled the automatons sometimes found on clock towers which displayed a deal more warmth and animation than did the Treadgolds.

Thankfully Lucy was spared this derision. She was liked by the whole company and much pitied for having such ill-favoured parents. Her match with Thomas pleased everyone and Tate Wilkinson spoke for all when he suggested that Lucy and Thomas should fill the vacant place with their own song and dance.

At first they both resisted this, Lucy thinking that it showed poor taste with Mr Treadgold so recently killed. But Tate and the others declared it to be in the best tradition of the theatre, and so 'Mr and Mrs Hammond' were to make their debut.

'I've been watching you for some time,' said Tate. 'You've produced some fine spun routines. You'll neither of you ever be in the opera, but you dance better than a penny booth, I'll say that for you. One or two appearances will be a good advancement for *Harlequin Sailor*. Let the public get to know you as a brace. See you start tonight m'dears. Hallelujah, Praise the Lord.'

Most men in the company habitually pulled at the bottle to fend off the qualms of the evening, Those denying the habit did not include Thomas, who took to the custom with readiness. Lucy like many wives, hoped that her love and support would prove mightier than his need for liquor. It was not to be so. Anticipation before the performance created anxiety, so that their first appearance as a dancing pair caused him misgivings.

'I know I shall let you down,' Thomas said irritably. 'You've been dancing all your life. I'm a fraud. No training. I shall be a mishap.'

'Stop, before I get angry,' said Lucy. 'You have natural capability and audiences love you. You're seeking sympathy and you don't need it. I have never sung in public before, so I have as much occasion as you to be nervous.'

As Tate had said, this was to be a harbinger of Harlequin and Columbine and they were careful not to reveal over much of those characters in this early display. Hurried examinations of the wardrobe produced two ideal costumes. They were both to be in blue. She as a shepherdess in a dress attended with black bodice, blue panniers and bonnet. He as a sailor in bell bottoms, blue jacket and a straw hat.

'Start with the country dance I've seen you practising,' said Tate. 'Then each give a song, you decide which, but let the accompanist know in good time. And mind you end with a hornpipe. Always a rouser that.'

The day passed with arguments on movements, keys of songs, interspersed with costume fittings and sewings, until the time to appear. Both were scared. Lucy tried to keep Thomas occupied so he did not tumble to the bottle. But an hour before their cue, he disappeared and she guessed he was in the tavern. She would not go to him, remembering the discord with Walter, but his absence increased her anger.

He arrived with barely five minutes in hand and she showed her agitation. 'Don't ever do this again. Your conduct is shameful.'

'I'm here, aren't I?'

'Yet in what kind of repair? Oh, how you add to my worries.'

'All will be well, my love, all will be well.'

And so it was, at the start. They stepped on stage to an unusually silent house. No bill had been posted of their appearance, no announcement made, so that for the time it took to walk from the wings to centre stage, there was an awkward moment of non recognition.

Then the cry went up,

'It's Puck!' shouted someone. 'And 'is missus!' another.

A round of cheers and clapping filled the theatre. Together Lucy and Thomas stood, hand in hand, smiling and bowing to the acclaim. Both waited as the noise continued, until a fiddler was heard drawing a chord on his instrument. The approbation stopped; an expectancy fell as the couple turned to face each other. He bowed neatly to her, she curtsied in return and they began a dainty Irish jig to a tune everyone knew. Clapping and stamping to the rhythm sounded from floor to ceiling. The dance lasted scarce five minutes, but the following applause was nearly as long. Thomas brought it to an end by leaving Lucy alone to take her bearing. After a brief hesitation she sang in a small but sweet voice, *My Mother Bids me Braid My Hair,* carefully attended by the fiddle.

Madame Catalani herself could not have received a greater ovation. It ended only when Lucy and Thomas changed their stage positions, she leaving him alone to sing.

The fiddler gave him a key note and reluctantly he began. His voice was husky, unmistakably affected by nerves. After a few notes he stopped. He cleared his throat. Another chord was given from the violin, but still he could not secure it. Once more he stopped.

The monster was come. It was here before him - the fiend with a thousand eyes. The disaster he was waiting for. It was like the time he couldn't climb the rope. The whispers were right, he was inept. He was only a prompter's devil with no business to be on the stage. He was lost, close to terror, unable to think until a voice came from the gallery,

'Come on Puck. Give us a tune!'

Great applause and the fiddler stroked the key note once more. Thomas lifted his head and began in a tentative but true tenor, *Here a sheer hulk lies poor Tom Bowling. . .* The sad shanty was the perfect choice. His voice grew in sincerity, until the sentiment of the words and music worked their spell and many in the house were tearful. An audience likes to laugh, but far outshining that, it likes to cry. And so it was. They cheered, they loved him, the more because he had overcome a dubious start.

Lucy joined him and as directed they ended with a boisterous horn pipe *The Drunken Sailor*. The roof was well-nigh raised. Bow followed bow, still they were not allowed to leave. Finally Thomas threw his straw hat into the audience and the joyous couple ran off. But they had to come back.

The Drunken Sailor was encored and could have been again and again had not Tate had the curtain dropped.

'Always leave then wanting more,' he said.

Those that could, gathered round them, showing pleasure at their success. The delight was genuine, and with it came the additional knowledge that this success was good for all of them. It was left to Tate to temper a note of caution.

Looking at Thomas he said,

'If you're set on throwing away a good hat every night, young fella-me-lad, I knock it off your wages.'

*

Thirty One. *Hurly-burly.*

To begin, the band of the King's Own Troop of Light Horse gave two grand concerts at the St Mary Gate theatre, Whitley offering the first for subscribers to the forthcoming season. Its success saw the second open to the public in the hope that those who had never been in the theatre before would take the opportunity of finding it was not the gateway to hell. Play acting may be the devil's doing but music was *all of heaven we have below.*

This proved not to be the case. The programme of marches, both English and Turkish, was stirring but hardly heavenly. Parade ground music intended for the open air when played in the confines of the small theatre increased in cacophony until a resounding finale was reached. Being a *'Battle Symphony'* it was complete with bugle calls and percussion depicting rifle shots, canon fire and explosions. For more sensitive listeners, particularly those of the nonconformist persuasion, this confirmed that the theatre was truly a place of infernal din; the temporary deafness inflicted for hours afterwards, sure proof of Satan's handiwork.

But overall, the patriotic sentiments pleased the majority of insentient concertgoers and the Whitleys looked forward to a lucrative partnership with Colonel Mundy. The cementing of this alliance seemed even stronger when they received a second invitation to a Saturday morning reception at the barracks, 'To Develop Cordial Relations between the Military and the Gentility of Nottingham.' Surely this would bring about their long sought for inclusion in the town's fashionable hierarchy

The morning was fine and the Whitleys' dress restrained. Cassy in her renovated French gown and Jemmy in his grey frock coat arrived with the other guests at the gaily decorated barracks. The band, now at a discreet distance, played light music as stirrup cup was offered by orderlies and an air of good humour prevailed. Surveying the other guests whose faces were unfamiliar, the Whitleys glided towards a group, when Jemmy stopped abruptly and grabbed Cassy by the arm.

'Quickly, turn round, walk the other way.'

'Why? What for?' asked the surprised Cassy.

'It's the damned Hamiltons,' said her husband. 'Here to promote their wretched offerings at the Rose, no doubt.'

But it was too late. At that moment Colonel Mundy and his wife had recognised them and approached, all smiles and hospitality.

'Mr and Mrs Whitley, how good of you to come.' Pleasantries were exchanged as the Mundys continued, 'Do come and meet the Hamiltons, though you'll doubtless need no introduction. You theatrical people are certain to know each other.'

There was no avoiding the encounter. Mrs and Mrs Hamilton and their three daughters stood together, costumed it would suggest for some Arabian Nights extravaganza. Formalities were exchanged. A tense quietude following until Colonel Mundy's wife said brightly to Mr Hamilton,

'We greatly enjoyed your performance last night.'

'We were honoured to have you and so many officers at our humble spectacle,' replied Mr Hamilton. His ladies giggled nervously behind their fans.

For the Whitleys this was a severe blow. That the Colonel and the military had patronised the Hamiltons before attending their theatre was an acute rebuff. There followed another stillness, broken only when Cassy enquired carelessly, 'What was the play on offer?' as if it was an item at the fish mongers.

'King John,' replied Mr Hamilton. 'Shakespeare,' he added.

'Shakespeare?' exclaimed Jemmy, as if he had not heard the name before. 'How bold of you to offer so big a play.'

'We do not give the full text,' said Mr Hamilton. 'We are sir, miniaturists, with but five of us our scale is small but flawless in detail.'

'We must come and see you, when we have a minute to spare.'

'Oh but you must,' said the Colonel's wife smiling at Mr Hamilton. 'That scene where you were about to put out the young prince's eyes, was dreadful, quite dreadful.'

'I can believe that,' said Whitley gravely. Cassy looked away.

The Colonel smiled remarking benevolently, ‘ Now, you theatre folk are sure to have so much to discuss,’ as he and his wife moved to their other guests.

‘Yes,’ said Mr Hamilton expansively, ‘even before we opened, Colonel Mundy was desirous to patronise a play. I sent my manager with the catalogue, (as is usual on such occasions), before I paid my *devoirs* to him. “Sir,” the Colonel said to me, “I must engage you. Name your terms. I propose to secure an exclusive number of evenings for the officers of my regiment.”’

It was rare for Jemmy Whitley to be at a loss for words, but this proved to be one such moment. But worse was to come. Mr Hamilton had scarce reached the end of his discourse, when they were joined by a gentleman having every appearance of a prosperous dealer in starch and hair powder.

‘Perhaps you don’t know my manager,’ said Mr Hamilton. ‘Allow me to introduce Mr Powell esquire.’

Brook Powell smiled. If the sudden meeting with the Whitleys surprised him he shielded it completely.

‘Mr and Mrs Whitley and I are old partners are we not?’ he said.

The word ‘not’ almost escaped Whitleys clenched jaw, but he merely acknowledged the new arrival.

‘Brook is our true anchor,’ enthused Mr Hamilton. ‘He cares for us like a guardian angel, does he not ladies?’ The question was answered with modest smiles hidden behind a gale of fluttering fans.

Whitley found his tongue. ‘Mr Powell’s services were always. . .’ he hesitated ‘. . . remarkable. What else have you been doing of late?’

‘Oh, did you not know?’ announced Powell. ‘I have been contriving a fairground enterprise. My protégé was Paddy O’Hara, the surprising Irish giant. Only twenty one years old yet he measures eight foot in height. A very well favoured young fellow. I managed him afore he went back to Ireland, greatly richer for the experience.’

‘And before that the ‘surprising child’ was it not?’ asked Jemmy. ‘But here you are with a new concern. Tell me, does this make you. . . legitimate?’

With his mouth firm closed, Powell made a series of sounds in his throat, that was possibly as near to a laugh as he ever achieved. This was followed by a glare which put Whitley in mind of a cornered rat. 'Yes I am legitimate,' he said, 'I no longer deal with Freaks!'

'Freaks!' complained Whitley, continuing to rage over Powell's insult as they walked home. This, with the implication that he was of equal standing with the wretched Hamiltons had ruined not only the morning but the entire day. 'Never was such insolence. I could have struck him on the spot.'

'I'm relieved you did not,' said Cassy. 'Best not provoke him.'

'His was the provocation. "Freaks"! And calling himself a manager.'

'That was the Hamilton's description.'

'Propounded by Powell I'll warrant. Well as I have said, we'll act the Hamiltons off the stage like the dogs they are. We'll pay them their *devoirs,* whatever that means.'

They continued with no words as they approached the square.

'They'll die the death at the Old Rose,' he said fiercely.

'Don't forget we played there once ourselves,' reminded Cassy.

'We had the sense to perform burlesque and comedy. Not Shakespeare. I say the Bard will make as much sense as Naylor and his Scottish songs.'

'Naylor was well liked there.'

'They won't last the week.'

'We'll see,' said Cassy.

Returning to the theatre they found Mr Grist sitting in the green room, a large volume on his lap, with others piled beside him. Slamming the book shut, he placed it with its companions and stood, drawing in his breath,

'By heaven,' he said, 'it is a monstrous confection.'

'Plumptre's play?' asked Whitley.

'Plumptre's play,' repeated Grist. 'I collected two sets from him yesterday. I cannot say I have sat up all night reading it, for I have never found anything more soporific. He should market it as a sleeping draught.'

'You do not recommend we play it?'

'Hah! Mind you if it were cut by a hundred fold it might make a farce. I fancied we might counterfeit a performance, then tell him what a success it had been. That way the poor fool might remain happy.'

'I fear he will insist on seeing it played. Doubtless ask for a performance in his bedroom Was he abed when you called?'

'He was. Mightily impatient for news. He asked when the rehearsals were to begin and where were the designs he was promised?. Perhaps if he were shown some suggestions it might placate him whilst my plan is underway.

'You have got the extra copies?'

'At my rooms, ready for submission to the Lord Chamberlain as I proposed. What we'll require is the letter from Marmaduke Pennell. You know, Whitley, for once I feel sorry for the Lord Chamberlain's examiners, being obliged to read the whole interminable play.'

The suggestion that Mr Plumptre be presented with some designs, seemed to Whitley a good one. Recalling the scenic models that Ceraccio had made sometime of late, he resolved to send them to Plumptre House to mollify the would-be playwright. Assuming the signor would be backstage with Mr Bracer, Jemmy was dismayed to find the signor was nowhere to be found.

' Never 'ere. 'ardly ever turns up,' said Mr Bracer. 'I pay 'im by the hour when 'e does, but I reckon it's them mucky pictures takes up all 'is time.'

'Mucky pictures, what do you mean?'

'I mean just that. Shocking, if you ask me. That there Armstrong hussy should be ashamed, the baggage.'

'Bracer, what are you talking about?'

'Perhaps it was while you was sick abed,' continued Bracer. 'The signor's been making a fortune selling pictures of that there Belinda, as naked as the day she was born. So called poses of 'er, with no clothes on. What's more she's living with 'im now. Disgusting I calls it. Need a good 'iding, both of 'em.'

The realisation that things were happening within his company of which he knew nothing troubled Whitley. His intent was always to have complete knowledge of backstage business for until now he had taken pride in caring for everyone from player king to spear carrier. His apparent neglect might be due to his illness and must be righted at once. He sought out Signor Ceraccio at his lodgings. Instead, on arrival he was greeted by Belinda Armstrong, which would appear to confirm her living with the painter.

'Good day, Belinda. Is the signor at home?'

'No he's not.'

'Out on a commission or some such matter ?'

'He's gone to arrange for the carrier. We're off tomorrow or the next day after. You can see for yourself.' Belinda opened the door allowing Jemmy to observe within the house, boxes, easels, canvases and numerous bundles clearly ready for an imminent removal.

'But where. . .and why?' he asked.

'Been promised a proper engagement. At the theatre in York.'

'York!' The sound of the word struck him to the quick. 'Is this Wilkinson's doing ?'

'You might say so. Most anxious to have us join him he is.'

'But you are both needed here.'

'Needed? That's a laugh. I've not had a decent part for weeks and Signor Ceraccio's treated no better than a lick-spigot. Well he won't be paid piecemeal no more. He'll be respected for the proper artist that he is and be rewarded accordingly.'

'This is a betrayal.' Whitley was shamed to hear himself using such a banality, but could think of nothing else.

'Pardon me sir,' said Belinda haughtily, 'We both have our futures to consider, which will not served by staying in this blind alley.'

'You are a wicked ungrateful girl.'

Belinda laughed. 'I expect I am. But several fine gentlemen are more than desirous of partaking of my good company and who knows where I shall end? It won't be here, that's for sure.' She shut the door with a slam.

Two weeks later, the admonished Whitley received a letter .

'We are both in York, Belinda Armstrong and Guino Ceraccio.'

He replied by return of post,

'Stay there and be damned.'

*

The loss of Belinda was unexpected and distressing. Whitley had mentally cast her as his Cordelia when he played Lear, because of her lightness of weight, discounting her lightness of voice. Although her Juliet was said by some to have been one of the loveliest ever seen, others complained it was the most inaudible. Her beauty was undeniable yet being seen and not heard on the boards indicated her talent was best employed in wider aesthetic spheres.

Signor Ceraccio had discovered this to his advantage and Whitley regretted angrily the loss of both him and the girl. He wondered if Wilkinson's eagerness to employ them suggested he had seen a capability that he had not detected himself. Was this another indication that his powers were waning?

Placing aside the problem, Whitley devoted his mind fully to the coming season. The main attraction was to be Mr Grist, whose Othello was anticipated with an excitement little short of a cut in taxes.

The season was to open with a gala for the benefit of Mr Grist, graced by the presence of Colonel and Mrs Mundy with the regimental band providing entr'acte music throughout the evening.

All seemed set fair on the night until Mr Bracer approached, 'There's talk of trouble,' he said in a sombre voice.

'Trouble?' asked Jemmy.

'I was in the Feathers last night. They were saying the 'amiltons 'ave been thrown out of the Old Rose. Laughed off the stage.'

Whitley was relieved for the moment. 'What happened?'

'*As You Like It*. Only they didn't. Mr and Mrs 'amilton playing the young lovers, I ask you. They said it were more like Father Time and Mother Goose.'

'How very sad,' said Whitley not without some satisfaction. His forecast had been right but it was always disquieting to hear of hostility towards any acting company.

'That's not all.' continued Bracer, 'It means Powell's lost 'is position as their manager. It's said 'e's seeking revenge. 'e's putting it about its all your doing. Saying you organised a gang to go and wreck the performance. That you couldn't stand the competition.

'But that's libellous.'

''e's on the warpath. You'd be best keep 'im out the theatre.'

'That can't be done. We may try to prevent him him coming, but it's impossible to stop him on the door without causing trouble.'

'Don't say I 'aven't warned you.'

The gala opening night of the season had become a fashionable occasion. Footmen bearing flambeaux, boys sweeping crossings to the pavement, unofficial playbill and fruit sellers adding to the press of playgoers as coaches arrived at the theatre. A strong wind caught clothing and wigs, as well as blowing out the few oil lamps that tried in vain to light the street. Attempts at re-lighting them added to the horde of humanity in the narrow space. Whitley had given instructions that if Powell or any of his colleagues were seen, their admittance was to be refused. But the crush at the door was so extreme that any form of exclusion proved impossible.

With music to be provided by the military band combined with Mr Grist's first performance as Othello, excitement was high. The gallery and pit had filled swiftly, where good natured banter indicated that an enjoyable night lay ahead. Even some of the boxes were early occupied which was rare and a sign that nobody wished to miss a minute of the delights in store.

Backstage, nerves were manifest from butterflies in the stomach to genuine nausea. These features were hidden beneath feigned gaiety and cries of 'break a leg' too numerous to count. Mr Grist was carefully blacked up. An ebony wig had been constructed to cover his scalp in tight bristles. Dark tights encased his legs convincingly, his face, neck and arms required the application of burnt cork. The supply of this commodity had been generously increased by the extra consumption of alcohol within the company.

For some unknown cause, the arrival of Colonel and Mrs Mundy was delayed and the earlier good natured mood in the auditorium began to curdle. To keep an audience waiting is always dangerous, as this evening was soon to demonstrate. Clapping and shouting broke out. Cries of 'Let's have a start,' and 'Why are we waiting?' began to sound ugly. Piercing whistles, stamping and kicking created a new, sinister atmosphere and the Whitleys grew anxious as they waited to welcome Colonel Mundy and Mrs Mundy.

'We've got trouble makers out front,' Jemmy said to Cassy, as he peered through the curtain.

'Is it Powell? I've seen no signs of him?'

'Never mind Powell. There's a group in the pit sitting with their hats firmly on their heads. I'll wager they're democrats up to no good.'

'Then we must start - Mundys or no Mundys.'

Following Whitley's urgent request, the playing of the national anthem by the regimental band was brought about. Its military conductor, splendid in full regalia, marched on stage to conduct his musicians. With an imperious command he brought forth a stirring drum roll for the start of the familiar tune.

All in the theatre rose, apart from the group of democrats who stayed firmly seated, their hats defiantly remaining on their heads.

The accord of voices raised together in 'God save our gracious king,' was quickly lost. Starting as a murmur of indignation, a swell of anger turned into the chanting of,

'Hats off! Hats off!' directed at the insolent minority.

Voices everywhere took up the menacing cry, 'Hats off Hats off!' in a rhythm as dangerous and threatening as war drums.

Inevitably when the miscreants ignored the command they were attacked, their hats snatched and thrown away. Attempts at retrieving the head gear turned into fisticuffs and fights quickly broke out. People fell as benches were overturned. Angry loyalists pushed forward to get at the democratic villains, whilst others scrambled to get out of the way. The inhabitants of the gallery looked down in delight at the disorder below. However, cries of encouragement resulted in factions being formed amidst the gods themselves which rapidly lead to conflict. Every kind of hat was seized and flung over the upper railings, where they descended like newly shot game birds, the owners desperate to retrieve them.

The onstage band, having forsaken the national anthem, attempted to restore order by playing military music. As is well known, such pieces encourage rather than reduce belligerency and it was only the want of a Scottish piper to inflame emotions further that all-out warfare was avoided.

The musicians watched the battle from the stage, as if from a grandstand. As the lowering of a curtain was attempted they put aside their instruments and being military men joined the fray in the role of peace keepers, but to little effect.

Initially, those in the boxes were bemused. The more judicious decided to forgo the entertainment and make for home, only to find that hostilities had spread to the foyer. Shouts of 'Death to the king,' countered with 'Kill the rebels,' and other slogans added to the uproar and distress. In time the loyalist faction in the pit gained ascendancy over the democrats who were roughly manhandled and thrown outside onto the street. The hurly-burly in the gallery took longer to resolve, it not being clear who supported which side. Slowly, a procession of bloody noses, broken knuckles, and torn clothing staggered down the staircase.

Anger did not end when once on the pavement. The expelled democrats shouted abuse at anyone not of their convictions, frightening some of the waiting horses into a bolt, which in turn saw their drivers in hectic pursuit of both steeds and vehicles.

In the midst of this disorder, Colonel and Mrs Mundy made the fatal mistake of arriving late at the theatre. It being a formal occasion the colonel was in full dress uniform complete with decorations that included a ceremonial sword. Alighting from their coach, unaware of the situation, the couple were for a moment flattered by the attention of the crowd. What seemed to begin as admiration, speedily revealed itself to be malicious with the colonel first being ridiculed and then attacked by the democrats. His sword was wrested from its sheath with one ruffian waving it dangerously in his face. Some of the band of musicians seeing the danger, pushed the terrified Mrs Mundy back into her coach whilst others tried to rescue their commanding officer. Poor Mundy was knocked to the ground, only to be kicked and rolled in the dirt, his sword used to cut away pieces of his uniform, taken as tokens.

One of the musicians, thinking himself on the battlefield. reached for his trumpet and sounded the call to arms. Fellow soldiers in sundry parts of the vicinity (mostly in taverns or other establishments) rallied to the summons as quickly as their legs or state of dress permitted them. The seriously injured Colonel Mundy was conveyed to his quarters, where he and his distressed wife received the care they badly required.

Eventually the trumpet call had been heeded by two of the town constables who, learning of the disturbance, arrived when calm had been restored. The crowd and most of the carriages were departed, for as it had become glaringly clear, the gala opening of *Othello* would not take place that night.

In accordance with the law, the following morning the violent outrages at the theatre were reported officially by the constables at the magistrates' court. As a result, their worships ordered that notice should be given to the theatre manager immediately to shut down the place of entertainment until further notice. On learning of this Brook Powell was greatly satisfied. The closure of the theatre had been achieved, without any effort on his part.

*

Thirty Two. *Tried before the last Lincoln Jury.*

WALTER TREADGOLD and JAMES OLDFIELD both former theatre comedians were indicted for feloniously stealing on the 4th day of September last one bay gelding price £12 the property of JAMES SWEENY.

JAMES SWEENY, prosecutor sworn.

'What is your profession?'

'I am a director of the Oxford Canal Navigation Company.'

'And you live in Stamford?'

'I do. I have a freight company of my own newly based in that town.'

'Tell the court what happened on the night in question.'

'I missed a bay gelding from my stable in the night between the 3rd and 4th of September. I had given up the horse for lost when two weeks later I went on business to Deeping St James where I saw the horse and knew it directly. It was in a field, put to a log in the custody of John Frewin.'

'How came the horse there?'

'John Frewin told me he had recently bought the horse for six guineas.'

'Are you acquainted with the prisoners?'

'I am acquainted with the prisoner Oldfield who for a short time worked in my accounting house.'

'Are you conversant with the prisoner Treadgold?'

'He asked me once for work as a copyist, but I refused him.'

'For what reason ?'

'He was not competent for my needs. He was trained only to be a dancing master which did not answer my demands.'

'Are the prisoners known to each other?'

'Yes. They are both previously comedians in the theatre, and I have often seen them drinking together.'

'Are you not conjoined with the prisoners, having sometime worked as a comedian yourself in the past?'

'I am not. I bring this charge only for the love and upholding of justice.'

JOHN FREWIN, witness sworn.

'I bought the horse from Oldfield when he said he had the one would suit me.'

'How much did you give for the horse?'

'I gave him six guineas in money.'

'When you were later approached by the true owner Mr Sweeny, how did he tell you it was his horse?'

'By the white marks on its forehead with a long tail and a full mane.'

'What did you next?'

'I described the seller of the horse and it became evident that it might be the prisoner Oldfield. Mr Sweeny told me that he was oft times to be found at a tavern in Stamford and desired that I meet him there to see if it was the exact man.'

'You went with him to Stamford?'

'I did. Together we saw the two prisoners at the King's Arms tavern where I recognised the prisoner Oldfield. Mr Sweeny then called for the constables and the two prisoners were arrested on his instructions.'

PRISONER OLDFIELD'S DEFENCE.

'I am a sometimes porter at the George Inn. I was approached by the prisoner Treadgold who asked me if I could take a bay gelding to Deeping St James where it was to be stabled awaiting a sale. It was a morning's walk to Deeping, meaning I had to lead the horse by hand for I am not able to ride a horse with no saddle. Treadgold told me that he would share with me half the cost of the sale for the doing of this.'

'Did you ask Treadgold how he came by the horse?'

'I did. He said it was his own property.'

'What happened when you were got to Deeping?'

'I found the stables were more costly than I had money for. So I asked Mr Frewin if he could give the horse a mash and allow him overnight in his field.'

'What said he to that?"

'He admired the good shape of the horse and when I said it was for sale, he said he should like to buy it. We agreed the sum of six guineas and I then returned to Stamford where I met Walter Treadgold, giving him three guineas being one half of the sale.'

'You sold the horse in the belief that it was Treadgold's own?'

'I did.'

PRISONER WALTER TREADGOLD'S STATEMENT:

The Prisoner changed his plea to that of Guilty in that on the 4th day of September last he did feloniously steal one bay gelding price £12 the property of James Sweeny. He admitted that he did persuade and inveigle James Oldfield to act as an accomplice into the selling of the same bay gelding without his knowing it to be unlawful. The prisoner spoke as follows:

'My Lord, at my first being taken into custody, I intended to plead "Not Guilty", but my mind is now altered. I beg leave to trespass on your Lordship's patience to speak of the character of James Oldfield, who acted in all innocence in that he believed the horse to be mine lawfully for the sale thereof.

I know him to be a pious, godly man and a good husband and father to his children. I hope that no penalty will be afflicted upon him because of my wrong doing and I support him for your Lordship's mercy.

I plead guilty to the charge of stealing the horse, I have no more to say, but recommend myself to the mercy of God and to beg your Lordship's prayers and those of the jury.'

Verdict

WALTER TREADGOLD: Guilty. Death.

JAMES OLDFIElD: Guilty. Jury recommended mercy.

*

Thirty Three *Chance governs all.*

The fairy was stuck. She should have flown away prettily into the fleecy clouds above Cloud Cuckoo Land but something was wrong with the hoist and she was swinging around like an angry spider

'What the bloody 'ell's 'appened?' asked the fairy who did not appreciate the jibes about hanging out to dry, nor the suggestions of being a fallen angel; she demanded noisily to be returned to earth.

The fairy was one of the local children who were recruited to play elves and goblins essential for *Harlequin Sailor*. With so many sprites running wild backstage Tate Wilkinson was reminded how much he disliked pantomime.

If the children were not carefully safeguarded there would be angry parents and magistrates investigating conditions behind the scenes. Yes, he hated pantomime but apart from this minor hiccup, *Harlequin Sailor* was going well, and the opening night less than a week away promised to be a landmark in his career.

Cloud Cuckoo Land was one of the new scenes created by Signor Ceraccio following his arrival in York. After long and difficult consultations, hampered by disparity with language, a new scenario had been devised. Such were the radical changes to *Harlequin Sailor* that at times it had come close to being called *Harlequin Becalmed* or worse, but somehow a plot was salvaged from the jumble of ideas and it was in the final stages of rehearsal. Of the original script, much had changed, with only the Tropical Island and the Underwater Palace still intact. Although the Ruined Abbey by Moonlight was retained, for some arcane reason it had turned into Cloud Cuckoo Land.

To his credit, Signor Ceraccio was trying to master the English language and both Mr Weaver and Mr Watson, the master painter and carpenter, sought to interpret his instructions. Sadly, the signor's endeavours often added to the confusion when, for example, he asked his assistant to,

'Listen to the colours. They are sounding too loud.' Or when some of his work came in for mild criticism he shouted angrily,

'Don't spoke. If you shall not like, I went.'

Miraculously, in spite of these difficulties, a beautiful production was evolving with many wonderful tricks and devices to delight the eye. Lucy and Thomas were a comely pair. Her singing and dancing combined with his acrobatics made a delightful team and Tate was proud that they had come together under his tutelage and guidance.

Although Signor Ceraccio had been lured initially to York by Tate Wilkinson, there had been others also seeking his services. The now famous Cupid and Psyche ceiling at Nuthall had become a celebrated work, admired by many, including the newly rich Lord Openshaw. This local connoisseur had commissioned the signor to decorate the interior of Skelton Jassy, his nearby Yorkshire mansion nearing completion.

Nor had Belinda Armstrong been neglected for by now she could be accurately termed - a beauty. Gentlemen visiting the signor's studio began to ask if they could stay awhile to observe her posing as the various nymphs needed for divers commissions. These requests grew in frequency until the artist and his model, realising the commercial benefit, decided that a fee could be asked for the privilege. A small stage was set up, complete with a brass rail and a red velvet curtain, behind which the young lady prepared herself for viewing. For a not insignificant price, the drapes were drawn to reveal Belinda in whatever guise the onlooker might request. Classical and Biblical subjects were popular, of which Eve was by far the most favoured.

In time, Lord Openshaw of Skelton Jassy became so enthused that he was willing to pay a large sum for Belinda to appear exclusively in any guise whatever at his newly built mansion. Astutely, Belinda made it clear that his lordship's wishes could not be granted without some commercial advance so that as the weeks passed, she was gifted with sundry valuables which she regarded as a security. When, as was inevitable, she came to share his lordship's bed her collection of knick-knacks turned into a most satisfactory endowment.

In the theatre, preparations had been going a little too well for it should have been recalled that even the fairest of days can end in storm.

And so it proved.

A letter, badly written on scrubby paper was delivered to the stage door. Addressed to Lucy, she had paid for the postage recognising the crude hand to be that of her brother Walter. The letter contained a bleak request for his dancing clothes to be got to him. The reason given was that he was to be hanged a week hence at Lincoln Castle.

Nothing more.

Lucy's near collapse on reading this, ensured that the news was rapidly heard by everyone. Many stood mute, observing her distress, unable to express their sadness at the tidings.

It was Fanny M'George who rushed in with ill-considered words,

'It must be a terrible mistake,' she said, 'There's sure to be an explanation. It will all turn out right, you'll see.'

Nobody shared this view which was taken as a foolish effort to dispel Lucy's awful news. After conveying his sympathies, Tate Wilkinson in his most avuncular manner recommended work as a cure.

'Yes it is a dreadful prospect,' he said, 'but the Lord will provide. Be thankful you've got *Harlequin* to perform in. That will guide you through safely. We open less than a week now and there's nothing better than performing to drive away sorrow, depend on it.'

Lucy sat still and silent with Thomas who, unable to bring her comfort said, 'I think that's right. However bad it seems, when you get on the stage you will probably feel better.'

'That's so,' said Fanny, desperately bright, 'Doctor theatre it's called. Cures all ills. Once you're in front of the footlights, you'll see.'

It was of no matter that the words were inadequate, for Lucy heard none of them. Cold from the news she sat trembling, until in a quiet voice she said, 'I must go to him.'

Thomas looked at her and then at the others, sharing their disbelief. He replied simply, 'You can't.'

Again Lucy appeared not to have heard, or if she had, not to have understood, 'I must go to him,' she repeated,

The five gentle words had the strength of a green shoot forcing its way through rock. With it, Tate Wilkinson realised that the girl's determination was a challenge to his sufficiency.

'What are you talking about? You can't leave and go to him,' he said aggressively. 'You are honour bound to play here.'

Lucy looked at him calmly, 'He is my kin, my brother, If he dies alone, what shall be left?'

There was no answering this. She should have said no more, but she continued, 'It is my place to be with him.'

On this, Tate pounced, 'It is your place to be here. There's many depending on you, my girl. Without you, there will be no play, no work for us all. Let the dead bury the dead. We'll have no more talk of your departing!'

Lucy stared at him, 'I must be with him,' she said as if explaining something to a child.

Thomas, his uncertainty increasing tried to reason, 'He did not call for you. He called only for his suit.'

'Which I must take to him.'

Tate, his voice rising in volume, broke in, 'Your brother wrote, "one week hence," There's no date on the letter. How long ago was that? Most likely he is already dead. Even if you left this minute, you cannot get to Lincoln in less than two days, more likely three. It is near winter, the roads are bad, the weather treacherous. Think on it.'

Lucy stood silent and gave her answer, 'I will hazard the risk.'

Near to desperation Tate turned to Thomas, 'Can you not reason with her? Forbid this folly?'

Thomas asked, 'What if we got there and found him dead?'

Slightly surprised Lucy answered, 'Tom, I'm not asking you to come. I shall go alone. You must remain here and play your part.'

Tate broke in. 'Yes, let her go alone, if go she must.'

Thomas almost laughed, 'No. Never.' To Lucy he said, 'Of course I shall come with you.'

'Hell and damnation!' Tate shouted. The likely absence of both Lucy and Thomas would bring catastrophe to the opening of *Harlequin Sailor*. Months of preparation were unravelling. His voice rose with unfamiliar fury.

'Your loyalty is here, not with that fleeing rascal, your brother. His time is come and you need to accept madam, that he has gone to the bad. Justice will have its due.'

He walked away unable to say more. But the talk of justice was intolerable for Lucy, as in truth she had no notion why Walter was to be hanged. She and her mother had assumed he had killed Treadgold, but they did not know for sure. Had he confessed to the murder? Unlikely, for all enquiries into the crime had come to nothing; the murder was declared unsolved and neither she nor her mother would ever inform on him. So why was he under sentence of death? Perhaps Fanny was right and it was a dreadful mistake. More reason why she must be with him, at least to learn the truth.

As Thomas said, the main purpose of the letter was Walter's request for his dancing suit. This was not uncommon; many condemned men chose to be hanged in their best attire.

For Tate's wife Jane this demand suggested an alternative which she put to her husband.

'I have decided it might help if I visited Mrs Treadgold,' she said. 'It could be that she, not Lucy, will take the suit to her son.'

'You can try,' said Tate truculently, "I doubt you'll succeed.'

Until it was revealed by Jane, Mrs Treadgold knew nothing of her son's sentence of death. Given the dreadful news, the mother showed no emotion, keeping Jane standing at the door until she was later admitted reluctantly. A recounting of the facts gained no seeming reaction and it was not until Jane told of Walter's wish for his dancing suit that eventually she spoke.

'What an improper idea,' she said. 'I am admonished by it.'

'As it is his very last wish. Would you take the suit to him?'

'Out of the question. You forget, I am a widow. My only means of livelihood is by my teaching. If I forgo my duties I shall find myself a pauper.'

When Jane explained that if Lucy and Thomas were to visit Lincoln, the entire theatre would be put in jeopardy, Mrs Treadgold's comment was, 'They must please themselves.'

'Do you not wish to see your son for the last time?' asked Jane.

'The letter he wrote was to his sister, not me, I think that conveys our standing.'

'He may have written to you and the letter gone missing.'

'If that is so, then my loss is to be endured.'

Jane was shocked at the woman's dispassion.

'Forgive me,' she said, 'that appears somewhat unfeeling.'

'I have always kept my temper in rein,' said Mrs Treadgold. 'If you are expecting me to weep and wail because of your tidings, I am sorry to be a disappointment. I shall deal with my sentiments privately when I am alone.'

With manifestly nothing more to be said the conversation ended. Jane returned to the theatre, expecting to find Lucy and tell her of her mother's inflexibility, but Lucy was not to be found. Instead, Jane Wilkinson discovered Tate in the worse temper she had ever witnessed.

Several bewildered children stood, wondering what was happening, whilst other company members were almost hiding in the darkness of the auditorium. Somewhere behind the scenes could be heard crashes and shouts, until Tate walked on stage pushing aside whatever barred his way.

'Go home, the lot of you! There'll be no more rehearsal today. The Lord alone knows when or what the next one will be.'

'Will you please to tell me what is happening?' asked Jane, attempting to bring about stability.

'Our leads have gone! Both of 'em! That is what is happening! With no sense of duty. No responsibility to others Quite the reverse. They are prepared to bring disaster on the lot of us. For that's what it will mean. Disaster!'

Jane asked no more. 'Come down,' she said to him gently, 'that we may talk about this.'

'No I will not,' shouted Tate. Seeing some of the children still staring at him in bewilderment he yelled at them, 'Clear off you little wretches!'

The children screamed and ran. Jane walked up onto the stage, 'How dare you take your anger out on the children.'

Tate looked at her, raised his arms in desperation and walked in an uneven circle, his head bowed like an exhausted runner until Jane took hold of him. At once he leaned upon her, grateful for support. Together they walked from the stage into an empty dressing room where they sat together.

Calmly she asked, 'What has been said?'

'I have made it plain to them both. If they walk out I will never have them back. Never! Furthermore, I shall sue them for breaking their bargain. If they plan to ruin me, then I shall ruin them.'

'Where are they now?'

'Doubtless they are repaired to Coney Street. A coach leaves from there tomorrow morning I'm told. If there are places they will take them. For sure that will be on the outside. In this weather! They will freeze before they get to Lincoln. They have no idea what travel is like in winter.'

'You cannot expect Tom to let Lucy go alone.'

'I am done with them! They are amateurs both. Performing only when it obliges them. There's no place for such hirelings in my theatre.'

Jane found herself nowhere. She understood her husband's fury. Great and expensive preparations had been made for the pantomime. What were they do? His talk of suing the young couple was futile, for they had no funds. What good would come by putting them in a debtors' prison?

There was no-one in the company could replace them. Another play would have to found, the public would be annoyed; their business would suffer.

And yet. She could not help but support Lucy's endeavour to see her brother for a last time. Given the situation, she would have done the same.

At the Black Swan, Coney Street, Lucy and Thomas waited for travel news. There was indeed a stagecoach leaving the next morning for London via Newark-upon-Trent. Priority was given to those going the full distance but it was not known if there were spaces for any making only part of the journey.

'If there is but one place I shall travel alone,' said Lucy.

Thomas's sufferance was under test. The determination of his new wife, was approaching obsession. He tried to bring reason.

'You will likely be on the outside of the coach among unsteady cases and boxes which shift with every lurch. All that protects you is a narrow rail. And in these strong winds overturning is not uncommon.'

Lucy would not be dissuaded. She knew of the dangers and how unlikely it was to get there in time, but she considered the alternative. To stay in York, dancing in pretty clothes, pretending to be a lovesick maiden when her brother was awaiting execution? No. She had to go. She had to try. To do nothing would bring remorse, certainly for the remainder of her life. Why did nobody see that?

Thomas was witnessing a determination that alarmed him. Her resolution was driven by grief; it being near to madness he must be with her until it had passed. They sat hands held tight, unaware of the attention of fellow travellers. Several people recognised them from the theatre, wondering what was the cause of their distress.

'Oh dear, whatever can be wrong? Poor things. So pretty when they dance together. Must be a lovers' tiff. What it is to be young!'

The landlord allowed them to stay through the night in the tap room, where they watched the fire die low, knowing it was the last warmth they would feel for days. At five thirty it was announced that there were outside places on the morning coach. A booking clerk took their names and payment.

Shouts and commands filled the early morning air. Prior to the time of leaving, porters were collecting luggage and parcels which were flung about regardless of their contents. Fifteen minutes before the departure of the *Improved London Rapid* the coach was brought round and the horses backed in. It was clear which people were to travel outside, for a group of men and women waited, their hats tied on firmly, with sacking and shawls draped over their shoulders. Six privileged passengers were allowed inside the coach and the doors shut fast. Two people elected to travel upfront with the driver, three others on the roof. The remaining three, including Lucy and Thomas, were with the guard at the rear of the coach in the large basket between the two back wheels. Packed tight with luggage the travellers settled as best they could, until at fifteen minutes past five o'clock, after shouts of 'Let 'em go,' and 'Give 'em their head,' the guard blew his horn, the driver cracked his whip and the journey began.

Although it was early October the weather was as clement as could be hoped for. Cold dry winds swayed the rattler on its speedy way sudden lurches due to holes in the road caused alarm with shouts and screams from both inside and out, followed by smiles of relief as the coach righted itself and progress continued.

There were four changes of horse which being well organised caused small delay. Two stops to pay the tolls were a greater hindrance, there being flocks of sheep and various carts also waiting their turn through the barrier. By the time Newark was reached the day had ended. Here the *Rapid* was to stop overnight at the White Hart Inn before its next stage to London.

The full tariff was greater than Lucy and Thomas could afford, but a modest evening meal was managed, with the night spent cheaply by sleeping in the stables. They found an acceptable dry space in an empty horse stall. Thomas looked at the galleries rising from the inn yard.

'This is where I first played Puck,' he said cautiously as they bedded down in the straw and hay. 'It seems long past.'

Lucy made no reply. This was the first mention of the theatre since they had left York. Thomas recognised that they were both mindful of the subject, each avoiding it for the sake of the other. The belief that Lucy was unaware of what they had abandoned would not leave him; on the very threshold of possible success she had asked that they jettison everything they had worked for.

He had followed her without question, because of his new devotion. Yet a small fancy was growing that he would regret this headstrong action; she should never have demanded so much of him. He feared that this nascent thought could grow into a resentment damaging their love. In alarm he put this aside. It must be dismissed. It was unthinkable. It could not be.

'Dame fortune smiles upon you,' said the jovial farmer at the White Hart breakfast table. He had heard that Lucy and Thomas were in need of transport for Lincoln there being no coach that day. Regardless that they had not eaten, he drank another cup of coffee with a last piece of pigeon pie, explaining that he had a team of pack horses shortly leaving for Thorpe on the Hill.

'Within hailing distance of Lincoln,' he said. I've newly delivered a load of corn and return this day with sundry goods. What coach fare would you have paid? I'll match that what e'er it be.'

'What load are you carrying?' asked Thomas.

'Mostly stone,' said the farmer. 'For repairs to the road, but I'll see that the ponies carrying you have only a half pack.'

'They will travel no faster than we can walk.'

'Take it or leave it. I depart in the hour.'

'No, we'll walk,' said Lucy quietly. 'The distance is not great. Aside to Thomas she said, 'Give no price to that pinchfist. The sooner we begin the better.'

In their favour was the road itself, the old Fosse Way, which being Roman was direct and obtained in good repair. A strong eastern wind blew hard and cold. The two held hands as they advanced, rarely speaking. At dusk they approached Lincoln seeing the three towers of the cathedral looming high ahead before darkness hid them.

With the final steep climb up to the castle, landfall was achieved. Now that they had arrived their unease increased; soon they would learn if Walter lived or not. The time of the journey could not have been bettered, for it had taken only two days, yet the fear of being too late was real and dreadful.

Lincoln Castle faced the cathedral. On arrival at the square between the two great buildings, clouds broke briefly allowing the bright moon to reveal the contrast between the huge structures. The cathedral with its tall delicate towers looked fair and kindly in the silver light, unlike the castle with its dark and oppressive scowl. Great nail studded doors to the castle gate house assumed the aspect of a mailed fist, tight shut, bereft of welcome.

Lucy and Thomas approached, looking for some method of making themselves known. A chained ring was pulled, sounding an indignant bell somewhere far within the walls. They waited but it produced no result. A second attempt brought no answer. Thomas beat his fists on the doorway but there was no response. For several minutes he kicked against the hard bleached wood, but to no purpose.

Was this how their journey was to end? An inviolable fort yielding them no knowledge of what had, or was about to happen?

‘We have to wait until the morning,’ said Thomas.

‘No,’ said Lucy, ‘tomorrow may be too late. We must make ourselves known tonight. There must be a way. . .’

As they stood with no mind of their next step, a passer-by carrying a large bundle of sticks on his back hurried on his way.

‘There will be no answer from there,’ he said. ‘Once it’s dark there’s no getting in or out. It’s easier to waken the dead.’

‘But we seek news,’ said Lucy. ‘We need to know if the hangings have yet been done. My brother you see, he’s inside. . . ‘

‘Your brother. Under sentence?’

‘Yes,’ said Thomas. ‘We’ve come in the hopes that. . .’

‘Too late,’ said the man. ‘The hangings were yesterday. In the castle yard. Three young men. You should have got here earlier.’

The man went on his way.

*

Thirty Four. *Grist to the Mill (pond).*

'It's an ill wind,' said Mr Grist, never afraid of a commonplace, 'turns none to good.' He sat back expansively in his chair as he and the Whitleys waited outside the magistrates' meeting at the Nottingham Exchange. It was the official enquiry into the recent disturbance at the theatre which had so far taken a full morning to hear.

'Pray do not talk of the wind,' said Mr Whitley. ''The recent gales have dislodged many slates from the theatre roof. We have water dripping in at several places.'

'Which adds force to my point,' said Mr Grist, 'had we been open to the public, there would have been seats that could not be sold. But seeing we are closed, the repairs can be carried out at leisure.'

'Leisure or not, I would rather there were none. Our revenue standing at nought, such outlays are luxuries we can ill afford.'

Jemmy Whitley was growing increasingly irritated by Mr Grist's predominance, especially where his wife was involved. His presence with them at this meeting had been against his wish, for it was really none of his business.

Whitley and his wife had been called to give evidence but Cassy had insisted that Mr Grist accompany them. Although Mr Grist himself had not been summoned before the justices, he behaved as if his was a vital presence.

'Yes,' Mr Grist continued, 'our period of closure has allowed detailed and unhurried rehearsal time, a welcome luxury. When we reopen, the standard of playing will be of a higher quality than ever.'

True, with the theatre closed there was little else to do but rehearse. *Othello* had been full ready at the time of the riot, all that it needed was an audience. In addition, three new farces to be played in the repertory were in place. Whitley had also used the opportunity to work at *King Lear* which he did in spite of Cassy's disfavour. He was, as he often insisted, more than old enough for the part and it was this that concerned her. Illness and recent setbacks were not good foundations for depicting the deranged monarch which she feared might well affect his own equilibrium.

Above all the renewed licence to perform was required, thus the verdict of the magistrates was anxiously awaited that particular morning. In spite of Alderman Fairlight on the committee, as the case was undergoing appraisal, there had been discerned a favourable mood so that when Marmaduke Pennell appeared from the meeting smiling broadly, it was apparent that the licence had been renewed.

'Some opposition,' he said, 'from the expected quarters but we've achieved it.' He waved a document which he next handed jubilantly to Mr Whitley. Jemmy was greatly pleased and smiled happily as Mr Pennell shook his hand and then embraced Cassy, kissing her warmly. His smile faded when Mr Grist also embraced his wife and gave her a kiss that was far too long and lingering for Jemmy's liking.

'One proviso,' said Pennell. 'In future, there must be a constable on duty at every performance for which the theatre will be a charged half a crown each night.'

'A small price to pay,' beamed Mr Grist, which was all very well for he was not the one paying it.'

'Fortuitously,' said Mr Pennell, 'it could well be the riot has been to our gain. For in my letter to the Lord Chamberlain concerning a certain dramatic property by Mr Plumptre' (he winked at Whitley) 'I have brought it to his lordship's notice that there has been a disturbance of late at the Nottingham theatre. My argument being that great care must be taken concerning the dramatic content of any future play. The passions of the public must not be further inflamed.'

'Hah,' shouted Mr Grist triumphantly, 'what did I say? It is an ill wind turns none to good.'

'Oh go shut your bone box!' said Jemmy sharply.

The theatre reopened in splendour, overflowing with fashionables. The houses might literally have been called - bumper. Elegance adorned the best seats, enriched the scene and gave life and animation to the actors. The toast of the evening was Leonard Grist. His portrayal of Othello transfixed all who saw it. Desdemona's murder and Iago's betrayals bought tears of anguish and gasps of dismay from scores of spectators. When the moor smote himself with his hidden blade, a shout of horror came from the same quarters. The fall of the final curtain brought deafening applause and rousing cheers; the triumph of the night was complete.

From then onwards every appearance by Mr Grist was greeted with the same excitement as a major overseas victory. Women of all ages fought to be as near the stage as was thought proper when the great Mr Grist strode upon it. Each night at his first entrance, clapping from adoring female hands frequently split their white kid gloves. Shouts, and it might be said screams, could be heard from female voices and not only from the cheaper seats. For several minutes the action of the play was held up as Mr Grist recognised the acclaim, whilst the other actors glowered with envy at the interruption. Nor did it finish there. In Shakespearean roles each of his major speeches was applauded with the enthusiasm usually reserved for successful politicians on election night.

Such adoration caused Mr Grist to be in great social demand. Smitten hostesses, knowing their enthusiasm was not shared by their husbands, organised elegant afternoon receptions in his honour when the menfolk were obligingly absent. In any case Mr Grist was always on stage at night which made him unavailable at other times. And for any respectable matron to invite the actor after the play would indeed leave her open to harmful speculation.

With so many invitations, Mr Grist decided to revive the custom of visiting some of his patrons privately to thank them for their support. This enabled him to make certain calls without arousing dubiosity of his real intent. These included a certain Miss Nevill, a lady of means who lived alone but for a maid servant. She had been so captivated by the actor’s mastery of his craft that she had bidden him to call upon her whenever he had a free hour.

When a new piece was performed for the first time, it became a habit for Mr Grist to call upon Miss Nevill the following day, for her appraisal of the play and his performance in particular.

'You were very fine,' said Miss Nevill, sighing contentedly one afternoon. 'Allow me to congratulate you.'

'Ever your humble servant,' replied Mr Grist.

'The resolve with which you began, so restrained until you reached that overwhelming climax in the final act. It left me breathless, quite breathless.'

'You are over generous,' said Mr Grist.

'Not a bit,', continued Miss Nevill. 'Which allows me to ask if you would kindly move to your side of the bed. Your prominence, delectable though it is, prevents me from reaching me turkish delights.'

'Forgive me. I am such a heavy clod.'

'Not one bit of it. What is the phrase now, "*well made by moonlight?*"' she giggled as she studied him, daintily placing sweetmeats between his smiling lips. 'Indeed sir, you are a feast in yourself. I cannot recall being so well served in many a day and oft.' She kissed him affectionately.

Mr Grist was touched, on what part of his person cannot be fittingly told.

'But you, dear lady,' he replied, 'have enacted a noteworthy part in our congress. Parts that are without parallel. Like this. . . and that. . . and above all, this. . .'

'You are wicked Mr Grist, quite wicked. But do my eyes betray me? You are getting dressed? Leaving so soon? Surely this must not be?'

'Alas, I regret it must be so. For I am called to the theatre within the hour. I must be there for three o'clock. '

'For what reason?'

'Sadly,' he said with a sigh, 'I have to rehearse.'

'Oh no Mr Grist. You have no need to rehearse. No need at all.'

Another of Mr Grist's patrons, Mrs Faraday, recklessly visited Mr Grist at his own lodgings, in order briefly to escape from her family of nine young children. At the time, her husband was with his regiment in Gibraltar. Unlike Miss Nevill, Mrs Faraday was by way of an intellectual mind and delighted in discussing the works of Shakespeare. One afternoon, they studied the text of *The Life of King Henry the Fifth,* concentrating upon the scene between the French Princess and what Mrs Faraday termed as her governess.

'I think it is the one scene entirely in French,' said Mrs Faraday. 'Do you think Shakespeare spoke the language?'

'His education is thought to have been well rounded,' said Mr Grist, 'It is believed he had the rudiments of Latin, so why not French or even Italian?'

'Do we take it then that Catherine is learning English to enable her to converse with Henry in his own language?'

'That is so.'

'Now then,' said Mrs Faraday with a quickening tone. 'Why is it that Catherine's tuition deals entirely with parts of the anatomy?
So very odd. You see, in my own case, if I were to join my husband's regiment in Gibraltar, I would doubtless attempt to learn some Spanish. To converse with the natives, don't you see. And I would not be learning about parts of the body. Not so, I would wish to discuss trade, or policies with the overseas colonies, certainly not using Spanish for *de nick* and *de bilbow.* '

'To what conclusion does this lead you, my dear Mrs Faraday?'

'Oh, it's yet another example of Shakespeare's genius. "*The confident and over lusty French,*" that's the clue. Yes, Catherine was being tutored to seduce Henry. Thankfully the scene ends when they have got no further than *de nick* and *de sin.* Heaven knows what might have followed.'

'A most ingenious theory,' said Mr Grist.

'Entirely my own.' As she left their bed, Mrs Faraday waited to be helped back into one of her nether garments. Noticing something unusual on her petticoat, she paused.

'Dear me,' she said, 'what is this? Black smudges, how odd.'

Mr Grist examined the marks on her garment, then looking chop fallen he said, 'Last night I played Othello. My ablutions seem not have been as thorough as I would wish.'

Mrs Faraday smiled. 'Pray take care Mr Grist. A blackened bodice could blacken my reputation.'

*

Never had Jemmy Whitley known such business. As soon as a new appearance by Leonard Grist was announced, the box office was encircled by theatregoers hungry for tickets. Grist fever gripped the town and comparisons were made with the great Garrick himself. Did not Grist's name bear the same initial? Had he not introduced an entirely new style of performance? Those who had seen both, maintained that Grist was by far the better.

Whitley was divided within himself. Who could deny that full houses night after night were not every manager's dream? But to have that dream dependant upon a man as vain as Grist gave him cause for anxiety. And where did Mrs Whitley stand in this idolatry? At times Jemmy found himself frighteningly close to replicating Iago's jealousy.

With the adulation of the actor so supreme, Whitley decided not to play Lear that season. To challenge the dominance of Grist might well leave him open to unfavourable comparisons. Reluctantly he admitted that Grist had descended upon him like some great migratory bird resting awhile upon a mill pond. But like all such birds he believed it would not be long before it tired of provincial waters and would fly away to greater seas. It was then that he would play Lear.

More welcome news arrived in the form of an official letter from the Lord Chamberlain addressed to Marmaduke Pennell,

'It has worked,' said Mr Pennell walking into Whitley's room, 'a burden has been lifted from your shoulders. It is the Lord Chamberlain's verdict on Mr Plumptre's play.' He read from an official document.

'It having been reported to me by the examiner of all Theatrical Entertainments, that a manuscript entitled . . .' here Mr Pennell broke off laughing, 'It takes much space for the title to be given, . . .' *being a drama in twelve acts. Regretfully it has been determined that the text contains scenes of both of an improper and immoral nature .'*

'I was not aware of that,' said Whitley.

'Perhaps you do not possess my barnyard mind. When I read some of the play I detected aspects that the Puritans could find highly offensive. It was as a demure member of the public that I lodged my complaints. How wise of Mr Grist to suggest that clever course.'

Whitley winced. 'What did you complain of? he asked.

'Let the Lord Chamberlain answer that,' said Pennell. '*The drama makes much of the sexual degeneracy of the Queen of Egypt. She is depicted as a wanton who dallies with the Roman head of state, bearing him an illegitimate son. She is shown later in another adulterous affair with the emperor's envoy, at the end of which they both kill themselves in graphic and deplorable squalor. It is the Lord Chamberlain's belief that the subject will be very distasteful and embarrassing in mixed company of all ages.*'

'Quite so,' said Whitley,

'There's more, *"it may well be that the depiction of such depravity and vice as normal practice within the ruling classes might start an unfortunate train of behaviour in the minds of the previously innocent. On these sensitive grounds a licence for the performance of this play is withheld indefinitely."*'

'Do you believe the play would lead to corruption and unrest?' asked Whitley.

'Never!. More likely the audience would die of boredom. But public morals have to be protected. We have had recent disturbances and must not hazard more. When next you see Mr Grist, do give him my congratulations for suggesting this approach. How well it has worked.'

Mr Whitley made no remark as he shook Mr Pennell's offered hand.

'Oh before I forget,' ended Pennell, 'my wife has asked urgently if you could get us seats for Grist's next performance.'

*

Thirty Five. *My brother's keeper?*

It was Thomas's turn to lie awake. The reassurance of having Lucy at his side gave him a moment's comfort before he remembered. True, they had agreed that money be spent for a bed that night. Lucy had protested faintly at the waste of their funds but shock, cold and exhaustion had claimed mastery over hesitation. They had found a modest tavern on Steep Hill where a more or less dry bed granted oblivion from yesterday's grim tidings. Sleep had been dreamless for him yet he wondered what fears afflicted Lucy with her brother new buried in a prison grave. He looked at her, still deep in sleep, her mind apparently not troubled by events. Distress would return when she woke. For when or where would they next find repose?

Daylight showed between gaps in the shutters with kitchen sounds coming through the floor boards. Soon he and Lucy would be gone from here; final enquires had to be made at the prison and after that their future was unknown. Would it still be possible for them to return to York? Beg forgiveness of Wilkinson and yet appear in the Harlequinade?

As he lay wondering what plan to take, a knock at the door was followed by the voice of the landlord's wife.

'There is hot porridge downstairs if you want.'

Thomas thanked her, but the woman had woken Lucy. She sat up in alarm, then on seeing him her body eased and she smiled sadly, aware of the melancholy of the day ahead. They were both fully dressed, having removed only their shoes before falling on the mattress the previous night.

'They have something for us to eat,' he said.

'No,' she said, as she sat on the bed, 'we must be at the prison at the earliest.'

Thomas sat beside her. 'Be sensible. Walter is dead. We are the living. We must eat while we can, our next meal might be far distant.'~

The castle clock struck eleven as they approached the prison doors. In daylight they looked no less grim, but it could be seen that high up within the ridged and studded wood was a small grilled aperture. After Thomas sounded the bell, a shutter behind the grill was opened and a rough voice asked, 'What?'

'We are here to ask of Walter Treadgold. We are his relatives. . .'

'Wait,'the shutter closed. Some muffled discussion could be heard. The shutter reopened. 'Name?'

'Treadgold. Asking after Walter of that name.'

With no reply the shutter was slammed shut.

As they waited Lucy said, 'I fear his body could have been given to those devils the surgeons. It is the custom in some parts.'

'That would prevent your having to view him,' said Thomas.

'But I want to see him, if he is not yet buried.'

The grill opened, 'Come back at noon. No entry till then.'

About to close the shutter, whoever it was inside observed a gentleman walking behind Thomas towards the prison gate. He looked to be a man of importance, perhaps an official, for he was smartly attired, carried a leather case and a fine walking stick.

'Morning Sefton,' said the gentleman approaching the entrance which was immediately opened for him. As the man stepped inside, Thomas gained a momentary foothold.

'We are not visitors,' he said. 'We ask after Walter Treadgold. He that was late hanged.'

'Noon,' said the voice inside. Thomas's foot was knocked away and the door shut firm, leaving the couple cast aside.

'Let us wait in the cathedral,' said Thomas. They walked across the square to where access was given by the south door of the great edifice. Again they found a place of worship to be of no solace. Instead of peace, its vast interior provided only disquiet and alienation. Uneasily they sat in the vaulted nave until the silence was broken by an organist starting his practice. The cascade of notes, chords and arpeggios was loud and disturbing. Lucy glanced at Thomas, in agreement they left and walked outside to the close.

By midday a small crowd had gathered at the prison gate. Mostly sad, downcast women with shawls over their heads holding baskets in which food and possibly comforts lay beneath a protecting cloth. One or two chatted solemnly together, but most stood alone in resignation before entry was obtained. With the first chime of the clock they came to life, moving forward as the door was opened grudgingly. Two warders let them pass individually after their baskets and persons had been examined and their identities confirmed. Lucy and Thomas held back until nearly all were inside, it was then Lucy spoke to one of the men at the door.

'We are here regarding Walter Treadgold.'

'Name?'

'I am his sister Lucy. I ask for news of his death, and to see his body.'

'In there.' An office was indicated with a nod of the head. The door closed hard behind. Rough hands ran down their sides, evidently searching for weapons. The small ill-lit room contained an upright desk, walls lined with shelves from floor to ceiling in which ledgers and registers of different ages and sizes were pressed hard together. A stern faced clock hung on the wall, its pendulum ticking like the footsteps of time itself.

'Treadgold?' asked the man at the desk, running a dark finger down a ledger. He paused, finding what he sought.

'Yes, Treadgold - Walter.' he looked up. ' You want to see him?'

'If he is not yet buried,' said Thomas.

The man shut the ledger loudly. 'In the common cell.' He coughed noisily. Lucy, unsure of what she heard, leaned on the desk for support.

'Why in there, if he is dead?' she asked.

'I said he's in the common cell, not God's acre.'

Lucy dared to ask. 'You mean he's still living?'

The man looked at her scornfully. 'We don't send the dead 'uns to the colonies,'' he replied. 'There's many of 'em die before final delivery though. If you want to see him you'd best make haste. Visiting is but half an hour and it's passing fast.'

Turning to Thomas Lucy asked, 'Does he mean he's living?'

Thomas answered soft;y,' We'll find out soon enough.'

Two numbered tokens were taken from a forest of wall hooks. 'Hand 'em back, when you leave.'

'Which way do we go?' asked Thomas.

'Sefton! Common cell!'

'All ready gone in,' complained Sefton.

'Last two this 'ere. Look sharp'

Lucy and Thomas followed down dark stone walk ways. The turnkey chuntered to himself, his keys jangling, his feet shuffling for he had already completed the distance some minutes earlier. Every few yards iron grilles were unlocked to be locked again behind them as they passed through. It had been cold outside, but in here it was worse; the air had the bite of acid that pinched the nose with a dampness that caught the throat. There were few sounds, apart from shouts and curses that reverberated on the vaulting of the passage. They reached a heavy door. The turnkey unlocked it. 'Twenty minutes.'

The door was secured behind them as they were left standing in the dark hold. For a terrible moment Thomas remembered his own time in prison, the desolation of the bullying blackness. Mumbled conversations, low sounds of crying and distress gave notice that somewhere other people were in the cell. They stood together waiting for their eyes to conform to the gloom. Time was passing; undetermined shapes could be seen either sitting or lying on heaps of straw. With a sudden new found energy Lucy went from one to the other, urgently hoping her search was ended.

'Walter? Walter? Are you in here?'

'Lucy?' a man's voice replied.

'Walter? Is it you?'

'What's left of me.'

Lucy fell to the floor embracing a dishevelled bundle of humanity she thought to be her brother. Looking closely she pushed back the long lank hair, recognising him behind the stained face and the straggly beard.

'I can't believe it. We thought you were dead - hanged,' she said hugging him, kissing him repeatedly.

'It was a close thing.'

'But you're alive. that's all that matters. It's a miracle.' She rocked him in her arms, kissing and hugging him in a fervour of joy.

'You're alive, you're alive,' she repeated like a mantra.

Swiftly growing tired of this, Walter pushed her away. When next he spoke, his voice was hard. 'Stop your moaning. It's of no comfort to me.'

'But Walter you're alive,' insisted Lucy, 'you've been spared.'

'Spared? I got clemency. That means transportation.'

Lucy was perplexed. 'But that's better than death, isn't it?'

'It's a terrible sentence,' said Thomas thoughtfully.

'Even so, it's not a hanging,' said Lucy. 'And it won't be for ever.'

Walter laughed harshly. 'Not for ever, you little fool. Fourteen years. Over the seas. That's as good as for ever.'

'Fourteen years? Good God.' Lucy was shocked. 'So very long.'

'Still pleased are you?' asked Walter.

Unable to say more Lucy turned to Thomas. 'Fourteen years,' she repeated in an attempt to hold back tears. Words between brother and sister had ended. In the lull they became aware again of the surrounding sounds of distress and despair from others in the darkness of the cell.

As if remembering suddenly, Walter asked, 'Where's my suit?'

'Your suit?' she was amazed at him. 'We didn't have time. We came in such haste.'

'Have you brought drink?' he asked. 'There's none in here.'

'Walter, we thought you dead until. . .'

'Stow it! Trust you to come empty handed.'

'See here. . ." Thomas began to show anger, but Lucy put a finger to his lips to stop further differences. Realising her brother was not to be humoured she knew the moment was come to discover what had brought him to this state. In a clear tone of voice she asked,

'I need to know about our father,' she said. 'It was you that killed him, was it not?'

Walter grasped her violently, slamming a hand over her mouth as he spoke in a rasping whisper, 'Keep quiet, you stupid bitch!'

Thomas moved at once, trying to come between them, but Lucy prevented him. Walter looked urgently round the cell, wondering if her words had been heard,

'Listen,' he said in a low voice, 'the charge was theft, no more. Know that. Horse theft.' He whispered urgently, 'Say more and you can yet put the noose about me. So hold your tongue girl.'

Until now, Thomas had felt compassion but with these last words his pity for the prisoner had gone.

'Lucy has given up everything to come here,' he said.

'Much good will it do,' replied Walter. 'The one thing I asked for she has not brought. Trust you to come and gloat over me.'

'We came to help as best we could. As for your suit. You'll have little need for fine clothes over the seas,'

'Don't preach to me you mealy-mouthed bastard,' said Walter. 'I've years of hard labour ahead, with no payment. Remember?'

Thomas moved away, drawing Lucy with him.

'There's little purpose in our staying,' he said.

Lucy hesitated. 'When will you be taken?' she asked.

'How should I know?' answered her brother. 'Tonight. To-morrow. Whenever they choose. There's no "by your leave" in here.'

Lucy made an attempt to embrace him. 'Then, good-bye . . .'

'Go to hell, both of you,' muttered Walter. Surrendering to his pain, he turned his back on her, dropping to the floor, his head in his hands to conceal his passion.

Lucy hesitated. She knew this was perhaps the last time she would see her brother. Rising slowly from the floor she looked at Thomas close to despair knowing that he was her only help.

'Come,' said Thomas. 'We can do no good here.'

Lucy coughed over the brandy. It burned her throat. She had always hated the stuff when on rare occasions of near fainting it had been given to her. Now she had to admit that the warmth generated was gratifying and the loosening of tension that followed was not unwelcome. Thomas, she noticed, had already emptied his glass.

They were in a good quality tavern, situated in the castle square. They had left the prison at the same time as the stylish gentleman who had been admitted earlier. With his smart case and walking stick he had raised his hat to them, for he understood they had been visiting Walter Treadgold. Kind heartedly, he declared his concern for them as relatives of the prisoner and offered to buy them drinks, a gesture that was welcomed by Thomas.

'Allow me to introduce myself,' said the gentleman as they sat together, 'my name is Stint - Jeremiah Stint. I am clerk and assistant to his honour Judge Tipstaff. It was Mr Justice Tipstaff who heard the case, as I'm sure you are aware. Yes, I advised your brother to change his plea to one of guilty, always expedient. Juries don't like having to sit through long confrontational trials .'

Mr Stint went on to explain that when Walter had been sentenced to be hanged, it was Mr Stint, himself a lawyer, who had arranged the alternative sentence of transportation.

He had persuaded Judge Tipstaff that Walter's crime was more of a misdemeanour than a capital felony and whereas many felonies ended in death, a mutation to overseas banishment was quite common. Why? Because so many sturdy young men were required in the colonies. What a waste it was to hang a fellow, when for the good of his country and himself, he had years of fruitful labour within him.

Whist explaining this to Lucy and Thomas, Mr Stint chose not to reveal that Judge Tipstaff had extensive holdings in Virginia which were in sore need of manpower. Moreover, his lordship was happy to reward Mr Stint financially for the regular supply of reprieved prisoners to work on his numerous plantations.

'Oh 'tis a fine life out there,' enthused Mr Stint disregarding that in reality it was unrewarded servitude. 'How old is Walter? Eighteen is it? The very best age. Just think when he is but two and thirty he will be a free man to make himself a fortune in the new world. Another glass of brandy? Potman! Three more brandies! Those sausages look very fine don't they? Can you be persuaded to take a plate of them with some onion gravy?'

Thomas and Lucy were puzzled by the unexpected philanthropy of this curious gentleman. Lucy refused the brandy when it arrived, but Thomas was glad of its coming. They accepted the sausages and whilst consuming them listened to Mr Stint's genial discourse.

'Yes, it will be from Whitehaven your brother will sail. To get there 'tis a long march from Lincoln across the Pennines, very punishing particularly in wintertime as of now. Which brings me to a matter I am sure will interest you. The journey to Cumberland is usually taken on foot and in irons - very cruel, very cruel. But there is the alternative of a journey by cart which can easily be arranged. Far more pleasurable, it goes without saying. . .'

Thomas and Lucy were beginning to appreciate the hidden design of Mr Stint, who after talking of the walk to Whitehaven was soon describing the transatlantic passage to the penal sentence.

' . . . kept in chains below decks in rough seas. An intolerable ordeal for the best of men. Whereas an ample cabin makes the crossing one of infinite superiority and can be obtained for as little as five guineas, payable to myself in advance. That together with the price of the cart to Whitehaven brings a cost of ten guineas to guarantee a style of genteel travel, which I know the young man's family will gladly afford. . .'

'We are all the family there is,' said Thomas, 'apart from his widowed mother who has nothing to do with him.'

'Dear me, tut, tut, how sad.' For the first time Mr Stint's tone sounded a mite more severe. 'Nonetheless, you are clearly people of a rank desirous to take care for your loved one. I could well accept a part payment of shall we say, eight guineas?'

'We are hard pressed to find eight pence Mr Stint.'

'Upon my soul how sad.' Mr Stint helped himself to one of the large sausages from Lucy's plate, 'That leaves me to think that perhaps we should reconsider the court charges that were laid against Walter. Theft was it not? Had it been a homicide. . .'

He shook his head sadly, dipping the sausage into a pool of onion gravy. 'The three young men who took the rope but yesterday were murderers as I recall. Had your brother's charge been the same, we would not be speaking of clemency at this moment would we?'

'No sir, possibly not.' said Thomas.

'Precisely. The law has a long memory and crimes unsolved can oft be re-opened with fatal consequences, if you take my intent,' said Mr Stint; the sausage finished, he licked his fingers and dried them on the table cloth.

'My dear friends,' he said, 'I must take my leave. Perhaps you will consider my proposition. Not too long mind, for it is an offer you cannot delay in accepting. The sooner the young gentleman is away, the better. For if more serious charges such as murder were brought back against him. . .' He shook his head. 'Here is my address, I can always be found in the cathedral close. My best wishes to your brother when next you meet.' He bowed and sidled off.

Lucy pushed away her plate. 'I'll eat no more of his food.'

Thomas drank up, 'Brandy's brandy what e're the source.'

'What must we do?'

'He sees we cannot pay.'

'But I fear he knows the truth about Walter.'

'He may.'

They left the tavern, again uncertain of the course to take. They were about to make enquiries about travel back to Newark, when a piercing whistle sounded behind them. It was the potboy from the tavern.

'You've been stinted I see. "Fed and said" by Jeremiah Stint.'

'Perhaps we have.'

'Stay clear of that villain. 'e 'overs around the gaol like a dog round its vomit. Tried to sell you fancies for a prisoner I'll be bound.'

'We are having none of it,' said Lucy.

'Rightly so. Real Captain Sharp 'e be. Brings 'em 'ere in the Cross Keys regular. And just like today 'e's departed without paying 'is due. Which amounts to some fifteen pence it must be said.'

'That's none of our doing.' said Thomas.

'Ah, but you 'ave partaken of the fare and not settled the account,' said the potboy. 'Mine 'ost 'as deputed me to obtain the sum owing.'

'But it was Stint's ordering.'

'And your swallowing. There's many will vouch for that.'

'Go hang yourself,' said Thomas. A second later he realised that the potboy held a knife to his stomach.

'One shout from me and the constables shall wait upon you. We are within close hailing distance of the prison. Pay up or it's the worse for you.'

'It's a plot,' said Thomas. 'You're in league with Stint yourself.'

'Be that as it may, you owe the Cross Keys fifteen pence.'

The potboy was joined by two men from the tavern. The trio

formed a menacing triangle round the young couple, leaving no choice but to yield. The proximity of the law together with a small press of spectators made it impossible for them to challenge their accusers. They were jostled back to the Cross Keys, where between them Lucy and Thomas having found the fifteen pence were afterwards roughly ejected into the square.

'The sooner we leave the better,' said Thomas. They had resumed their original intent, which was to enquire when there was next transport for Newark. Coaches rarely ascended the cathedral hill and so they walked to the lower part of the town. 'It is horrible to leave Walter in this way. Whatever will happen to him?' said Lucy sadly.

Thomas stood in her path so she was halted.

'Have no pity for him!' Lucy saw a fresh determination in her young husband's attitude.

'Wilkinson was right,' he said. 'He has gone to the bad. There is no saving him. You can do nothing. Now we must try and retrieve what we have lost. If we can get to Newark and then to York, we may well be reunited with Wilkinson and our careers with him.'

'But that man Stint may do harm to Walter.'

'I think not. It won't serve him to get Walter hanged for if he did he would lose his transportation money from the judge. Lucy, you must rid Walter from your mind.'

'Be rid of him?' she thought. Could she ever be rid of him and his ingratitude? Was he a worthless cause? Weariness impeded her reason. She could not think of it now. Perhaps in time, if they got back to York. . .

It being no more than sixteen miles between the two towns, they decided to walk to Newark the next day. Before that, even though their funds were almost gone, they settled to stay another night at the inn on Steep Hill, for it meant on the morrow they would begin their trek refreshed and fed.

Leaving before dawn, the day broke bright with a strong wind from the north which assisted them in the direction they were taking.

Gusts of wind grew in frequency, abruptly rushing them forward into involuntary sprints to avoid being blown over. They laughed at these antics until the wind became a gale. It no longer helped them forward for they found themselves repeatedly hit by squalls almost hurling them into ditches. Clouds increasingly fast overhead, turning from light to dark predicted a menacing turn of the weather.

The terrain changed from openness to woodland. Shouting above the tempest they were aware of the dangers of overhead falling branches. A black line lay drawn across the road ahead which as they neared was found to be a fallen elm lying direct in the way. Carefully they managed to climb through its tangled branches avoiding the serpentine roots.

'No coach will be able to pass this,' said Thomas. 'The passengers will have to walk. A good thing we paid no fare.'

They walked warily under the tormented trees, the gale roaring as it swept its way through the upper branches. Then the rain came.

It was mixed with hail and in little time their clothes were saturated as the storm created new punishments. It added weight as it penetrated to their skin. But, in spite of its malevolence the wind behind them had speeded their journey and they arrived in Newark before nightfall. Once again they found hospitality at the White Hart. Here they were able to enjoy some warmth as their outer clothes were removed and before the the coming of the night dried before a fire. After a modest supper they slept in the same stable where two nights earlier they had huddled together.

Next day was dark and cold with the rain continuing ceaselessly. Several roads in the town were under water and there were reports of flooding in many parts, bringing few good tidings to those wanting to travel.

'There will be no travelling north today,' announced the inn keeper. 'We had trees blown over between here and Grantham last night, and there are stories of others blocking the highway to York, as well as floods. You best make plans for a further stay in Newark .'

So there would be no reaching York in time for the play, a defeat bringing a disquiet that neither could admit to the other. Her passions now fled, Lucy knew she should acknowledge the consequence of her demands. Yet how insufficient it was merely to ask forgiveness; rather she needed to make amends for her hasty judgements and to rejoice that Thomas with his benevolence had stayed with her. Was now the time to reward his constancy, by conforming to his wishes? But what were his wishes, what was it he wanted? She waited, hoping he would tell her.

'I think,' he said, 'we best go to Nottingham. I know it there. On the way are several villages where we could stop if the weather forces us. The theatre isn't up to the quality of York, but if Whitley is still in charge, he might have something for us.'

*

Thirty Six. *Accidental Circumstances.*

> *Lord Ogleby:* How's this - by what right and title have you been half the night in that lady's bedchamber?
> *Lovewell:* By that right that makes me the happiest of men; and by a title I would not forgo.
> *Fanny:* I could cry my eyes out to hear his magnanimity.
> *Lord Ogleby:* I am annihilated!
> *Lovewell:* And now, my dearest Fanny, we are seemingly the happiest of beings. . .

The final scene of *The Clandestine Marriage* was bringing Mr Willis's benefit night to its conclusion. The happy ending always preferred by audiences fast approached; appreciative laughter was to be heard from pit to gallery as Mr Grist in the comic role of Lord Ogleby once more delighted the house. The one flaw in the evening was that the role of Lovewell, the ardent young husband, was not being played by Mr Willis. For although it was his benefit, that gentleman was held in the debtors' prison.

Mr Willis was an adequate enough actor, but like many in the profession had fallen into debt and thus into prison. At very short notice the part of Lovewell, a youth of no more than twenty, had been taken up by Mr Whitley, almost treble that age. The magic of theatre had just about enabled him to get away with this duplicity, which Mr Whitley attributed to his mastery of the actors' craft. Other more critical minds said it was grotesque and trust the old fool to think he could bamboozle the public.

Not surprisingly, Whitley was much relieved when next day a young actor arrived at the theatre enquiring for work. Imagine also that relief when it was found that the young actor was Thomas Hammond no less. 'Tom! Tom!' Whitley embraced his young friend, 'you are indeed, welcome. My dear boy! And who is this ? Your wife d'you say? Lucy is it?'

The excitement at their arrival brought forward most of the company to discover what was happening. Dora Proctor, as might be expected, wept fulsomely as she greeted Thomas with moist kisses, whilst simultaneously taking the measure of Lucy. Mr Bracer shook his hand and said he was glad to see him for it was apparent that he too was truly pleased by his return. Cassy looked at him critically, 'You're far too thin,' she said, 'and how worn you look. Is this what married life's done for you?'

'News of your success comes before you,' said Dora. 'We have heard about your Puck. It is known far and wide.'

This was not true, for most members of the company knew nothing of the young man being so eagerly welcomed. Mr Grist had no idea who he was and thought the emotion on display most excessive.

Thomas and Lucy were taken to dine at a good tavern and following the meal, Jemmy questioned them carefully about their acting experience in York. He, at least, had heard reports of Thomas's success as Puck, but was not yet sure if he was experienced enough to play straight juvenile leads. He was the right age and had the looks but what of his ability? Deciding to take a gamble, he placed a copy of *Clandestine Marriage* on the table.

'Here it is, my boy, the perfect role for you, young Lovewell. We next perform the play two nights hence, I shall want you word perfect for rehearsal in two days.'

'In two days? asked Thomas.

'At your age I learned *Hamlet* in three days.'

'And forgot it in four,' said Cassy acidly.

Lucy and Thomas laboured together as he put to memory the part of Lovewell. He was pleased to be offered the role but sad there was as yet no work for Lucy.

'I fear I'm more a tumbler than an actor,' he said struggling with the text.

'Fiddlesticks! You're a fine actor, when you've a mind to it. You told me you learned Puck overnight.'

'It's a smaller part and I don't know how I did it.'

'By using your memory. The part of Lovewell is not big. Come now, Act Five. I'll read in for Fanny. Your cue is, *Mr Lovewell, this situation may have very unhappy consequences. . . .'*

Thomas hesitated. Lucy said, 'Your line is. . .'

'Don't tell me. Dammit I knew it last night. *That fate o'errules. . .'*

'Wrong. *But it shan't. . .'*

'Ah yes. *But it shan't - I would rather tell our story this moment.'*

They worked hard, both weary after the recent grim happenings in Lincoln. They gave no reason for their arrival in Nottingham, neither sought for sympathy following their long walk in bad weather. Thomas, as Lovewell, had only one hurried rehearsal during which Mr Grist, walking through as Lord Ogleby, observed him closely.

'You're not going to do that are you?' he asked at one point.

'I thought I might' said Thomas.

'It will get a laugh.' said Mr Grist.

'Yes.'

'Be warned young man. You take laughs from a comedian as warily as meat from a lion.'

He frowned at Tom, yet not without some sympathy. Shortly after this, Mr Grist left the rehearsal for the remainder of the afternoon, once more fuelling rumours of his dalliances.

Lucy paid small heed to such tittle-tattle, for her fears were increasing that Thomas was relying on drink to ease the learning of his lines. She never saw him take it, he was growing artful, but he repeatedly managed to slip away quietly and she knew for what reason.

Despite this, on the night Thomas gave a tolerable performance as Lovewell and everyone agreed it was better to see a personable young fellow as a lover then the fraudulent efforts of Mr Whitley. At the curtain, Mr Grist took his dominant share of the applause leaving Thomas to realise that in spite of Whitley's welcome, he was merely a replacement for Mr Willis who would expect his role back once he was free from a debtors' prison.

This came sooner than expected. Whilst Mr Willis's benefit had not completely freed him from debt, a pooling of funds from relatives enabled him to purchase his liberty. Once released from gaol Mr Willis quickly resumed his acting career, which deprived Thomas of his.

All was not lost though. A new turn was needed for the entr'actes. Until then, a Mr Southgate had performed his celebrated egg dance, in which he danced blindfold over a dozen eggs. It happened that Mr Southgate was often drunk and of the twelve eggs he began with, sometimes as few as five remained intact. The resultant wreckage was cleaned up quickly, but left a treacherous surface. It was when Mrs King had laid her length during *The Tragedy of The Fall of Rome,* that Mr Southgate was dismissed and the vacancy made known.

Thomas and Lucy swiftly offered their services. Until then, Thomas had not had an opportunity of displaying his gift for comic tumbling which had so pleased audiences in York. Auditioning before Mr and Mrs Whitley as well as Mr Grist and with the aid of a fiddler, they re-created the act that had been so favoured up north. Beginning with the Irish jig, they went straight into *The Drunken Sailor* hornpipe. They were good, and several company members drawn by the music applauded favourably at the close.

'Very well.' said Jemmy Whitley. 'We'll try you for three nights. Let's see what the public makes of you.'

'We sing as well,' said Lucy.

'Yes,' said Thomas. 'I sing "Tom Bowling" and Lucy sings . . .'

'Work it out with the fiddler,' said Jemmy.

'But I need a sailor's suit. And Lucy needs to be. . .'

'Go see Mrs Kenna,' said Cassandra as they left for the rehearsal room; for in a few nights' time Mr Grist was to appear as *Richard III,* a role he assured everyone was quite the best in his repertoire. Whitley was to support him as Buckingham with Cassy as Queen Margaret, parts that neither of them had played for years and which they had to relearn hurriedly.

The sailor suit for Thomas was not difficult to find, but there was no shepherdess costume to be had for Lucy. Still with a mouth full of pins, Mrs Kenna looked along her dress racks.

'I've got this mantua might do. You want something that moves nicely, don't you? Want it for tonight? Mmmm. I can't touch it for two days. I've got crook-back Dick to be ready for Wednesday.

Other costumes were considered but thought unsuitable. Ultimately there was one found what might be a possibility.

'How about this?' asked Mrs Kenna. 'It would move nicely I'd say. You'll be dancing won't you?' She held up a yellow gown.

'Saffron,' she said, 'nice with the Navy blue. It closes centrally so you'll need petticoats, but for dancing they would move very nicely.'

'What's your opinion?' asked Lucy.

'It should move very nicely,' Thomas smiled.

The theatre fiddler was accommodating and knew their tunes by ear. With him they went through their programme twice and all seemed well set for the coming evening. Thomas felt at ease in the sailor suit, but Lucy was unhappy with the saffron gown. She found it voluminous and hard to control, but Mrs Kenna who watched their run through approved the look of it.

'It moves nicely on stage,' she said. 'You'll soon get used to it. If not, I'll make something after crook-back Dick later in the week.'

Their debut went well and the house liked their presentation. The applause whilst nowhere near as rapturous as York, was friendly and warm. Whitley watched them from out front. He was not one to over enthuse knowing that praise always led to requests for more pay.

'Coming along nicely,' he said.

Until now Lucy had only known the theatre in York; she found the scale in Nottingham smaller and less likeable. Tate Wilkinson's administration was far better organised and she was critical of much, including the untidiness everywhere. In addition she cared little for the town, comparing it unfavourably with York. Both knew that if they had stayed there, by now they would have been so much happier playing the leads in *Harlequin Sailor,* but neither spoke of the matter.

Lucy wrote to Fanny M'George telling her where they were and hoping for news of their standing with Tate Wilkinson. Fanny's reply was brief. She missed them both, but Tate Wilkinson had sworn never to employ them again. *Harlequin Sailor* had opened a week late, with their roles recast by a young couple (not nearly as good) but the pantomime had been a great success due to the fine new scenery.

Now there would be no returning to York. Their future lay with Whitley's company, dancing in the intervals like the Treadgolds, but with no dance school to enlarge their salary.

*

'Of course it's not like me to pass judgement,' said Lady Grandby, 'but there comes a point, when a line has to be drawn.'

It was the turn of Mrs Greaves to be hostess to the Tory ladies' group whose monthly gathering was again making plans for future social events. Under Mrs Greaves' vigilant supervision, her tea caddy had been unlocked and the precious leaves infused in a new Worcester teapot. It was the very latest teapot, one with the raised chinoiserie pattern; the display of this costly acquisition being the main reason for Mrs Greaves inviting friends that afternoon.

'I'm in full agreement,' she said in reply to Lady Grandby, quietly furious that not one of the company had passed comment on her teapot.

'Not only must a line be drawn,' continued Lady Grandby, 'but something has to be done.'

'What are we talking about?' asked Mrs King whose deafness was increasingly bad.

'We're talking about Mr Grist, the actor,' Mrs Bentley said loudly.

'Oh he's very good. I saw him last week in, what was it now . .?'

'We're not talking about his stage performances, we're talking about his behaviour - elsewhere,' said Mrs Greaves, crunching a crumpet.

'Oh,' Mrs King was confused.

'In my view it's female laxity that's at fault,' said Lady Grandby. 'The Nevill woman has always been a slattern.'

'Isn't that a little unkind?' asked one of the ladies in the group.

'It's Mrs Faraday I worry about,' said Mrs Bentley. 'Whatever will she say to her husband when he returns from his tour of duty on Gibraltar?'

'I thought you were talking about Mr Grist,' said Mrs King, 'what's this about Miss Nevill and Mrs Faraday?'

Lady Grandby sighed impatiently. 'Tell her, someone.'

Mrs Greaves said loudly, 'Mr Grist has been *dallying* with them.'

'He's rallying? Oh dear, has he been ill?' Mrs King was at a loss.

'Liaisons. With the inevitable consequences,' explained Mrs Greaves. 'Both Miss Nevill and Mrs Faraday are with child by him.'

Mrs King was rather lost, 'They're wild with him, did you say?'

'They've both got a jack in the box. And they're his,' said Lady Grandby, stirring up a whirlpool in her teacup. Had she used the worst language imaginable, the effect could not have been more shocking. Jaws dropped, as did at least one Bath bun.

'Well I never did,' said Mrs King.

'You must be the only one,' said Mrs Greaves under her breath.

'Speak for yourself,' replied Lady Grandby.

'Are you suggesting . .?'

'Ladies, ladies,' said Mrs Bentley. 'Let us not stoop to the level of the market place. I'm sure none of us here has behaved improperly. "Lead us not into temptation," after all.'

'Best remove the temptation,' said Lady Grandby

'Hear, hear,' said Mrs Greaves.

'How can that be done?' asked the the others.

'Disapproval must be shown,' declared Lady Grandby, now commander in chief of the meeting. 'Miss Nevill is certainly not one of our circle, all the same in my opinion she should be shunned.'

Silence appeared to denote agreement.

Mrs Faraday and her dalliance with Mr Grist was then considered. It was thought likely that when General Faraday returned from his two years active duty, his brood of nine children being increased to ten might give rise to questions. On the other hand as Mrs Faraday herself had said, her husband rarely took a head count and might not notice the augmentation at all.

'We're losing the point,' said Lady Grandby forcibly, 'which is how we deal with Mr Grist. He is a thorough profligate. A married man needless to say, they're always the worst. In my view he should be run out of town.'

Such strong opinion created a further lull, broken by what sounded like the tinkling of sleigh bells but was, in truth, the anxious stirring of teacups.

Eventually Lady Grandby was asked how this might be achieved.

'By driving him off the stage,' she pronounced. 'It's quite

common for an actor to be booed off stage when he performs badly. We'll boo him off stage because he's performed badly in our genteel and respectable town.'

'I'm not going to boo anyone,' said Mrs Bentley. 'My husband would be horrified.'

'I don't suggest we do it ourselves. There are other ways of achieving these things. I, for instance, have two footmen who would be glad to have a night off at the theatre, especially if they were instructed to disport themselves badly.'

'Ah yes,' said Mrs Greaves , 'my stable boys have already been warned about unruly behaviour. And if I were to pay them for it. . .'

'Very well,' said Lady Grandby. 'It just remains for us to look at a playbill and arrange what night we can be rid of Mr Grist. And what night I can spare my footmen to carry out the ridding.'

'Who's married her footman?' asked Mrs King.

*

Whitley was confident that *Richard III* would be a big draw. For once he reversed the order of playing and placed the comedy at the start of the evening with the tragedy in the second half. Expectation was high and the house was full. The farce of *Love Makes a Man* had gone down well. Grist had offered to play in both pieces, saying he thought it would show off his versatility to appear first in a farce before depicting the villainous Richard. Whitley dismissed the idea as vulgar and played in the farce himself.

The entr'acte was much liked, Whitley being well pleased with Lucy and Thomas's performances. They provided a diversion of good quality; their dancing and singing fast becoming a favourite. It helped that they were young and pretty and Whitley was thinking that he should devise more musical items to exploit their talents.

After taking their bows Thomas began to lead Lucy down to the dressing room, but she held back.

'No,' she said. 'Let's watch Mr Grist. It's his first night.'

'He gets enough adoration without us adding to it,' said Thomas.

'I only want to see the beginning. Anyway if we rush off we're going to be like my parents. We should stay and be sociable.'

'You do as you please,' said Thomas, leaving to go down alone.

Partly out of anger, for she knew he would be drinking downstairs, and partly out of curiosity she decided she would watch Mr Grist's opening speech. Then she would join Thomas.

She stood at one side in the wings to hear the famous soliloquy. The space was crowded with the cast waiting for their cues as well as others also hoping to catch the celebrated lines. The house buzzed expectantly, always a good sign, until a drum roll requested order and all attention was given to the stage.

The curtain rose. Grist strode on, bent with deformity, his walk a crab-like hobble. An enthusiastic round of applause greeted his arrival. He took centre stage, regarding his audience with indulgent malice and with a delicious snarl began:

'*Now is the winter of our discontent,*
Made glorious summer by this sun of York;
And all the clouds that loured upon our house
In the deep bosom of the buried. . .'

What sounded like a post horn or a bugle brought Mr Grist to a sudden halt. The offensive blast of noise was the signal for an eruption of boos, cat calls and shrill-toned whistles from the gallery.

Mr Grist had become inaudible. He had never known such a thing and he was astonished. His misshapen aspect disappeared as he stood upright and regarded the audience in disbelief. For a full minute the pandemonium prevailed, until a second blast of the horn brought about complete silence. This was almost more troubling than the uproar. For here was the great actor, utterly alone and vulnerable before a full house breathless to know what he would do next.

Mr Grist cleared his throat, once more assumed his deformity, wiped his feet as if about to run a race and tried to continue.

'*Now are our brows bound with victorious wreaths,*
Our bruised arms hung . . .'

There came a second signal But this time there was no din, just a broadside of nuts, orange peel, apple cores and more dangerously empty bottles and stones thrown from the front row of the gallery. Mr Grist shielded himself from the onslaught his hands hiding his face as, in disbelief, he retreated up stage. This caused anger and confusion in the auditorium.

Shouts of, 'Shame,' 'Get them out of here,' came from the boxes.

Mr Grist seemed unsure of his next move. How could this be? What had he done to merit this? With one foot he pushed aside some of the debris and sent a bottle rolling towards the footlights. The house waited. . .

For those watching in the wings, there was consternation at the disturbance. Applause was expected, instead there was disapproval of the leading actor for no obvious reason. All those crammed together tried to see what was happening without crossing the sight lines. Everyone pressed forward in an attempt to witness the spectacle.

Lucy, not familiar with the different lighting system, found herself pushed roughly against the vertical batten of oil lamps. Her elbow caught one which fell, spilling its contents down her dress and onto the floor. Here it smashed, surged into flames, igniting some of the rubbish that lay there - as well as her dress.

On the stage it appeared Mr Grist was about to start again when a fearful scream came from the wings. Two actors, forgetting convention, backed onto the stage ahead of the young woman who followed, her saffron dress burning fiercely. There was a short moment of horrible beauty as red and orange flames, rising to twice her height, consumed the yellow fabric.

Lucy beat at the blinding heat with her hands, desperately twirling in a parody of a pirouette to escape her torment. Whilst others cried out in terror, she made no sound. Not until the dreadful moment, that her fair hair turned fleetingly into a halo of fire, crackling with black smoke. Then and then only, did she scream in terrible anguish, her arms flailing wildly as her skin was scorched.

It was all so swift. She fell, but the blaze persisted. Mr Grist, impacted with shock, beat at the flames with his bare hands in an attempt to extinguish them. From somewhere a cloak was found which he snatched and used in an attempt to try and smother the fire that still engulfed the young woman lying at his feet.

Watched with horror by the audience, incredulity held people in their seats for a brief moment. Then the realisation of danger struck fear.

With a harsh rumble like cattle stampeding, there began a rush for the doors. The theatre rapidly turned to panic. Whitley ran onstage asking for calm and trying to assure the crowd that there was no danger.

Benches fell, chairs upturned, doors blocked, people pushed forward in their haste to be away from the danger. The stairs were worse affected with several falling down to be trampled upon by those behind, surging forward regardless of the safety of others. Shouts from the wiser tried to keep order, saying there was no fire in the auditorium itself. Clothing was torn, feet were stamped upon, bruises inflicted by those normally 'genteel,' until some ten minutes later a shamefaced crowd of people stood outside in the dark wet street, relieved but mortified by their behaviour.

Thomas had no knowledge of what was happening. Drinking in the dressing room, he and two colleagues were aware that the audience was behaving badly. This was nothing new and there were amused comments that for once Grist was having a rough ride.

Calls of 'fire' swiftly cleared their heads, fetching them hurriedly upstairs to the stage. Here was chaos, shouting and crying, smoke, buckets of sand and water being thrown as still Thomas knew nothing. Some, seeing him, drew apart as if he was a hazard himself. It appeared that the peril was passed, the fire put out, until he saw Mr Grist leave the stage, his costume burned, his hands horribly blackened. Grist looked at Thomas and sobbed as he passed. He tried to touch him in a kind of comfort, but his hands, scorched by fire prevented this. People stood in a file, a bizarre line of honour, leading Thomas to where she lay.

He knelt by the charred remains, sickened by the awful stench of smouldering cloth and burned flesh. The heat from her body prevented him from touching her. He raised his hands in the air, gazing with disbelief.

All he could think was that ten minutes ago, he had been dancing with her.

She had looked so lovely. . .

*

Thirty Seven. *Exeunt Omnes.*

At the Old Rose on Bridlesmith Gate, *The Wonderful Spotted Indian Youth* was doing good business. Brook Powell had learned a lot in the art of presenting curiosities of nature. After the disaster of the surprising child and the disappointments with the Irish giant, he felt he had found a method that would draw in the curious to see his 'rarities', a term he much preferred to 'freaks.' Forsaking the fairground, the trick he found, was to treat the undertaking as if it was a theatrical initiative with separate evening performances. Following his failure with the Hamiltons and their scenes from Shakespeare, Jud Drinkwater, landlord at the Old Rose, had been looking for a new attraction, After all, he had made his best room suitable for entertainments, providing a stage complete with curtains and seating for more than fifty customers.

So Drinkwater and Powell had formed a partnership to provide a less artistic form of diversion at the tavern which would attract custom from those with more inquisitive taste. Performing animals were considered but this meant probably sharing the profits with a trainer which he would not countenance. However, Powell did purchase a small monkey which he thought might be of future use.

Not long after, he had found, quite fortuitously, an entire new curiosity. In a sad state of neglect, but with careful persuasion he had got the 'rarity' to appear in public. Immediately he set about advertising the enterprise.

WONDER! ALL ALIVE! WONDER!

To be seen in a commodious Meeting Room at the Old Rose.

THE WONDERFUL SPOTTED INDIAN YOUTH!!! .

Born of Black Parents in Jamaica: he is perfectly well proportioned; his head is covered with black and white wool; his breast, arms, legs &c are of a delicate WHITE equal to any European, spotted and inter-mixed with BLACK resembling that of a beautiful leopard. He has been exhibited before the Royal Family, Nobility &c with Universal Applause.

One reason for the success at the Old Rose was that it was the only entertainment to be had in the town following another closure of the theatre which, after the fire, the magistrates had again shut down until further notice.

Lucy's violent death had deeply shocked everyone. Her funeral was held at St Peter's church, where she was interred in the churchyard. Some days before the service, a letter had been sent to Mrs Treadgold in York giving her the news with the date fixed for the burial. She had replied to say how distressed she was but quite unable to make the journey because of the bad weather. Also it was impossible to leave her dancing school, which she was at present obliged to run single handed.

But it was for Thomas that was the overriding concern. He had become entirely mute with grief when after the terrible night, he was inconsolable in his sorrow. Finding Lucy on stage, he would not be parted from her charred body, wildly fighting off anyone who approached him. Force had to be used eventually, so that her corpse could be decently removed.

She was taken down to a dressing room where Thomas fell into a dumb struck silence, rejecting every approach by locking the door and sitting alone with her body for hours. His friends were afraid to leave him and kept him company through much of the following day. Seeing that he refused every kind of help, they eventually coaxed him back to his lodgings, persuading him to try and sleep under the care of Mrs Stirrup.

From then, he was nowhere to be found. It was unknown for days what had become of him. Some said he had left Nottingham but this was not thought likely, as his belongings, such as they were, still remained at his lodging house. He had his own key and Mrs Stirrup reported that he came back some nights long after she had retired. 'Always drunk,' she said, for she would find him next morning insensible on the bed, Lucy's few possessions at his side. Food that she took to him remained untouched and although she kept watch, by some means he evaded her scrutiny.

'It's not to be borne,' she said. 'Coming and going at all hours, drunk all the while. He's weeks behind with his rent, and I won't tolerate it.'

When next she saw him she would give him his notice she said, but this was not to be, for at some time he returned stealthily to remove his few belongings, after which no-one knew where he had gone.

Lucy's death was a near intolerable burden for Leonard Grist. Not only had he seen it happen so closely, his efforts to save her had left him badly injured. His hands were severely burned, also part of his face was caught. His eye brows, lashes, and much of his hair had gone, although the surgeon who treated him believed he would not have facial scars once the skin had healed. His hands were different, and it was thought they would take longer to cure. All that could be offered was an ointment to be applied with bandages which it was impossible for him to manage alone. Dora Proctor, still considering herself an authority on such matters, did the dressings for him daily. She wondered why he had not sought help from Miss Nevill or Mrs Faraday, but this Mr Grist refused to do for reasons he would not disclose. Instead he stayed aimlessly at the dark theatre unsure of his future, as was everyone else.

*

'Quite dreadful,' said Lady Grandby. 'It goes without saying one would not have wished any harm whatever upon Mr Grist himself. The man merely needed to be taught a lesson. Besides, my footman told me the fire and the girl was a quite separate accident.'

'But if we had not brought about the uproar,' said Mrs Bentley, 'none of this might have happened.'

'Not at all,' said Mrs Greaves. 'The unfortunate burning of the girl was not of our doing. In the first place they say she'd no business to be on the stage when she was She'd finished her performance and should have been with her husband.'

'That's right,' Mrs Bentley said. 'They say she'd been warned many times about the danger of fire. The cause was her own way-wardness.'

'Yes, I heard that,' said Lady Grandby. 'Sheer carelessness.'

'She was a bad lot,' added Mrs Greaves. 'My sister in York, goes to that theatre regularly. She wrote telling me that the girl and her so-called husband had walked out without a by your leave, leaving poor Mr Wilkinson with a play he had written specially for them. Left him high and dry they did, facing ruin.'

'What did he do?' asked Mrs Bentley.

'Oh, he found others soon enough, after which the play went ahead. Some sort of Harlequinade I believe. My sister saw it recently and thought it very foolish, though the scenery was pretty she said.'

'The whole thing's best forgot,' pronounced Lady Grandby. 'A sorry business. Any rate Grist is gone and nobody's going to miss him.'

'Who's going to kiss him?' asked Mrs King.

Just when it appeared possible that Alderman Fairlight and his magistrates might grudgingly renew the theatre licence, reports came from London of a worse mishap at the Haymarket Theatre, where eleven people had been killed in a crush during a visit by their Majesties. Immediately, more regulations to avoid similar catastrophes were ordered, delaying a new opening indefinitely.

Austere sermons heard in most chapels, whilst by no means exploiting the situation, discouraged patronage of theatres because of their perils. As a result, the Ladies' Assembly Rooms increased in favour, where whist and quadrilles were found more wholesome and less dangerous than the playhouse. Realising their decline in popularity was severe, the Whitleys decided to bring forward their spring tour by taking the company to Retford in the hope for better business in that town. This had the additional benefit of distancing Jemmy from the wrath of Mr Plumptre, who was reported to be seeking both damages and revenge following the rejection of his dramatic masterpiece.

Leonard Grist did not go to Retford. Because of his injuries he was not able to act. Also, his humiliation on stage, combined with the damage to his looks, had left him fearful of facing the public - for the present. More seriously, hearsay regarding his amatory exploits had turned him into something of a social pariah; in short he had fallen from grace and he decided it was time for him to start afresh - elsewhere.

This was not immediately possible because of his burnt hands. At the start he had been reliant upon Dora Proctor to change his dressings, but her leaving with the company, left him unable to do this for himself.

He became confined to his lodgings where he stayed to avoid recognition. He employed a maid to come in daily to cook and see to his wounds. The girl, though willing enough, was not skilled in nursing duties, so that Grist quickly fell into a despondency. For the first time in his life he found that he was lonely. Conversation with the maid was limited, his days were spent reading (turning the pages was difficult) and he quickly exhausted his small collection of books. Unhappy in this solitude he began to go out after dark to spend his evenings in the less salubrious inns of the town where he hoped his identity would not be uncovered.

One night he found himself at the Old Rose where the exhibiting of the wonderful spotted Indian youth was taking place. Though the prospect of looking at a monstrosity was not to his taste, Leonard Grist decided it might help relieve his pain and boredom, so he paid his six pence for the last showing of the night. The place he entered was filled with men and women drinking and smoking clay pipes which added to the haze of an already fetid room. A fiddler playing popular ditties asked from time to time, 'Any requests my friends? A ha'penny for your favourite air.'

A young woman already sitting at the front, clearly by prior arrangement called out, 'Give us *Lumps of Pudding* and dropped a coin into the fiddler's tin which Grist reckoned would be retrieved later.

The fiddler played the old tune enthusiastically and the girl with a coarse voice sang loudly, encouraging the audience to join with her. After some desultory clapping at the end she asked if there were any further desires for a song. A woman called, 'Let's have *Come Sweet Lass,* '

'Yes, that's a good'un,' and as the fiddler began, the girl took his tin asking the woman for her ha'penny.

For fifteen minutes the hearty singsong continued with Grist thinking it was a strange prelude for viewing the wonderful spotted Indian youth, until the young singer crooned the sentimental song *Oh,*

Jenny, Jenny, and skilfully quietened the gathering. When the signing ended, there was a lull, after which a tin gong was sounded behind the curtain, through which stepped Mr Powell.

'My lords, ladies and gentlemen,' he began in an absurdly pompous tone. 'With humble pride it is my privilege to present for your inspection and jurisdiction, one of the sensations of the age. The wonderful spotted Indian youth.' There followed another bang of the gong, and the fiddler began to play some false sounding Turkish march to which was added the very bad playing of a flute or perhaps it was a common penny whistle.

'His name is Fernando and he was born into slavery of black folk in Jamaica.' Here Mr Powell repeated most of the premise which could have been read in the press advertisement, until he concluded with, '. . I give you the remarkable, the wonder of wonders - Fernando.'

He drew the curtain revealing the wonder of wonders dimly lit, by an oriental lamp hanging above. Fernando stood with his back to the audience. He wore a short toga which left one shoulder and his legs bare. His jet black wiry hair could be seen with an area of startling white to the one side. He turned slowly revealing a strange piebald face, mostly black which had one eye and a cheek more of a mottled cream colour than white.

The audience gasped at the unsettling sight. Mr Powell took a candle which caught the gold of Fernando's circular earrings.

'See ladies and gentlemen how parts of his skin are as white as that of any European. Observe though how his left leg is of the colour of pure ebony with unusual ivory areas, whilst the other is the total opposite giving the curious likeness of a black leopard. You will notice how horribly he still wears a cruel manacle around the ankle of his black leg. A symbol of the slavery he once endured.'

With melancholy indifference Fernando looked at his beholders, until lowering his head slightly he drew from the folds of his toga the small monkey.

At once this took the fancy of the audience, perhaps drawing attention away from his aberrations, so that when Fernando fed the small creature with a piece of fruit, he gained a murmur of appreciation. Mr Powell again spoke.

'I regret you can only be given a short glimpse of Fernando, for ladies and gentlemen, you will appreciate he is highly sensitive and shy of his appearance, especially being as he is in a strange foreign land.'

With that he closed the curtain and Fernando was hidden from view. The gong was again struck, the flute mercifully ceased and the fiddler struck up the jolly air of *Fill ev'ry Glass,* signalling an end to the performance.

Mr Grist did not wait to see how satisfied the patrons were for he had noticed one thing. Fernando had two fingers missing on his left hand.

'Under no circumstances,' said Mr Powell. 'Even if I allowed it, being a foreigner he would not understand a word you said.'

'Mark here,' said Mr Grist, 'either I see him or I go direct into the tap room and tell everyone of your hoodwinking.'

'But you're in the profession,' said Mr Powell, 'you know we trade in deceit and illusion. . .'

'I don't give a rabbit's scud for your trade. I want to see young Thomas.'

'He'll have gone by now. . .'

Mr Grist moved swiftly as if to start revealing his findings to the tap room. 'I shall shout it from the roof tops. . .'

Mr Powell capitulated. 'Very well. Follow me.'

They walked from the stage through a door into a scullery at the rear of the tavern. It was cluttered with broken furniture, jettisoned clothing, empty bottles and the monkey locked in a small cage. On a table lay the discarded toga, the wig, the manacle and earrings. At a stone sink Thomas, near naked, was washing stains from his face and body with pump water. He looked at Grist with no sign of recognition and ignoring him, continued with his ablutions.

'Whatever has driven you to this?' asked Mr Grist.

There was no reply from Thomas. Grist saw that he was shivering, for it was bitter cold with a door open to a yard and doubtless the pump water near freezing. Had his hands not been bandaged Grist would have tried to help, all he could do was take a towel from a nearby peg and wait until Thomas was ready for it. The towel, filthy and sodden, looked as if it had not been washed in months. In anger, Grist retraced his steps to the tap room and finding the landlord demanded a clean towel.

'I want no argument,' he said angrily, 'a dry cloth this instant or I reveal your Fernando for the fraud that he is.' Drinkwater looked indignantly at Grist, but handed him a cloth from the bar, little better than the one in the scullery.

Thomas dressed slowly. Quaking with cold, he put his clothes on with difficulty, his skin being not properly dry with much of the stain remaining on his arms and legs.

'You need a brandy,' said Gist. 'Can I get you one here, or do you want to go somewhere else?'

Thomas signalled to the direction of the parlour and the two men returned to where the performance had been given earlier, sitting in a dim corner. Grist returned with two glasses of brandy clutched to his chest unable to grasp them with his bandaged hands. He bent to place them on the table but they fell and smashed onto the floor.

'I can manage to carry one, but not two,' he said lamely.

Thomas stood, walked away and returned with two fresh glasses.

'You put me to shame,' said Grist. 'But please allow me to pay.'

'It's my stand,' said Thomas brusquely. He drank his brandy at one go, then looked at the broken glass on the floor, moving the shards with his foot. Grist was at a loss for conversation. He did not want to mention the pitiable exhibition he had just seen, but as he looked at Thomas he saw some of the stain was still visible on his face. Eventually he asked,

'What do they pay you for this?'

'A shilling a night. Drinks on top.'

'How long will that last?'

'Dunno.'

Grist felt the deadness of stalemate settling upon them. Thomas was the next to speak, 'Do your hands hurt?' he asked.

'Yes,'said Grist. As if to change the subject, he asked impulsively, 'Why on earth are you degrading yourself, appearing as a freak?'

'It's my fancy,' replied Thomas.

'No. You can do better than this. It's nothing but a fraud.'

Thomas paused. 'It's what I'm fit for.'

Grist was about to argue with this, but then Drinkwater came with a brush and pan to sweep up the broken glass.

He looked at Thomas, 'I've told you don't come in 'ere. If folks get to see you close to, they'll likely recognise you.'

'I'll soon be gone,' said Thomas.

'See that you are,' said the landlord.

'Before that,' said Grist, unhappy at this exchange,'bring two more brandies. And I'm paying for them.'

Drinkwater appeared placated. As they waited Grist asked,

'Do they give you board here? Somewhere to sleep?'

'No I've not got nowhere. My landlady threw me out long past.'

Grist was troubled. Even though it was the way of the theatre to be up one minute down the next, he was upset to see this degradation. When the new drinks arrived he struggled with his bandaged hands as he felt in his pocket for payment. The bandages came apart.

'Can you find the money in my pocket?' he asked Thomas.

Thomas felt and put several coins on the table. The landlord took his due. Grist, without success, attempted to retie the bandages.

Saying nothing, Thomas reached across, took his hands and fully unravelled the dressings . He saw how hurt the actor's hands still were as he gently rewound the bandages and tied them.

'You have a dexterity,' Grist noted as he watched with gratitude, 'in spite of . . .' He thought better and said no more.

'There's much can be done with a finger and thumb,' said Thomas. 'But you can't tie a knot with only one hand.'

He finished the task. 'That should last a while. How will handle things tomorrow?'

'I've a maid comes in once a day, prepares me a meal and changes my dressings.'

'Is that sufficient?'

'It has to be.'

'How do you manage getting dressed? Washing. Having a piss.'

'I've got into a way of things. One does.'

Thomas said unexpectedly. 'You were the only one that helped her. The only one.'

Grist faltered before replying. He was astonished by the suddeness of the remark. Remembering the terrible accident he replied, 'I was nearest,' he answered. 'That's why.'

Words failed them once more. The drinks finished, Grist thought there was little purpose in staying. He stood to leave.

'All the same, you tried to help her,' said Thomas.

With nothing more to be said, Grist put a hand on his shoulder. There was some money remaining on the table, he pushed the coins towards him.

'Here,' he said, 'find yourself a good lodging. For tonight, at the least. Make sure you don't spend it on drink. A good meal would do you no harm.'

Thomas took the coins.

That night Mr Grist found increased difficulty in caring for himself. The bandages on his hands had been well tied, perhaps too well tied, for he was unable to undo his buttons because of this. He could neither dress nor wash himself properly and he found it humiliating to ask the maidservant for more help. He could not light a candle, hold a knife, certainly not use a corkscrew. Writing a letter was impossible and the girl was small help, being unable to write or read. She changed his dressings, but with none of the aptitude Thomas had shown and within an hour they were come undone.

Awake much of the night, he thought about Thomas. He wondered why Whitley had not taken him on the road. Perhaps he had no wish to go after the awful death of Lucy. Was that the reason? Poor lad, to lose her in that sudden and terrible way. For once in his life Grist thought about the welfare of another. Thomas had shown promise as a performer and should not degrade himself in a grotesque side show. He'd said he had no lodgings, which must mean he was sleeping roughly, whereas he had a room to spare. Male company might be advisable for a change.

Before dawn arrived, Grist had made a decision.

He went back to the Old Rose that night, but not to watch the bizarre performance which now sickened him, instead he went straight to the scullery at the rear hoping to avoid both Powell and Drinkwater. He timed his arrival to be at the conclusion of Thomas's last appearance. Whilst waiting for him he discovered the substances with which he turned himself into the side-show. Boot blacking and wood tar to stain his skin. It was so crude. Had he no idea of make-up? Did he know what damage he was doing to himself?

When Thomas came into the scullery to get washed and changed he showed no surprise at seeing Grist.

'You again is it?' he asked. 'Have I got an admirer?'

'I don't admire the methods you use for this sad business.'

'It's cheap and it works.'

'You'll burn your skin using such stuff.'

'Burn? Then you'll know about that.'

Grist spoke carefully. 'Thomas, would you come and look after me for a while? You could be a great help whilst I am incapacitated.'

Thomas paused as he continued with his washing. 'Have you not noticed? I have employment.'

'I can offer you a decent place to sleep, warm water to wash with.'

'Sounds like charity,' said Thomas.

'It's not charity. I ask for your assistance. You tie a bandage well.'

'What you want is a nursemaid.'

'Tom I can offer your board and keep, whatever suits you. But no drunkenness. I won't have that. You can go on appearing here if you want. I'd rather you didn't of course, but that's for you to determine.'

Grist thought of something else. 'I can give you guidance on make-up. Obviously you know nothing about it. Also help with your acting skills.'

'I know what that means.'

'What?'

'Never mind.' Thomas continued to wash and get into his every day clothes. Once dressed, he was about to return to the tap room.

'Don't go back there,' said Grist. 'Come with me. Start now, at once. That would benefit us both, don't you think?'

Grist could not believe he would refuse. How could he continue with this degrading routine? Surely what he offered was preferable.

He was surprised at how much he wanted him as a companion. He was weary of trying to manage alone.

'Please.' he said, 'I need your help.'

Thomas looked hard at him before replying. 'When your hands are healed, your hair's grown back and the skin stops peeling off your face, you'll go back to one of your doxies won't you? Your bad looks don't matter with me, is that it?'

Grist realised the truth in this. 'I would like to have your company for a while,' he said, 'If you could tolerate mine.'

'Where d'you live?'

'Park Row, one of the new houses beyond the old town wall. I have rooms there.'

Running his hands through his rough dishevelled hair, Thomas answered, 'For a while you say?'

Grist nodded.

'That means a day or so,' said Thomas. 'Very well, for a while.'

Thomas moved in. Grist's style of living took him aback. His lodgings were in well furnished rooms, one floor of a new mansion overlooking parkland. Each morning the housemaid came to clear up from the previous night, remove ashes from the grate in the living room, and see that a fire was ready for when Mr Grist arose. She prepared the main meal of the day which was taken about noon. It became Thomas's task first to wash, shave and help dress the actor, change his bandages and at the day end assist him to bed. In addition he wrote letters for him, cleaned his footwear and did the marketing. After two or three days a routine had developed.

Thomas appeared at the Old Rose until the customers grew tired of the novelty, or perhaps began to detect trickery. Powell showed no interest in him once their collaboration was ended and allowed him to take possession of the monkey, chiefly because it had bitten him more than once. Thomas had developed an affection for the little creature and was annoyed when Mr Grist refused to have it in his rooms, insisting that it remained stabled and in its cage. With the use of a cord he took the animal out for walks in the nearby pastures, where he began to teach it tricks. Up to this time it had had no name, so it was logical that the monkey became known as Fernando.

As Grist began to recover, a congenial friendship formed between the two men, with Grist, being older and more experienced, as the senior. Whilst not a master and servant situation, Grist's greater theatre knowledge cast him in the role of instructor. It well suited him to have a young consort, for secretly he saw a time when Thomas could be of use to him; helping perhaps as a dresser, should he rise to the heights of his craft.

They became at ease with each other. Thomas quickly found he could jest with the older man. Finding Grist privately scrutinising himself in a glass he said, 'Don't worry, you'll soon be the fairest in the land,' Grist had to laugh, covering his anxiety on the state of his appearance.

During spare moments Thomas began to rediscover his skill as a tumbler. He hung ropes from a garden tree which he shinned up and down, devising new tricks. On fine days they walked together in the nearby park where he showed off his abilities which now included the monkey as part of the routine. When he saw that Thomas had trained the creature to be clean, Grist allowed Fernando indoors where its antics were the source of amusement helping raise their spirits.

In time Grist decided that Thomas was not really an actor. He was something more unusual. His talent was as a knockabout, in a territory totally apart from his. It was not long before Grist said to him,

'Let me admit there was a time when I thought you to be a threat. But I was wrong. You are not a threat because you are not an actor. So far your voice is not good, it needs training though you sing sweet enough. Your acting may become tolerable with experience. But the truth is Thomas, you are a born tumbler, which I am not. If you were a good actor I confess we would not be friends, as I care not for rivalry. Yet I like you full well because you are a tumbler of genius.'

'When the good weather arrives,' he went on, 'we must leave here. My lease on these rooms ends shortly and I believe we should plan ahead. Perhaps in years to come we shall regard this time as an entr'acte in our careers, coming at the end of the first act with the best - yet to come.' Together they made plans.

One evening to celebrate their devising of a strategy, they invited as a guest, Mr Bracer. Whitley, being on tour, had left him in charge of the empty theatre, aware of the dangers threatening it. The meal ended after many glasses of wine and spirits. Mr Bracer, mellow in his cups said to Thomas,

'I recall when you first arrived at the theatre. When you were copying play texts. Christmas Eve it were, when you thought you was alone, but I heard you on the stage holding forth like you was Garrick himself.'

Thomas reddened, for he too recalled the event.

'There he was,' Bracer told Mr Grist, 'calling out, "I will give such scenes, such songs." ' He laughed. 'Such scenes, such songs . .'

'Did he by jove?' smiled Grist, pouring more port from the decanter. 'I'm uncertain about the speeches and the songs are as maybe.' He looked at Thomas as he drank. 'Shall I divulge our plans?' he asked.

'If you think fit,' said Thomas, following Grist with the port.

Mr Grist cleared his throat, 'I have never been a man for partnerships. Early in life I discovered from hard experience that matrimony was not for me. Until now, my philosophy has been, "He travels fastest, who travels alone." So it comes to me a surprise when today my young friend Thomas and I are entered into a partnership. Or do I mean an alliance. . a confederacy. . it might even be a collaboration?'

'Make up your mind,' said Thomas his head slowly drooping to the table.

'No, the word I seek is a - friendship.' Mr Grist looked at Thomas, almost soberly. 'For we are of use to each other. So long as we are both understand that. It does well for us to be partners.'

'You said friends,' corrected Thomas, close to sleep.

Mr Bracer, staring into his glass asked, 'You said you had plans. What are they ?'

'Plans. Yes,' said Grist dramatically. 'Thomas and I plan an assault on the city of London,' We shall attack and capture the stronghold with the brilliance of our artifice. No more for us the provinces. The hinterlands have lost their charm, henceforth the metropolis beckons. '*There is a tide in the affairs of men, which, taken at the flood, leads on to fortune*. For Thomas and I that tide is nigh.'

Fernando, perched on the back of Thomas's chair, finished the piece of orange he was eating and clapped his hands together as if in agreement.

Mr Grist smiled at the monkey, belched loudly then collected himself.

'Do we seek fame?' he continued, 'that will o' the wisp, that faithless harlot? Perhaps we do. Do we seek fortune? Yes I believe we do seek fortune. For fortune is more than monetary gain. It is both health and wealth and. . .' This time a fit of coughing stopped him momentarily.

'Good fortune attend your endeavour.' mumbled Mr Bracer.

Leonard Grist, his throat now cleared, addressed his two fellows with a voice that rattled both the glass and the cutlery,

'Together we shall storm the citadel! Either we shall take it or perish in the attempt. The two of us - Thomas and I!'

Bracer murmured, 'To Thomas and you'

Thomas stirred and looked up, raising his glass, but only an inch or two, 'To you and me.' Then he added.

'Not forgetting Fernando,'

'Not forgetting Fernando,' agreed Mr Grist.

*

Note.

Several incidents and characters in this novel are taken from biographies and newspapers of the 18th century

Both Jemmy Whitley and Tate Wilkinson were actor/managers who ran theatrical circuits based in Nottingham and York respectively; the latter wrote two lively autobiographies from which some episodes have been taken. The confrontation in chapter 27 between Wilkinson and Griffiths is from volume four of T.W.'s memoirs. The characters of both these actor/managers are my invention, and I hope no disservice has been done to either of them.

The opening performance in Nottingham of Addison's *Cato,* with the subsequent arrest of Wheeler and the following riot happened early in 1763 and was reported in the *Nottingham Journal.*

Marmaduke Pennell, one time mayor of Nottingham, is thought to have built both the Mary Gate theatre and the Ladies' Assembly rooms on Low Pavement.

Plumptre House, Bulwell Hall and Nuthall Temple were real houses, long demolished. The portrayal of those that lived there is entirely fictitious, although the builder of Nuthall Temple was in fact the local MP, Charles Sedley.

The liaison between actor Mr Grist and Miss Nevill is reported in *Abigail Gawthern's Diary 1750-1810,'* where Grist was described as a *clever sensible man.* Miss Nevill bore him a daughter even though he was a married man. In later life the two married and were accepted into 'polite' society, a reminder that this was a more liberal time before the censorious Victorian era.

Several advertisements e.g. for the 'Surprising Child', and the 'Spotted Indian Youth' are exactly as they appeared in the local press of the time although the ensuing episodes are fabrications.

Riots were endemic to Nottingham for the hundred years from the middle of the eighteenth century. A military presence was required for most of this time to try and keep the peace although the building of the barracks came later than I have suggested.

For the rest, all other characters such as Tom Hammond, Lucy Treadgold, Lady Granby, Mrs M'George, Mr Powell and Mr Sweeny are complete fabrications. ~ M.P.

Bibliography:

BREWER, John: *The Pleasures of the Imagination. (English Culture in the Eighteenth Century.)* Harper Collins 1997.

COLLIER, Jeremy: *A Short View of the Immorality and Profanity of the English Stage.* London 1698.

DICKENS, Charles: *Sketches by Boz.* London 1836.

FIELD, Henry (ed) *The Nottingham Date Book.* Nottm 1880.

GAY, John: *The Beggar's Opera* and *Polly.* London 1728.

HARTNOLL, Phyllis (ed): *The Oxford Companion to the Theatre.* O.U.P 1951.

HAMPDEN, John: (ed) *Eighteenth Century Plays.* Dent 1928.

HENSTOCK, Adrian: (ed) *The Diary of Abigail Gawthern of Nottingham 1751-1810* Thoroton Society, Nottm 1980.

HODGKINSON, J.L. *The Early Manchester Theatre.* Blond 1960.

LEE, PICKETING & HELFER (editors) *New Penguin Guide of the Theatre.* Penguin Books 1998.

McCONNELL STOTT, Andrew: *The Pantomime Life of Jospeph Grimaldi.* Canongate, 2009.

McINTYRE, Ian: *Garrick.* Allen Lane, Penguin Press 1999.

MOODY & O'QUINN (ed): *British Theatre 1730 - 1830.* C.U.P 2007.

NICOLL, Allardyce: *British Drama.* *(5th Ed.)* Harrap, 1962.

NICOLL, Allardyce: *The World of Harlequin.* C.U.P. 1963.

PRICE, Cecil: *Theatre in the Age of Garrick..* Blackwell, Oxford 1973.

ROSENFELD, Sibyl: *Strolling Players & Drama in the Provinces 1660 - 1765.* C.U.P. 1939.

ROSENFELD, Sibyl: *A Short History of Scene Design in Gt Britain* Blackwell, Oxford. 1973.

TREWIN, J.C.: *The Pomping Folk in the Nineteenth Century Theatre* Dent, 1968 .

WARWICK, Lou: *Drama That Smelled.* Hull 1975.

WILKINSON, Tate: *Memoirs.* (4 Vols) London 1790.

WILKINSON, Tate: *The Wandering Patentee.* (4 Vols) London 1795.

*